P9-DOD-540

3 5674 05586349 3

Chase Branch Library
17731 W. Seven Mile Rd.
Detroit, MI 48235

OCT - - 2015

CH

THE THEORY OF DEATH

Also by Faye Kellerman

Murder 101

The Beast

Gun Games

Hangman

Blindman's Bluff

The Mercedes Coffin

The Burnt House

The Ritual Bath

Sacred and Profane

The Quality of Mercy

Milk and Honey

Day of Atonement

False Prophet

Grievous Sin

Sanctuary

Justice

Prayers for the Dead

Serpent's Tooth

Moon Music

Jupiter's Bones

Stalker

The Forgotten

Stone Kiss

Street Dreams

Straight into Darkness

The Garden of Eden and Other Criminal Delights:
A book of short stories

With Jonathan Kellerman

Double Homicide

Capital Crimes

With Aliza Kellerman

Prism

THE THEORY
OF DEATH

A Decker/Lazarus Novel

FAYE KELLERMAN

wm

WILLIAM MORROW
An Imprint of HarperCollins*Publishers*

This book is a work of fiction. The characters, incidents, and dialogue are drawn from the author's imagination and are not to be construed as real. Any resemblance to actual events or persons, living or dead, is entirely coincidental.

THE THEORY OF DEATH. Copyright © 2015 by Plot Line, Inc. All rights reserved. Printed in the United States of America. No part of this book may be used or reproduced in any manner whatsoever without written permission except in the case of brief quotations embodied in critical articles and reviews. For information address HarperCollins Publishers, 195 Broadway, New York, NY 10007.

HarperCollins books may be purchased for educational, business, or sales promotional use. For information please e-mail the Special Markets Department at SPsales@harpercollins.com.

FIRST EDITION

Library of Congress Cataloging-in-Publication Data has been applied for.

ISBN 978-0-06-227021-4 (hardcover)
ISBN 978-0-06-243744-0 (international edition)

15 16 17 18 19 DIX/RRD 10 9 8 7 6 5 4 3 2 1

As Always: For Jonathan
And welcoming Judah

CHAPTER 1

I NEED A FAVOR."

Nothing by way of introduction, but then again phone etiquette—or any kind of etiquette—had never been the kid's strong suit. Decker knew who it was. McAdams had been calling him off and on since he left Greenbury PD for Harvard Law, mostly to bitch and moan. His complaints rarely centered on school studies. Instead, they had way more to do with his schoolmates and people in general.

"Shoot."

"It's reading period up here. Finals are in two weeks. Can I crash at your place and study down there?"

"Sure, you can come here. But I can't guarantee how quiet it'll be."

"I can use the libraries at the five colleges. And there is an invention called earplugs. In any case, I need to get out of here."

"Is everything okay?"

"I'm fine. I'm just sick of the place. You know me. I'm not a good team player."

"Not one for study groups?"

"Weren't you the one who said that groups were only as good as their weakest link?"

"I might have made that remark."

"There are a lot of weak links around here, Old Man. I'm better off away and on my own."

"How long were you thinking of staying?"

"Ten days to two weeks. I promise to behave myself. No complaining."

"You know what they say about making promises you can't keep."

"Yes or no?"

"You're always welcome, Tyler. When would you like to come down?"

"I'm on a bus."

"A bus?"

"I didn't feel like making chitchat with a limo driver."

"Aha. I didn't figure you for slumming it."

"God forbid. It was a last-minute decision. I figured if worse came to worst, you'd kick me out. And even if you kicked me out, Rina would just invite me back in. So actually this call is a mere formality."

Decker smiled. "Well, thanks for the heads-up."

"Can you pick me up?"

"I'm at work, Tyler."

"What about Rina?"

"She's working today as well."

"Surely someone can cover for you to pick up a fellow officer who was shot in the line of duty."

The bus station was over a half hour away in Hamilton. Not that Decker was doing much. A long silence ensued. "I suppose I could send someone." An even longer silence. "Or I suppose I could pick you up myself."

"You just want to hear me say 'please.' "

"Go for it, kid."

"Please."

"What time are you getting in?"

"In forty-five minutes. And don't be late. I'm a stickler for punc-tuality."

THE SKIES WERE gray and threatening with temperatures in the high thirties. The highways had been cleared of snow from the last storm, but there were still pockets of ice on the asphalt. Still, it was good to get out of the station house. The new heating system was far from perfect. Most of the time it was stifling hot except for a few areas that were still freezing cold. The winter had been milder compared to last year, but in the Northeast that still meant the usual white landscape against dark tree trunks and ice in the woods and lots of bare hard ground and dead grass in backyards. Rina had planted an indoor garden of herbs and tomatoes that she lovingly tended to in their sunroom. Lately she had been talking about getting a dog—a Pug or a Papillon. Something portable so when they visited the kids and grandkids, they could cart it around. Decker was a little more hesitant, but something small would be doable. He liked animals as long as they had four legs. In his decades working for law enforce-ment, he'd had enough of the biped kind.

Decker pulled up to the station just as the bus was arriving. He stretched as soon as he got out of the car. Being cramped behind the wheel of a compact for a half hour took its toll on all six feet four inches of his body. That and being older, although he felt in good shape. He still had a headful of white hair, his bushy mustache still held hints of its original red color. His spine was straight and his brain was working: What more could he ask for?

Although he talked to the kid almost weekly, he hadn't seen him in five months. When Tyler got off the bus, Decker immediately noticed changes. He was still a slender guy, but he appeared as if he had been working out. His chest was broader and his neck seemed to have grown in diameter. His dark brown hair sat a few inches above his shoulders, long but not coiffed. He needed a haircut. His intense hazel-green eyes scanned the platform, and as soon as he saw Decker, he managed a hint of a smile.

When Tyler had left Greenbury last August, he had healed from his gunshot wounds. But even so, there were remnants of what had happened. Tyler walked with a small limp, discernible but only if you looked for it. Given enough time, it would disappear. The memory of what he had gone through was another thing. Decker relieved him of his duffel.

"Welcome home."

A full smile. "If this is home, I'm in trouble."

Decker threw his arm around the kid. "Well, then how about 'welcome back.' "

He let go with a deep sigh. "Man, I feel better already. Like I can actually take a breath without it being debated. How's Rina?"

"I haven't spoken to her yet."

"Oh." He made a face. "She won't mind my sojourn?"

"Relax, Harvard. You're among friends."

"First time in a long time. How's Greenbury been doing in my absence?"

"Humming along. And after last winter, I'd like to keep it that way."

"True that."

The two men stopped at the car. Decker unlocked the doors and Tyler threw his knapsack in the back. He slipped into the passenger seat. "So nothing interesting?"

Decker started the ignition and turned the heat on full blast. "We were called to a death, but it was natural causes: an eighty-one-year-old man who died of a heart attack. The daughter phoned it in. She hadn't heard from him in a few days. It wasn't a pretty scene."

"Poor guy."

It was the first time that Decker ever heard Tyler express sympathy. "Yeah, it was kind of sad. How have you been?"

"All right."

"Been doing any target practice?"

"A little. I haven't had a lot of opportunity to go to the range. Law school takes up a lot of time."

"The first year is the toughest."

"Tedious. It does require an attention span. Some parts I actually like. That was surprising."

"What interests you?"

"Criminal law . . . what else. But to really understand criminal law, you need to really have a good grasp of tort law, and that is bor-ing. And that's most of first year. Ah well, it's just hurdle jumping." He turned to Decker. "Good to see you in the flesh, Old Man. You're looking well for your age."

"No need for the qualifiers. You're looking good as well. You've been working out."

"It gives me time to unwind." He raked his hair with his fingers. "I know. I need a haircut. I'm thinking of shaving my head."

"Whatever for? You've got a good mop. There's time enough for being bald."

"It's a pain in the ass to get haircuts. I suppose I'd have to shave my head regularly to keep it looking smooth. I hate doing maintenance on myself. If it wasn't for social convention, I'd be walking around in torn pajamas, wearing newspaper on my feet."

Decker laughed. "Then it's good you have the money to be labeled as an eccentric rather than a nutcase."

"Yeah, that is the only difference, right?"

A call from the station house came through the car's Bluetooth. Decker depressed the button and the speakerphone kicked in. Mike Radar's voice.

"Where the hell are you?"

Decker said, "What's going on?"

"Where are you?" Radar's voice was still tense but it dropped in volume.

"I went to pick up Tyler McAdams from the bus station. He's in town for a few weeks."

"Hi, Captain."

"Hi, Tyler. You doing okay?"

"I'm doing fine."

"Good. Decker, how far are you from the Elwood exit off the highway?"

"Around ten minutes. What's up?"

"I'm gonna give you the directions that were given to me and I'll meet you there. The kid can come as well."

"What's going on?"

"We've got a dead body, that's what's going on."

WITH ALL THE turns and U-turns and the missed forks in the dirt road, it took about a half hour to get to the remote spot in the forest. Once Decker found the clearing to park the vehicle among the other police vehicles, it took Tyler and him a few minutes to hike through the copses of bare trees to the crime scene spot.

The department had amped up its professionalism. This time there was actually crime tape that looped around the tree trunks encircling the body. There were three uniforms guarding the scene who handed out shoe covers, gloves, and evidence bags. He and McAdams slipped on the foot and hand protection and Decker ducked under the tape. The ground was covered with a layer of fresh snow and the group had the good sense not to disturb the shoe print that led to and from the corpse. Lots of other tracks zigzagged across the area—deer, hare, wild turkey, and fox.

It was a nude male, prone and slightly twisted to the left. He appeared to be around five ten, between a hundred and forty and a hundred and fifty pounds. No obvious marks on his torso, legs, and arms—except for the rips and tears in the flesh that were probably due to animal activity. His abdomen had been torn open as well. Squatting down, Decker noticed lividity, the blood pooling to the bottom of the corpse. When he felt the skin, it was cold, but the body was far from frozen.

He took several pictures of the body with his cell phone. Then he gently brushed away the surface powder that covered the corpse's head. Once this was done, Decker was studying a roundish face, blue eyes, auburn, straight hair, full lips, a weak chin, and an open mouth with all of his front teeth intact. There was a single shot to the right temple with semifrozen blood splatter on his face and shoulders.

Decker stood up. A revolver lay inches from his right hand, fingers curled as if he'd been grasping the gun. A neat pile of clothes sat around two feet from the body. Shoes had been placed next to the clothing. Decker tried his phone but there was no reception. He turned to McAdams. The last time the kid had seen a body, he had turned queasy. "Are you okay?"

"Not too bad. Probably because we're out in the open and it doesn't stink too badly."

"Fresh air is good."

"The body is gruesome." McAdams looked at Decker. "Animal activity, right?"

"Probably." Decker turned to Lauren Hellman, the uniform that was closest to him. She was in her thirties with blond curly hair and brown eyes. "Who found him?"

"Anonymous call to the police station. No reception here, so whoever called had to get out of the woods first."

"The police system must have pulled up the cell number."

She smiled. "Of course. When we called it back, we got voice mail—someone named Carson. Captain said it sounded like a teenage boy. He left a message that it was the police and to call back immediately. Even if the kid doesn't call back, we'll figure out who it is."

"I'll need to interview him. The victim doesn't look too far out of his teens himself."

"College kid?" McAdams suggested.

"The colleges haven't reported anyone missing to us."

"Do they do that?"

"If it's been more than a day or two, they do. But this may be less because the body isn't frozen." To Lauren. "Anyone touch anything?"

"No, sir."

"Clothes were like that when you came down?"

"Yes, sir."

"Okay. Has the coroner been notified?"

"I believe Captain Radar called up the New York Coroner's Office. I don't know if he's called any criminal investigative division."

"No need. We can handle this," Decker said. "It's not like last year's murder."

Lauren raised her eyebrows. "Thank goodness for that; right, Detective McAdams?"

"Right."

"I didn't know you were back."

"Just for a couple of weeks," Tyler said.

"Looks like you came just in time."

Decker said, "He's not here in an official capacity."

"I'm not?"

"I thought you had studying to do."

"Study, schmudy . . ." He grinned and rubbed his gloved hands together. "What can I do for you, Old Man?"

"If you're serious, take out your phone and take some pictures of the clothing and shoes. I'd also like more pictures of the body before I go through the pockets. I also want to do a little measuring."

"Right-o."

Decker measured the distance between the body and the clothing, and the distance from his right hand to the gun. Once everything was recorded, he squatted down and began to search through the pockets, disturbing the pile as little as possible. Empty as in not even a scrap of paper. He stood up and brushed off his pants. "We have a John Doe." He turned to McAdams. "What's your take?"

"Because I have so much experience."

"Answer the question."

The kid thought for a few moments. "Suicide or a murder made to look like suicide."

"Why suicide?"

"Uh . . . gun's near his right hand and the wound is on the right side." McAdams squatted and looked at the wound. "Stippling on his temple. If we checked his right hand, we'd probably find gunpowder residue. No apparent bruising or strangulation to indicate a struggle."

"Okay, what else?"

"I just got here. Cut me slack for jet lag."

"You came from a city in the same time zone."

"Minor details."

Decker smiled. "If we assume it was a suicide, Mr. Doe had to walk to this spot on his own two feet because I don't even see any tracks from a bike."

"There are lots of shoe prints, however."

"So let's look at the tracks. These . . ." Decker pointed to a set of shoe prints. "This comes out of the copses and stops right here. There's not a lot of detail in the print, most of the tread has been obscured by snowfall and its subsequent melting. There are a few good ones under a tree canopy. Meaning he walked here before it snowed last night."

McAdams said, "These tracks, on the other hand . . . these come from the opposite direction. There are lots of them and the tread detail is much sharper. They're more recent, like in this morning."

"Exactly. Our anonymous caller and probably a friend because there are two sets of tracks. They stop at about four feet from the body. Then they U-turn. And you notice that in the turnaround, we get bigger strides."

"They're running away from the body."

"Exactly." Decker thought a moment. "If this was a murder, I'd expect to see some evidence in the snow . . . like drag marks next to the tracks."

"Maybe the murderer smoothed out the drag marks and let the snowfall cover up the rest." A pause. "Do you think it's a murder?"

"It's an odd place to commit suicide. Usually suicide victims want their last stand to be very visible."

McAdams nodded. "What do you think about the nudity?"

"Good question. Going out of this world like he came into the world." Decker shook his head. "The first thing we need is an identity. Get lots of face pictures because if we don't find ID, we're going to have to do this door to door."

"Or college to college."

"Or college to college," Decker said. "After that, get some close-up photographs of all the prints in the snow—human and otherwise. Then when you're done with that, take molds of each different shoe print you find."

"Do you have a kit?"

"In the back of my car." Decker paused. "Do you know how to take a mold?"

"Never done it before, but I'm sure I can figure it out."

"It's a little tricky to do in the snow. You need a deft touch. Even so, it won't be perfect since ice melts. I'll show you how to do it. It's not hard, but you need to make sure the mixture is completely smooth and bubble-free. And you have to work fast before it starts to set up. I'll tell you what, McAdams. I'll do the detailed ones under the tree that were probably made by our victim and you do the ones that were probably made by the anonymous caller and friend."

"Sure." While McAdams was snapping pictures, Decker walked back to Lauren. "Has anyone found a car, motorcycle, or even a bike? This spot is deep in the woods. Unless he lived in a cabin somewhere, I'm assuming he took some kind of transportation to get him in this vicinity."

"No one found any vehicle, but we haven't checked beyond the immediate area."

Decker started looking for vehicle tracks. He didn't find anything. McAdams walked over. "I took about twenty pictures of his face. Before I go on to the shoe prints, do you want to look-see?"

Decker scrolled through the snapshots. "These are good. When we get reception, we can send them to my computer at the station house and make some leaflets from them for ID purposes." He fished out keys to his car. "After you're done taking snapshots of the prints, go fetch the kit."

"Yes, boss."

"You don't have to do this, you know."

McAdams smiled. "I'm fine, Decker. When I'm not fine, I'll let you know."

"Fair enough." Decker regarded the high-tops on McAdams's feet. That was good. But he wasn't wearing a scarf or a hat or gloves other than the latex gloves provided to him to prevent evidence contamination. "Go put on some warmer clothing, Tyler. You're gonna need it."

"We'll be here for a while."

"Yes. Hypothermia is the enemy."

"I'll fetch some warm stuff from my duffel."

"Since when did you become so agreeable?"

"Don't worry. I can turn very quickly."

"And you're sure you want to do this? Mike Radar will be down soon. You can take the car and he'll drive me back."

"Are you trying to get rid of me?"

"Not at all. I could use another set of eyes."

"Ones without cataracts?"

"Your funeral is destined to be a very small affair."

McAdams shrugged. "I'll be right back with the kit."

"How good are your Boy Scout skills?"

"They're horrible, but I can get GPS on my phone."

"I don't think we can get good reception. If not, I have a compass."

"Wow, that's really old-school."

"I am old-school. Go suit up and I'll show you how to take a shoe-print mold. And don't attempt to take all of them . . . pick out the best one you can find per shoe. I don't want us running out of material. We'll meet up when we're both done." Decker pointed to a set of single footprints that trailed into the forest. "See that?"

"It looks like footprints."

"The person was walking not running and they only lead one way. Once Mike gets here to direct the forensics, you and I are going to take a little hike."

CHAPTER 2

KID WAS WAY too young to end it all." Radar shook his head while staring at the body. "I'm assuming suicide, but I suppose we'll have to wait for the autopsy."

The coroner was John Potts—a sixty-five-year-old retired doctor who began a new career servicing the small towns of upstate New York. His lab was fifteen miles away in the bigger burg of Hamilton, where the bus station was located. He said, "What I can tell you is that there doesn't seem to be any kind of blunt-force trauma, strangulation, suffocation. There are no other bullet wounds other than the one shot to his right temple, and no stab wounds. Of course, with all this animal activity, something might have been eaten away. Then there's the tox screen, of course."

The captain nodded. Radar was in his late fifties, a tad less than six feet tall, a strong build except for a slight paunch. His face was saggy with light eyes, thin upper lip covered by a gray mustache, and a cleft chin. He raked whatever white hair he had left with his fingers. To Decker, he said, "What do you think?"

Decker said, "Single gunshot with no other bruises or wounds. Probably suicide. And it probably happened in the late night or early morning. I'll split the difference and say around midnight."

Potts looked up. "What drew you to that conclusion?"

"Flurries fell around two A.M. He was dead before that happened because he had been covered by a light sprinkling of snow. The exposed skin is cold and hard but there is still warmth underneath with nothing frozen solid except for the toes and fingers. Also, in my experience, this isn't something people do during the daytime. They think about it, they get drunk and start brooding, and then they crawl away to end it all. When you do a tox screen, I bet you'll find alcohol or drugs. How close am I to your time estimate?"

Potts had already put a thermometer into the liver. "From eleven last night to three this morning using an average outside temperature of twenty-five degrees."

"If it's suicide, it's an odd duck," Radar said. "Alone and naked in the deep part of the forest. This isn't going out in style. It's more like 'don't anyone take notice of me.' " To Potts: "What do you make of it?"

"My department is the how, Mike." Potts stood up and snapped off his gloves. "Your department is the why." He nodded to his assistants to load the body onto the gurney. It was a five- to seven-minute walk to the clearing where the van had parked. The coroner said, "I'll have to thaw the body thoroughly before I can do the autopsy. It shouldn't take too long to get him on the slab. Even so, it'll take at least a couple of days if nothing else comes up." A pause. "Poor kid. And you have no idea who he is?"

"Not yet."

"I'll keep you updated when I know something." Potts rubbed his arms and hurried to keep up with his assistants.

Radar turned to Decker. "What's next?"

"Do you mind finishing off the forensics?"

"Not a problem. What's your plan?"

"McAdams and I are going to follow the pathway and see if we can figure out how he got here. It's a long way to come by foot."

"There isn't any vehicle nearby. If he walked, it was an all-day affair. Maybe he camped out."

"That could be. It's cold but easily survivable with the right clothes and provisions. Anyone check Missing Persons around the area?"

"Ben Roiters is on it. He's working from a desk in a warm place, the lucky stiff."

"Luckier stiff than this one," McAdams added.

Radar's face turned sour. "Are you officially working, McAdams? If so, I'm going to figure out how to pay you."

Decker said, "He just happened to be in the car with me when you made the call. He's giving me the day and then he's back to civilian life. He has finals to study for."

"Ah, law school," Radar said. "How's that going?"

"It's going."

"So you're not working for the department."

Decker answered first. "No, he's just here for the ride."

McAdams said, "Uh, last I heard, I'm of my majority and capable of making my own decisions."

"This isn't why you came down here," Decker said.

"Things change, Old Man. As you always say, flexibility is a virtue."

"I don't remember saying that."

"So you *are* working on the case?" Radar said.

"I'll work with Decker if he wants me. If it's a suicide, it won't take long to wrap it up, right?"

"Once we find out who he is," Decker said. "If it's not suicide, it gets complicated. I'm not pulling you away from your studies."

"Not to worry. I could probably take the exams right now and pass . . . albeit a low pass. Besides, I could use a break for a day or two. Clear my head of all that legal nonsense."

"So are you working or not?" Radar asked.

"Yes, I'm working. And don't worry about the money. We'll use the bartering system. You can teach me all you know about ballistics, fingerprinting, and blood splatter pattern, and I'll give you my time gratis. But only if the Loo wants me around."

"You can tag along today." To Radar, Decker said, "Did you find out the identity of the anonymous caller?"

"Carson Jackson, age sixteen. The other set of footprints probably belongs to Milo Newcamp, also age sixteen. They claim they were out hiking, but they were probably hunting illegally."

"Hunting what?" McAdams asked.

"Turkey, fox, deer . . . which would be okay except it's not hunting season. They're coming down to the station house with their parents at around six in the evening."

"Tell them to bring the shoes they hiked in this morning."

"You've got shoe prints?"

"We do," Decker said. "We'll probably be back by then. I don't want to be here in the dark. It's disorienting enough in the daylight. Plus there's no phone reception. If I'm not at the station house by six, come look for me, *please.*"

"I'll do that." Radar smiled.

Decker looked at McAdams. "Give him your phone."

"What?"

"You have the snapshots of our victim on your phone."

"So do you."

"You have more. Give it to him."

McAdams made a point of sighing as he handed his phone to Radar. Decker said, "When you get to your computer, could you download the snapshots and send them to my computer? Also have someone make leaflets with Doe's picture so we can start passing them around."

"Do you think he's local?"

"McAdams thinks he's probably a student at one of the five colleges of upstate. I suspect he's right. Since no one has reported him missing, I want to pass the pictures around the campuses. If you could get someone to grease the skids at the colleges, we can move efficiently."

"I'll call in the mayor. He'll want to know what's going on . . . especially after last time."

"Yeah, I have a feeling he doesn't like me very much," McAdams said.

"On the contrary, Tyler, your father just donated more money for a new emergency computer system."

McAdams turned to Decker. "Did you know about this?"

Decker was staring at the depression where the body had sat. "Pardon?"

"Never mind. What are you looking at since there is no longer a corpse?"

"I was just wondering what was so bad in his life that he couldn't bear to wake up and face another day."

THE SUN WAS casting long shadows as darkness waited in the wings. The footprints had stopped in a thicket of bare oaks, the trees identifiable by the brown, dead lobular leaves that they had shed during the fall. Decker's feet sank into the patches of snow and earthy detritus: clammy and cold. Neither he nor McAdams was wearing hiking boots. Decker broke a ski heat pack and gave it to McAdams. Then he broke another one for his numb feet. His gloved hands and covered head were warmer, but not by much.

McAdams looked around. "There's nothing out here and the ground is covered with leaves and snow. How are we going to figure out what direction he came from?"

"I don't know and it's getting late."

"Pack it in?"

Decker didn't answer. "The bottom of John Doe's pants were wet but not muddy. If you were tramping through all this slush and leaves, there'd be some muddy residue on the cuffs, don't you think?"

"Well, he had to have trudged through some of it because his shoe prints stop here."

"I certainly don't see any tire tracks." Decker thought a moment. "The guy comes out to the woods and kills himself away from civilization. He has no ID, nothing to give us any idea who he is."

"He wants to go out anonymously."

"Yeah, and a car would ruin the anonymity. You can't lose a car. It's too big to hide and it can be traced. The same with a motorcycle."

"Okay."

"Look at all the dead stuff on the forest floor, Tyler. Between the leaves and the snow cover, you could easily bury a bike and no one would probably notice until next spring if at all."

"Gotcha. So where do we start digging?"

"Like I said, his pant cuffs were wet but not dirty. I'm saying he buried it somewhere near his footprints." Decker picked up a long stick and gave it to McAdams. Then he found another one. "You sweep the area to the left of the footprints, I'll sweep the right."

There were a lot of tree roots, but after ten minutes of searching, Decker hit something solid about a hundred yards from where the footprints disappeared. He took off his winter gloves and slapped on the latex. Then he bent down and brought the object to the surface, shaking off leaves and dirt and bugs. The bike was painted electric blue and had ten gears. Definitely not a mountain bike: it was meant for short distances like tooling around downtown Greenbury.

"It's a Zipspeed," McAdams stated.

"The bicycle rental place?" Decker said.

"Exactly. You can see the logo on the front fender. I've rented their bikes before. The company specializes in franchises in college towns."

Decker studied the handlebars, the seat, and the wheels. He found what he was looking for etched into the wheel rims of both tires. "We've got an ID number: 19925."

"I don't have anything to write it down with."

"Doesn't matter. The bike comes back with us. It's evidence."

"We're lugging it back with us?"

"Well, you are." He handed the bike to Tyler. "You're younger and stronger."

"I was shot."

"That pity card was used up a long time ago. When we get it back, call up the local Zipspeed office while I talk to our hikers who found the body."

"The place will probably be closed by the time we get back."

"Then you find who's in charge and get them to open up."

McAdams held up the bike. "How do we get this back to town? It won't fit in the car."

"It'll fit on top of the car. I've got some bungee cords in the trunk."

"Suddenly law school doesn't seem so bad."

Decker laughed. "You can beg off any time you want, Harvard."

"I know. I guess I forgot how much tedium is in an investigation. But it's better than the tedium in law school right now."

"It's your choice. You can think about it as we walk back to the car. It's getting late. So get a move on."

The kid heaved a big sigh and picked up the bike. "Why does this always happen to me? Caught between the devil and the deep blue sea."

"You can't fight the devil." Decker put his arm around his shoulder. "So you might as well learn how to swim."

CHAPTER 3

THE BOYS WERE all arms and legs, gangly in the way that teenage boys are before the muscle comes in. Carson Jackson was fair-haired with adolescent acne. He looked like his mother, who sat next to him, throwing her son poison arrows with her eyes. Milo Newcamp was short with scruffy hair and a long nose, and was accompanied by his father. Both parents were impatient to get the interviews over. Their expressions were weary, conveying that the boys had been in trouble too many times before. Decker had placed them in one of the two interview rooms at the station house. It held a rectangular table and six chairs surrounded by unadorned walls painted off-white. The room did have a one-way mirror that had been installed five years ago. Decker had only been with the department for a little over a year, and in all that time, he never remembered anyone sitting on the other side while an interview was being conducted.

Once the shoe prints had been taken off of the teens' boots, Decker started the interview by asking them the basics: time, place, reason for being there on a school day, where they came from, where they were going. Then he went over his notes.

"So you both decided to skip school and go for a hike."

"It's not the first time they've been truant," Carson's mother interjected.

"Okay," Decker said. "Mrs. Jackson, I'd like them to answer the questions. Once I'm done—and it shouldn't take too long—you can deal with your boy however you want."

"Let's just get it over with, Julia . . . again." Mr. Newcamp frowned. "We've both got better things to do."

"That's for certain." Julia muttered, "Morons!"

Decker said, "So you boys biked to the forest and started the hike around eleven, leaving your bikes in a thicket off Millstone Road."

Again the boys nodded.

Decker looked down at his notes. "And you weren't on any mapped trail?"

"No, sir," Milo said. "But we've hiked the backcountry before."

"From where you started to where you ended up, it's about fifteen minutes." Decker looked up. "What took you so long?"

Milo's father chucked the back of his son's head with two fingers. "Tell them what you were doing. They probably went hunting. No matter it isn't hunting season and it's dangerous to go shooting when you can't see the orange jackets. Idiots!"

"Mr. Newcamp, let me ask the questions so we can all get going with the rest of our day," Decker said. "So you found the body."

"Yes, sir." Milo answered for both of them.

"And then what did you do?"

"We couldn't get phone reception. So we turned around and went back to our bikes and went home and called from there."

"Not home," Mr. Newcamp said. "You went to the Arby's until school let out." Again he chucked his head.

"Ow!" the boy exclaimed.

Decker said, "Stop hitting him, okay? You're in the presence of the police." Newcamp looked down, another sour look on his face. Decker continued. "Did either of you touch the body to see if he had a pulse?"

The boys shook their heads. Milo said, "His face was covered with snow. He wasn't moving. I didn't want to mess anything up."

Decker leaned across the table. "We didn't find anything on the body, boys: no wallet, no cell phone, no pad, no backpack, and no personal identification." A pause. "This is important, so don't lie. Did either of you take anything?"

The boys shook their heads emphatically and said no several times.

"You didn't go through his pockets?" Decker said. "Because if you did, we'll find your fingerprints." Not always the case, but the kids didn't know that.

"No way, no way," Carson said. "We just got the hell out of there."

"We ran back, sir," Milo said. "I don't want nothing to do with a dead body."

Yvonne Mastino came in and handed Decker a note. The boys' boot prints matched the casts from the shoe prints in the snow. "Okay," Decker said. "I have what I need for now. You can pick up your hiking boots and go home. I might have a few more questions later on. With your parents' permission, I want to keep your rifles at the station house until hunting season begins."

"Good idea," Julia Jackson said.

"That's so unfair!" Carson protested.

"Shut up, Carson." To Decker, Julia said, "I'll bring his in tomorrow."

"Ditto," Newcamp said. "Better it's here than one of you shooting someone and going to jail for manslaughter. Idiots!" He started to hit his son's head but stopped himself. "Are we done?"

Decker nodded. The four of them got up and left. He turned off the tape recorder just as McAdams came into the room. "Anything illuminating with the kids?"

"Just stupid teenagers playing hooky."

"No one was in the Zipspeed office, but I got hold of the clerk and he looked up the numbered bike on his computer. It was rented by John Smith."

"A pseudonym, y'think?" Decker said.

"I dunno about that. The clerk claims that no one rents without a driver's license left on file as security."

"So he got a false license with the name John Smith."

"Or his name is John Smith," McAdams stated. "I got one bit of news. The name might be fake, but the form that he filled out had his student ID number. According to that, he went to Kneed Loft."

Of the five colleges of upstate, Kneed Loft was the smallest. It specialized in math/science/engineering, but it was still considered a liberal arts college rather than a technological institute like MIT or Caltech. Decker said. "Let's grab some flyers. We can start there."

"Um . . . question. Have you told Rina that I'm in town?"

"Yes."

"And it's okay?"

"Yes, it's okay. For some odd reason, she likes you." Decker stood up. "Let's go."

"Do you think the kids took anything from the crime scene?"

"Like a laptop or phone? They said no and I believe them. You saw how tidy the pile was, clothes neatly folded and stacked. If they did some rifling, the clothes would have been messed up."

"They could have straightened the clothes afterward."

"McAdams, have you ever been in the average teenage boy's room? Meticulous is just not in their vocabulary."

THE FIVE COLLEGES of upstate were their own entities with their own security and their own secretive methods of handling crime, the offenses usually centered around students getting drunk and getting into trouble. There was the occasional crossover, usually when the incident was too serious for the colleges to handle. Such was the case last year when a student of Littleton College, a senior named Angeline Moreau, was found murdered in an off-campus residence.

The college had been more than happy to punt to the local police. Greenbury wasn't used to dealing with big-city crime, and the town hadn't had a brutal whodunit in years. It was Greenbury's good fortune that Decker had signed up six months before the case broke, having recently hung up his shield as a detective lieutenant for LAPD.

The architectural styles of the five colleges were as different as the institutions. Duxbury was the oldest and the biggest, constructed during the mid-1800s with its imposing limestone and brick buildings. The women's college, Clarion, was built in the twenties: cleaner lines and more intimate buildings. Postwar Morse McKinley specialized in government, international affairs, and economics. It resembled a dingbat fifties apartment building that had metastasized into collegiate dormitories. Littleton was the eco-friendly fine arts and theater college where Decker and McAdams had spent the majority of last winter, investigating an art heist that had turned deadly.

Kneed Loft's architecture was brutal sixties design when ideas and thought reigned supreme and aesthetics ranked in desirability with the military-industrial complex. It was a block-long rectangular bunker of brick and brownstone with small, square windows. Decker had never been inside its hallowed halls. There hadn't been any occasion for a visit.

It was almost eight in the evening by the time he and McAdams arrived at the college. The temperature was in the low thirties with a breeze that was dry enough to chap the lips and sting the eyes. A black starry sky canopied the white lawns of the sprawling campuses. The administration offices were closed and it would probably take a number of phone calls to get them to open. Since the college was small—six hundred students total with six dormitories—it was easier to pass around flyers and see if any identification could be had by facial recognition.

The residences were named after twentieth-century scientists: Fermi Hall, Bohr Hall, Einstein Hall, Planck Hall, Goddard Hall, and Marie Curie Hall lest anyone think that Curie was referring to her husband, Pierre. The first dorm they came across was Planck Hall. It was two stories of dreary, functional brick devoid of charm and style. Since neither Decker nor McAdams had access keys, they knocked on an unmanned glass door and of course got no response because it was doubtful that anyone heard them. A minute later, a student swiped her residence card and the two detectives piggybacked on the open door, coming in after she had bounded up the stairs.

The first thing that came into view was a Volkswagen Jetta sitting in the foyer. How they got a full-size car in a lobby was anyone's guess. Behind the driver's seat was a steel robot with a sign around his neck, dubbing him Rupert. He wore a beret, sunglasses, and driving gloves. The students coming in and out of the dorm walked around the car as if it was a completely natural phenomenon.

The rest of the lobby was the usual college mess: used bottles of beer and spirits, discarded red cups that had held beer and spirits, pizza boxes, stale french fries and other assorted old takeout, overflowing trash cans, and outerwear strewn about the floor. Since there wasn't much fresh air circulating other than the door opening and closing, the garbage reeked.

"Phew!" McAdams waved his hand in front of his nose. "Poor Rupert. Should we start with him since he seems to be the eyes and ears of Planck?" Tyler bent over and showed the flyer of John Doe's postmortem to the robot. "You know this guy?" He paused. "It might help to take off the shades, dude."

Decker smiled. "Let's start upstairs and work our way down."

They climbed to the second level. Most of the doors were open and the space was a cacophony: music, human voices, and mechanical noises that sounded like hammering and drilling. They started on one side and it didn't take long for John Doe to be identified by Damodar Batra, a senior with a duel major in math and mechanical engineering.

"Oh shit!" Batra stared at the picture, his mouth agape. "Is that Eli Wolf?"

He had pronounced the name *E*-li—long E, long I. Decker said, "Spell it for me."

Batra complied. He was short in stature with black straight hair and a dark brown complexion. Sitting cross-legged on his bed, he had headphones around his neck, and surrounded by two laptops, a phone, and a tablet. "What happened?"

"Is Eli a friend of yours?"

"Kind of. Eli really doesn't have friends per se. He's kinda schizoid, but that's more of the norm here than not."

"So how well do you know him?"

"It's a small school and an even smaller math department. We've taken some classes together. Now that we're seniors, we have different advisers, so I don't see him so often. We're both busy." A pause. "My God, he looks . . . dead." He looked up. "He's dead?"

"Yes, he's deceased. This is a postmortem picture."

"God, that's totally fucked up!" The boy seemed genuinely shocked. "What happened?"

"We're still evaluating," Decker said. "What can you tell me about him?"

"Not much. We weren't like the best of friends but we certainly knew each other."

"What was his major?" McAdams asked.

"Theoretical math." Batra's jaw muscles bulged. "I believe he was

doing some postgrad work on Fourier analysis and Fourier transforms."

Decker turned to McAdams. "Any idea what that is?"

"Not a clue." Tyler looked at Batra. "Please explain in simple
English if possible."

"Fourier did work on temperature gradients like about three
hundred years ago. Heat travels from hottest point to coldest point
and how fast it travels is dependent on the material. The way to explain this mathematically was figured out by a guy named Fourier.
He took complex waves that make up things like temperature gradients and broke them up into simpler sine waves. You guys know
what a sine wave is, right?"

Decker said, "I believe trigonometry was a prerequisite for Harvard."

"You went to Harvard?" Batra asked.

"He did." Decker pointed to McAdams.

"Amplitude, frequency, and phase," Tyler said.

Batra laughed. "Do you know about eigenvalues?"

"Nope. But I know enough first-year tort law to sue almost
anyone."

"You're in law school."

"That is the unfortunate case, yes." McAdams pointed to Decker.
"He, however, is a full-fledged attorney."

"About thirty years ago," Decker said. "Can you give me a layman's definition of an eigenvalue?"

"It's easier to give you a mathematical explanation. It involves
matrices and nonzero vectors, which mean nothing to almost everyone in the universe except weirdos like me. The point is, all of this
stuff starts out theoretical but it has very practical applications."
Batra looked up. "Eli had a great, great mind. He could picture complex math like gradients, vectors, and matrices in his head. It was a
gift. What happened to him? Was it an accident?"

"Why would you think it was an accident?"

"It wasn't an accident?" This time, Batra seemed genuinely stunned. "He committed *suicide*?"

"I'm not sure," Decker said. "Did he seem depressed lately?"

"Not to me. If anything, he seemed very okay. I know his thesis was going well."

"It sounds like you know Eli better than you think."

"Everyone in our class knew about Eli. He was . . . exceptional."

"Who was his thesis adviser?" McAdams asked.

"Theo Rosser—he's chairman of the department. Eli also worked with Dr. Belfort and Dr. Ferraga. He could have worked with anyone. He had the entire mathematics department in awe."

"Would you have phone numbers for any of them?"

"Uh . . . hold on, I'll see if they have something listed in the faculty roster." It took him a few minutes to find what he was look-ing for. "Nothing for Rosser beyond office phone number. I have Dr. Belfort's cell number. She's my adviser."

"First name?" Decker asked.

"Katrina Belfort." He recited the digits out loud. "Hope that helps."

"It's a start," Decker said. "And you have no idea who he might have hung out with?"

"He didn't hang out with anyone. He was always in the library working on something that no one else understood."

"He had to eat," McAdams said. "Ever see him in the dining hall?"

"Sure . . . sitting alone most of the time. Sometimes he'd be sit-ting with a group of people, but I think that had more to do with availability of chairs than anything social. Or it could be that they were picking his brain. He was a helpful guy." He thought for a moment. "You know, you might want to contact Mallon. They sort of hung out."

"Is Mallon male or female?"

"Female . . . not that it mattered to Eli. Or to Mallon, for that matter. She's pretty much a loner herself. Katrina Belfort is her adviser as well, so I see her occasionally at meetings."

"So you both have the same adviser?"

"Yes. Mallon, Ari Weissberg, and me."

"What is Mallon's last name?" Decker asked.

"Euler. Spelled like the mathematician but pronounced Youler instead of Oi-ler. I think she has a distant relationship to the great one."

"Where can we find Mallon?" Decker asked.

"She's in Marie Curie. You want her cell number?"

"That would be helpful."

Batra gave it to them. He shook his head. "God, this is horrible. I've got to take a minute to absorb it. Is there anything else?"

"Yes, and this is important," Decker said. "You have just identified our John Doe as Eli Wolf. Are you sure it's him?"

"Almost positive. But if you want further corroboration, keep passing flyers around."

"First we're going to talk to Mallon Euler. If she identifies him as Eli Wolf, then we'll start doing notification."

"His parents. Shit, that's bad."

"I'm asking you to sit on this until we've contacted them. Do you happen to know where we can contact Eli's parents? Maybe there's a family phone number in the student directory?"

"I don't think there's a family phone number because I don't think there's a family phone. I seem to recall that Eli Wolf's family is Amish."

CHAPTER 4

THIS TIME, THE vehicle sitting in the lobby was a 1970 bronze Cadillac Eldorado convertible. The dummy, again wearing shades, sat behind the wheel, costumed in complete livery.

When McAdams offered Mallon Euler the flyer, she looked at the paper but refused to hold it. She sat cross-legged on her bed, her face revealing nothing. She wasn't much of a person if physical substance were the criterion. She was elfin: small, painfully thin, heart-shaped face with pixie short blond hair, and deep blue eyes. She wore a sleeveless blouse even though the room wasn't hot, showing off her stick arms, and denim shorts. Hotel-type slippers on her feet.

Decker said, "Do you know him?"

A nod of the head. Her eyes suddenly watered. They went from the flyer, to McAdams's face, then back to the flyer.

"Who is he?" Decker said.

Her focus was still on the flyer. "He's dead?"

"Yes." Decker waited, but no response came. "Who is he?"

"Eli."

"Last name?"

"Wolf . . . Elijah Wolf."

Decker turned to McAdams. "Two IDs and that's good enough for me." To Mallon: "Where did he live, Mallon? Which dorm?"

"Goddard Hall."

"Do you know the suite number?"

"Twenty-five."

"Does he have a roommate?"

"A single. He's a senior. Most seniors have singles." She looked at her lap. She whispered, "What happened?"

"That's what we're trying to figure out."

"When did it happen?"

"I'm not sure of the exact time. We found him this afternoon in a remote section of the woods—off the Elwood exit from the highway. Any idea why he might have been there?"

"None. I don't even know where Elwood is." She continued to stare at her lap as she talked.

"Were you and Eli friends?"

"We had similar academic interests."

"That doesn't preclude friendship."

She looked up, then down. "We talked research."

"What kind of research?"

"Math."

"How often did you two speak?"

"All the time."

"But you don't consider him a friend."

"I don't have friends." A quick glance to McAdams and then she returned her eyes to her knees. Another tear escaped from her left eye. She brushed it away. "But it doesn't lessen the pain of losing him—his mind." She spoke in a hush. "It's so horrible."

Another tear followed by another. Decker handed her a box of Kleenex. "When was the last time you saw Eli?"

"Yesterday."

"What time?"

"One in the afternoon. We met for lunch at the dining hall."

"And how did that go?"

"The usual."

"I have no idea what the usual is, Mallon."

"We talked math."

"Anything different about Eli's behavior?"

"No."

"Did he seem upset or depressed?"

"Not at all."

"Preoccupied?"

"No." Eyes went to Decker, to McAdams, and then downward. "I'm not good at judging emotional states. But to me, he seemed fine . . . maybe even a little . . . upbeat. Things were going well with his thesis. That much I know."

"Did you see him regularly?"

"Yes. At least twice a week."

"So who called whom to meet for lunch?"

"I never call anyone. We texted."

"Before I forget, what's his cell number?"

The girl recited the digits robotically. To McAdams, Decker said, "Can you call the number?"

"Already on it."

Decker returned his attention to the girl. "Who texted whom?"

"I texted him. I was stuck on something and asked him to take a look at my work."

McAdams hung up from the call. "Hmm . . ."

"Voice mail?" Decker said.

"Disconnected . . . and there's no new number."

That was consistent with suicide: the kid was checking out. Decker said, "What's your research?"

Her eyes slowly lifted to his face. "It *was* fractals."

Decker asked McAdams, "Any ideas what a fractal is?"

"I do, as a matter of fact," McAdams said. "They're repeating patterns found in nature."

"I have no idea what that means."

Tyler scrunched his forehead. "Suppose you have a three-leaf clover. And you examine one of the leaves of the clover and discover it's lobed into three sections and the lobe looks just like the clover in miniature, and then you look further at one of those lobes, and it's also in three sections. Etcetera, etcetera, etcetera." He looked at Mallon for confirmation.

"More or less correct," she said.

"And that's what you're studying?" Decker asked the girl.

"No. I was working with the mathematics of fractals and the theory of roughness. My interests have morphed into Fourier analysis and transforms."

"Which is what Elijah Wolf was studying," McAdams said.

"Eli has changed his focus of interest a few times, but yes, we were using the same mathematical formulas although we were doing very different things. When we spoke, he was mostly helping me, not the other way around."

"So you don't know exactly what he was studying?"

"Something using Fourier transforms." Mallon wiped a tear from her eye. "I wish I paid more attention. But like I said, he was helping me."

"And Dr. Rosser was his adviser," Decker said.

"Yes. That shows you how brilliant he was. Dr. Rosser only has one student per grade at the most. He's the chairman of the department, so he could have his pick. But he wouldn't pick me even if I had been as smart as Eli. He hates women."

"He does?"

"Just ask Dr. Belfort. She's my adviser."

Decker nodded. "Is there anything else you can tell me about Elijah Wolf?"

"He had a real gift." The tears were back. "He'll be missed terribly."

"Mallon, do you know anything about his family?"

"No."

"I was told he was brought up Amish."

"Mennonite."

"Oh." Decker paused. "You knew he was Mennonite."

"Yes."

"So you do know something about him." She answered with a shrug. Decker said, "Did he ever talk about his background? His evolution from Mennonite to math genius?"

"He didn't speak of his past much if at all." Mallon lowered her eyes. "I didn't pry. I wish I had."

"Okay." Decker smoothed his mustache. "So why did he tell you about his religion? What was the context, if you remember?"

"Of course I remember. He taught me how to play rook and crokinole. He told me they were Mennonite card games and that he had come from that community."

"Anything else?"

"Other than how to play the games, no, nothing else."

"So you don't know where geographically he's from?"

"No."

"You didn't ask him?"

"No." She bit her lower lip. "His accent seemed local."

"He had an accent?"

"By accent, I mean his speech pronunciations and patterns. I have a good ear for that. By the way you talk, it's obvious you're from the West, but you have a slight, slight southern twang. If I had to guess, I'd say eastern Louisiana or western Florida."

"Gainesville, Florida. Smack in the middle of the state. But my mother grew up closer to Louisiana."

McAdams broke in after looking up information on his phone. "Wow, lots of Amish in upstate. They come here because farming land is cheaper than in Lancaster." He looked at Mallon. "Are you sure he wasn't Amish?"

"He said Mennonite," Mallon said.

McAdams was still retrieving info on his smartphone. "There are a few small Mennonite communities upstate."

Decker said, "Mennonites are more modern than Amish. There's a good chance that his family has electricity and a phone."

"I'll get on it," McAdams said.

Decker turned to the young woman. "I'm going to need to notify his parents, Mallon. Please don't say anything to anyone until I do that very unpleasant task. Can you sit on this until I do?"

"Of course. I don't talk to many people anyway. I don't gossip."

Decker handed Mallon his card. "Well, if you *hear* gossip or if you think of anything else no matter how small, please give me a call."

Mallon stared at the card. Finally, her spindly fingers took it.

Decker said, "Thank you."

McAdams said, "Sir, can I have a minute alone with Ms. Euler?"

The request took Decker by surprise. "Of course."

As soon as Decker left the room, McAdams stowed his smartphone and said, "Okay. So where do I know you from?"

Mallon stared at him. "What makes you think you know me?"

"Obviously I don't *know* you, but we've met before. I don't remember, but you do. You keep staring at me. So where?"

"Philips."

McAdams was confused. "Really?"

"Really."

"Sorry, I don't remember the circumstance. You're a lot younger than I am. And I kind of kept to myself."

"Not always."

"Did I insult you or something? I've insulted many people in my day."

"On the contrary, you gave me the sagest advice that anyone has ever given me."

"Now there's a switch." McAdams paused. "Now I'm curious." He waited. "Please?"

"I had just started ninth grade. I was a year younger than anyone else and of course I was being bullied as usual. Ellen Harold, Mackenzie Gregory, and Misha Greenwood."

"I know Mackenzie. Her brother and she grew up around the corner from me. Nasty piece of work. Both of them actually. What'd I do?"

"It was after they stole my phone for the third time. I was crying and of course they were making fun of me for crying. And you came along and said, 'Mackenzie, stop torturing her.' She gave you some sass but there was no bite behind it. They left, but I was still crying."

McAdams furrowed his brow. "I can't imagine anyone getting sympathy from me."

"I didn't."

"Okay, that's consistent."

"I said to you, 'All I want is for them to like me.' I was sobbing by this time. 'All I want to do is fit in.' And you know what you said?"

"I haven't a clue."

"You said, 'They'll never like you and you'll never fit in.'"

McAdams laughed. "Okay. That sounds like me."

"But then you said—and here's the wise part—you said, 'But if you concentrate on your studies, you can make something of yourself. And while they still won't like you, maybe they'll respect you.'"

"Wow. I said that?"

"You did."

"Completely out of character. You must have caught me at a weak moment."

Mallon's lips curled in a semismile. "When you walked away, I asked you your name and you said it didn't matter. But I found out your name anyway. Last I heard you were off to Harvard."

"That happened."

"And now you're a cop?"

"That happened as well." McAdams checked his watch. "I need to get back to my boss." He picked up his briefcase. "I'm glad things worked out for you, Mallon. And if it's any consolation, Mackenzie has been in rehab twice."

"It means nothing. I don't waste my time figuring out how to exact revenge."

"Then you're one step ahead of me." He pointed to the card still in her hand. "Do call him if you think of anything."

Mallon said, "How did he die?"

"That's still an ongoing part of the investigation."

"Did he die alone?"

McAdams's smile was tinged with sadness. "Mallon, we all die alone."

CHAPTER 5

WHAT WAS THAT all about?" Decker and McAdams were walking toward Goddard Hall, located across from Marie Curie. The two dorms were separated by a strip of brown lawn and ice. McAdams raised the collar on his coat.

He said, "She looked familiar."

"More like you looked familiar to her. She kept stealing glances at you. Do you know her?"

"Not personally. She went to Philips Exeter."

"Ah, another rich kid."

"No, she was a scholarship who was bullied by the rich kids. Apparently I once interceded on her behalf and it left an impression on her."

"That was nice of you. What did you do?"

"Gave her a pep talk. Honestly, I don't remember." He stopped and turned to Decker. "I just wanted to make sure that if I did know her, I wouldn't hurt the investigation."

"Like she wasn't a former one-night stand who had nasty things to say about your sexual predilections?"

"I should be so lucky."

Decker smiled. "I need a phone number for Elijah's parents, Tyler. I have to make the notification."

"Yeah, you don't want that hanging over your head. I don't know what to tell you, boss. Doesn't seem like Elijah had any intimate friends who would know about his private life."

"I agree. So while I search his room, why don't you hunt around the college and see if you can dig up some kind of official with late office hours who can help us out with getting the parents' phone number."

"I can do that. If this is a typical college, there's probably some old perv administrator lurking in the hallways."

"Tread lightly, Tyler."

"Hey, Old Man. Who has more familiarity with these kinds of places? You or me?"

"You win, hands down."

"I can handle myself." He smiled but it lacked glee. "The kid shot himself, right?"

"Looks that way."

"It wasn't murder, right?"

"We'll know more once we've done the postmortem."

"Meaning you haven't ruled murder out."

"I haven't ruled anything out. Are you nervous?"

"Just saying my gun skills are still primitive."

"We don't need guns right now."

"You're sure about that?"

"I can't guarantee anything, but I'm not packing." Decker paused. "Or we could both go to Elijah's room to hunt around."

McAdams licked his lips. "I know I'm being paranoid. I'll get you a phone number if it exists and meet you at his room."

"It's not paranoia, Tyler. It's a healthy dose of caution."

"I haven't even thought about it in months." A pause. "Just being here . . . it brings back memories. But I'm fine. I'll deal."

"It's okay to be nervous. Anyone who has ever had an encounter with a bullet is nervous. It's why I'm so paranoid about my surroundings. Death never gives anyone a second chance."

THE VEHICLE OF choice for Goddard Hall was a rocket ship—no surprise there. The robot wore a NASA helmet and something resembling a space suit. He was completely vertical, strapped with a five-point seat belt, his imaginary eyes looking into the ethers.

Since Eli's room was locked, Decker had to round up a resident assistant who used the passkey—in this case an electronic card—to open the door. The RA, named Alistair Dixon, had gone to Kneed Loft as an undergraduate and was currently working on a two-year master's thesis, something about a mathematic model for commodities trading. He was stocky with a round ruddy face, beige eyes, and brown curly hair. He knew Eli as everyone knew Eli: as a genius who lived in his research and merely existed in the real world. Dixon also called in the authorities from the college because he knew he was in over his head. He said, "I really do think we should wait for someone to escort us into Elijah's room."

Decker looked at his watch. "I understand, but I've got to move this along. Please open the door."

"I guess as long as you don't touch anything." Dixon pushed open the door. "You really should check with the residency dean before you go around snooping."

"Snooping?" Decker gave him the ferocity of his eyes. "The boy is dead and I want to find out why. And while you're at it, ask your residency dean if he has Elijah's parents' phone number. We don't have it and they don't know what happened yet."

"Holy crap!" Dixon paled. "Who's going to tell them?"

"That would be me unless you're volunteering."

Dixon's complexion had turned gray. "He's really dead?"

"Yes."

"God, that is horrible!"

"Yes, it is." Decker stepped inside the dorm room.

Elijah Wolf was compulsiveness personified. There wasn't a speck of anything out of place. The room had been cleared of just about everything. On an empty wooden floor sat a bed, a desk, and a desk chair. The closet had no door. Jackets and shirts were neatly hung, jeans were folded on a shelf, and shoes were lined up on the floor with toes pointing inward. There were also two folded towels in the shelf along with a hanging terry-cloth robe and a pair of slippers.

His desktop was bare except for a gooseneck lamp, a tissue box, and a printer. No sign of his computer. Decker opened the desk drawer: pencils in a box, pens in a box, and two big rubber erasers. There were two storage drawers on either side of the kneehole. The one on the left was a repository of bathroom products: a six-pack of toilet paper, two boxes of tissues, Tylenol, Advil, Claritin, and Benadryl. Nothing that could be resold for profit, nothing that could be used to steel oneself against impending death.

The right-hand storage drawer was completely empty. He gave it a shove to close it but it bounced back open. The second time, he shut it slowly and it closed and latched.

On the wall over the desk were bookshelves lined with math books. He took them out one at a time, ran through the pages, turning the books upside down to see if any loose papers dropped to the floor. Once again, he didn't find anything. The books themselves were more formulas than words and he couldn't understand any of it.

The bed had been neatly made up. Decker searched the pillows, the mattress, the frame, and underneath the bed, finding nothing. He searched the windows, the floorboards, the walls, nothing underneath the frame, nothing underneath the pillow or mattress.

The boy had done a thorough job cleaning out his personal effects along with any remnants of personal life. Decker knew that math was a pencil and paper thing, but surely the boy had some electronics other than a phone. Did he hide them? Did he chuck them? Did someone out there know that Eli would no longer need them and helped himself?

Something was bothering him . . . well, a lot of things were bothering him, but there was an idea just out of reach in his brain. As he was finishing up, a petite woman with dark, almond-shaped eyes and black, straight hair came marching through the door. She seemed to be around fifty, wearing a black skirt, a green sweater, black knee-high boots that must have been custom made because her feet were exceptionally small. She stuck out her hand.

"Zhou Lin. Dean of residency and student life."

"Detective Peter Decker, Greenbury police."

She shook his hand vigorously. "What is going on?" Decker explained to her why he was here and showed her the picture of Elijah Wolf. She gasped and brought her hand to her mouth. "Oh my God. That's horrid! What happened?"

"We're not sure."

"Suicide?" She was kneading her hands.

"Nothing has been ruled out. Did he appear to be a candidate for suicide?"

"No, not that I know of."

"Are suicides common here?"

"Not common, thank God, but Kneed Loft is a high-pressure environment. It's not like the other colleges. You can't bullshit your way through subjects like topology, thermodynamics, or structural engineering. You either know what you're talking about or you don't. For those who are shaky, we try to intercede at every level; tutoring as well as therapy. But there is that rare occasion when the student is not doing well and he or she feels they've let everyone down. Especially in the Asian culture, where failure is not an option. I know what I'm talking about."

"I'm an observant Jew. We also have norms."

"Not even close, Detective. Jews have guilt: we have shame. To me, guilt is internalized. Shame is something that's foisted on you like a faceful of dog shit. And that's why we're a bunch of fucking Goody-Two-shoes, pardon my language. Not each and every one of us—we are over a billion people—but with our brainpower, we should be leading the world in innovation. Good Lord, how many greats have had failure? Like one hundred percent?" She shook her head. "I'm ranting. I'm nervous. What happened to poor Elijah? You can't tell me. Ongoing investigation, right?"

"Was Elijah one of those kids who couldn't take the pressure, Dean Lin?" Decker asked.

"Actually, it's Dean Zhou. Lin is my first name. Chinese have the surname first."

"Yes, right. Sorry."

"As far as academic pressure with Elijah, I always thought he was immune. He was so engrossed in what he was doing he didn't have time to feel shame or guilt or anything like that." She looked at the RA for confirmation.

"Absolutely," Dixon said. "Eli was brilliant. As I remember him, he was the one who helped other people. But his profs would know more than I would."

McAdams walked into the room and handed Decker a slip of paper. On it was written the names Ruth Anne and Ezra Wolf along with a phone number.

"Right," Decker said. "I'll give them a call." He introduced Tyler to Alistair Dixon and Dean Zhou Lin. Hands were shaken all around.

"Did you find anything?" McAdams asked Decker.

"Nope. Place has been cleared out. It's especially unsettling because this guy was all about math and I haven't found a scrap of paper with numbers or formulas. No computers or pads left behind, either. I can't see him junking his electronics. Maybe he gave them away."

"Even if we did find them, he might have cleared the hard drives. Betcha we wouldn't have found anything meaningful."

"Sometimes it's the little stuff that's meaningful. I'd like to know what happened to them."

"Are you done?" Zhou asked.

"For now." But Decker remained rooted where he was.

McAdams said, "What's bothering you, sir?"

"You're getting good at reading people." Decker held up a finger. He walked over to the desk and pulled out the drawer on the left—the one with the toiletries—and then closed it gently. It clicked into place. Then he did the same maneuver with the right-hand drawer. It bounced back open. He then closed it slowly and forcefully and it finally locked. Then he opened it again.

He lay down on his back and examined how the drawer was attached to the desk. There was a simple lever that should have released the drawer from the mechanism that held it in the desk. It was jammed or had been monkeyed with. The drawer would simply not disengage.

"What are you doing?" Zhou asked.

McAdams said, "He's looking to see if he can pull out the drawer because he suspects that something's behind it."

"Very good, Harvard."

"Harvard?" Dixon said.

"It's a private joke," McAdams told him.

Decker pulled the empty drawer as far as it would go. He tried to insert his hand in the space between the back of the drawer and the back of the desk, but his hand was too big.

"Anything?" Lin asked.

"I don't know," Decker answered. "It could be that the drawer was crammed and something fell behind it."

"I don't see Eli as much of a crammer," McAdams said. "But I can see him hiding something."

"I agree," Decker said. "But I can't get my hand behind the drawer."

"I can try," Dixon offered.

"How about if I try?" the dean said. "I have tiny hands."

"It's a tight squeeze," Decker said.

"I've been in many tight squeezes and have always come out on top." She bent down and inserted her tiny hand and fingers over the top of the back end of the drawer. "There is something . . ." She stretched her arm as far as it would go, pulling out a wad of around twenty pieces of paper stapled together. Then she shook her arm out and looked at her find. "Here are your formulas." She started to look over the pages, but Decker gently pried them from her hands.

"This may be evidence."

Zhou looked annoyed. "Of what?"

"Who knows? Thanks for your help."

"I could help more if you'd let me look over the pages."

"How about if I look?" Dixon said.

The dean looked at the RA. "I can take it from here, Alistair. And don't say a word about this. We will announce it in due time."

"Uh . . . okay."

"That's your cue to leave," Lin said.

Dixon gave a forced smile then decided it was inappropriate. "Bye."

After he left, Decker did a quick scan through the pages, then gave them to McAdams. "Anything familiar?"

"It's like Greek or Latin. I can read it, but it means nothing."

The dean said, "I could tell you a lot in just a quick glance. For instance, I saw Fourier transforms."

"Which we knew he was studying," Decker said. "Let me look them over first and make sure I'm not missing something crucial. Before I show anyone anything, I need to call the parents up and see them personally. At some point, if it's not germane to Eli's death, you can certainly look over these pages, Dean Zhou. And I'd like to think if I need your help with the numbers, you'll be available."

"Of course. I still don't understand why you wouldn't want me to help you out now. I thought time in police cases matters."

"It does. Thanks for your offer. I'm sure I'll get back to you on it."

"You don't trust me?"

"I'm just a wary guy," Decker said. "But I hope you don't take offense. I'm a cop. It is my sworn duty to be suspicious."

CHAPTER 6

EVEN THOUGH THERE were six official detectives in Greenbury PD, everyone pitched in with major assignments in potluck fashion. Over the past year, Decker's duties had run the gamut: from a grisly homicide almost a year ago to traffic patrol when power lines had fallen in an ice storm. Before McAdams left for school, he and Tyler shared a partners desk in the same area with Ben Roiters and Kevin Nickweed. Now that Tyler was gone, his desk had become spillover for the three of them.

He wanted to make the notification from the landline at the station house. The call lasted a few minutes, and after he hung up, McAdams knocked and then came into the office. He noticed Decker's grim face.

"How was it?" Tyler said. "Stupid question."

"I'm going to their house tomorrow at lunchtime—around ten in the morning because they work very early. I offered to come up tonight, but the father said it was too late. He had to get up early and he needed his sleep."

"Wait." McAdams furrowed his brow. "You just told him his son is dead and he's worried about his sleep?"

"People grieve in all sorts of ways."

McAdams looked at his watch. It was a hair past nine. "How far away do they live?"

"About an hour."

"You could be there in an hour and they're not interested? They must be really alienated from their son."

"Don't know because there wasn't a whole lot of conversation over the phone. It felt like as I was talking, the father was nodding on the other end. Listening but had nothing to say. It could be shock. It could be cultural. It could be he's suspected that this phone call was a long time coming." Decker sighed. "I'm tired emotionally. I need to call it a day."

"Sure . . ." McAdams made a sour face. "What the hell happened to my desk?"

"You didn't expect us to leave it as a memorial, did you?"

"You could have kept it neat at least." He picked up a pile of papers. "What is all this crap?"

"Those are Ben's cases. You'll have to ask him about it."

"You let Ben pile up his shit on my desk?"

Decker spoke to the ceiling. "Someone needs dinner." He stood and put his arm around the kid, but Tyler shook him off.

"Nuh-huh. Don't give me that fatherly act of yours. You have betrayed my trust."

"How can I make it up to you?"

"I have to think about that one." He turned to Decker. "How about if you put a picture up of me on your piano?"

Decker laughed out loud until Tyler told him he was serious. "Okay, then." Decker cleared his throat. "Send me a snapshot of your good side and I'll gladly include you as part of my family. Can we go? I'm starving and Rina is waiting for us with dinner."

"I will eat dinner with you but only for Rina's sake."

They donned their coats, scarves, and gloves and headed into Decker's Porsche. The car was the sole part of Tinseltown that he had brought along in the move to upstate. He drove it only to work and back, but it reminded him of his younger years and that was always fun. He never thought of himself as much of a mechanic, but lately he enjoyed tinkering with the beast.

The temperature was in the twenties, and it was a clear night with a cold wind whipping needles into the face. Decker warmed up the car's motor and then cranked up the heater. "All kidding aside, thanks for helping me out today."

"Truth be told, you did me a favor. It felt good to get away from school and think about something else." A pause. "I can come with you tomorrow to wherever you're going."

"I'm fine flying solo, Tyler."

"I'm sure that's true, but I wouldn't mind coming. I'd like to see how you conduct an interview with bereaved parents. And FYI, I can study very well in a moving vehicle. I don't get carsick, in case you're wondering."

"I wasn't wondering. But you need to concentrate without distraction."

"You'd be surprised how distracted I can be when I'm alone. You'll keep my nose to the grindstone. Besides, you just might want a second opinion."

"A second opinion on what?"

"On the family, of course. Maybe they didn't approve of his current life. Maybe Eli had an argument with his dad. Maybe that's what drove him to suicide."

"I think you're projecting."

"Of course I am. Anybody would eat a gun rather than listen to my dad spout off." A pause. "I mean it *is* a suicide, right?"

"On the surface, it looks pretty textbook. We should have the report by tomorrow or the next day." When the kid was quiet, Decker said, "What's on your mind?"

"The sheaves of paper that we found. They were stapled together. I don't think they accidentally fell behind the drawer. I mean the front sheet got a little crinkled from pulling up the packet, but the rest of the papers were pristine."

"He was hiding them, I agree."

"So then what are the papers about? And do they have anything to do with Eli's death?"

"I think the first question is why would Eli be hiding anything?"

"Maybe it was his research." McAdams paused. "Maybe he hit upon something so important that he didn't want anyone to see it, including his professors, who might steal his ideas and claim them for their own."

Decker stopped at a light. "The reverse is maybe he stole the papers from someone else and was trying to pass them off as his own."

"He felt guilty about it and decided to kill himself. He does come from a community where there are strict moral rights and wrongs."

"I don't know, McAdams. Why not just tear up the pages and move on?"

"Maybe it was too late. Could be he already handed them in to his professor. To backtrack would expose him. Maybe he couldn't take the shame."

"Then why did he bother hiding the pages if he already handed something in to his professors?"

"I'm not saying that's what he did," McAdams said. "Just that we should find out what he was studying and compare his known papers to the ones he was hiding. Maybe they're the reason behind the suicide."

"You're itching for something big, aren't you."

"Not necessarily big. Whatever it is, it's more interesting than studying tort law." McAdams took off his jacket in the overheated car. "What about a code?"

"What code?"

"Maybe the math isn't his research. Maybe the math is a code for something illegal."

"Now we have Eli being part of a syndicate?"

"I'm not saying he was a major-ass criminal, but there is a lot of drug dealing in the institutes of higher learning. Surely you know that."

"The papers are filled with math formulas."

"They are, but we don't know what they represent," McAdams said. "We need someone trustworthy to look them over. What do you think about giving them to Dean Zhou? Do you think she's trustworthy?"

"I haven't a clue. She did seem anxious to see the papers. I agree with you, Tyler. We need to interview his professors first to find out what Eli was studying. We get some copies of his work and compare it to the papers he was hiding. Because for all we know, the hidden papers may have nothing to do with his thesis."

"But we need someone who understands math. That shouldn't be a problem. We both know a certain Harvard math professor who has been useful in the past. I find him trustworthy. What do you think?"

Decker said, "I don't see Professor Gold pilfering other people's work. He's a full professor, tenured, and well respected."

"But then again, he ratted us out to the authorities."

"But he did it to protect us. We might as well go to him since I don't know anyone else."

"Okay, then it's settled," McAdams announced. "First, we talk to Eli's professors and try to get some copies of his research since we can't find his laptop—which, by the way, is still bothering the crap out of me. Once we do that, you can call up Professor Gold and we can take a trip to Boston."

"So you're calling the shots now?" Decker said.

"You always tell me to take initiative."

His plan was dead-on except that Decker had reservations about taking the kid away from his law books. He did have exams to pass. "This is the deal, McAdams. You study tomorrow while I interview Eli's family. We'll assess where you are in your studies tomorrow evening."

"How can you assess where I am?"

"I can't. So I'm going to have to rely on your honesty. If you say you can take a day off to travel to Boston with me, I'll take you at your word and we'll go together."

"Fair enough."

"Besides, you did say you can study in a car. It might even work to your benefit. A day will give you time to amass questions. Once we're up north, you can just ask your law professors for clarification."

"I don't ask questions in school, boss. I've never once raised my hand, gone to office hours, or joined a study group. If I'm called on, I usually know the answer, and the few cases I didn't know, I didn't try to fudge or guess. I said out loud in front of everyone that I'm not sure, but I will look it up after class and get back to you. And I always did get back. I e-mail them the answer I should have known in the first place. If I can't figure out this stuff on my own, I shouldn't be in Harvard Law."

"That's a fine policy for school, Tyler. But on this job, I would hope that you'd ask me for help. You'd better ask me for help. It could be life and death."

"I know that better than most." McAdams stared out the windshield. "Police work is on-the-job training. You can't learn it in books. So of course I ask you questions. With academic issues, I sink or swim on my own."

"Fiercely independent."

"It's hard to break away from Black Jack McAdams, but I try." He sat back in the seat and sighed. "Lord knows that I try."

MCADAMS FELT MORE at home with the Deckers than he did with his own parents. After he had been shot, he had moved into the spare bedroom for almost two months as he recovered. The house was done up in a typical New England B-and-B style with chintz wallpaper and gleaming hardwood floors. The living room ceiling had been opened up to the attic rafters, giving the area a larger feel.

All that winter, Rina had not only nursed him back to health, but she had also taken part in some of the investigative work with him. The case was solved but the ending was unsatisfying. Nothing had been neat. Such was McAdams's introduction to real police work.

His relationship with Decker was mentor/mentee. While he admired the old man more than he would dare admit out loud, McAdams's relationship to Rina was different. She was part mother figure, but she was also part friend. It surprised him that a religious woman who covered her hair and knew the Bible by heart could be so insightful and act so ordinary.

She greeted him with a hug—something not every religious Jewish woman would do—but that was just Rina: warm and friendly, quick-witted and rock-solid dependable. Tonight she wore a blue sweater and a black skirt that ended midknee. A black beret sat on her head. Her feet were in slippers.

"Your room is set up," she told him. "Let me know if you need anything."

"Thanks. I'll be fine."

"Hungry?"

"Starved." McAdams hoisted his duffel. "Let me get rid of this."

"Sure. Unpack and I'll see you in a few minutes."

Rina walked into the kitchen, where Decker was picking at the rice pilaf. She said, "Ah, ah, ah."

Decker kissed her lips. "Tastes good. We're starving."

"I'm hungry, too." She spread the rice onto a big platter and put the roasted chicken on top. There was also a bowl of green beans. Baked apples were still in the oven. They both heard water running. "You want to take a quick shower as well?"

"I'll do it after dinner," Decker said. "I'll get a hotter shower if I wait. We really should get a bigger water heater."

"I'll call someone."

"Get a couple of prices. Even in a small town, you can get competitive bids."

"Not a problem. So what's going on with the body in the woods?"

"He's a college student and it's probably a suicide."

Rina frowned. "That is so sad. You have a name?"

"Elijah Wolf. He's from a Mennonite community."

"Oh dear. Did you contact his parents yet?"

"I did."

"How do you do that? It must eat you alive."

"It does, but someone has to do it. I'm visiting the parents tomorrow, hoping to find out more about him. They live about an hour from here. I spoke to the father. He didn't say much. Could be shock, but it could be cultural."

"What does the father do?"

"He has a farm. That's all I know."

"How religious are they?"

"No idea, but they do have a phone."

"Are you taking Tyler with you?"

"No, no. He came down here to study, not to get involved in this case. I don't want to be the reason he did poorly on his exams."

"So you're driving up-country alone?"

"Talking to the boy's parents isn't a two-person job."

"I'm not questioning your detective skills, Peter. I'm not working tomorrow and I was wondering if you wanted company." She sighed. "I guess I just want to help."

"You are a help just being who you are." Decker kissed her forehead. "Actually, it's a good idea."

"What is?"

"Keeping me company, coming up with me. You can talk to the mother. As one religious woman to another, you'll probably get more out of her than I would."

"If she's able to talk, that might be true. If I were her, I'd be a basket case. I'm sure she *is* a basket case."

Rina handed him the plate of chicken and rice. She took the bowl of green beans. They went out into the dining room and placed the food on the tabletop.

"If she and I happen to wind up together, I'll keep the conversation light. Food is always a good icebreaker. I can talk recipes for hours. It's the primary bond between your mother and me. We should visit her. She's old and frail. The bonus is Florida." Rina consulted her smartphone. "At present, it's sixty-eight degrees."

"After I'm done with this mess, I'll ask for a little time off. Since I worked on Christmas and New Year's, Mike will be amenable."

"Good. So I'll come with you tomorrow?"

"I'd love it. Thanks for offering."

"No problem. When are we leaving?"

"Around nine-thirty."

"Perfect. I won't have to rush."

With a wet head, McAdams walked into the dining room. "Man, that looks good." He sat down and put his napkin on his lap. "I haven't eaten all day. I'm beyond starved and into famished territory."

After ritually washing, Rina and Decker sat down. Everyone filled their plates. Conversation was kept to a minimum as they ate. Afterward, Decker and McAdams cleared the table while Rina served the baked apples. When they all sat back down, Decker said, "Rina's going with me tomorrow."

"To the Wolf farm?"

"Yes."

McAdams shrugged. "I see I'm being replaced once again."

"Stop that," Rina said.

"At least it's someone competent."

Decker said, "Your competency isn't at issue here. You need to study. When I go up to Boston, I'll take you with me, okay?"

"Goody, goody." McAdams cut the apple into smaller bites. "So when are you going to interview Eli's math professors?"

"When I get back. Sometime in the late afternoon."

"I'd like to come with you. I've been around professors more than you have and I might actually be of help."

"It's a fair point. Let's see how far you get with your books."

"Whatever." McAdams wiped his mouth, got up from the table, and cleared his plate. "I'm going to try to rip off a couple hours of studying." He turned to Rina. "Thanks for dinner and thanks for putting me up."

After he left, Rina said, "He's dying to come with you."

"It's more important for him to study. Besides, by the time we come back, I'm hoping the postmortem will be done." Decker stood up and stretched. "Give me a better idea of what I'm working with. I don't want a repeat of last year: something small turning into something big and dangerous."

"Understood." Rina got up. "You look beat. I'll load the dishwasher. Take a shower."

"No, I'm actually okay. I'll finish up here and you relax." Decker looked at his watch. "We did dinner in twenty-eight minutes. By the time I'm done, I should have plenty of hot water. I like long showers. They help me clear my head. And being that we are no longer in a drought zone, I can indulge myself without feeling like I'm scoffing at some environmental water-protection law conjured up by some Green Party fanatic who drives a Prius and shops organic at Whole Foods."

"You're working yourself up. Go take your shower." She gave him a gentle push. "I'll put the kettle on. I just got some loose-leaf exotic Indian tea at the organic coffee and tea store. It has ginger, cardamom, and ginseng. It's supposed to revitalize the flesh as well as the spirit."

Decker smiled. "That sounds good to me. At my age, I can use all the revitalization I can get."

CHAPTER 7

DRIVING THROUGH RURAL upstate in the winter, Decker passed landscapes of white and brown, so different from the verdant fields that were in place a half year ago. Crops of lettuce, kale, cabbage, onion, beets, carrots, and oversize pumpkin had been stocked in every farmer's market as recently as late November. Snowfall had come later this year, plus it wasn't as harsh as last winter.

The farming communities varied in size and modernity, from those that employed the latest equipment to oxen yoked plows. Decker didn't know where Elijah's parents fit in, but the phone number suggested they didn't eschew electricity. Rina was staring out the passenger window as Decker waited until he had a chance to safely pass a buggy.

"Another world," she said. "Not unlike the one you encountered when we first met."

Decker gave her a hesitant smile. "A little different. At least these communities are producing something."

Rina slugged him. "We produced scholars. And there has been

a real sea change in the Orthodox yeshiva world, just saying. More and more of them are encouraging their students to pursue advanced secular education."

"It only took what? About two hundred years?"

"Now you're just being contentious."

"I don't deny it. It's fun to tease you." Decker paused. "Do you ever miss the insular life?"

"No. It was what I needed at that time, but I didn't like being disconnected from the real world. Even at the time, I knew I wasn't going to stay. I'll tell you one thing that surprised me. I love living in a small town. It's so manageable. And with the colleges nearby, I feel we get the best of both worlds. What about you?"

Decker gave the question some real thought. "I must admit it's still an adjustment. I often wake up with the anticipation of what's going to await me at work. And then I realize it's going to be same old, same old."

"You didn't expect to be called down to a crime scene yesterday."

"True, but even so, there's not a lot of detection work involved."

"So you think it's suicide?"

"Probably."

"But you don't know why."

"No, I don't. If I hunt around, I'm sure I'll find out he had depression issues. It doesn't seem like a spur-of-the-moment decision. And unless someone wants me to look further, it's really not up to me to find out why he killed himself."

"What about those pages you found tucked away in his desk?"

"Not really my business, either, unless it's a suspicious death."

"What if they had something to do with his suicide?"

Decker thought about that. "Let me get back to you on that one." He smiled. "I'm not complaining, Rina. I like the quiet life." A pause. "It's certainly better than being shot at, but obviously that can happen anywhere."

"That is indeed the truth." She leaned over and kissed his cheek. "Can you stop off at the next Dunkin' Donuts? I'd like some fresh coffee."

"Sure."

They found one ten minutes later on the main strip. There was a Dunkin' Donuts, a DQ, a two-show movie theater, a library, a grocery store, a store specializing in livestock feed and equipment, a dress and fabric store, an appliance store—new and used—a city hall, and several diners, all of them specializing in pie. The parking was diagonal except for the hitching posts for the buggies. The population included some Amish, some moderns, and some in-betweens.

"You want a cup?" Rina asked.

"Thanks. I can get it."

"No, I'll do it. I want to stretch my legs." She came back a few minutes later with coffee. "Here you go." Rina took out a large paper bag that she had brought from home. "Want a sandwich?"

"No thanks, this is fine."

Rina took out an apple, made a blessing, and bit in. "Sure you don't want anything to eat?"

Decker patted his stomach. "Does it look like I miss a lot of meals?"

"You look great."

"For my age."

"I didn't say that."

"You thought that."

"I did not! We both look great. No asterisk 'for our ages' necessary."

"Easy for you to say. You're way younger than I am."

"Even more proof why you must look great." She leaned over and kissed his cheek again. "You snagged yourself one hot, terrific babe."

THE WOLF HOMESTEAD was ten minutes from the main highway, in a patchwork of snowed-under farms. There were some greenhouses, and what they grew behind the glass panes was anyone's guess. Judging from the farmers markets, the hothouses probably had tomatoes, cucumbers, beans, and squashes. There were also chicken coops, pigsties, and sheepcotes. No hogs in sight, but the sheep were grazing, chowing down whatever brown grass and detritus remained from the fall crops. While the area certainly wasn't Gainesville, it was vaguely reminiscent of Decker's childhood: simpler times and simpler needs and much, much quieter.

As they inched closer to the appointed address, the Wolf spread fanned out into lots of acreage, with a barn, two windmills, several chicken coops, and a sty. There was a corral and paddock, but no horses in sight. Around twenty sheep roamed around the grounds. Beyond the farming area were orchards of deciduous trees that were bare at this time of year. From the distance they looked like apple trees. New York ranked second in U.S. apple production, just behind Washington State.

The main house was polished-looking—three stories fashioned from whitewood siding and fieldstone—and fronted by a dirt driveway that held an old, black Lincoln Town Car. Decker parked behind the car, killed the motor, and he and Rina walked up to the front door. He knocked and a woman in her late forties or early fifties answered the door. She was around five-foot-five, with blue eyes, apple cheeks, and a sprinkling of freckles across her nose. Small wrinkles and spiderweb lines framed her mouth and her eyes. She wore a long brown dress with long sleeves. Most of her light brown hair was tucked into some kind of netting.

Rina had on a green sweater and a denim skirt that covered her knees and black fashion boots. Her dark hair had been secured under a black beret. While the two women weren't dressed similarly, they both were dressed modestly. Decker took out his identification. "I'm Detective Decker of the Greenbury Police Department."

The woman nodded with her eyes on Rina's face. "You're here to talk about Elijah."

"Yes, ma'am. I'm very sorry for your loss and I'm also sorry to intrude at this time. But it's better if we talk now. This is my wife, Rina Decker."

Rina held out her hand. "I'm very sorry for your loss, Mrs. Wolf."

"Ruth Anne." The woman touched Rina's hand with barely any pressure. "Come in, please." Leading them into a small and immaculately clean and homey living room, she pointed to a sofa upholstered in a soft, muted orange print. "Can I get either of you some tea or coffee?"

"I'm fine, thank you," Decker said.

She turned to Rina. "Mrs. Decker?"

"It's Rina and tea would be lovely, thank you."

Five minutes later, she came out carrying a tray. She poured tea for both Rina and Decker. "Just in case, Detective."

"Thank you."

She gave a brief smile. "My husband and son should be in soon. I'm making lunch. We adhere to a strict schedule, otherwise things don't get done."

"Can I help?" Rina asked.

Ruth Anne looked at her. "Forgive my boldness, but you're Jewish, aren't you?"

"Yes, I am."

"You're dressed differently than the others."

"You mean like the Jews in Squaretown? Yes, I do dress differently from them."

"I was thinking more like the Jews in Monsey."

"Jews run the gamut in their religiosity. Some might consider me fanatical, while others would consider me heretical."

"I can understand that."

"I came along to keep Detective Decker company." Rina stood, teacup in hand. "Perhaps it would be better for him to talk to your husband without my presence. Let me help you in the kitchen. It's probably a place where we're both familiar."

The woman nodded. "Of course."

Rina gave a quick glance to Decker and followed Ruth Anne into the kitchen. The woman immediately picked up a knife and began chopping vegetables for a salad. Rina said, "Would you like me to do that?"

Ruth Anne immediately put down the knife and turned her back to Rina. She placed her hand over her eyes. Rina couldn't hear her crying but she could see her shoulders heaving. "I'm so sorry."

"I'm . . ." Ruth Anne waved her hand in the air. "I'm fine." She pivoted back, her still eyes wet. "I'm all right. Yes, you can chop the vegetables. Put them in the bowl. My men like a big salad."

Silence ensued for the next minute. As Rina chopped, Ruth Anne took out a pan and four chops. She said, "How many children do you have?"

"Between the two of us, we have four children. They're all grown."

"Married?"

"Two married, two are engaged. We also have a foster son who has parents but stayed with us for around three years. We're still very close. And you?"

"Five." A pause. "We had five children. Elijah was number two."

"I heard he was a brilliant boy."

"He was always bright."

Rina nodded and began dicing a tomato.

"Bright . . . but not brilliant, at least not right away." Ruth Anne looked up at the ceiling. "Elijah changed when he was fourteen. He was riding in the backseat of a car, along with his older brother and a friend who was driving." A long pause. "It was a terrible accident. The driver was killed and my eldest son, Jacob, broke his left leg. But he was otherwise okay, praise God. Elijah was wearing a seat belt but there was impact. He was in a coma for two weeks. We almost lost him. It was touch and go."

She recited the story with a flat voice. Rina said, "That must have been so earth-shattering."

"At the time, I thought it was the worst thing that could happen to a parent. Now I see I was wrong." Ruth Anne put the chops in an oiled pan.

From the aroma, Rina knew it was pork. She kept chopping vegetables, but stopped drinking the tea. Even though it was silly, it was hard to be around the smell.

"Elijah changed after that," Ruth Anne continued. "Before the accident, he was friendly, popular, and outgoing. Afterward, he became withdrawn and quiet. Very uncommunicative. He buried himself in a world of numbers."

She flipped the meat over. Grease splattered on the stove top.

"My husband is a very laconic man. He always thought that Elijah was a frivolous boy. He and Elijah used to butt heads all the time. After the accident, my husband was pleased with the change in his attitude. He thought the accident had shook some sense into the boy, showed him that the world wasn't a silly place. He was pleased that Elijah had become so serious." She shook her head. "But I knew something was wrong. Elijah wouldn't talk to me except to say he was fine and his perspective had changed." A pause. "He stopped going out. He stopped seeing his friends. He stopped doing anything social."

She threw up her hands. Then she placed the pork chops on a paper towel to drain the grease and turned off the fire.

"When it came time for college, Ezra wanted him to stay close to home and go to community college which is just ten minutes from here. That way, he could still help with the farm. That's what his brother did. I wanted him near to keep an eye out. But it seems that Elijah had entered some kind of state math contest. It caught both of us by surprise that he even knew about such things, let alone took the initiative and entered it without our knowing about it."

She divided the chops onto two plates.

"He came in first place."

"That must have made you so proud."

"It did. But it was a mixed bag. We . . . 'we' meaning Menno-nites . . . we keep a low profile. After the contest, the letters began to arrive . . . full scholarships from Harvard and Princeton and MIT and so many others. People found out. People began to talk."

"It's hard when you're a private family and you're suddenly thrust into the spotlight, even a good spotlight."

She nodded. "I had reservations about sending him away. I didn't want him holed up in some small dorm room working with formulas during all his waking hours." Her eyes moistened. "I wanted him to have a meaningful life with a wife and children and his own land."

"I understand," Rina said.

Ruth Anne regarded her with fierce eyes. "Do you?"

"In traditional communities, family is everything."

"Yes, it is. Not that it matters now." She stared up at the ceiling. "I really lost Elijah six years ago. It would be one thing if he had been happy with his new life. But he seemed so . . . I don't know how to describe it. He became so withdrawn and secretive. Almost paranoid, but I found out that sometimes people can be that way after brain injuries."

Rina nodded.

"His only focus was on his math. His world became very small. He had wanted to go to Princeton, because they have a top math department and they had this professor who Elijah wanted to study with. Ezra refused. He didn't want a big university to subvert our values and lead him into a life that we didn't approve of. Kneed Loft was a compromise. It was an hour away and also had an excellent math department. Plus there was another professor there that Elijah said he'd work with."

"Did he give you a name?"

"No. After the accident, he didn't talk to us beyond the basics.

After much consideration, Ezra allowed him to go to Kneed Loft, but only after he worked a year on the farm because he was only sixteen. So he worked his year without complaint and then he left."

A long pause.

"And he never really came back." She bit her lower lip. "During his first year, he came home for Christmas and Easter. After that . . ." She shrugged. "Never saw him unless I visited, never heard from him unless I called . . . I got a cell phone so I could text him. It was the most likely way he'd answer me."

"What about his father? Did he call him?"

"I do believe they haven't exchanged a word in the past two years." She turned to Rina. "If you have children, you know that they can be very different from one another."

"Absolutely."

"So . . . there you have it." Ruth Anne paused. "Still . . . even with all the changes, I can't understand why he would kill himself. He never seemed depressed. His world had become math, but he seemed to like what he was doing. He seemed to be all right. The last time I talked to him, he even seemed lighter of heart. Shows you what I know."

"It's not a matter of knowing, Mrs. Wolf. The mind is mysterious. Even when people seem transparent, we know they're not."

"Your husband." A long pause. "Is he talking to people about Elijah?"

"I believe he is. You can certainly ask him questions."

"Not in front of my husband."

Rina paused. "I'll give you his cell number if you'd like."

"Why not?" Ruth Anne took out a scrap of paper and a pencil and Rina gave her the number. "You never know what you need, right? Not that I'd even know what to ask him." She folded the number and placed it in her pocket. "Thank you."

"Can I ask you when you last spoke with Elijah?"

"It was a month ago. His research was going well. He didn't seem at all down. Maybe he hit a setback. If he had, he certainly wouldn't have told me about it." Her eyes leaked tears. "Now it really is in the past. Are you done with the salad?"

Rina nodded. "Do you have dressing for the salad? I'll be happy to toss it."

"Just add a little olive oil and lemon."

"Sure." Rina began mixing the greens.

Ruth Anne wiped her eyes. "I know that God has tests for all of us. And I have no idea why He's testing me. But that's all right. I'm strong. Elijah was weak. Even as a boy, he always depended on Jacob to get things done. Why would God test such a weak boy? Surely He can pick on stronger people."

Rina shrugged. "Sometimes our understanding as well as our faith elude us."

"Isn't that the truth." She turned to Rina. "I am so angry! I'm angry at God, I'm angry at Elijah, I'm angry at Ezra, I'm angry at the world. And it isn't good. I have children. I can't be this angry person and do right by them." She stared at the ceiling. "I just don't know where to turn or what to do."

"When my first husband died, I was very angry as well. I had two little boys to take care of and I couldn't see how I could manage. But I did."

"How?"

"The passage of time. Ultimately I reconciled with God. I didn't want to lose my faith because selfishly it was helpful to me."

Ruth Anne didn't answer. They both heard a screen door open and close. She said, "The boys are here. Can you take the salad out for me?"

"Of course."

Ruth Anne looked at her. "I'm assuming you'll tell your husband what I told you. I want you to tell him, but I don't want Ezra to know what I told you."

"Whatever you want. And if you want to keep everything confidential, I won't mention it to Peter . . . Detective Decker. I'll tell him we talked food."

"No, no. Tell him everything. Maybe it'll help him understand Elijah. Because I certainly didn't understand my son at all."

CHAPTER 8

MCADAMS IGNORED THE doorbell. The Deckers weren't home and nobody except the police department knew he was in town. But by the third chime, he was irritated. He rose from the dining room table where he had spread out his papers and books. Maybe they were expecting a package. Or maybe one of their many children had dropped by for a pop-in visit, although he suspected that they had keys. Most likely it was a nuisance call. To him, all calls were nuisances.

Swinging open the door, he was face-to-face with Mallon Euler. She was dressed in a Windbreaker over a thick sweater, black jeans, and high-tops on her feet. Her hands were covered but her head was bare. He tried to hide his surprise but he suspected he wasn't doing a good job. "Hi there." He stepped outside. "Detective Decker isn't in. Can I help?"

"Actually, I came to see you."

A pause. "Sure. If you give me a minute, I'll phone the station house and we'll talk down there."

"It's personal."

"O-kay." His mind was racing. He looked at his watch. "Wow, it's past noon. No wonder I'm hungry. Care to join me?" She smiled. It didn't seem angry or happy, just a facial gesture. He shrugged. "While you decide, I'll get my coat and shoes."

"You could invite me in."

"I'll just be a moment." He closed the door in her face and immediately called Decker's cell. It rang four times before he picked up. McAdams said, "Sorry to bother you. Are you with Elijah's parents?"

"Yes. Is everything all right?"

"Mallon Euler just showed up on my doorstep . . . rather, your doorstep, wanting to talk to me." McAdams started lacing up his boots. "It doesn't take a genius to figure out where I'm staying, but it does take a modicum of effort. Plus, she doesn't want to talk at the station house. She says it's personal. And in case you're wondering, I haven't invited her inside. But I did invite her to lunch." He pulled on his jacket and gloves. "Is that okay?"

"Seems reasonable. Save the receipt and we'll pay for your expenses. Find out what's on her mind."

"How's it going with you?"

"I'll let you know when I get back. Call me if you have any questions."

"Will do." He clicked off his cell phone and walked outside. "Let's go toward campus. More places and choices. What are you in the mood for?"

"Whatever you want." Her voice was testy. "I'm not hungry."

"Okay. Let's just walk and we'll find something."

"You could have invited me inside."

"It's not my home and it's not my place."

"I'm sure Detective Decker wouldn't have minded."

"Maybe not, but he wasn't here to make that decision." McAdams stopped and faced her. "Or if you don't want to eat, we can talk on a park bench. It's a little cold, but I'm dressed for it."

"Why don't you trust me inside the house? Are you that arrogant to think I'm going to throw myself at you?"

McAdams laughed. "I am arrogant, but that was the last thought on my mind. Look, Mallon. I'm not officially on the case. But I'm not officially *off* the case. If you don't want to talk at the station house and you don't want to talk in a restaurant, pick a place as long as it's semipublic. I'm just trying to be professional, that's all."

She didn't answer, stared at the tip of her shoe sweeping over the hard ground.

"Or you can change your mind about talking to me." Mallon stared at him and then she bolted ahead. Not knowing what to do, McAdams followed. "What's up?"

"Nothing." She faced him with tears in her eyes. "Let's go Indian. I'm a vegetarian."

"Great. I love Indian."

They walked a half mile until a collection of storefront cafés and bistros came into sight: three square blocks of eateries and shops catering to the college crowd. Rajah's was on Harvard Street closest to Duxbury, the oldest of the five institutions.

Once inside, McAdams's nostrils were filled with the pungent aromas of exotic spices. Mallon did a once-over of the place and chose a table farthest from the entrance and closest to the kitchen: the warmest and noisiest spot in the restaurant. Even before they had managed to park their butts on chairs, a server in a black shirt and black jeans was already there with naan on the table.

The server smiled. "Buffet?"

"Yes," Mallon answered. "Unless you want to order off the menu?"

"Buffet is dandy," McAdams said.

"Two chai?" the server piped in.

"Yes," Mallon told him.

"With milk?"

"Yes," Mallon barked out.

The server didn't seem to notice her anger. "Right away."

She sat down while McAdams hung up the coats on a provided hook. When he came back to the table, he noticed she was sulking. He rubbed his hands. "I'm really sorry about Eli."

She looked at his face and then at the tabletop.

"We're still in the dark. Anything that you'd like to tell us would be helpful."

"I don't know anything. If I did, I would have told you yesterday."

"Did he seem depressed or worried lately?"

"No. I already told you that."

"Maybe on reflection, you thought of something?" No response. McAdams said, "Okay. I'll stop pressing you. I hate being pushed and I imagine you don't like it either. Talk when and if you feel like it. I am legitimately hungry, so I'm going up to the buffet." He stood and so did she. "Would it offend you if I ate meat?"

"No."

McAdams filled his plate with tandoori lamb, basmati rice, raita, fresh cucumbers and tomatoes, the dal of the day, sag paneer, and fresh mango and orange slices. She filled up on vegetables, fruits, and salads. When they both sat back down, Mallon said, "Thanks for asking."

"Pardon?"

The waiter came by with two piping-hot chai teas. "Anything else?"

"Water," McAdams said. "Do you have garlic naan, by the way?"

"Yes, sir."

"Could you bring an order?"

"Right away."

After he left, Mallon said, "Thank you for asking whether or not I'd be offended if you ate meat."

"No problem. Don't want you to lose your appetite. If someone eats eggs in my presence, I get a little queasy."

"Eggs?"

"One of my half sibs has an anaphylactic reaction to eggs. Luckily I'm just sensitive to them. I can eat them in baking and cooking, but I can't eat like a plain egg without getting sick."

Mallon nodded. "Must be hard to do brunch with you."

"I don't go out a lot, so it's not a problem." He looked up and took in her face. She hadn't bothered with makeup except for a little mascara and lipstick. The blush on her cheeks was probably from the cold. As hard as he tried not to notice, he did. She was a very pretty woman in that waifish way. "You want to tell me what's on your mind or do you want to finish eating first?"

"Don't be too blunt."

"I would think you'd appreciate it. Math people are usually no-nonsense. It's the social-science people that love the ambiguity. They can discuss minutiae for hours and seem very happy about it. It used to drive me crazy, listening to people who loved to hear themselves talk."

"Everyone wants their fifteen minutes."

"Right you are."

She put down her fork. "How's this for bluntness? Do you have anything new in regard to Eli?"

"No, I don't."

"I heard you found a stack of papers with formulas hidden behind his desk."

"Word gets around." McAdams didn't bother to look up. "Who told you that little ditty of info?"

"Why should I tell you anything if you hold back on me?"

"It wouldn't be very professional if I just gave you random facts."

"You're really into this professional thing."

"I try to do a good job in whatever I do."

"Bully for you."

"No need to be hostile."

"I'd like to see those papers."

"That decision is not up to me, Mallon." McAdams's brain was whirling. He didn't want her to seize up, so he had to say something encouraging. "But if you tell me *why* you want to see them, maybe I can make a case for you."

She didn't speak right away. She played with her rice, shoving it around the plate. Finally, she nibbled a few grains. "I have a feeling those papers have to do with my research. I wouldn't want them falling into the wrong hands."

"I can understand that."

"So you'll let me see them?"

"Not my decision. But I'll tell you this. Decker is keeping them off-limits to anyone in the school until he knows what's in them. We're both aware about plagiarism and academic stealing."

"So show them to me. I can tell you what they're about."

"I'm sure you can. But I think Decker wants someone not associated with the school to look them over."

"See, that's the problem, Tyler." She leaned over and grabbed his hand. "If it is my research, I don't want any third party seeing what I've done. The chance of someone hijacking research is very high."

McAdams extracted his hand and studied her face. The blush in her cheeks had reddened. Her lower lip was trembling. "No one is going to steal your research, Mallon. I promise."

"How can you guarantee that?"

"Because I know the man who we'd like to show the papers to. He's a full, tenured professor at Harvard. He doesn't need to steal any research."

"That's what they all say."

"Let me talk this over with the boss. Maybe I can have someone contact you after he's looked at the papers, okay? You tell him what you're doing. He'll know right away if it has something to do with your research."

She bit her lower lip. "Who is this guy?"

"Someone trustworthy." McAdams speared a piece of lamb. "Why do you think that Eli was hiding your research?"

"Eli was secretive whether it was his research or anyone else's papers. It's not that our professors routinely steal data. But reading other people's research . . . sometimes it gives them ideas that they later claim to be their own."

"Has this happened at Kneed Loft before?"

"It happens everywhere, Tyler." She leaned over again. "I can call you 'Tyler,' right?"

"Sure."

"If you went to Harvard, you probably know that academia is a very evil profession."

"Evil's a little strong. More like amoral."

"No, 'evil' is the right word. There are some people that will do anything to get a name, an award, or even to get published. Stealing is the quickest way to tenure if you haven't had a novel idea in years. Professors routinely steal and plagiarize. At the very least, they take over first authorship when they've had nothing to do with your research."

"As unfair as it might be, Mallon, professors are entitled to put their names on any research that came out of their labs."

"That is total bullshit!"

"I agree. But that happens all the time. How else do you get a million publications to your name?" A pause. "Plagiarism and stealing are different animals. Do you know for sure that this has happened at Kneed Loft?"

"I have very strong suspicions."

"And you've never told anyone?"

"I told Eli."

"No one in authority?"

"And get blackballed from every major graduate school?"

"Right." A pause. "Do you think that idea stealing had something to do with Eli's su—death?"

"It was suicide?"

"I didn't say that."

"You started to."

"No, I didn't. I started to say suspicious death."

"So you think there was foul play, as you guys say in detective speak?"

"Every death that's not natural causes is suspicious. We don't have the coroner's report. I can't tell you anything more because I don't know. Let's go back to my question. Do you think someone was trying to steal Eli's research and claiming it for his or her own?"

"I think that stealing ideas is always a possibility—his ideas or my ideas."

"Do you think it had something to do with Eli's death?"

"Possibly."

"Are you worried about your safety?"

"I can take care of myself."

"What do you mean by that? You're not worried or you are worried but you can protect yourself."

"That's very Socratic, Tyler."

"Answer the question."

"I'm not worried for my personal safety but I am worried about my research. If you really want to get a feel for Kneed Loft, Eli's death and what's going on, you should check out the math department one by one by one."

"How many people are we talking about?"

"All the professors and the grad students."

"Kneed Loft has grad students?"

"It has a few graduate departments and math is one of them. You can get a Ph.D. in theoretical math there. It's not as prestigious as the big universities like Princeton and Chicago and Berkeley, but I suppose it worked for Eli."

"He was going for a Ph.D.?"

"He was studying math. I think the degrees for him were incidental."

"How big is the math department?"

She did a quick mental calculation. "There are fourteen professors and ten grad students." A pause. "Yes, twenty-four in total. You should look at every one of them."

"Could you narrow down the search for us?"

"No, I can't. In case I'm wrong, I could be accused of slander, so I want you to treat everyone equal. And maybe in your inquiries, you'll find other evidence of wrongdoing."

"I'll talk to Detective Decker about this. It would help if I had more information. It's hard to investigate people on someone else's say-so without a shred of evidence."

"You have your evidence. Eli hid those papers from someone."

"Maybe he was hiding them from you."

Her blue eyes darkened. "You're being deliberately provocative."

"I'm just asking questions," McAdams answered. "You're very interested in the case. That makes us interested in you."

Tears formed in her eyes. "I'm trying to help you."

"I know, Mallon. But if you choose to get involved, you open yourself up to all sorts of possibilities."

She continued to eat in silence. Then she said, "I know you're only doing your job."

"Mallon, what personal thing did you want to talk to me about?"

"Nothing other than what I told you," she whispered. "I feel more comfortable talking to you than Detective Decker. Same age and a history and all that."

What history? McAdams thought. "Okay. Feel free to call me if something else comes to mind, no matter how trivial."

"When will you find out if it's a suicide or not?"

"I don't know. That's Detective Decker's domain. You can call him, also. He's very easy to talk to." He glanced at her plate. She had barely eaten. "Not hungry?"

"Not really. I'm done."

"Then I'll call for the check."

When he took out a credit card, she said, "I can pay my own way."

"I'm charging it to the department. So unless you want to make a contribution to the police department to the tune of seven dollars and ninety-nine cents, which is what the buffet costs, let me take care of it."

"You won't get into trouble?"

Suddenly she was concerned for his professionalism. He smiled. "No." He raised his hand and the server was over a minute later with the check. McAdams stood up, fished a twenty out of his wallet, and left it on the table. Then he tore off the bottom part from the check for a receipt.

"If you think of anything else . . ." He gave her his card.

She reluctantly took it and together they walked outside and stood in front of the restaurant.

McAdams said, "I think we're going in opposite directions, so I'll say good-bye."

"Thanks for lunch."

"Anytime."

"Even if it's not business?"

Her smile was seductive. He said, "Take care, Mallon."

"Tyler, I don't mean to sound like a jerk. I'm sure most of the professors at Kneed Loft are honest. It's just . . . it's hard to know who to trust."

"You're protective of your work. I totally get it."

"The difference between failure and success can often be just a single thought." Her eyes moistened. "I'm not there yet, Tyler. Eli was helping me. He was the only person in that entire place I could trust. Now that he's gone, I've not only lost a sounding board, I lost my lifeline to sanity. I have no one else to turn to. He was the only one who understood. I don't know what I'm going to do."

She began to weep openly. She fell against his chest. For a moment, he froze but then he realized they were out in public, so no one could take it the wrong way. He put his arms around her as she sobbed on his shoulder. "I'm so lost without him."

"You're a brilliant girl, Mallon. You'll be fine."

"You don't know that."

"I don't know, but I suspect that's the case." He patted her back. "Call me. Even if you just want to talk."

She pulled away. "Do you mean that?"

"I do. I'm very good at listening." He smiled. "It's talking that gets me into trouble. If you're around me long enough, eventually I'll piss you off."

"Join the club. Every time I open my mouth, someone gets angry with me. I can't help it. I just say what's on my mind." She sighed. "So here goes nothing. I like you, Tyler. Obviously I had a school-girl crush on you for years. But now we're both adults and I'd like to see who you really are. Can I take you out to dinner?"

McAdams's head became foggy. He should have expected it, but he didn't. He didn't want to put her off. He suspected she was up to something. So taking her out to dinner while the case was still open was out of the question. But later on . . . if she was still genuinely interested . . .

He let out a small laugh. "When all of this is over and I'm done with my own finals, that would be a yes."

"What finals?" Her eyes narrowed. "I thought you were done with school."

"No, actually I'm in law school." When Mallon made a face, McAdams said, "Yeah, yeah, I know. It's one of those necessary evils for me."

"Where is law school?" When he paused, she said, "Figures. What are you doing here in Greenbury?"

"Officially I am a Greenbury cop who is currently on leave. Unofficially I'm here studying at the Decker place because it's quiet and I can concentrate."

"So you're not working officially, then."

"No, I *am* working officially."

"Either you are or you're not."

"It's complicat—"

"Oh please!" She mocked, " 'It's complicated.' " She shook her head. "Don't be so pedestrian."

"See, I'm pissing you off already." He checked his watch. "What was that? Like five minutes?"

She laughed. "Maybe less."

"I can't do anything socially with you until Eli's case is closed. Call me or Detective Decker if you think of anything that might help us."

"I will—now that I have some motivation for you guys to finish up." She lightly kissed his lips. Then she kissed him again with more bravado. "I've been wanting to do that forever." She walked away, leaving him standing alone with his fingers on his lips. Then he ran his fingers through his long hair and blew out a stream of hot air that misted in the cold.

This is not good, he thought. *This is really not good.*

CHAPTER 9

BY HIS DRESS, Ezra Wolf could have been Amish: white shirt, dark pants, suspenders, and hat. He was about five ten with a slim build but thick arms. He had short, ginger-colored hair, blue eyes, and facial hair that did include a mustache. Wolf had walked through the door with a young man in his twenties with the same coloring—red hair and blue eyes—but who was taller and thicker across the chest. He wore modern clothing: denim jeans and a maroon, long-sleeved T-shirt. The duo's feet were shod in socks, probably leaving their boots in the mud room. Silently, Wolf and the young man sat down at the dining room table.

Decker introduced himself and then Rina. "Thank you for agreeing to meet with me."

Ezra Wolf nodded, but remained silent. The young man took over. "Jacob Wolf." He stuck out his hand, first to Decker, then to Rina. "I'm Eli's older brother. We're two years apart."

"I'm very sorry for your loss," Decker said.

"Thank you."

"Grace," Ezra announced. After a short invocation, the two men began cutting up their chops.

Jacob said, "I know you want to ask questions. It's fine."

Ezra kept eating. Ruth Anne sat with her eyes on the tabletop, her top teeth gently biting into her lower lip.

"You're not having lunch, Mom?" Jacob asked.

"Not hungry."

No one spoke. Then Decker said, "I know it must be difficult to talk right now."

Ezra spoke up. "When can we bury our son?"

"If nothing new comes up, I'm hoping in a few days."

"What could come up?" Ezra asked. "He killed himself."

"We don't know for certain, Mr. Wolf. The coroner makes the final ruling."

"Do you think he killed himself?"

"If I had to guess, I'd say yes."

"Then there's nothing more to discuss." The man put down his fork and stared into space. "Why you're here is a mystery to me."

"I wanted to come here personally and tell you how sorry I was."

"That's very kind of you," Ruth Anne said. "We appreciate it."

"Anything you can tell me about Elijah would be helpful to our investigation."

"What investigation?" Jacob asked. "If you think it's a suicide, what's there to investigate?"

"There is something else," Decker said. "We found some papers hidden behind one of the drawers in his desk. I guess I'm trying to figure out if the papers were significant to his death."

"Does it matter?" Ezra said. "My son is gone."

"Mr. Wolf, nothing I do will bring him back. And if you think there's nothing to talk about, I'll respect that."

Since no one answered him, Decker turned quiet. He had to go along with the family's decision even if he disagreed with it. Jacob broke the silence. There was rancor in his voice. "Since he left for college, he hasn't kept in touch."

Decker nodded.

"That's the truth," Ezra said. "We haven't seen Elijah in years." He looked at his wife. "When was the last time he came down?"

"Four years ago for Easter."

"He was a good boy." Ezra picked up his fork and stabbed the salad. "Not as much stamina as Jacob. The boy wasn't cut out for farm life. But he worked without complaint. After he went to the college . . . we didn't seem to matter anymore."

"He cared in his own way," Ruth Anne said.

"Oh, he'd send us money . . . not that I ever asked." Ezra shook his head. "Why would I need his money? Maybe giving us money was his way of keeping in touch. I don't know."

Decker paused before he spoke. "He sent you money?"

"That's the truth," Ezra said.

"It was odd," Ruth Anne said.

"Very odd," Ezra confirmed. "First couple of times, we tried to return it. He just sent it back, so I stopped trying. I never touched it. Put it in the bank in case he wanted it later. But he never asked for it."

"Can I ask how much?"

Ezra turned to his wife. "What was it? Like a thousand a month or something for the last two years."

"A little more," Ruth Anne said. "Maybe twelve hundred."

"That's a lot of spare cash." Decker tried not to look surprised. "Any explanation where it came from?"

"I called him and asked about it," Ruth Anne said. "He said he had a job and he didn't need it. He decided to send it to us."

"What kind of a job?"

"He was working beyond his scholarship requirements. His tuition, room, and board was paid for by the college. I think Ezra's right. It was his way of keeping in contact."

"Okay." Decker wrote it down. "I know this may sound like I wasn't listening. I understand that you didn't keep in contact. But I'm asking it anyway. Did you have any idea of what Elijah was working on in his math?"

Ezra shook his head. "Even when he still lived at home, I didn't know what he was doing. I can do calculating in my head. Never needed to write anything down, but what he was doing with the formulas and letters was way beyond my ken."

"You sound like you're good at numbers," Rina said. "Did Elijah ever try to explain it to you?"

Ezra eyed Rina, and then eyed Decker. "I asked him once or twice. I was lost within a few minutes."

Jacob said, "Something with vectors and complex formulas and matrices. I couldn't tell you the specifics because I didn't understand them, either. He tried to explain it to me once, but I couldn't follow him. I'm also good at numbers. When I went to community college, I always got A's. I'm thinking of becoming an accountant actually."

"You'd make a fine accountant," Ruth Anne said.

"He makes a fine farmer, too," Ezra said.

The room went silent. Finally, Jacob said, "Eli's mind was on another planet. After a while, we just didn't have much to talk about other than the weather."

"He was a good boy," Ezra said.

"I didn't say he wasn't." Jacob was snappish. "Just that math totally consumed him." He had finished his lunch and put down his fork. "Thank you, Mom. It was really good."

"I have cake if you want it."

"No, I'm fine. Save it for dinner."

"What about you, Ezra?"

"If you're offering, I'll take a piece."

Ruth Anne stood up. "Can I get either of you some cake?"

"No, thank you," Rina said.

Decker said, "I'm fine. Thanks."

"How about a refill of tea for both of you?"

"Sure," Rina said. "I'll come help you."

"No need." Ruth Anne's smile was fleeting. "I'll be right back."

No one spoke until Ruth Anne came back with a pound cake and tea. It took a few minutes to serve and pour. She sat down and Ezra took a forkful of cake. "It's good."

"Thank you." She turned to Jacob. "You sure you don't want a piece?"

"If you bring it out, you know I'm gonna eat it."

Ruth Anne smiled and served him a slice.

Jacob said, "It's delicious. Lemon?"

"Yes. Fresh lemons."

"At this time of year?"

"Guess California or Florida had some extra that wound up in the local barn market."

The men ate in silence. Decker said, "Jacob, were the two of you close growing up?"

"We were brothers. We shared a room. I was the serious one. He was a goof."

Decker sipped his tea. "From what you've told me, it doesn't sound like there's anything goofy about him."

"He changed radically after the accident." Jacob finished the cake in four bites and took another piece. "He stopped being the class clown. Maybe he realized that life wasn't infinite. He got very serious with his studies. His true genius came out."

"What accident?" Decker asked.

"Car accident," Ezra said. "Jacob broke his leg."

Jacob said, "My injury was nothing compared. My friend who was driving was killed and Eli was in a coma for over a week."

"That's horrible," Decker said.

"It was a test from God," Ruth Anne said. "We almost lost him.

At one point, the doctors talked about brain surgery for the pressure in his head. Luckily, it didn't come to that."

Ezra said, "After the accident we did lose him in a sense. He stopped talking to us."

"That's not so," Ruth Anne said.

"He stopped talking to me and that's the truth." Ezra looked at his son. "Maybe he talked to you."

"Dad, he didn't really talk to me, either." Jacob put down his fork. "But I don't think it was anything personal. He just changed. Math became his life. Once he won that contest, he became totally devoted to his studies."

Ezra wiped his mouth and stood up. "We should get back. We're putting up a new coop. We try to do all the repairs in the wintertime when we're not farming."

"Makes total sense," Decker said. "There never seems to be enough hours in the day to get things done."

"Or enough daylight," Jacob added.

"Now, that's the truth," Ezra said. "You ready?"

"Yep."

Ruth Anne said, "I wiped the mud off your boots."

"Thank you, Mom," Jacob said.

"Yes. Thank you." Ezra stuck out his hand. "Let me know when I can bury my son."

"I will, Mr. Wolf." Shaking of hands. "Once again, I'm terribly sorry for what happened."

The man sighed. "It was a terrible decision, what he did. I don't know what he was thinking. But no matter what the church says about him and his sins, he's still my son." He tipped his hat to Rina. "Nice meeting you, ma'am."

"Likewise."

Decker said, "Jacob, what contest did Elijah win?"

"Some statewide math contest. He came in first, which is remarkable because it included New York City. He didn't even tell us about it. We found out after the fact. I was really mad. He should have told us. But that was Eli. Impulsive. He didn't always think things out . . . obviously."

"He shouldn't have done it." Ezra's voice was soft. "But he was still my son. I won't turn my back on him even if the reverend says we can't bury him in the cemetery."

"I already talked to Reverend Deutch, Dad. There won't be a problem."

"When did you do this?"

"Yesterday. After he called. I didn't want you to worry about it."

"That was very considerate of you, Jacob." Ruth Anne's eyes welled up with tears. "Please excuse me." She got up and retreated to the kitchen.

Ezra said, "I'll be back in a moment."

Decker thought that the old man was going to comfort his wife. But Ezra went in the opposite direction, down a hallway. Rina stood up and started gathering dirty dishes. Jacob said, "You're a guest. You don't have to do that."

Rina said, "I don't mind." She left Decker alone with Jacob.

Decker turned to the boy. "I'm so sorry."

Jacob shrugged. "He hadn't kept in contact for a while, but it doesn't lessen the hurt. I tried to keep up the relationship. I called him after Dad gave up. It was mostly one-sided. I told him he needed to keep in touch. I told him he needed to call the folks. He always said he would, but he never did."

"This might be a painful question, but do you think there was a reason why he chose to distance himself from the family?"

"We weren't important to him anymore. Just a bunch of farmers . . . what did we know."

Decker nodded. "I apologize for my intrusive questions."

"I don't take offense. It's your job. I tried not taking offense with

Eli, but sometimes it was hard. He was one of those guys who made promises he never kept. I don't think it was out of meanness. He just probably forgot."

MCADAMS SWITCHED THE phone to his other ear. He was talking to Iris Beaufont, who remembered him instantly. No surprise there because he had spent half his time at Exeter in places other than classrooms and clubs. Not that he didn't have friends; he did—a few guys from his neighborhood and even a girlfriend that he took to the prom. She was now a lawyer and worked for the Miami PD office defending drug dealers. She had been one of his forty Facebook friends before he shut down his account. Truth was McAdams had always been more comfortable with people his parents' ages.

Iris said, "According to the records, Mallon Euler was here for two years. It appears she left after her sophomore year."

"Any reason why she left the school?"

"I have no idea, Tyler. I shouldn't even be divulging this information to you."

"I'm an official detective now."

"And official detectives have search warrants."

"Only in the movies."

"Anything else I can help you with, darling?"

"Is Dr. Kent still head of the math department?"

"It would take an ambulance and a gurney to relieve him of his duties."

"Do you have a number for him?"

"It's one thing for me to look in the computer files. It's another to give you his phone number. But I will tell him that you called."

"You're a doll. Thank you."

"So you're still with the police? I heard you were in law school."

"From whom? My dad?"

"Your sister."

His *half* sister. "Ah, Danielle. She's fourteen already?"

"Sixteen."

McAdams let out a laugh. "How's she doing?"

"Give her a call and find out."

"Yes, Mother."

"*Are* you in law school? I'm in charge of updating our alumni list."

"Yes, I'm in law school."

"Where, darling?"

"Harvard. And I'm sure that's way more impressive to your parents than my police work."

Under her breath, she muttered, "Not to me."

McAdams smiled although Iris couldn't see it. "Law school is a promise I made to my father and my late grandfather. Actually, I don't hate it. Obviously I'm not entirely divorced from investigatory work. Hence the phone call."

"Why are you interested in Mallon?"

"Can't tell you." McAdams paused. "Is she related to the famous Euler?"

"Great-great-great-grandniece. It says on her application. And that's all I'm going to tell you since you're being stingy with your information."

"So she left the school at fifteen . . . and you have no idea where she went?"

"Did you just hear what I said?"

"How did she get on in school? I know she was bullied."

"How did you know that?"

"She told me."

A long pause. "If you know the girl, why are you asking me these questions?"

"I know the girl, but I trust you."

"Flattery will get you everywhere. Yes, she was bullied in her first year. She was in the nurse's office all the time, although her injuries weren't physical. Her second year, I didn't see her as much. Perhaps she learned how to deal with the idiots. Perhaps the girls found someone else. You know we do the best we can, but we can't control the minutiae of behavior. And girls are always getting their feelings hurt even if they're not bullied. It's always best for kids to figure out how to handle themselves. Of course, if there is anything physical, we have to step in."

"And with Mallon, there was nothing physical?"

"Nothing is noted in her records. As far as I can remember, there was nothing that required intervention."

"She's brilliant. Could she have gotten into college early?"

"I don't know. She never answered any of our questionnaires after she left."

"Could you ask around for me?"

"I'll do what I can, which won't be much. I've got to go, darling. I'll tell Dr. Kent to call you."

"Thank you, Iris."

"You can thank me by dropping by on Career Day."

"Oh please. The place must be overrun with parents and alumni who are lawyers."

"Lawyers, yes. Cops are another story. Surely you can tell us something interesting that will keep us awake for once."

"If you can fill in the blanks about Mallon, I will be happy to talk to you about investigation work—or what little I know about it."

"I'm sure you know plenty."

"Enough to keep you entertained. I'll even bring a pipe and a deerstalker hat for ambience."

"We have a uniform no-smoking policy. Even Sherlock would be forced to comply."

"What would Sherlock Holmes be without his pipe?"

"A bland do-gooder just like the rest of them. But you know how it is in institutions, Tyler. Rules are effing rules."

CHAPTER 10

AS SOON AS McAdams heard the car pull into the driveway, he came out of the house and waited on the porch. It was a little past two in the afternoon and his studying had been slow going since he had returned from lunch and spoke to Decker about Mallon Euler. He wasn't sure why he had such an uneasy feeling. Part of it was suspicion, but he was savvy enough to realize that part of it was attraction. It had been a while since he had felt soft lips and vulnerability. The women he knew in university were identical to the men: smart and all about the competition. He had nothing to offer any of them other than his sarcasm and snobbery, which was guaranteed to keep everyone at arm's length.

Rina got out of the Porsche and waved. Tyler waved back. "What ho, as Bertie Wooster would say."

"What ho right back at you." Rina bounded up to the front door. "Where is Jeeves when you need him?"

"Sure be nice to have someone bring me tea and solve my problems." McAdams shook his head. "I am wondering about the wisdom of my coming down here."

Decker walked up to the porch. "Yeah, let's talk about that." He threw his arm around the kid and the three of them went inside the house. "You need to go back to Boston, put some distance between you and the girl."

"If she's determined, she can still contact me."

"If she's rational, she'll know it'd be inappropriate. I am concerned about stalking."

"She's not . . . I didn't get that feeling. But I'm not too good at reading people."

Rina gave Decker her jacket. "You can hang this up while I make coffee."

"Fair division of labor." Decker turned back to McAdams. "She already has a thing for you from the past. Just go back up and finish out your term."

"I should have told her no—or that I have a girlfriend or I'm gay. Anything except to agree to go out with her." He hit his head. "What was I thinking?"

Rina said, "She threw you a curve ball."

"She seemed so uninterested yesterday."

"You do realize that she was talking to us in a tank top and shorts," Decker said. "She made no move to change into something more suitable considering we were the police."

"Yeah, I should have picked up on that. Damn those women and their wily ways."

Rina said, "I'm going to fix myself a snack. Anyone hungry?"

"You know I'll eat whatever you bring out," Decker said. "I'm hopeless."

"I'll fix something healthy."

"Not too healthy."

"I've got some leftover cookies."

"Who doesn't like cookies and coffee?" McAdams said.

"And there lies the problem." Decker patted his belly.

"I'll be back in five. You can start without me, but then you'll have to fill me in."

"Will do." Decker turned to McAdams. "Reception wasn't great, Tyler. Tell me what happened again."

He recapped the conversation. "When she asked me out, I should have just said no. What I told her is that when I'm done with finals and the case is resolved, I'd go out with her. And then she kissed me. Twice."

"And you don't think she's a stalker?"

"I think she's way more interested in the hidden papers. She thinks it's her research and she doesn't want it getting in the wrong hands. Plus, if I go back, I'd feel like I'm escaping something I should be able to deal with."

"Tyler, you're not even supposed to be here. The case is getting in your way."

"No, it's not." When Decker gave him a look, McAdams said, "Okay, it is. I've spent the last half hour trying to trace her from Exeter to Kneed Loft. It seems she left high school after two years."

"And?"

"I don't know. Could be she started college early. I have a call in to an old math teacher at my school. Maybe he can help because it doesn't say in her records."

"You're spending *way* too much time on this. You have to go back to Cambridge anyway in what? Ten days? Just bite the bullet."

"Yeah, okay." McAdams was sulking. "As long as I'm up there, how about if I take Eli's papers with me and have Dr. Gold look them over."

"Perfect. But once you're there, stay there."

"Fine, fine," McAdams said. "I'll go back up first thing in the morning."

"There should be a five-thirty bus going up to Boston. You have plenty of time to catch it."

"I'm too tired to bus it. I'll rent a car and go in the morning. One day won't make a difference."

Rina came in with the coffee on a tray and looked for a clear spot on the dining room table. She pushed aside a pile and put down the tray.

McAdams said, "I'll clear my papers so you can set up for dinner. As a matter of fact, I'll set the table. I know my way around your kitchen."

"Sure, help me out, but please don't bake. Last time you stayed with us, I gained five pounds."

McAdams gave her a sly look. "I was thinking pecan bars."

"Don't you dare. What's going on?"

"Tyler is leaving in the morning," Decker said.

"Boss's orders." The kid made a face. "Where are you off to, Peter?"

"Kneed Loft. I've got an appointment with Eli's professors."

"I'll come with you," McAdams said. "Mallon's interest in the hidden papers has piqued my curiosity. And I'd like to get a better idea of what Eli was actually doing." When Decker gave him a look, Tyler said, "I promise I'll leave in the morning."

Rina said, "Let him come with you, Peter. It's probably better than the girl showing up at the house again."

"Sure, why not?" Decker shook his head. "Come on. You can take notes on your iPad."

"Just like old times."

"Don't get shot."

"I'll do my best."

EVEN THOUGH IT was cold, they decided to walk. The air was bracing and it woke up Decker's sluggish mind. It felt good to move, especially after a long car ride. The sky was clear and blue and the sun had melted the thin layer of snow that had fallen yesterday. The two of them had to skip over the numerous water and mud puddles. McAdams had borrowed a hat, and because they were walking quickly, he began to sweat underneath. He took it off and raked his fingers through his overgrown locks. He was squinting in the glare of the sunlight as Decker gave him a detailed recap of the conversation in the Wolf house.

McAdams said, "Wow. How long was Eli in a coma?"

"About a week."

"Closed head injury. The brain swells and all sorts of things can happen. It accounts for his major personality change."

"Yes, I thought about that," Decker said. "What about his sudden genius? Could brain trauma account for that?"

"I'm not a doctor, so I don't know. Offhand, I would think that it's not going to make a limited thinker into Descartes. But if the family has a predilection for math—and it seems like they do—maybe the changes in his brain enhanced what was already there."

"I was looking up brain injuries on my phone during the ride home. Rina was kind enough to drive. There is precedence . . . people after a concussion suddenly emerging from the trauma with an enhanced sense of taste or smell or other things. Sometimes the changes are permanent. But sometimes they're not."

"Depends on the nature of the injury."

Decker nodded. "Did you know that GIs get a lot of closed head injuries even if they're not a hit directly to the head? They wear helmets, and while the headgear protects them from flying debris, it also puts the head in a confined space. The vibrations can rattle the brain. Sometimes their personality changes are due to brain injury rather than the horrors of war."

"You'd know more about that than I would."

"Yeah, war is very loud. I remember when our pilot was attempting a putdown of the chopper in active fighting: the rotors of the

Huey combined with the explosions and the spitfire of the machine guns. You can't hear yourself think, let alone communicate, which of course is essential. Anyway, that isn't what happened to Eli. He wasn't in combat. I'm just thinking that the kid might have been suffering from depression brought on by neurological changes."

"Hence the suicide."

"I didn't see any pain meds other than OTC in his dorm room. Certainly no antidepressants. I was looking for them."

"Maybe his religion frowns upon their use."

"Maybe. We'll get a tox report from the coroner, even though it's pretty obvious that the shot to the head was the cause of death. I want to see what the kid had in his system."

"Do we have a coroner's report yet?"

"I don't know." Decker made a quick call to the station house. "The report isn't in yet. Kevin Nickweed is on it. I didn't ask for a quick turnaround. That's standard when you don't ask for high priority. And this isn't high priority."

McAdams said, "What do you think about Eli sending money to his parents?"

"Could be he was working for the math department and had no use for the extra money. Or like his father said, maybe it is his way of keeping in contact or atoning for his lack of interest in his family."

"On the other hand, if Eli wasn't working for the math department, maybe he was making money illegally and wanted to shunt it somewhere safe."

"I don't know, McAdams. From what we've heard, Eli doesn't seem like the type to engage in illegal activity."

"If he had brain injuries, maybe his inhibitions were lowered."

"Sure. But twelve hundred a month seems like a small amount of money to take a risk on screwing yourself up."

"What if the twelve hundred was the tip of an iceberg? Like I said, maybe that's what the hidden papers were about. Some kind of code."

"Elijah Wolf, the Mennonite-cum-math-genius-cum-what? Drug dealer?"

McAdams smiled. "Maybe not drugs, but there are a lot of other illegal shenanigans to get sucked into. We've got a guy who's a whiz at numbers. Maybe he had some kind of blackjack system. There are a lot of Indian casinos up and down the eastern seaboard."

Decker thought a moment. "Gambling isn't illegal. And why give it to his parents? And also, why the consistent amount every month?"

"Maybe he made a lot more and it's hidden somewhere. Maybe he gave his parents the same amount to make it look like it was from a job. Or maybe his parents weren't telling the whole truth." McAdams became animated. "If he was a gambler, maybe he hooked up with the wrong people. Maybe Eli did something that he thought would tarnish his genius image and felt suicide was the honorable way out. Or maybe he was forced to shoot himself."

Decker was quiet.

"What?" McAdams said.

"I was just thinking about the death scene. His fingers were curled but he wasn't holding the gun."

"Why is that significant?"

"There's a phenomenon when you shoot yourself. If you're tense when you do it, your fingers get a lock on the gun and go into rigor. It's called cadaveric spasm. His fingers were curled but he dropped the gun. It isn't unheard of to drop the gun. It's just one of those things that you think about if you're a detective. If he were forced to shoot himself, he'd be tense and he'd be more likely to be gripping the gun. Of course, if he had taken drugs beforehand, it could have relaxed him."

"Or given drugs against his will."

"So you think his suicide had something to do with getting involved in something criminal?"

"It happens, right? That seemingly good people go bad."

"Of course it happens."

"Especially considering that Eli probably had sustained brain injuries."

They kept walking. Decker said, "I do like your shenanigans-with-numbers theory. A guy who's good with formulas could be useful in a number of unsavory activities—counting cards in blackjack, poker playing, bookmaking. He could probably shift the odds in his head at a moment's notice."

"How about this?" McAdams held up a finger. "Automated stock trading. Everyone in that industry is looking for the next big thing in algo trading. Maybe Eli found it."

"I like that, Harvard. Do we know if he was working in the industry?"

"No one has mentioned it."

"We haven't been asking the right questions." Decker thought a moment. "Twelve hundred a month doesn't put him in the high-roller category."

"Like I said before: maybe it's the tip of the iceberg."

"Last I heard, automated trading was legal."

"It is legal."

"Do you know how it works?"

"In a nutshell, it generates tiny, tiny profits from zillions of automatic trades to produce big profits."

"And there are specific firms that specialize in this type of trading?"

"Usually that's the case. These firms usually don't make major markets because they move in and out so fast." McAdams took out his smartphone and looked up Algo Trading on Wikipedia. "Algo firms break up big institutional trades in major companies into more manageable sizes."

"Do they affect the stock prices?"

"Not as much as you'd think. Algo companies take in relatively small profits compared to the overall market trading, but they are responsible for a large percentage of the market volume. This big-volume trading can lead to a phenomenon known as flash crash if things go awry."

"Like that guy in the UK around five years back."

"Yeah in 2010. Navinder Sarao. Exactly." McAdams put away his phone. "I can delve further if you want."

"If I need more information on this, I'll ask you to do it, but only after your finals."

"Sure." He stuck his hands in his pockets. "If Eli had hit upon an algorithm that was highly profitable, it might explain why Mallon is so interested in those hidden papers."

"It might explain why *everyone* is so interested: Dean Zhou, Alistair Dixon the RA, and Eli's professors."

"Which professors?"

"So far we have Theo Rosser, Dean Zhou, and Katrina Belfort all willing to look the papers over under the guise of being helpful."

"Where does Katrina Belfort fit in? Who told her about the papers?" McAdams hit his head. "She's Mallon's adviser. Did she call you or did you call her?"

"Belfort, you mean?"

"Yeah."

"I called her. She was on Eli's advisory committee but she had to resign due to other obligations."

"Like what?"

"She didn't say. I only talked to her for a minute. I'm going to try to catch her this afternoon. I also talked to . . ." He checked his notes. "Dr. Aldo Ferraga. He was also on Eli's advisory commit-tee. All three of them—Ferraga, Rosser, and Belfort—were pretty shaken up when I spoke to them over the phone."

"How can you tell emotions over the phone?"

"You get a feeling for what's righteous after doing it all these years. I can still be fooled, though. My first impressions aren't always spot-on."

They walked in silence. Then McAdams said, "Are you referring to your first impression of *moi*?"

"God forbid!" Decker stifled a smile and put his arm around the kid. "What in the world gives you that idea?"

"I can do without the sarcasm, Old Man."

"What sarcasm?"

"And your children still speak to you?"

"Every single one of them. And as they get older, I've gained stature and IQ points. Someday even your father won't seem so bad."

"I don't dislike my father." A pause. "I don't actively like him, but no one does."

"You may like him more when you're a dad."

"Doubt it. God, me a dad. Pity my poor children. They don't stand a chance."

"Oh, I don't know about that. You may rise to the occasion."

McAdams laughed to himself. "For an old guy, you're okay, Lieutenant."

Decker was taken aback. "High praise."

"As high as I'm capable of giving."

CHAPTER 11

ENTERING KNEED loft—four stories of unadorned brownstone punctured with prison-size windows—Decker checked the directory. Engineering and applied sciences occupied the bottom floor, computer science held the second tier, physics and chemistry shared the third floor, and applied and theoretical mathematics reigned supreme on the fourth.

The interior of the college was pure function—tiled floors, low acoustical ceilings, long hallways, small classrooms with a whiteboard and stark, wooden desks along with a stale musty smell of too much radiator heat and too little fresh air. Decker and McAdams did a couple of two-steps, dodging speed-walking students with their eyes on the floor. They took the elevator to the fourth floor, a replica of the ground floor they had just traversed.

A woman with blond hair, dressed in workout clothes, was locking up Katrina Belfort's office. She had an athletic build of developed arms and developed calves.

"Dr. Belfort?" Decker asked.

"Yes?" When she stood up straight, she appeared to be around five eight. Hazel eyes, high cheekbones, and a big chin. A pretty woman bordering on handsome. "Oh . . . you're the detective?"

"I am. Peter Decker of Greenbury police. This is my partner, Detective Tyler McAdams."

"Right." She checked her watch. "I totally forgot. It's been a crazy day." She checked her watch again. "Uh . . . hold on." She unlocked the door and ushered the men inside. "I can't spare a lot of time right now. Things are just too hectic."

"With Eli's death?"

"Of course with Eli's death! That gave everyone a shock and then some."

"You didn't see it coming?"

"Of course not. If anything, he seemed more . . . relaxed. Probably because his thesis was going great and he was into things that excited him."

"What kind of things?" McAdams asked.

"Math things, I would imagine." She paused. "Eli was reserved . . . cautious with what he talked about. I didn't have as much to do with him in his upper-division studies as I did when he was a freshman."

"Why's that?"

"Well . . ." She looked at her watch. "Oh hell, here goes nothing. Eli was a prize student. He was brilliant. Any faculty member here would have killed to work with him because he had such great promise. But to the victor goes the spoils. It was assumed from the start that he'd work under Dr. Rosser even though his interests coincided more with me than with him. But since I'm low woman on the totem pole and likely to remain that way, I could only stand by and watch."

She shook her head angrily.

"It was clear to all of us that Eli was unhappy working with Rosser. He even hinted about switching to me. Of course, that sent Theo into a rage. I backed down. I not only backed down, I took myself off Eli's thesis committee." She gave a dismissive wave. "I'm not saying Theo is to blame. But he certainly was insensitive to Eli's needs."

"When did this drama happen?"

"It wasn't drama on my part. Theo makes drama out of everything. It happened about a year ago. Since then, Eli seemed to adjust. Maybe he had a rapprochement with Rosser. I hope so." Her eyes suddenly moistened. "Not that it matters now."

Again, she glanced at her watch.

"I really have to go." She swiped her cheeks with her hand. "I'm sorry. This is very difficult to talk about."

"One more thing," Decker said. "I'm hearing some contradictions. Elijah was happy about how his thesis was progressing so well and Elijah was unhappy working with Dr. Rosser who was his thesis adviser."

"Like I said, he seemed to adjust to reality. Look, Eli's emotional swings were in millimeters not miles. He had an almost flat personality, which isn't unusual for students here. He was more interested in math than anything else, and if the math was going well, he was fine." She opened the door. "Anything else?"

"Maybe we can talk another time when you're not so rushed."

"Good luck with that. I'm always in a rush." She stepped out in the hallway and waited for them to follow. Then she locked her door and exhaled. "Terrible, terrible, terrible what happened. He will be missed."

"Did he ever talk about his parents to you?" Decker asked.

"I didn't even know parents were in the picture. For all I knew of his personal life, Eli could have been an orphan."

THE OFFICE OF Professor Theo Rosser, Ph.D., was spare and clean with a small window that looked over a mud-filled expanse that turned into lawn in the springtime. There was a small sitting area with two wooden chairs, a large uncluttered desk, and a leather desk chair. The walls were filled with diplomas, awards, and accolades. The door was wide open but the professor was nowhere in sight.

"What now?"

Decker checked his watch. "He said three-thirty."

"Academic Standard Time." McAdams was checking out his credentials. "He got his Ph.D. from UCLA. The two of you can bond over the Pacific Ocean."

"What year?"

"Nineteen-eighty-five."

"Thirty years in academics."

"It's clear that Belfort hates him, but he must have something going for him other than his ability to pick brilliant students," McAdams told him. "Look at all these awards."

"Are they prestigious awards?"

"No idea. But I don't think he'd put them on his walls unless they were coveted." The clock on the wall said three forty-five. McAdams said, "How much longer should we wait?"

"I'm not in a hurry. Give it another fifteen minutes."

"What about Eli's other adviser?"

"Aldo Ferraga. We didn't connect, but I did leave a message. We'll see if he calls back."

With a gust of energy, a balding, thin man blew into the office. He placed his briefcase down on the desk. "So sorry I'm late." He took off his coat, hanging it on a coatrack. "Feel free to take off your jackets and sit down. It's just been one of those days." He let out a sigh. "That's to be expected after such a terrible tragedy."

He sat down in his leather desk chair and threw his head back. "What a terrible waste." He looked up. "I'm Theo Rosser. Chances are you could guess that without being a detective."

"I'm Detective Peter Decker, Greenbury police. This is Detective

Tyler McAdams." Hands were shaken all around. Rosser appeared to be in his mid to late fifties. His eyes were milky, his thinning hair was gray, and he had a stoop-shouldered doughy build. "Thanks for agreeing to see us on such short notice."

"Yeah, sure." Rosser shook his head and sat up. "Was it suicide? That's what everyone is saying."

"The coroner hasn't made a definite determination."

"What do you think?"

"I leave those things to the experts," Decker said. "Did you know Eli well?"

"I was his primary adviser. As such, our conversations usually revolved around his research."

"What can you tell me about him?"

"His brilliance is . . . was indisputable. As far as what I thought about him . . . quiet, serious, dependable, an original thinker."

"How'd he get along with others?"

"Math isn't a social subject, Detective."

"Did he have friends?"

"I wouldn't know much about his life outside of his work. He didn't say and I didn't pry. He could communicate. His presentations, though complex, were well thought out. He was helpful to other students in the lab."

That jibed with what Mallon Euler had told them. Decker said, "You don't have departmental social functions?"

"Of course we do." Rosser thought a moment. "He was at our Christmas party about a month ago." A pause. "That was unusual."

"He usually didn't participate?"

"Not usually. But he was there, and after a few beers, he was actually quite amicable. He seemed in a very good mood. Things were going well with him in school. That's why this suicide . . . we were all in shock when we heard about it yesterday. It doesn't . . . I don't know. Maybe he had a hidden life that I didn't know about."

"Did he bring anyone to the party?"

"It wasn't really a party . . . just something the faculty does to make our upper division students comfortable."

"Did he bring anyone with him, Professor Rosser?"

"No, I don't think so." A pause. "He spent some time talking to Mallon Euler. She's also in the department . . . very bright. Not like Eli, but quite gifted." Another pause. "He looked like he was trying to calm her down. Mallon can be . . . excitable. I do know that he was helping her out with her thesis. He had patience with her, I'll say that much. Perhaps they were an item and I was unaware."

"It's a small department for you to be unaware of who's dating whom."

"Social acuity isn't my forte, Detective."

McAdams said, "Was Eli helping out anyone else besides Mallon Euler?"

"Eli helped anyone who'd ask for help. He was too nice, if you ask me. I was always afraid that people would take advantage of him."

"In what way?"

"He would spend too much time in helping others and not enough on his own work. But I never said anything because with his own assignment, he was always on time or early. Things came easy to him."

"What was Eli working on?" Decker asked.

"It involves a lot of complicated mathematics. Unless you're in the field, you won't have any idea what I'm talking about."

McAdams said, "A friend of his told us it has to do with Fourier analysis and eigenvalues."

Rosser furrowed his brow. "Which friend?"

McAdams looked up his notes. "Damodar Batra." When Rosser waved him off, Tyler said, "Eli wasn't researching eigenvalues?"

"Only as a starting point. Do you have any idea what Fourier analysis is or what an eigenvalue means?"

"It has to do with a relationship between matrices and vectors," McAdams said.

Decker said, "The mathematics was beyond me, but what I took out of it was a paring down of complex things into simpler parts. What was interesting to me as a detective was the practical applications: the eigenface and eigenvoice recognition. You take a bunch of real faces, assign a value percentage to each part of the faces—like sixty-three percent of this nose, and thirty-seven percent of that nose, and then put them together to make a totally new face. It's basically a computerized identity kit except you have a lot more features to draw upon. Those percentages of the features were called eigenvalues."

"It's interesting what sticks in people's minds," Rosser said. "Of course, that's what you'd be interested in."

"Could you get a little more specific on Eli's research in layman terms?"

"First of all, it's hard to explain in layman terms. You need the mathematics. Secondly, his research is still ongoing."

"Meaning there are still original publications to be had from what Eli was doing."

"He was part of a team, Detective. We share the work, we share the credit. Any paper he might have produced would have had multiple authorships. His theories were not developed in a vacuum. And what does his research have to do with his terrible, untimely death?"

"I don't know if it has anything to do with it," Decker said. "I suppose you heard that we found hidden papers—a stack of them actually—stuffed behind Eli's desk in his dorm room."

"I have heard. I'd like to take a look at those papers. I need to make sure he wasn't compromising anyone else's research."

"I have a lot of people who are interested in looking over those papers for the same reason."

"As his adviser, I would know right away what he was working on. I just want to make sure he wasn't poaching someone else's thesis."

"That's an odd thing to say," McAdams told him. "Why on earth would you think that Elijah—who was your most brilliant student—would poach someone else's thesis?"

"I don't think that. I just want to make sure." Rosser's face tightened. "There's an easy way to solve this problem. Just let me see the papers."

Decker said, "I appreciate your need to keep your research within the confines of your lab, but you also need to realize if those papers are important to his death, I have to keep them under lock and key as evidence. Is it possible for you to give me something that Eli already made public so I can compare it to what we found behind the desk?"

"How could you tell—as a layman—if it was similar or not?"

"I couldn't, but we know people who could."

"Just give my research away?" Rosser shook his head. "No thank you."

"That's why I said something previously made public."

"It was only made public within the lab. It certainly wouldn't stop poachers from stealing what might be in those hidden papers."

"Professor, we're taking the papers to someone at Harvard. That's a given."

Rosser turned red. "To whom might I ask?"

"Someone who doesn't need anyone else's research for tenure," McAdams said.

"We've used him before," Decker told him. "He's not about to poach your research. If for no other reason, he'd now be under scrutiny."

"Cold comfort."

"Let me promise you this," Decker said. "If you supply us with some papers of Eli's research and the hidden papers turn out to be relevant to your research, I'll make sure you get them before anyone else. What do you say?"

"Do I have a choice?"

"Of course you have a choice. You can say no. But the best choice you have is to cooperate."

Rosser sighed and sat back in his chair. "I probably sound like I'm making a mountain out of a molehill."

McAdams said, "You're being protective of your work. We understand academia."

"I have tenure," Rosser said. "It's not for my personal gain. But not everyone in my lab is as lucky. I have students who are applying to very prestigious graduate programs. I have master-level students who are using my data to try to further their careers at other universities, and I have assistant professors here who are trying to get tenure. If privileged data were to get out, it would screw up people other than me."

"I appreciate where you're coming from," Decker said, "but that isn't our intention. The tragedy just happened a day ago and we don't quite know what is or isn't relevant."

A long pause. "Let me sleep on it. Let me think about what I can give you that would do the least amount of damage." Rosser sighed. "Anything else? I'm completely jammed up today. Eli's death has thrown a monkey wrench into everyone's schedules."

"How specifically are you dealing with Eli's death?"

"We've formed several ad hoc committees to meet with students. I've asked for a counselor to come down. Math people aren't noted for emotional exuberance but that doesn't mean that the kids aren't affected. It's a mess right now. So if we're done . . ."

"I do have another question, Dr. Rosser. Did Elijah have a paid job doing work for the math department?"

Rosser furrowed his brow. "He worked as a TA in several lower-division classes as part of his tuition. He was here on a free ride, you know."

"I do know. Did he work in the department for spare change? Well, a little more than spare change."

"What are you getting at?"

"Eli was sending home around twelve hundred a month to his family. He said he got it by working a job for the math department. Maybe he kept a little for pocket money. So if you assume that, maybe he was making even more."

"Twelve hundred a month?"

"Yes, sir."

"I have no idea where it came from. Maybe someone else in the department hired him on as a research assistant." A pause. "Strange that he wouldn't tell me, but as I said, we kept our conversations on his thesis. I suppose you can check with the bursar's office."

"Thanks, I'll do that."

Rosser seemed troubled. "I don't mind his working for someone else other than me. But he should have said something. Do you know who he might have been working with?"

"No idea whatsoever."

"Well, if it was someone in my department, I'd like to know about it. I don't like people working with my students behind my back."

"I understand."

"So you'll tell me if you find out anything?"

"Let me find something of significance first. Right now I'm just trying to piece together who Elijah Wolf was."

"Do the police always delve so deeply in a suicide?"

"I do what I think is necessary for my peace of mind," Decker said.

Rosser made a point of looking at his watch even though there was a wall clock in the room. "Anything else?"

"Not at the moment. Thank you." Decker gave the professor his card. "Call me anytime. My cell is on the back. And please let me know about your decision to share some of Eli's research. It may prove invaluable to all of us."

Rosser flipped the card over a couple of times. "I'll call you and let you know."

"I'm taking the hidden papers to our professor tomorrow," McAdams said. "Just to let *you* know."

"What time?"

"I'm leaving around two in the afternoon." When Decker looked at him, McAdams just smiled.

"Who is your professor? I don't think you ever told me a name."

"Privileged information."

"There are only so many people in a math department."

"If you ask around, we can't stop you," McAdams said.

Decker said, "Thank you for your time."

"Not a problem. You can see yourself out."

As soon as they walked into the hallway, Decker said, "I thought you were renting a car and leaving in the *morning*."

"Guess I'm not a morning person."

"You told me you didn't want to go out in the afternoon. You told me that if you left in the morning, you'd be more on your game. You told me that the only reason you are staying tonight is to get a good sleep. Either you're lying or stalling or all of the above."

"All of the above."

"Cool it with the snide talk. You're beginning to piss me off."

"You know, Decker, no one except my nanny has ever given a damn about me. It's way too late for me to develop a father figure now."

"I'm sure you can take care of yourself." A pause. "But if you screw up and your dad finds out you were working with me, he'll be major league pissed. And with some justification. You should be studying, Tyler. You should be concentrating on your tests, not running around trying to make sense out of a senseless act and being stalked by a crazy math girl in the process."

"She hasn't called me once since our lunch, FYI." McAdams looked at his phone. "Okay. She only called me once."

"Look, kiddo, if it's all the same to you, I'd rather not be on your own father's shit list."

McAdams smiled. "I've been on it many times and I'm still here to tell the tale. Actually, I consider it a place of honor."

"Of course you do," Decker said. "Pissing off one's parents is a time-honored tradition. You seem to have extended the tradition to me. I don't know whether to take it as an insult or a compliment."

McAdams gave him a small punch in his arm. "What the hell, Decker. Live large. Take it as a compliment. And I still expect my picture on your piano."

Decker said, "Get me a damn picture and I'll put it up. Should I start calling you 'son,' McAdams?"

"Only if you pay my tuition."

CHAPTER 12

THE WINTRY NIGHT was long and quiet and McAdams was finally able to slip into the zone. Sitting at the desk in the Deckers' living room, he focused his eyes and mind on the intricacies of first-year law. Outside, snowflakes were dancing under the porch light. Inside, it was warm even though the fire was almost out: just a hint of flame, a waft of pine wood, and the occasional crackle of a splitting log. The fireplace, like the radiator, was mostly for atmosphere anyway. The real heat was coming from an updated forced-air system. Rina and Peter had gone to sleep hours ago. They kept the house a tad on the chilly side, but he was comfortable with a sweater on his chest and some single-malt Scotch in his belly courtesy of a rare bottle he packed before leaving Cambridge. In the wee hours of the morning, having plowed through about a third of the material, he felt good enough to call it quits.

He was in that drifting-off-to-sleep state when he heard his cell ring. At first he thought he was dreaming, but then the nasty intrusion refused to quit. Groping around, he found his phone, ripped it from the charger, and managed to croak out a hello, which was unusually civil for him at this ungodly hour. The voice on the other end was female and frantic. Her speech was way too fast for his brain to process. Even though he couldn't understand the words, he had a pretty good idea who was speaking.

"Mallon?"

"Yes, of course. Have you been listening to me?"

"It's three in the morning and you woke me up. You want to go a little slower?"

In a panicked voice, she said, "My . . . room . . . has . . . been . . . ransacked . . . can . . . you—"

"I get it. What do you mean ransacked?"

"Do you want an *OED* definition?" When the line went silent, she took a deep breath and said, "Tyler, you've got to come down here. I'm on the verge of hysteria."

He managed to suppress a sigh. First things first. "Where are you?"

"Not in my room. I just got the hell out of there. I haven't even called campus police yet. I just ran."

"Okay." He began to pull on warm clothes. "I repeat. Where are you?"

"I'm at a twenty-four-hour café about a block from campus. Do you think I'm safe here?" A gulp of air. "Please come rescue me. I'm . . ." She burst into tears.

"Just hang on and stay put. I'm dressing as we speak." He had on a sweatshirt, jeans, and socks and was lacing up his boots. "I'll go wake up Detective Decker. We'll be right down. What's the name of the café?"

"Insomnia."

"I know it. I'll be right there."

"Can you stay on the line with me, Tyler? I'm petrified. And the worse thing is I don't know who I should be scared of."

"I'll stay on the line. Just yell if you need me to talk."

"If I'm yelling, it's too late."

"Mallon, I can't get ready holding a phone up to my ear. I'm going to put the phone in my pants pocket, so that's why I said to yell. It'll be about five minutes. Just hang, okay." He slipped his phone into his pocket and gently knocked on Decker's bedroom door. He knew that the detective was a light sleeper: years of responding to emergency situations. A moment later, Peter opened the door a crack. His hair was a mess but his eyes were alert.

"What's wrong?"

"Mallon Euler's dorm room was ransacked. She's at an all-night café. She's on my cell line. She asked me to keep the line open until we get to the location."

"Okay. Tell her we'll be right down."

"I heard that," Mallon said from Tyler's back pocket.

"Good," Decker answered.

McAdams took his index finger and made circles around his temple. Then he shrugged.

Decker shrugged back. "Give me a minute."

"If you toss me your keys, I'll warm up the car."

"We'll take Rina's car. It's in the driveway. Keys are in her purse."

"Got it." McAdams grabbed his winter jacket and braced himself for the cold night air. It wasn't as arctic as he thought: the high twenties according to the car's external thermometer. By the time Decker arrived, the car was spitting out warm air and the windshield had been cleared of powdered snow. McAdams had already moved into the passenger seat.

Decker shifted the car into drive, pulled it into the street, and took off slowly. It was cold enough to freeze water under the snow and that meant black ice. It was his second winter in upstate Greenbury and he was almost used to driving in inclement weather, but it did require more concentration.

Within five minutes, they had parked outside the café. Mallon came out before they reached the door to the place. She was bundled in a pea-colored, quilted coat, her head covered by a hood rimmed with fake fur. Jeans covered her legs and boots on her feet. "It's probably easier to walk from here. I'm assuming you want to see my dorm room."

She stormed off. They were going at a very fast clip. Decker had on solid shoes but it was still slippery underfoot. He said, "Did you call campus police yet?"

"I thought I'd leave that up to you."

"What time did you notice your room was disturbed?" Decker asked.

"As soon as I came back. It was a little before three."

"Where had you been?"

"Library."

"It's open all night?"

"Not Bennington. It closes at eleven. Pascal's is open all night because it has the computer lab." She was huffing and panting. "It's a good place to work because it's only open to upper division and it's quiet."

"When did you leave your dorm room to go to the library?"

"Around ten."

"Did you notice anything unusual when you left?"

"No."

"No one who looked like he or she didn't belong?"

"No. But I'm not always aware of my surroundings."

"And you were gone between ten and three."

"Yes."

"But you can't narrow it down further than that."

"No."

"Maybe someone on the floor saw or heard something."

"Maybe, but I didn't stick around to ask questions." She stopped by the door to her dorm building. Her breathing had quickened.

Could have been the aerobic walk: more likely it was fear. She swiped her card and the three of them went up the stairs. With a gloved hand, Decker opened the door to her room.

The place was a mess even by college dorm standards. Drawers pulled out, mattress lifted and shoved off her bed, closet emptied with most of her clothes lying on the floor. Decker stuffed his gloved hands into his coat pocket. "Look around. See if anything of value was taken."

"I don't own anything valuable. I'm a starving student. The only valuable things I have are my phone, my laptop, and my research papers. And since Eli died, I keep everything with me at all times."

"No jewelry, no loose cash, no—"

"Nothing!" She sat down on the floor and huddled into a corner, still swathed in her outerwear. Her eyes moistened but she didn't say anything.

Decker continued to look around without touching anything. "So what do you think the person was looking for?"

"No idea."

"Take a guess."

"I can only surmise he was either looking for my research or for me, and both imply evil intent."

"You think it's a he?"

"He, she, I don't know."

"Whoever it was, this wasn't methodical."

"Meaning?"

Decker shrugged. "When I see a mess like this, I think that someone is looking for drug money. In a petty theft, the perpetrators don't usually commit crimes with people milling around. I don't think it was kids."

"So who then?"

"Like you said, someone looking for something you have." He paused. "Don't get offended, but to my eye, it looks staged."

Mallon glared at him. "You think *I* did it?" She turned to Tyler. "What about you?"

"I came when you called," McAdams said.

"That doesn't mean you believe me."

Decker said, "I didn't say you staged it, Mallon, I said it looked staged." He took off his gloves and hat. It was warm inside the room. And quiet. Decker had never been in a dorm when it was almost silent. "Could be someone was trying to scare you." He turned to her. "Who'd want to scare you?"

"I don't know! Between Eli's death and this mess, the asshole is doing a good job."

Decker glanced at his watch. "Do you have a twenty-four-hour emergency line for campus police?"

Slowly, Mallon took her laptop out. Her hands were still gloved and were shaking. "I'll look it up." She recited the numbers. "Can you call . . . please?"

"Of course. But first I'd like to poke around your floor and see if someone heard or saw anything. It would be easier to do that before I called campus police down."

Tears streamed down her cheek. "Whatever you think."

"I don't know how much I'm going to get out of a bunch of college kids who probably just fell asleep. I suppose the good news is that most of them are probably in their rooms." He looked at McAdams. "I can probably do this by myself. You can go back to the house."

"I'm too wired. How can I help?"

"If that's the case, you scour the rooms to the left and I'll go right. Ask if they saw or heard anything going on in Mallon's room."

"You're leaving me *alone*?" Mallon asked.

"Leave your door open," Decker said. "Nothing's going to happen." He picked up a corner of her mattress and slid it back onto the bed frame. "Lie down and try to rest even if you can't sleep." He offered her his hand to help her up.

From her corner, she stared upward. Then she clasped his hand and he pulled her to her feet. She bent down and picked up her covers. "I can't stay here."

Decker said, "We'll work that out later. But I need you to stay here right now. I'm sorry, Mallon. This must be very frightening for you."

More tears. "It would help if I knew who the bogeyman was." She looked at McAdams. "Sorry for waking you up."

"No, no. You did the right thing," he said. "It's not a problem."

They walked out of the room. Decker took a survey of the hallway. Mallon's room was smack in the middle, making it even a more unlikely candidate for a random break-in. There were eight to ten rooms on either side and twenty rooms on the other side of the hallway. The canvassing was compact and shouldn't take that long. He said, "Did you bring a notepad, Tyler?"

"Uh, no, but I have my phone."

Decker tore out several pages from his pad. He gave him a pencil. "It's easier to write by hand than to type on a screen that small. Let's start inward and work outward."

Tyler dropped his voice. "You think she's being straight?"

"She seems genuinely shaken." Decker exhaled. "Let's see what we can find out."

THE FIRST ROOM was occupied by a young man who returned to his dorm room at around one after a beer fest with his buddy in Goddard Hall. He didn't see or hear anything.

Going down one room to the left: it was occupied by a woman. Again, no see 'um, no hear 'um. By the fourth room, the constant knocking was bringing people to their doors, asking questions. Most of them were shocked by the ransacking as well as clueless. But Decker did hear a couple of reports that proved to be interesting.

"The only person I saw going out of Mallon's room was Mallon."

Decker was talking to Kelly Liu. She was twenty-one with short, clipped black hair and oval black eyes. She must have weighed around eighty pounds. She lived five doors down.

"When was this?"

"Around midnight."

"You're sure about the time?"

"No. It could have been later. I was coming back from a late study session and I saw her coming out of her room."

"And you're sure it was Mallon?"

She paused. "I think so."

"Did you see her face?"

"Well, not really. I just assumed it was her because it was a woman."

"So you're sure it was a woman?"

"I think so."

"Did you talk to her?"

"I don't remember. I think I said hi. We didn't have a conversation. She seemed like she was in a hurry."

"At midnight?"

"She was walking fast. People are pretty wired right now. It's the week before finals."

"What was the woman wearing?"

"She had on a jacket. Jeans probably. I don't remember her shoes."

"What color was the jacket?"

"Dark." A pause. "I think it was a hoodie. You can talk to Jayden. He was with me."

"Where does he live?"

Kelly pointed to a door.

Decker nodded and handed her a card. "Call if you think of anything else." He knocked on Jayden's door. The young man who answered was dark-complexioned with a full dark beard and a turban. Jayden's last name was Khalsa. He related the same story as Kelly Liu.

"But you're not positive it was Mallon."

"No, I am not."

"Was it definitely a woman?"

"I would think. If it was a man, he was very slight. Mallon's very slight. I assumed she was Mallon. But I didn't see her directly."

"What was she wearing?"

"A brown hoodie jacket. I thought that was odd . . . coming out of the room wearing the hood. A light jacket for the weather."

"Kelly told me that she appeared in a hurry."

"Yes. She was walking fast."

"Anything else?"

He shook his head. "No."

Again, Decker gave the young man his card. After an hour of talking to the kids, he met up with McAdams and compared notes. Tyler also had heard a similar story of someone noticing Mallon going in and out of her room between twelve and one in the morning. He said, "So what do you think?"

"The people I spoke to were pretty sure it was a woman because of the slight build." Decker smoothed his mustache. "Mallon keeps insisting that she doesn't have anything of value except her research. I don't know why Mallon would stage a break-in, so I'm thinking maybe someone was after her research."

"Maybe Mallon staged it for attention."

"I don't know, Tyler. Her reaction seemed real." Decker turned to the kid. "You still should leave to go back to Boston. I'm going to call campus police now. Go back to her room. I'll be there in a minute."

"What specifically do I tell her?"

"Don't tell her anything just yet." When Decker had finished the call, he went back to Mallon's room. "How are you feeling?" he asked her.

"A little numb."

"I called campus police. Someone should be here soon. Are you comfortable staying in your room by yourself?"

"Uh . . . like no."

"Okay. Do you have a place to stay other than your dorm room?" McAdams said.

"What do *you* think?"

"A friend?" Decker suggested.

"Do I seem like I have friends?" The room was silent. "Never mind. I'll figure something out."

Decker said to Tyler, "You can go home and get some rest. I'll wait for campus police."

McAdams crooked a finger and the two men went outside. He whispered. "I'm fine, Decker. You've got a job. I don't. Go home and tell Rina what's going on and switch cars with her. I'll wait with Mallon. I'll even help her clean up. She's way more likely to talk to me than to you."

"I'm sure you can, but I don't want you alone with her. People who aren't stable misinterpret everything."

McAdams sighed. "If you think the ransacking was legitimate, boss, I don't want to leave her alone."

Decker thought for a long time. "You go back to the house. I'll wait with her."

"Then what?"

"Let me think." After a minute, Decker said, "She can come crash at the station house until we can figure this out. We've got a bunk there. Beggars can't be choosers. You go back to the house and rest."

"Way too buzzed. What can I do?"

"You can study until it's time for you to leave."

"Decker—"

"I don't need anything right now, Tyler. I'll just wait with her until campus police makes their report. That'll take some time. Then I'll come home for breakfast and try to hunt down Aldo Ferraga."

"Why?"

"If Mallon is telling the truth, someone ransacked her room. Maybe someone was looking for the pages we found. Maybe someone was looking for other research. Dr. Rosser hasn't been forthcoming. Katrina Belfort seems too busy and Eli wasn't her student. Maybe I can get something out of Ferraga."

"Let me call him up in the morning," McAdams said. "One less thing on your plate."

"Yeah, fine. Thanks." He fished out the keys to Rina's car. "Take the Volvo back to the house. I can walk."

"What about Mallon? She might be carrying a suitcase. You take the car. I'll walk back."

"I'm sure she'll pack a small wheelie thing. I'm old but I betcha I can handle it. Go home and get some rest."

"I'll call you if I get hold of Ferraga."

"Fine. I can see that you want to get involved. I hope it's not because of the lady."

McAdams stared at him. "What makes you say that?"

"She's pretty. And how long has it been since you've had a date?"

"Could I punch you without being put up on insubordination charges?"

"Just making you aware, Tyler."

"No need for that, Old Man. Believe me I'm *painfully* aware."

CHAPTER 13

I T TOOK AN hour for campus police to conduct and finish a break-in report. Once that was done, it took thirty minutes for Mallon to clean up her room, shower and dress, and then pack a small bag. It was a little after six in the morning when she and Decker walked out of the dorm. Outside was the kind of cold that turned noses red and fingers numb. As they walked to the station house, a glorious dawn began overhead, the skies bursting with reds, pinks, and oranges. Decker was wheeling a small carry-on bag for her while she walked with her head down and her eyes on the sidewalk. He asked her if she was hungry. Her answer was a shrug.

"When was the last time you've eaten?" he asked her.

"I had lunch yesterday with your detective or whatever he is."

"He's a detective. He was here before I came on to the department."

"He told me he's in law school."

"He is," Decker answered. "The station house has coffee and a couple of vending machines. Not too tasty. So if you want to grab a muffin or a bagel before we go, I'm fine with that. I'll pay."

"Who can resist such an offer?" When Decker didn't respond, she said, "Thank you." Her eyes watered. "I'm not myself. Or maybe I am myself and I'm just a rude person."

Decker smiled. "Eat something, Mallon. You'll think more clearly."

"Maybe. Bagelmania is just down the street."

"Let's go." When they got there, Decker handed her a twenty. "Could you get me an onion bagel and cream cheese and a black coffee? I'd like to phone my wife."

Mallon sighed. "I hate to be a pain but can we eat inside Bagelmania instead of the station house? It's probably a little nicer."

"Sure. I'll join you in a minute." He managed to call Rina, punching in the correct numbers with thick gloved hands. "Hey there."

"Hello, stranger."

"Did Tyler update you?"

"He did. Are you all right?"

"I'm doing okay, thanks for asking. Where is Tyler now?"

"He went out about fifteen minutes ago."

"Where?"

"He didn't say. But he did take your car."

"Swell."

"He told me you're trying to decide if the ransacking was staged or not."

"Several witnesses say that they saw Mallon leaving her dorm room when she was supposedly not there. But no one got a good look and no one spoke to her, so maybe it wasn't Mallon. I'll try to dig out a witness who saw her at Pascal Library between twelve and one in the morning."

"Are you leaning toward one conclusion more than the other?"

"She did seem upset. And I can't think of her motivation for trashing her own room."

"Getting attention from Tyler?"

"Yes, that is a possibility. Or maybe she stole research from Eli

Wolf and is trying to take the suspicion off herself. But if that was her reasoning, all she did was cast suspicion *on* her. The plan is to take her to the station house until she can make suitable arrangements with the school to live somewhere else."

"How long will that take?"

"I don't have a clue."

"You know you can bring her here."

"That would be a bad idea. Besides, aren't you working?"

"I am, but only a half day and not until noon. Maybe I could get something out of her." A pause. "You know: woman to woman."

"I'm sure you could get blood from a turnip. But she isn't invading our personal space."

"Why are you even investigating the break-in, Peter? Isn't that a job for campus police?"

"You're absolutely right." Decker paused. "She called, so we came, especially since this happened on the heels of Eli's death."

"You're a kind man."

"You mean a sucker."

"I mean that despite your gruff exterior, you genuinely care."

"Call the pope and nominate me for sainthood."

"Take a compliment, Peter."

"Thank you, dear." Decker checked his watch. "I'm going to grab a bagel with her. See if I can learn anything else. I'll talk to you later. Keep warm."

"It's around eighty degrees in the house."

"It's around twenty out here. You know, in this advanced age of electronic communication, it's a shame they haven't figured out how to redirect temperature over the Internet."

SHE WAS ENGAGED with her laptop when Decker came inside. He sat down and spread a thick layer of cream cheese over his bagel. He ate about half when she finally looked up.

"I got about twenty e-mails asking me if I'm all right. That's twenty more than I usually get." She slammed her laptop shut. "I have class in a couple of hours. Then I have a meeting with my adviser at noon. Maybe the smartest thing for me to do is just stay in Pascal until then."

"Are you okay with that?"

"I'll call Tyler if I'm not." She looked at him. "Or I can call you. I'm sure you think that I'm a stalker, but I'm not."

"Mallon, we have to talk about your housing."

"I'm not going back to my dorm room."

"You need to call campus housing and find a temporary bed."

"I don't want to stay on campus. At least not alone."

"I'm sure they can get you a roommate."

"Until I know what's going on, I don't want some stranger living with me."

"I'm sure it would be a student at the college."

"Even worse. Someone looking over my shoulder trying to steal my ideas."

Paranoid? Or does she really have enemies? "You'll have to find accommodations. I'm out of suggestions. Any ideas?"

"I'll just sleep in the library."

"That is not sustainable."

"I can stay with you."

"That would also be a no."

"You let Tyler stay with you."

"Yes, I do. He's a coworker. You are not."

She made a face. "Well, I don't know what to tell you."

"Who is your adviser again? Katrina Belfort?"

"Yes. I tried for Dr. Rosser but he's too *busy*. He gave me Belfort probably figuring that a woman should only work with a woman, the pig."

"He told me you were very gifted."

Mallon's face registered shock. "For your benefit. He hates me."

"How do you get along with Dr. Belfort?"

"Good, actually. I call her 'Katrina.' She's on a first-name basis with most of her students."

"Maybe you could stay with her? You can't be afraid of her stealing your material because she already knows your research."

"Not all of it."

"But she knows what you're working on. What do you think? Do you feel comfortable enough to ask her?"

"I don't know."

"Then it's campus housing, Mallon. Unless you prefer the police station or a homeless shelter."

"At least at those locations, no one will steal my work." She shrugged. "I guess it doesn't hurt to call." She looked in her contact list and then touched the name. The line rang several times until the voice mail kicked in. "Hello, Katrina, it's Mallon Euler. I'm sure by now you heard about my mishaps. I was wondering if I might ask a favor. Could you call me back?" She recited the numbers and then hung up. "I don't know where she is at seven in the morning, but she isn't answering her cell."

"I have to go to work. Do you want to come to the station house or would you rather go to Pascal?"

"I'm feeling a little calmer now . . . more like drained." She looked around. "I'm actually okay here at Bagelmania. It's public and it has Wi-Fi. I'll stay here until my first class at nine. I'm due to see Katrina at noon anyway. I'll be fine . . . I hope."

Decker gave her his card. "Feel free to call, Mallon."

"Where's Tyler?" She asked the question with appropriate casualness.

"He's going back to Boston this afternoon."

"You mean Harvard?" When she didn't get an answer, she said, "Say good-bye for me. You know, it's the second time he's come to my rescue. That's two more times than anyone else in my feeble life."

MCADAMS WAS AT the station house, sitting at Decker's desk, feet propped up while he was writing on his iPad. He wore a black turtleneck, black cords, and boots on his feet. "I tried sleeping. It was useless, so I came here. I drove your car back, so you're all set. Dr. Ferraga called me back. You're meeting with him at eleven-thirty." He held up a folder. "Elijah Wolf's autopsy report. The coroner ruled it a suicide."

Decker stared at him. "Can I sit down?"

"Sure. Pull up a chair." Decker swatted McAdams's shoes off the desktop.

The kid stood up. "I wouldn't need to use your chair if you would have left my desk alone."

"I cleared off my stuff. Sit down and stop griping."

McAdams complied. "I got a call from Dr. Kent this morning."

"Who is he?"

"Math teacher at Exeter. He remembered Mallon. She left because she applied to college early. He wrote her a recommendation. He said she was very gifted in math."

"So nothing sinister about her leaving?"

"No."

Decker paged through the autopsy report. "Pretty straightforward. Nothing from the tox screen. Of course, it's the regular stuff. He could have taken a more exotic drug."

"What do you think?"

"I think it was suicide." He put the report down. "I'll go see his parents tomorrow. Give them the news in person."

"What do you think happened?"

"No idea. It's especially curious because Dr. Rosser reported him as being more social within the last month."

"Saying his final good-bye to those who helped him?"

"Could be." Decker sighed. "What a shame."

Even Tyler looked pensive. "Yeah."

"Anyway, that's that." Decker looked up. "I take it you booked a car to drive you back to Boston?"

"I'd like to stick around until tomorrow. I can even come with you to visit Eli's parents."

"Tyler, you promised to go back. It's where you belong."

"That is debatable. Besides, I have a very good reason for sticking around. Dr. Gold can't meet me until tomorrow late afternoon. That is, if you still want to bring Eli's hidden papers to him. I'm hoping maybe we'll get something from Rosser by that time."

It was a valid point. "All right. I'll take you up north tomorrow."

"I appreciate it, boss."

"Well, we might as well know what Eli's papers were about. Maybe that'll provide some answers to why he did it. After that, I'm kicking you out of the house."

"I'm a pain, I know."

"No, you're not a pain." Decker was silent. "Let me ask you something. And it's sincere."

"Uh-oh."

"Why are you doing all this busywork with me when you have no intention of going into law enforcement?"

"You don't know that. Even I don't know that. The only thing I do know is I'm not doing a nine-to-five desk job. I'm just too damn restless."

"Most of detective work is a nine-to-five desk job."

"No, no, no. You sit at a desk, but you don't do a nine-to-five desk job. There's a difference." A pause. "I'm going to graduate law school. I'd be stupid if I didn't. And I will pass the bars—bars as in plural—because there's lots of money for me when I do. And maybe I'll be a lawyer. Or maybe I'll be a real detective in a real city. Or maybe I'll finally go to Hollywood and write that Oscar-winning screenplay. The world is my playground, Decker. Don't be the one to stifle my dreams."

"If your dream is to become a cop, you're aiming low."

"Aiming low definitely fits the idle rich." He gave Decker a forced smile. "So as long as I'm staying another day, I'd like to come with you to talk to Dr. Ferraga."

"Sure, come with me."

"And I have the time to go with you to visit Eli's parents. It's on the way back to Cambridge."

"Sure." Decker thought. "I might as well come with you to Cambridge."

"Makes sense."

"Take a notepad, McAdams. It's easier than writing on your iPad."

The kid held up a spiral pad. "I got it out of your desk. I hope you don't mind."

"Like it matters if I minded?"

"Yeah, you're right. I'd take it regardless of your feelings. I was just practicing at being polite."

CHAPTER 14

WAS NOT ELI'S primary adviser." Aldo Ferraga spoke with a slight singsong Italian accent. Decker had looked him up before the interview. The professor had been in the country over twenty years. "I know you spoke to Dr. Rosser. I'm sure I have nothing to add."

"But you did work with Eli, being on his thesis committee."

"It is a small department. I'm on quite a few committees." Ferraga was short and slight. He had light eyes that were red-rimmed, and he sported a full, dark beard. He wore a white shirt with no tie, brown pants, and a brown corduroy jacket with suede patch pockets. Brown suede loafers on his feet. The blazer was more than just an affectation. It was cold in his office.

"I'm going to visit his parents tomorrow," Decker told him. "Would you like me to relate any kind of a message to them?"

"You have not talked to the parents?"

"Not since the official ruling."

"It was a suicide?"

"Yes, it was ruled a suicide."

"Then it is a tragedy—for any young person. It is especially sad when it is a young person with so much promise. He had an unusually superb mind. He will be missed."

"Did he seem troubled to you?"

"Intense yes, but not troubled. I saw Elijah as a gentle boy. He did not have the killer academic instinct. He was happy to help anyone who needed it."

"Socially awkward?"

"Not so much for this department." A pause. "At the Christmas party last month, he was quite engaging . . . talkative"

"He was studying Fourier analysis?"

"He had decided to focus on Fourier transforms, actually."

McAdams tapped his pencil against his notebook. "That's upper-division math."

"Yes."

"So it's an advanced field of study."

"I wouldn't say advanced. It is a basic field for any mathematician. I suppose it depends on what you do with it to make it advanced."

"What was he doing with it?" McAdams asked.

"You'll have to ask Dr. Rosser."

Decker said, "He's not all that forthcoming."

"Many academicians take a proprietary interest in their students."

"Especially one who was hiding papers behind a desk drawer."

"Yes, I had heard. You have the papers?"

"I do."

"But you refuse to show them to any of us."

"Too many people want to know what is in them. It's safer to show them to someone outside the university to prevent plagiarism."

"Providing that your outside source is trustworthy."

"Dr. Mordechai Gold at Harvard," McAdams said.

Ferraga smiled. "Of course. And when you find out what the

papers are about, perhaps you can relate to all of us what could be so valuable that Elijah felt the need to hide his work. From our limited conversations—we did have a few conversations, yes—it did not appear that Eli was on the verge of a major breakthrough."

"But you wouldn't know for sure."

"No. I do know that he was taking his research into different directions."

"What kind of directions?"

"More applied than theoretical. Not surprising. Eigenvalues and Fourier transforms have many practical applications."

"Such as?" Decker laughed. "Let me back that up. I have no idea what a Fourier transform is."

"Why would you know?" Ferraga said. "I don't know how to question a witness."

"Can you explain anything in layman's terms?"

"Specifically, it is applied integration to turn a function of time into a function of frequency—sine waves or cosine waves for instance."

"And what kind of practical applications would use this?"

"Anything that has a chart. Anytime you have a complex shape and you want to see the composition of it, you would use Fourier transforms."

Ferraga paused.

"I don't know if this is true or not. I don't want to start rumors, so this is strictly off the record. But I've heard that Elijah was working with Lennaeus Tolvard for the past year."

"Why off the record?"

"In Kneed Loft, it is frowned upon to choose one primary adviser and then work with someone else."

"It's certainly not going to hurt Eli's reputation anymore."

"But it may impact Lennaeus Tolvard."

"Why would a professor care if any student worked with someone else?" McAdams asked. "Isn't curiosity a good thing?"

Ferraga looked long-suffering. "We are all very busy, Detective. Once we take on a student and that student is part of our lab, he or she is expected to work with us, not take our information elsewhere."

McAdams said, "Turf battles."

"More like stealing intellectual property, Detective."

Decker said, "Could you spell 'Lennaeus Tolvard' for me?"

Ferraga complied.

McAdams said, "If Eli was working with this Tolvard, it could explain why he hid his papers behind his drawer. He didn't want anyone finding out that he had found another mentor." He looked at Ferraga. "What would have happened if Eli had wanted to switch advisers?"

"As I said, once a student is in upper division and has chosen an adviser, it is frowned upon to switch."

"So he wouldn't have been allowed to switch?" McAdams asked.

"It is doubtful that any faculty member would have agreed to the switch. It would have to be on the fly—pardon, the sly. Be on the sly."

"And you don't have any ideas what Eli and Tolvard were working on?"

"Tolvard's appointment is in the physics department. His specialty is cosmology. The applications for Fourier transforms in outer space are endless. I suspect that this wasn't part of his thesis although you'd have to ask Dr. Rosser about that. I suspect he was doing this on his own because the field interested him."

"And you don't think Dr. Rosser had any idea about it?"

"I'm sure he has heard the rumors, the same as I have. How he dealt with it?" Ferraga gave a shrug.

Decker said, "If Eli had done something with Tolvard, who would have owned Eli's research? Rosser or Tolvard?"

"Ah, that is an interesting question. If something was published, I would suspect both would get authorship. But who would be the primary author, I don't know."

"Eli wouldn't get primary authorship?"

"Of course not. He'd get some recognition, but the primary authorship goes to his supervisor."

"So if he published with Tolvard as the lead author instead of Rosser, that would create a problem."

"Yes, of course. But I doubt that a turf battle would lead to his suicide."

"How about if he were mentally unstable to start?"

"You're in the wrong department, Detective." Ferraga looked at his watch and grimaced. "The Kneed Loft Psychology Department is on the third floor."

THE COFFEEHOUSE AT Kneed Loft was lined with walls of whiteboard filled with indecipherable equations. Students bounced up and down between their seats and the boards, writing things down as it occurred to them. Their work was visible to everyone. In this day and age, privacy had become a rara avis.

McAdams took a sip of his espresso. "Looks like Eli was doing a big no-no. But even if he was, I don't see why that would lead to his suicide."

"Neither do I," Decker admitted. "And it's not up to the police to discover why he did it."

"So you're done looking into Eli's death?"

"Any further probing is counterproductive. We'll see his parents tomorrow, and that's that. Since you're going to Harvard anyway, we'll take the papers to Gold. See what they're about. But I doubt if it'll have anything to do with his suicide."

"So what's on tap now?"

"I'm going back to the station house. I've got a couple of small burglaries I'm working on. Electronics stores. I've got some CCTV to look through. You can go home and study."

"Or I can talk to Lennaeus Tolvard."

"If he talks to you, he's not going to admit that he was working with someone else's student."

"I can still try."

"Sure, if you think that's a better use of your time than studying for your finals."

Mallon Euler burst through the door, loaded down with two carry-on suitcases and a knapsack strapped to her back. She was with Damodar Batra, the senior who first identified Elijah Wolf through a postmortem photograph. She was talking animatedly, but then she stopped in what appeared to be midsentence when she saw Decker and McAdams. She wheeled her suitcase over to their table. Batra was in tow, wearing a ski jacket, jeans, and boots. Mallon still had on her pea coat from this morning.

"She was a no-show," she announced. "God, that pisses me off."

"Uh, the she being Katrina Belfort, correct?" McAdams asked.

"Yes, Detective McAdams, that is *correct!*"

"No need for the snappish attitude," McAdams answered.

"I happen to be a little bit more than concerned," Mallon went on. "I can't reach her by phone, text, e-mail, Twitter, or Facebook. And no one has seen her this morning. After what happened last night, I'm nervous."

Decker said, "Did you call campus police?"

"She doesn't *live* on campus, Detective. She lives in town. I believe that's your territory."

"Do you have her address?"

"Bluejay Lane." She recited the numerals. "Could you stop by like in right now?"

"Sure." Decker stood up. "Did you find a place to crash, Mallon? You can't go around living like a turtle with your home on your back."

"Damodar invited me to stay with him until I've found another place. We trust each other since our research is totally orthogonal."

"Completely," Batra added. "We were just going to grab coffee before we moved her in."

"If you find out about Dr. Belfort, can you let me know?" Mallon asked. "It's not like her to miss a meeting."

"She is very prompt and very meticulous," Batra added.

"I'll swing by . . . let you know." To McAdams, he said, "Are you coming?"

"I thought I'd stick around here," McAdams said. "Maybe talk to Professor Tolvard."

"Ah, so you've heard the rumors, also," Batra said. "That Eli was working with Tolvard."

"I've never heard that," Mallon said.

"You're more theoretical. I'm more applied. So I have my fingers in both areas. And I hear things."

"What have you heard?" McAdams asked.

"Just what I said. That Eli was working with Tolvard."

"Any idea on what?"

"Nope, but since Tolvard is in the outer space department of physics and Eli was working on Fourier series—"

"Fourier transforms," McAdams corrected.

"Ah, so he redirected his interests from theoretical to applied. And now that makes total sense. He was probably doing something with cosmic rays."

"Isn't that verboten . . . to switch advisers?" Mallon said. "God, if it isn't, I'm done with Katrina."

"I don't think he formally switched," Decker said.

"So he was doing it on the DL," Batra said.

To Mallon, Decker said, "Why are you done with Katrina Belfort?"

"She's a nice woman, but she never has enough time for me. It took me nearly a week to get an appointment with her and she's my adviser. What's going to happen when I really need her in a month or so?"

"Never choose a professor that doesn't have tenure," Batra said. "The underlings are too busy and there's too much temptation for them to rip off your ideas."

"It's just odd that she hasn't shown up anywhere," Mallon said. "And after last night, I'm very nervous."

Decker put on his jacket. "I'm on my way."

McAdams stood as well. "I'll walk out with you." After they left the coffeehouse, Decker said, "I'll let you know if I find out anything at Belfort's house. You let me know if you find out anything significant about Eli and Tolvard. It's called being a team player."

"That isn't my forte."

"What is your forte?"

"Getting under people's skin. It's a good skill to have as a detective."

"Then I'll say this, Tyler. It's certainly the one skill that you mastered beyond excellence."

CHAPTER 15

THE HOUSE WAS a turn-of-the-twentieth-century bungalow. It featured white wood siding, blue shutters and trim, a small porch with a chair, and a planting area for flowers that was currently under a blanket of snow. There was a shoveled pathway to the door, where multiple footprints were rounded out by a thin layer of snow. The rear of the house backed up to woodlands. Decker walked up to the front door and knocked. When no one answered, he took off his gloves and retrieved a set of lockpicks from his jacket. Kneeling down until his eye was in line with the keyhole, he inserted the first pick into the lock and felt for the tumblers to click into place. He was working away when he heard a male voice.

"Excuse me. Can I help you?"

Decker turned around and stood up. He brushed off his knees, now dusted with snow. "Police." He took out his badge and the man gave it a once-over. He appeared to be in his late seventies or early eighties with white thin hair sticking out of the front of his green

Celtics snow cap. He had pale, blue eyes with weathered skin and a stooped gait. "And you are?"

"Harvey Calloway. I live across the street."

"I'm looking for Katrina Belfort. She didn't show up for work this morning and her colleagues are a bit concerned. Have you seen her this morning?"

"No, not this morning."

"What about last night?"

"No, not last night, either."

"Would you know when was the last time you saw her?"

He gave the question honest thought. "A day or two ago. I usually take a very early morning constitutional and I come home just around the time she leaves for work."

"And what time would that be?"

"Around seven-thirty."

"Is she a friend of yours?"

"Just an acquaintance. We exchange morning salutations. 'Hi, Katrina. Hi, Harvey.' She picks up our papers when we go out of town to visit our daughter. By 'we,' I mean the missus and myself. Katrina says she likes picking up our papers because she doesn't subscribe to any newspaper and it's a treat for her to read them in the morning with her coffee. I asked her why she doesn't subscribe to the local paper. She told me she just gets her news off the Internet. It's a generational thing."

He held up a finger.

"We did get her a subscription to the *New Yorker* for Christmas. Actually it was the missus's idea. Katrina was very appreciative. She made us a cake. Very professional. One of those thin layered things with lots of cinnamon and spice. I think she said it was a Dutch kuchen. She had some Dutch blood in her. Anyway, it was a delicious cake even though we didn't need the calories."

"Sounds like you two were pretty friendly," Decker said.

"Just because I'm a friendly guy. I talk to everyone. What's going on?"

"Like I said, her colleagues were concerned that she didn't show up for work today." Decker paused. "Does she seem to have a lot of friends?"

"She isn't the party type, if that's what you're asking. You think something happened to her?"

"No idea. I just want to take a look around because her no-show is unusual." No one spoke. Decker said, "You've been in her house before?"

"A few times . . . to thank her for the cake, for instance."

"So you can come in with me, tell me if the house looks like it did the last time you went inside. Just don't touch anything, okay."

"Is that allowed?"

"It wouldn't fly if this were LAPD. Neither would picking her locks. But this isn't Los Angeles. It's a small town, and when the folks here don't show up for work and no one can contact them, I get concerned. You don't have to go in, Mr. Calloway."

"No, no. I want to help."

"Okay. This should only take a few minutes." Decker bent down and finished picking the lock. It sprang open, but there was a chain lock preventing the door from opening all the way. That was usually an indication that the person was inside the house. It was also possible that she left via a back door. "Hold on." Decker closed the door partially and, with a hook, managed to displace the chain from the slot.

He opened the door into a tidy living room stocked with old-fashioned furniture that could have come from Grandma's attic. More than likely, the pieces came with the house. There was a curlicue oak-framed couch with white and blue iris upholstery, an oak coffee table, and a couple of used wing chairs. There was a desk piled high with papers and an oversize computer monitor, and behind it was a bookshelf filled with academic texts. Several framed photographs: her with a blond man with long hair, both with full smiles and holding skis and ski poles. There was another photograph of an older couple framing the blond man and Katrina. Lastly, in a silver frame, there was a head shot, Katrina's chin resting in her hand. Decker slipped on a latex glove and picked up the ski picture. "Boyfriend?"

"No idea."

"Okay." He put it back down. "Does the house look tampered with?"

"Not at all."

The living room was divided from the kitchen by a marble countertop. Decker glanced at the kitchen. Nothing was out of place. The food in the refrigerator wasn't old or rotten. He said, "I'm going to have a look around."

"Can I come?"

Decker took in a deep breath. No foul odor indicating a dead body. But it was cool inside. "It might be better if you waited for me here. I shouldn't be more than a minute."

"Okay."

"Just please don't touch anything or sit down . . . if that's okay."

"I'm fine."

It took around ten minutes to do a preliminary search, and everything appeared to be in order. The house had two bedrooms with one bathroom that was off the hallway. The beds were made, the bathroom was clean, and the back door was locked. Decker went back to the living room. "We can go now."

"Anything suspicious-looking?"

Decker shook his head no. "I'm going to look around back and trample through the woods a bit. I'd hate to think she was out there with a broken leg or something, waiting to be rescued."

"Can I come with you?"

"No thanks. This is a police job."

"Can you let me know if you find anything out—good or bad?"

"Of course."

"If you need to warm up, I'll put the kettle on."

"I may take you up on that. I'm fine for now."

The two of them left by the front door with Calloway going back to his house. Decker retraced his steps through the house and left by the back door. The rear yard was small and covered with snow. But it did tell a tale. The snow layer was anything but pristine. No clean footprints but a lot of upheaval with bumps and lumps all over.

Like someone was covering tracks.

Decker stared at the yard for a minute, trying to decide what to do next. He took out his phone and called McAdams. "What are you doing now?"

"I'm studying for finals in the café at Kneed Loft, waiting for Lennaeus Tolvard to call me back for an appointment."

"Keep studying. I'll talk to you later."

"Wait a minute there, pard. What's going on with Dr. Belfort?"

"She's not in and her house looks undisturbed. Go back to your studying."

"You didn't call me just to say everything's okay. What's going on? Truth, please?"

Decker owed him that much for being a good cop. "Her backyard looks hinky. The snow layer has been messed with, like someone was trying to erase footprints or drag marks. I say that because her house backs up to the woods and I'm wondering if her body might be there. I'm going to go poke around."

"Peter, wait for me."

"No need."

"You called me. That classifies as a dangled carrot."

"Okay, I'll wait. But get here soon. I'm cold."

"I'm in a coffee shop. I'll bring coffee."

"Make it a large. I have a feeling we're going to be here for a while."

IN ANY SEASON, woodlands hiking was tricky business. There was a sameness to the forests and it was very easy to get disoriented. Plus, phones often didn't get good reception, if they got any at all. In freezing weather, when the trails were iced over and each step had to be made with care, Decker knew that getting lost was not an option, especially with Tyler in tow. He opened his car trunk, pulled out his survival backpack, and looped it over his shoulder. It had water, thermal packets, freeze-dried food, and most important a warm change of clothing. He had a compass, a pad of paper, a camera, and some evidence bags.

The woods in winter were fifty shades of gray and none of them sexy: stark, colorless, and bleak. Thousands of bare trees sat in snow, their roots buried under scattered detritus and rotting flora. Evergreens and pines were scattered among the deciduous trees, and Decker got a hint of Christmas aroma depending on how the icy wind blew. And the entire place dripped water: cold and clammy.

McAdams shifted on his feet. "How long do you reckon to be out there?"

"A couple of hours. Thanks for the coffee, by the way. Are you warm enough?"

"I'm fine. Do you want me to carry that, Old Man?"

"If you're going to call me Old Man, then yes, you can carry the pack." Decker took it off and gave it to McAdams.

"This is heavy."

"You offered."

The kid smiled. It opened up his face. McAdams was a good-looking boy: a thin patrician face, long straight nose, hazel eyes, and normally short, dark, curly hair. Girls would think him handsome if he'd lose the perpetual scowl.

They took their first tentative steps into the woods. Decker looked around. Some areas were more protected than others, which meant the snow layer was uneven. No shoe prints to be seen, but there was the same disturbance that he'd found in the backyard. He looked around and sipped coffee.

"What are you thinking?" McAdams asked. "That she was killed and dragged into the woods out back?"

"I didn't see any evidence of a murder scene in the house. Nothing upended and no overwhelming smell of bleach or antiseptic. But I didn't take a microscopic look."

"So maybe she was taken into the woods at gunpoint and the bad guy shot her there?"

"I don't know, Tyler." Decker paused, then pointed. "The snow has been messed with between those two trees going up the hill. Let's go there and have a look."

They walked a few minutes without talking, the snow crunching under their feet. Decker trudged slowly, looking up and down and to and fro and left and right. Not likely he'd find anything of evidential value, but at this point in his life, it was a habit. They seemed to be trodding on a natural trail with the ground underneath somewhat free of rocks or roots. The snow was deep but he could still feel the ground under the soles of his boots. As they climbed high and went deeper, the temperature dropped and an arctic mist rose from the ground. Visibility was curtailed.

"This is creepy," McAdams said. "This doesn't bother you? It's like flying blind."

"Then we're lucky we're walking and it's in daylight."

"You are intrepid."

"This isn't the wilds of Africa." Decker stopped to survey his surroundings and check his compass. "Let me just take down a few coordinates."

"I was never one for camping."

"Growing up like you did, I'm not surprised." Decker looked at him. "We're about five minutes from civilization. Nothing's going to happen to us."

"What if the yeti isn't a myth?"

Decker laughed. "C'mon, Tyler, let's go this way."

The old man led and the young lad followed, the two of them walking for another ten minutes deeper into the bowels of the woodlands. The trek was slow and slippery, the gelid mist stinging the eyes, the temperature cramping the muscles and numbing the face. Decker kept his eyes focused on the disturbed ground until they reached a copse of trees.

He stopped.

The ground was covered in puddles of snow and dead foliage. But he could see clearly that the location had been the target of recent activity. There were wild animal tracks: foxes, rabbits, deer, vultures and maybe a bear too stupid to hibernate. Decker's nostrils perked up. "I'm definitely smelling some kind of carrion."

"I can't smell. I think my nose froze."

"Let's follow my nose. It can't be too much farther."

"Oh joy."

"Don't get sick on me, McAdams. You might have gotten a little soft these past months."

"I'm fine." He adjusted the straps of the backpack. "I think."

Decker motioned him to the right. They walked a couple of hundred yards, and as they did, McAdams said, "Yeah, I'm smelling something now." More walking. Tyler covered his nose with his gloved hand. "God, that's putrid."

"Yeah, it's pretty bad..." Decker stopped in his tracks. "Oh dear God."

They were both looking at the half-eaten nude corpse. Most of the torso was gone and had become an empty bowl of blood and torn guts. The neck had been eaten through as well, leaving a decapitated head that had rolled several inches from the body. The legs and arms had sustained numerous bites with chunks taken out of the flesh. She had been nude, but her clothes lay piled neatly beside her body, reminiscent of Elijah Wolf. Winking from under the detritus was something metal.

Decker squatted down and brushed a few leaves aside. He was staring at a 9 mm Ruger stainless-steel pistol. He left it where he found it and took out his compass. He made a small map on his pad of paper and then he looked up. "Let's go back and call it in." He looked up at McAdams, whose skin tone was pale and ashen and not from the cold. "You okay, Tyler?"

The kid nodded. "This isn't pretty bad. It's very, very bad."

"It is." Decker took a swig of coffee. "Drink."

"I don't think . . ." He did a dry retch and swallowed hard. "I'm . . . okay."

"You're gray, Tyler." Decker took out a camera and began snapping pictures. "Catch your breath and drink the coffee. It'll help because if something's going down the gullet, other things can't come back up."

"You think so?"

"Are you going to heave?"

"No." Another swallow. "I'm fine." To prove it, McAdams took out his iPad and began taking pictures as well. Looking through the touch-screen camera was helpful.

He could pretend he was watching Netflix.

CHAPTER 16

DO YOU KNOW who she is?" Stella Grady worked in the hospital morgue in a bigger town near Utica. It was her day off and she was kind enough to schlepp to Greenbury to act as the coroner. She was tall and big-boned with short dark hair, dark eyes, and a square chin. She was wearing a heavy coat with big boots, the soles encased in blue shoe coverings to prevent contamination. Underneath she had on blue scrubs. She was in a crouch.

"I believe she was Katrina Belfort, but I have to get her ID'd by someone who knows her," Decker said. "Belfort is a professor at Kneed Loft. She didn't show up for work today and that's unusual."

"I hope someone can identify her. There's been lots of animal activity all over the body and the head's a mess."

"I'll pass around the least gruesome postmortem face I have. I'd like to at least put it on what's left of the neck and torso so it doesn't look so awful. We have a gun. Do you have a gunshot wound?"

"We've got a large crater here." Stella handled the head delicately. "Something blew out the back of the skull."

"Like a short-range gunshot from a Ruger?"

"Very possibly." She regarded the gun in the bag. "I have to examine this more closely, but I get a feeling that something else was at play besides a single gunshot wound."

"So you're not thinking suicide?"

"Not sure what it is yet, Detective. This could have been one well-placed bullet, but the occiput is an odd area to shoot yourself. It can be done, but it would be an awkward hand position. What about the gun? You saw it in situ. Did it look like it was dropped from a suicidal hand?"

Decker regarded the crime scene. "It was almost buried in dead foliage . . . like it sank under. I have to think about it. There have been so many disturbances at the scene from animals that I haven't a clue what was the original position of the gun. Any estimated time of death?"

"I obviously can't use the liver. Whatever is left over is frozen. Normally it takes a while for the entire body to drop to these kinds of low temperatures, but because she's in bits and pieces, everything would be sped up." She stood up. "Judging by the torso and the amount of fresh flesh . . . maybe last night to early morning."

"Thanks. That's a start."

"Can we start gathering up the remains? It's going to take time to transport the body parts down the hill and into the van."

"Yeah, sure, go ahead." Decker turned to McAdams, who was taking photographs on his iPad. "Yo, Harvard."

The kid looked up. "You haven't called me that in a while." A smile. "Perhaps the moniker means you want my professional help."

Decker smiled back. "This is the plan. I'm going to stay up here with Forensics. I'll need a couple of people to canvass the area— maybe someone saw or heard something last night."

"I can do that."

"I've got Karen and Kevin on it. I have another assignment

for you that'll be equally time-consuming. So you tell me if you want in."

"Of course, I want in. We've got a genuine crime." A pause. "This isn't suicide, right?"

"Nothing's been ruled out yet. But to me, it looks staged to look like a suicide—the gun, the nude body in the woods with the clothes around."

"Elijah Wolf."

"Exactly."

"So maybe we should take a second look at his death."

"We will, but only after we've taken a first look at Katrina's death. We've only seen her once. I'd like another ID. Do you have a decent shot of her face on your iPad?"

"I got plenty of head shots . . . no pun intended."

"I need you to take the best ones you have. Go to Kneed Loft and get her identified by two sources who knew her better than we did. I'd suggest Ferraga and Rosser since we've talked to them recently."

"The head isn't attached to a body. It's really gross."

"We're going to put it back on the neck and put a scarf around it so we don't make people sick. And while you're at Kneed Loft, find out where Rosser and Ferraga were last night."

"What about Dean Zhou?" McAdams said. "She was eager to get her hands on Elijah Wolf's papers."

"Right. Get her alibi. Belfort also had students—Batra and Weissberg and Mallon. Talk to them as well."

"We know where Mallon was."

"After three A.M. we know where she was. Between ten and three, she said she was at Pascal Library. Go see if you can get people to place her at the library during the entire time she said she was there. We have someone sneaking into her room around midnight. Maybe it was Mallon slipping back to her room to change bloody clothing."

McAdams nodded. "And if no one can vouch for her?"

"Then she's a suspect. We need to find out about Belfort: her relationship to her students and colleagues. Her personal relationships. Did she have a boyfriend, girlfriend, or was she having trouble with anyone specific?"

"What about Theo Rosser? He hated her."

"He didn't say anything against her. It was more like she hated him. That's why he's on the suspect list. I also want to know if she was in debt. Was she doing something dishonest? Did she have any bad habits, and lastly, is there an ex somewhere?"

"We're treating this as a murder and not a suicide."

"It's a very, very suspicious death. I'll be here at least a couple of hours, so you've got some time. Come back to Katrina's house at around three-thirty and we'll go through it with a fine-tooth comb. If you get hung up with something, leave a message on my phone. I don't have reception here, but I'll pick the message up when I'm back in civilization."

"Got it."

"I'm hoping you're still planning to leave tomorrow, Tyler. Unfortunately for everyone, this throws a big wrench in my time schedule. I may not be able to drive you up because I might not get to Eli's parents until Thursday."

"What about Gold?"

"Oh, right. You can take the papers up to him when you go back. I just won't be able to come with you."

"Or we could both see Gold on Thursday."

"The way things are going, Harvard, that's a big if. You really need to get back to your former life." When McAdams didn't answer, Decker said, "Am I talking to deaf ears?"

"What?" McAdams quipped.

"Very funny."

"I'll be fine. Just make sure I don't get shot again."

"That is *not* going to happen."

"Then I'm a happy camper. I'll see you at Belfort's house around . . . three-thirty?"

"Sounds good. By then, the light will be fading and we won't be able to do too much out here anyway." McAdams hesitated. Decker said, "What is it?"

"You really suspect Mallon Euler of this?"

"I have no opinions yet."

"If you really do suspect her, I'll show her the face and see how she reacts."

"Let's hold off. Her room was ransacked and she seemed pretty shaken. If she was involved with this mess, we'll show her the post-mortem photos at a more opportune time for us. If she wasn't involved, there's no sense giving her nightmares that'll last a lifetime."

AS SOON AS Rosser saw the photos, he turned pale and his hands started shaking. "It looks like a grotesque version of Katrina Belfort."

The man was ashen. Beads of sweat had congregated on his brow. He wiped his face with a tissue. He wore a dark green sweater and brown corduroy pants. Scuffed penny loafers sat on his feet. He tried to talk but words caught in his gullet.

McAdams said, "Do you need some water?"

"No . . . thank you." Rosser was still trembling. "How did this *happen*?"

McAdams wasn't sure if Rosser meant what was the method of death or what were the sociologic circumstances that led up to the death. In either case, the question was probably rhetorical and didn't require an answer. He pulled up a chair and sat down. "How well did you know her?"

"She was a colleague." He shook his head, his eyes faraway. "We didn't socialize outside of the department, if that's what you're asking. Whatever spare time I have, I spend with my wife." He wiped his face again. "God, this is awful." He regarded McAdams. "Was it suicide like Elijah?"

When unsure how to reply, McAdams answered the question with a question. "What makes you think it's suicide?"

"I don't know. That's why I'm asking you."

"Was Dr. Belfort close to Eli?"

"Not that I know of. She had been on Eli's thesis committee, but she excused herself due to other commitments. Aldo Ferraga took her place. But I was his primary adviser."

Questioning a person was harder than McAdams had thought. He was used to jumping off Decker's train of thought. "Who else was on Eli's committee?"

"There were three of us: Aldo Ferraga, Lennaeus Tolvard, and myself."

"Lennaeus Tolvard?" McAdams hoped he sounded genuinely surprised.

"He's in the physics department. It isn't a must obviously, but it's looked favorably upon when you round up an outside professor for your committee. I guess after Katrina resigned from Eli's committee, he took it upon himself to recruit Tolvard."

"Tolvard." McAdams paused. "I've heard the name before." Rosser said nothing and McAdams didn't push it. Until he had a definite direction, he should stick to what Decker told him to do. "Who were Katrina's students? We'll need to talk to them."

"I know she's the primary adviser for Mallon Euler. I sent Mallon to her because I was just too busy. And I was trying to help Katrina build up her research lab and I thought Mallon was a good choice."

"Did you send her anyone else?"

"Not personally, no. I believe she had three students in her lab: Mallon, of course. I think Ari Weissberg was also one of her students, although I don't think he was happy being there."

"Why not?"

"Her lab was just getting started. If you want to get into a top-tier program, it's better to be in a lab where the professor is tenured. Not that there was anything wrong with Katrina. She was extremely bright. Just . . . untested, I want to say."

"You said three students. Who's the third student?"

"Oh yes. Damodar Batra. He was her first student. They seemed to get along very well . . . maybe too well."

McAdams perked up. "Meaning?"

"He had been seen going in and out of her house. During daylight hours, mind you, but it is unprofessional to hold meetings with your students at your residence."

"I see," McAdams said. "Do you think professional turned to personal?"

"Nothing to indicate yes or no for that one."

"Speaking of personal relationships, did Professor Belfort have a boyfriend?"

"Not that I know of."

"Who were her friends?"

"I don't know anything about her social life outside the college."

"But you knew that Damodar Batra came over to her house."

"It's a small department in a small college. Things get around. But truly, I don't know about her social life. At the few departmental parties we've had, she had always come alone."

McAdams thought a moment. "How long has Dr. Belfort been with the college?"

"Two years. We had a search committee for candidates. It does the interviews, but all tenured faculty votes for final confirmation."

"Who was on the search committee for Dr. Belfort?"

"I was, as was Aldo Ferraga. The third member at that time was Michael Mannix, who has since left for UC San Diego. Can't say I blame him with these winters. We knew he was leaving. That's why we were searching for someone. We needed to fill the void and Katrina's specialty was similar to Michael's."

"Which was?"

"Probability theory. Over the course of the year, Katrina's interests had changed to fast Fourier transforms, which can relate tangentially to probability theory. Whenever you're working with the market fluctuations, you're working with probabilities."

McAdams said. "*Fast* Fourier transforms deal with fluctuations in the stock market?"

"Potentially yes."

"Could you explain what Fourier transforms have to do with the stock market?"

"Do you know what Fourier transforms do?"

"They change functions from time to frequency and break down complex waves into simple ones."

"Very good. Have you ever seen a graph of a stock within a single session of daily trading? The x-axis is time and the y-axis is the price. The stock has a daily high and low and everything in between the two numbers."

"Yeah, it kind of zigzags like a bunch of thunderbolts."

"Exactly. If you're a day trader, it would be an advantage to know what kinds of waves make up the zigzag. The highs and lows would be characterized by the amplitude of the wave, and the frequency would characterize the space between the amplitude. If the frequency is long and the amplitude is low, the stock isn't undergoing a lot of change. But a lot of stocks are volatile. If you knew the waves making up the pattern, in theory, you might be able to predict the stock's next move: either up or down. And that would be tremendously helpful, especially in day trading, where fortunes can be made and lost within seconds."

"So anything that can give you an edge on where the stock is going will help with the bottom line."

"Theoretically yes."

"Okay. Was Dr. Belfort plying her trade—her theoretical knowledge by day trading in the market?"

"I have no idea, Detective."

"What about Elijah Wolf? Was he doing day trading, too?"

"Elijah?" Rosser made a face. "His research didn't reflect any of that nonsense."

"You think it's nonsense?"

"Day trading is nonsense. It's a fool's game. Glorified gambling."

Silently, McAdams agreed with him. "When was the last time you saw Dr. Belfort?"

Rosser sighed. "Sometime yesterday morning. We had been talking about Eli. She was still very upset. So upset that I wondered at the time if there wasn't something else going on."

"Like what?"

"Well . . ." Rosser sighed. "Batra wasn't the only student seen coming and going from Katrina's house. Not that I want to speak ill of the dead. But if you think it has some bearing on what happened to both of them, I feel it incumbent to say something."

"Do you think she was having an affair with either boy?"

"How should I put this?" A pause. "After observing Katrina for the past year . . . well, she liked her admirers. Math is generally a department of young men. She was low person in the faculty, but she had her acolytes in the classroom."

"Okay. I'll talk to Batra. Anyone else I should speak with?"

"I'd say Batra is a good starting point."

"And the last question, Dr. Rosser. Could you tell me where you were between ten last night and, say, three in the morning?"

"*Excuse* me?"

"Routine question, sir."

"I was sleeping . . . well, not at ten. I was doing work at home until one and then I went to bed."

"And your wife was with you during the period?"

"She went to bed earlier ... around eleven." He stared at McAdams. "I did not leave my house."

"You were working on your computer?"

"Mostly by hand. My computer was hardly on."

"Could I take a look at your computer? It might verify your time frame. And if you e-mailed something, it would show where geographically you were working." Again there was silence. "Just a peek at your laptop—"

"I work on a desktop," Rosser said.

"I can come to your house to look at your desktop." McAdams waited. "It would help eliminate you as a suspect."

"That is ridiculous."

"I could come tonight ... get it over with."

"How about if I call you? I'm very, very busy."

"Whatever works," McAdams said. "I would think you'd do anything to get out of this mess."

"I'm not in any mess, Detective. You can't seriously suspect that I had anything to do with this ghastly affair."

"What I think is immaterial. I'm just saying that it's in everyone's interest to cooperate."

Rosser said, "I'm not hiding anything, I'm just busy. These past days have been horrific. Just give me a chance to settle my department. I'll call you, Detective."

He sounded disingenuous. To McAdams, insincerity counted as a lie.

CHAPTER 17

THE SUN WAS sinking fast and there wasn't much that Decker could do in the fading light other than secure the area, which was done with a tent. Theoretically, it would block animal activity, but since the area still contained bits of blood and remains, the canvas wasn't going to dissuade hungry, feral creatures from tearing down the structure. Decker made his way back to civilization with its heat, electricity, and phone reception. Katrina Belfort's backyard was lit up with police spotlights. The temperature was dropping rapidly, and although Decker had packed hand and feet warmers, there was still numbness and pain in his fingers, toes, and nose. Because of last year's murders, the police department had secured official crime scene tape, which had been placed across the front and back doors of Katrina's house and around the perimeter of the yard. Detectives/police officers Karen and Kevin—known as K and K—were chatting under the backyard porch, comparing notes when Decker walked into their conversation.

Karen, the newest addition to Greenbury, was in her fifties, a transplant from Chicago PD. Like Decker, she wasn't quite ready to retire, and since McAdams officially had left for law school, there was room for one more. She was tall with a weathered face holding blue eyes, sharp cheekbones, and a beak for a nose. Her avian features were more eagle than sparrow. Kevin Nickweed was large and big and had been with Greenbury much longer than Decker. At one time long ago, he had been an experienced detective in Milwaukee, but since his homicide skills were a bit rusty, he was happy to let Decker take the lead.

Kevin said, "The most interesting thing I picked up from neighbors is that Katrina often had people coming in and out of her house."

Karen concurred. "Especially on the weekends."

"Lots of parties?" Decker asked.

"No one talked about loud noises, just that she had visitors."

"Young, old?"

"Mostly students," Kevin said. "The same students by the descriptions: probably two or three males and one female, the girl described as average height, very thin with short blond hair."

"Mallon Euler," Decker said. "What about the boys?"

"One was Indian, the other two were nondescript white males— average height and weight. Their dress was the usual student stuff— jeans, sweatshirt, boots, and a backpack. One of the white kids was usually on a bike."

"Damodar Batra was probably the Indian. He's one of Belfort's students. So was a guy named Ari Weissberg. Elijah wasn't officially her student. And she wasn't on his committee anymore. But he still could have visited her. I'll get pictures for you to get a definite ID with the neighbors."

Karen said, "I also got reports of an occasional visit from a thirtyish blond guy who was good-looking."

"Ditto," Kevin said. "One of the neighbors who told me that also remembers a car occasionally parked in front of her house late at night."

"Oh?" Decker perked up. "What kind of a car?"

"A sedan. She couldn't get more specific than that. I tried. I even showed her pictures of cars on my phone. She just kept shaking her head."

"But she knew it was late at night." Decker paused. "Any information about the *occupant* of the car?"

"Never saw anyone, except once, she saw someone leave around two. It was dark and the person was bundled in a coat and scarf. She just assumed it was one of the kids."

"Students wouldn't own cars," Decker said.

"So maybe it was the blond guy," Karen suggested.

"She didn't see a face?" Decker asked.

"Nope."

"Well, that is really a shame!" Decker clapped his gloves to get circulation in his fingers. "Okay, what about the night of her death? Any luck?"

Karen said, "The people I talked to were fast asleep by twelve and didn't know anything about an incident until this afternoon when they saw all the official cars."

Kevin said, "Mostly the same except there was Belfort's next-door neighbor to the north. You'll need to talk to her. She had trouble sleeping last night and got up to read around two or three in the morning. She decided to make herself a cup of herbal tea and she peeked out the back window. She saw something moving across her backyard. She couldn't make out anything specific because the backdoor light was off in Katrina's house. But she didn't think too much about it because she thought it was an animal . . . low to the ground and not walking upright like a human."

"Low to the ground," Decker repeated. "Someone dragging a body through snowdrifts would be bent over."

"Like I said, you should talk to her."

Decker said, "So regular visitors were three or more students, a blond guy, and our mysterious occupant of a sedan. What about females closer to her age?"

Karen shrugged. "Nope."

Kevin said, "Same here."

"Okay," Decker said. "Good work. Go to the station house, get warm, and write it all up on the official forms: names, address, telephone numbers, and statement."

"No prob, Pete," Kevin said. "Do you need it tonight?"

"Yes, I do. Just leave your reports on my desk."

"What are you going to do?" Karen asked.

"I'm going to go inside the house, warm up, and hunt around for signs of a crime."

Kevin looked around. "Where's Robin, Batman?"

"At Kneed Loft poking around."

"I thought he was in law school," Karen said.

"He is, but you know how it is. People who break the law are a hell of a lot more interesting than the guys who uphold it."

WHEN ATTEMPTING TO interview students, McAdams realized quickly that they didn't stick around in any one place for too long. Damodar Batra committed to three locations at the time of Belfort's demise: his dorm room, the library, a party in Goddard Hall, and . . . oh yeah, he went out to get a pizza at around eleven because all the party food was gone and he was hungry. He had probably been noticed by a zillion people and all of them probably couldn't remember where or when they saw him.

Mallon was a little easier to pin down because she claimed she was in one space—the library—and there were people who did remember seeing her there. But they didn't remember exactly what time or for how long. That kind of precision—when the person remembers it was exactly two because the church clock rang out—usually exists only in fiction.

Katrina's final student was Ari Weissberg. He was on a bus coming back from Boston last night after visiting friends at MIT. He claimed he arrived at his room around midnight, studied a little, and then went to sleep around one. He did say hi to a few people but he doesn't remember exact times. The only thing that McAdams could confirm was that the kid arrived at the Hamilton bus station at 11:30 P.M. It took at least thirty minutes to get back. Beyond that, the trail faded to black.

As far as faculty, McAdams had placed two calls to Dean Zhou and she had yet to call back. Her whereabouts went to the top of his list. He did manage to catch Aldo Ferraga in the flesh. The man was in a rush and appeared distracted. He had allotted five minutes for an interview before heading to a faculty meeting, which was going to deal with Katrina's horrible "accident" in the woods.

"Why do you say it's an accident?"

The man combed his curly hair with stubby fingers. "Who would want to murder her?" He sounded peeved. "She was a hardworking woman and this is a very small and safe town. The whole thing is crazy!"

"Did you know her well?"

"I knew her. She was a colleague and she was nicer than most. Ambitious, of course, but if you want to get tenure, you have to be ambitious."

"Have you ever seen her outside the school?"

"My wife and I had her over for dinner. She had us over for dinner. That kind of thing."

"Often."

"No, not often. A few times."

"Did you know what her research was about?"

"Of course. Fourier transforms."

"Like Mallon Euler."

"Which is precisely why Rosser thought that she and Katrina would be a good match. Now, if you'll excuse me—"

"You told us that Elijah Wolf was working on Fourier transforms. I had heard that his primary interest was fractals."

"Ah, yes, in the beginning, but he switched to Fourier transforms mid junior year. He began showing a keen interest in applied math. I told you and the older detective all this this morning."

"That was about Elijah Wolf. This is about the untimely death of Katrina Belfort. We're talking again to everyone who knew her. So you may have to endure a little repetition." Ferraga was silent. McAdams said, "If Eli's interests were changing, maybe he was secretly meeting Katrina Belfort to talk about Fourier transforms."

"I wouldn't know, but I wouldn't be surprised. Katrina often invited students over to her house just to talk." A long pause. "And she did speak very fondly of Eli."

"How fondly?"

"I suppose it doesn't make any difference now." A sigh. "Katrina wanted to be his primary thesis adviser. I know she wanted him to switch from Rosser because Eli seemed to be gravitating in her direction."

"How'd that meeting go?"

"What do you think? There was a shouting match. Rosser was furious. He almost had Katrina fired, which he could do because she was on probation. A few of the faculty intervened, including Dean Zhou and me. Suggesting a student change primary advisers is not a reason for dismissal. When cooler heads prevailed, the matter was dropped and no one spoke of it any further."

"But you think he was still seeing Belfort on the sly?"

"It's possible."

"This morning, you told me that Eli had turned to Lennaeus Tolvard, working with him on the sly."

"I said I *thought* it was possible. The man was on Eli's thesis committee." Ferraga checked his watch. "I must go now."

"One more question, sir. Where were you last night between ten and four in the morning?"

"Me?"

"We're taking statements from everyone, Professor. It's nothing personal."

"I certainly hope it is not personal." He cleared his throat. "I was home with my wife. She can vouch for me. I went to bed later than she did, but I never left the house."

Same alibi as Rosser. McAdams said, "Could I take a look at your phone and laptop? It might be able to alibi you if you used either one of the electronics at home."

"I don't need an alibi because I didn't do anything. And I didn't make or receive any phone calls last night. I don't even think I used my computer. Most of my computations are done by hand." He stopped talking and regarded McAdams's eyes. "I need to lock up. I'm already late for my appointment."

"Of course," McAdams said. "Thank you for your time."

Ferraga escorted him out. "Next time make an appointment. Then I won't be so rushed."

"I would have done that but these are extraordinary times, don't you think?"

Ferraga didn't answer. He locked the door, picked up his briefcase, and walked away without so much as a good-bye.

"ROSSER TOLD ME that her students came to her house," Decker said. "That syncs with what the neighbors told us."

"He also said that Belfort liked her admirers. I think Rosser was trying to paint her as a flirt, maybe even more. What do you think?"

Decker and McAdams were standing in Katrina Belfort's living room. Decker had been going through her most recent calls on her cell phone while the kid was scrolling through her computer. "I don't honestly know. He clearly didn't like her. Good job with the interviews and alibis, by the way."

"I do my best." McAdams was trying to break into her e-mail with little success. Her computer was one wall after another of security. Even her word-processing files needed a password. "Do you think she was having an affair with one or more of her students?"

"Wouldn't be the first time," Decker said. "Although I am curious why Rosser was leading you in that direction. Maybe he was hiding his own affair behind the accusations?"

"I thought about that," McAdams said. "Maybe the love loss bit was a ruse. Or maybe he was jealous of the others. Katrina was a good-looking woman. Or maybe she was carrying on with more than one person."

"Or she could be legitimately helping her students. She hadn't lived in Greenbury for very long, no signs of a busy social life, maybe her work was her life. I can tell you this much. She had roughly the same phone calls over and over—Mallon, Damodar, Ari, Elijah Wolf when he was alive . . . then you have Rosser, Zhou, and Ferraga. There are also lots of calls to someone named Ryan." Decker looked around the room. Then he held up the photograph of Katrina and a young man in skiwear. "Our missing link?"

"Maybe. Give a call."

Decker stared at the picture. "He looks younger than she is." He continued to study the picture. "Of course!" He slapped the photo. "They look alike. The eyes, the lips . . . the identical smile."

McAdams stopped what he was doing and looked at the picture. "Right. Brother and sister."

Decker didn't answer right away. Then he said, "Look at Katrina's face for a moment, Harvard. Tell me what you see." When McAdams picked up the glam shot, Decker said, "No, put that down and look at the ski snapshot. Who does she look like besides the guy standing next to her in the picture?"

McAdams studied her face. "Are you thinking Mallon Euler?"

"Same long face, roughly the same height. Belfort's build is bigger, but under a hoodie you couldn't tell that. If she was covering all that long hair, I think she could easily pass for Mallon."

"If it was Katrina who broke into Mallon's room, what could she be looking for?"

"Maybe she thought that Mallon might have a copy of Eli's papers. Or maybe she was trying to spook Mallon?"

"But why?"

"I don't know. I'm just shouting out suggestions." Decker held up the phone. "Let's see what Ryan has to say, if anything."

The line was connected, and after four rings, it went to her voice message.

You've reached Ryan, you know what to do.

Beep.

"This is Detective Peter Decker of the Greenbury Police Department. Please call me back as soon as you get this message." He recited his cell number and hung up the phone. He pointed to the computer. "Did you find anything worthwhile in that hunk of metal?"

"Not yet. I'd probably have more success if I took it with me and studied it in your house."

"We shouldn't take it home. It's evidence."

"One night."

"We'll deal with that later. Right now let's have a look around. Make sure we haven't overlooked a crime scene."

"You don't think she was killed in the woods?"

"She might have been poisoned here and dragged into the woods. If that were so, the house would be the primary crime scene. How about if you rummage through the kitchen and bathroom cupboards and cabinets and see what kind of pills and poisons are lurking about. I'll check out the living room and bedroom, go through the drawers, and look for signs of a struggle."

"Everything looks pretty darn neat, Deck."

"That's why I said I'll look for *signs* of a struggle, Harvard. I'm searching for all the tiny cracks. Eventually I'll find a leak. With crime, there's no such thing as watertight."

CHAPTER 18

SOME PEOPLE MAINTAINED neat rooms in their public spaces, but the drawers and closets of their bedrooms were dumping grounds. Not so with Katrina Belfort. Her desktop was clear except for the computer and monitor and everything stored below had been organized. While McAdams poked around in her bedroom, Decker pulled out the drawers's contents and sifted through the printed matter. He mostly found bills, old receipts, and bank statements organized by dates and categories. All of the amounts going in and out suggested a reasonable life. Her academic work was contained in the bottom two drawers—papers with indecipherable formulas except to those in the know—and two neatly typed-up articles, both of them having to do with longitudinal studies of stock prediction using fast Fourier transforms. There were also a few cover letters to academic journals, explaining her topic and submitting her work for publication.

There were no personal letters, but people often correspond in texts, tweets, and e-mails. He hoped her phone and computer would divulge some hints as to what had happened in the woods.

A half hour later, McAdams emerged from the bedroom, holding a sheet of paper with a latex-gloved hand. "I think you need to see this."

He handed the paper to Decker. Smack in the middle of the sheet were the lines

I can't go on anymore. The pain is too much.

It was typed using the same font and letter size as Belfort's peer-review articles: Times New Roman with a magnification of twelve.

"Where'd you find this?" Decker asked.

"In a nightstand drawer. Just opened it up and there it was," McAdams said. "It's rather nonspecific for a suicide note."

"First thing I'm interested in is what kind of pain. Did you go through the bathroom yet?"

"I did."

"Did you find any prescription medication?"

McAdams took out his notebook. "Aleve, Tylenol, Claritin, Benadryl, Sudafed, vitamins—organic, by the way. One vial of erythromycin with two tablets inside . . . she didn't finish her course, bad girl."

"So there was nothing to suggest that she was on pain relievers for a physical condition. Anything to suggest psychological pain? Anxiety or depression medication?"

"Just what I told you, boss. She was on birth control. It might suggest a boyfriend even if there were no pictures of him in her house."

"Sure. We need to explore it further. What about illegal stuff?"

"As a matter of fact, she had some loose joints in a plastic bag in her nightstand—the one not with the note."

"How many joints?"

"A half dozen. I counted them. More recreational user than dealer."

"I agree. What about poisons?"

"Nothing in the bathroom, although I suppose you can OD on Sudafed or Benadryl, especially if you mix it with booze."

"I haven't checked the kitchen yet. Maybe she was a secret boozer."

Since the house was open plan with no walls, the living room, the dining room, and a tiny kitchen were all one space. McAdams started by looking in the pantry while Decker opened the refrigerator. Inside were a half gallon of milk that hadn't reached its expiration date, ditto with the orange juice, fresh fruit and salad vegetables in the bin, fresh cheese, and several packages of deli meat. Decker smelled it—nothing rotten or off. He checked the freezer, which was equally well stocked: frozen juices, fruits, pie crusts, cookies, lots of boxes of one-dish meals like lasagna, pot pies, stews, and several cartons of chicken breasts with green beans and roasted potatoes.

"There's about a half-dozen wine cartons in the pantry. Two Buck Chuck. Also two used bottles of whiskey. Chivas and Jim Beam, which is bourbon actually."

"What about under the sink?"

McAdams squatted. "Dishwashing liquid, Cascade, sponges, Drano . . ." He opened the bottle. The chemicals burned his eyes. "Looks full. Nothing here suggests depression." He stood up and stretched. "Nothing suggests that this woman's life was falling apart."

"And yet something in her life got her killed. If we think the note was faked, we have to figure out who would fake it and who would type it out on her computer. It has to be someone she knew well. Tyler, do you think you'll be able to hack into her computer?"

"I honestly don't think so, but I'll give it the old college try."

"Okay, let's do this. Detach the keyboard and the mouse from the computer. I want our crime scene unit to dust it for prints. If it hasn't been tampered with, we might get something beyond smudged prints. We'll take the desktop to the station house after we've dusted the on/off button for prints. Keep at it for a while. See if you make any headway. I'll meet you there and I'll pick up dinner for us. Just give me a little time."

"Last winter the station house at night was one step above an igloo."

"The heat's been fixed to the point where you have to open a window to breathe. You'll be fine."

"You know, if things were permanently deleted from her files, I know I won't be able to recover them. But a pro could possibly recover the files from the hard drive if they weren't written over."

"If we have to, we'll hire a pro. Just do what you can. Take the computer in the car. I'll walk into town, get some grub, and meet you back at the station house."

"Why don't we just go together? Or are you not done yet?"

"I think she was shot in the woods. But I also think she might have been knocked out and dragged up there before she was shot. I want to look around for evidence of a struggle here—in the house."

"The place is spotless."

"I know. And it doesn't reek of disinfectant. It could be that there wasn't enough blood spilled in the house to warrant a whole-sale cleanup of bleach. Maybe just a roll of paper towels was sufficient. All I'm saying is that if she was murdered here, I'll find evidence."

"Want me to stay and help?"

"Thanks but no. You crack the computer, Harvard, and I'll do the searching. Let's play to our strengths."

ARTIFICIAL ILLUMINATION WASN'T daylight. Each had their advantages and worked in different spectrums. Something visible in daylight often blended into surroundings under a lightbulb and vice versa. It was always advisable to look at the scene under all sorts of conditions.

The house took on a cozy quality at night—the neatness, the fireplace, the pillows and throw blankets. The wood floors were recently swept and the tabletops were dust-free. Even the picture frames were polished. The rule of thumb was that women kill in the kitchen, but are killed in the bedroom. So that's where Decker started his search.

His cell rang . . . a number he didn't recognize. "This is Decker."

"Detective Decker?"

"Yes. Who am I talking to?"

"Ryan Belfort. You asked me to call you right away. Is my sister all right?"

"Mr. Belfort, where are you calling from?"

"My office. What's going on?"

"Where is your office, sir?"

"Manhattan. You're making me nervous."

"Mr. Belfort, I'm so sorry to tell you this, but your sister has died—"

"Oh my God! What the hell happened?"

"Mr. Belfort, this conversation would be best face-to-face. Is it possible for you to come up north to Greenbury?"

His voice became a whisper. "I just spoke to her yesterday."

"When?"

"Around four in the afternoon. This is insane. I can't . . ." His voice faded into silence.

"What about your parents, Mr. Belfort? If you give me a numb—"

"It's just Kat and me. Our parents died in a car crash six years ago. Kat was both mother and sister to me." His voice cracked. "What *happened*? Was it an accident?"

"No, it wasn't. Right now we're ruling it a suspicious death."

"Murder?"

"Murder or suicide—"

"Suicide's impossible!"

Emphatic in his statement. Decker said, "Why do you say that?"

"Kat wasn't suicidal. If anything, she was happier than I'd seen her in a long time. She liked her job. She liked living in a small town. She liked her students. She was impressed by their intelligence."

"Did she mention specific names of students?"

"No, she didn't. Do you think it was one of her students?"

"We're not sure. Did she talk to you about her students?"

"Just to say it was a diverse group and she liked that. I can't fucking believe . . . this is fucking nuts! You can't tell me anything?"

"I'd like more information before I put my neck out there. I don't want to mislead you or tell you something wrong. I promise you when I know more, you'll know more. And it would be beneficial to talk to you face-to—"

"This is just . . . horrible." He was quiet. "I'm stunned."

"Mr. Belfort, was your sister with your parents when they had their car crash?"

"No, she wasn't."

"Do you know if she had been suffering from physical pain?"

"Physical pain?" A pause. "As far as I know, she was at the peak of health. We went skiing about a month ago. We're both avid skiers."

"And what about emotional pain—depression or anxiety."

"Everyone gets depressed or anxious from time to time."

"I'm talking about something crippling—"

"It wasn't suicide! I'm positive!"

"I have to ask these questions. I'm sorry if they touch a nerve. You said she liked her students. What about other relationships? A boyfriend, maybe?"

"If there was, she didn't say anything to me about it. I do know there was a fling around three years ago—Jason Logan. He was a math professor at the University of Maryland. The breakup was cordial. She wasn't serious about him. He was twenty years older and married. I wasn't happy that she was involved with a married man, but as far as I knew, it didn't get in the way of her life."

"Okay." Decker was writing as fast as he could. "And as far as you knew, they were no longer in contact."

"They weren't in contact. Kat would have told me if they were."

"Has she mentioned anyone else in the last three years?"

"Not really. She always told me that once she was hired as faculty, she was too busy with her research to pursue relationships. Do you have evidence that says differently?"

"No, I don't. What about friends?"

"I wouldn't know. I suspect she was too busy for intrusive friendships."

"Can you think of anyone who might want to do her harm, sir?"

"No one."

"And you're pretty certain she wasn't in any . . . compromising relationship?"

"I couldn't swear, but I don't think so. I will tell you this. She wasn't *depressed*!"

"Is there any way that you could come up to Greenbury, Mr. Belfort?"

"To claim the body? I suppose I'll need to do that."

"We're not ready to release the body." God no, they weren't ready to do that. There was no way Decker was going to tell him about the mutilated corpse until he had to. "I'd still like to speak to you in person."

"Is it absolutely necessary?"

"It would be helpful," Decker said.

"It'll have to wait until the weekend. I'm in the middle of litigation and the office is crazy now. Is there any way you could come down to New York City?"

"Possibly on Sunday. Would that work?"

"Possibly. Call me on Sunday."

"Thank you, Mr. Belfort. I'm sorry, but I do have to ask you where you were last night. I need to eliminate you as a suspect."

A bitter chuckle. "I was in the office until eleven, and then I went home and went to bed around two. As I said, we have some pressing litigation."

"Anyone that can verify your whereabouts?"

"At the office, I had to sign out of the building. Home? As far as home, the night doorman was on duty. George Ellison. You can call him if you must."

"Thank you for your cooperation and for answering my questions. And again, I'm sorry for your loss."

Belfort paused. "Detective, I don't know every single detail of her life. But I do know as surely as the sun rises in the east that Kat didn't kill herself."

Decker took in a deep breath and let it out. "That's why I asked you if your sister had enemies . . . who might hold ill feelings toward her."

His voice dropped to a whisper. "No idea whatsoever. But you'd better find him before I do."

"Sir, Mr. Belfort, leave the case to—" He stopped talking when he realized he was speaking to a dial tone.

CHAPTER 19

DECKER MADE TWO lists.

Why it could be suicide:

1. Single shot to the head. Bullet from the gun? Probably.
2. A suicide note.
3. No evidence of another crime scene—yet.
4. Her house was in order . . . TCB before she left the planet?
5. Recent suicide of Elijah Wolf. Did she do a copycat? Was it related?

Why suicide is doubtful:

1. No evidence that Katrina's life was falling apart. Home of a clear-thinking individual (see number 4 why it could be suicide).
2. The single gunshot to the head was at an odd angle for a suicide.
3. The removal of her clothing. An attempt to make the suicide look like Elijah Wolf's death? If she had PCP in her system, it could have elevated her temperature and she took her clothes off. Check with toxicology report.

4. No mention from students or colleagues of drug or alcohol abuse. Probe this angle.

5. Suicide note was nonspecific: staged?

He read over the lists several times. If there was *anything* that suggested the slaying happened inside the house—and that would include OD or poison—Decker was determined to find evidence. He carried two pairs of glasses with him. One was for reading print that was too small for his older eyes. The other pair had even greater magnification. He used that pair when searching for clues. He gloved up, snapping the fingers into place, and went to work.

With the exception of the kitchen and bathroom, there was wood flooring throughout, covered by scattered area rugs. He put on his evidence glasses and searched the wood for scratches and bleached spots where someone might have wanted to scour and scrub away blood. When he didn't find anything obvious, he moved to the area rugs. Squatting, he hunted around for wet spots. Nothing. Then he stood up and carefully moved furniture off the rugs. Then he lifted the rugs and checked the padding underneath. Nothing damp or sticky. He checked the upholstery on the couches and chairs, removing pillows and cushions to view and feel the framework, but found that everything was utterly normal.

Next he moved on to the small tiled kitchen that led to the back door. The floor looked clean and dry over the grout. Even so, he sprayed the small surface area with luminol and turned off the lights. There were intermittent spots of neon blue, but these kinds of markings were more associated with tiny bits of animal matter that also glowed under luminal. So did some food products. A gun shot wound or a stabbing would have lit up the floor.

Decker moved on to the bedroom. He checked the current bed linens: dry. He pushed aside a queen-size mattress to look and feel underneath the springs: dry. He checked out the bathtub for yanked-out tufts of hair in the trap: relatively clean. He sprayed luminol inside the tub to see what hadn't been washed away. Again, the bath held a few muted spots here and there that were more likely to be dead skin than fresh blood.

He gave the bathroom a quick once-over. It contained a tub/shower combo. When people are attacked there, they often grab the shower curtain for support, yanking it off or tearing it. The shower curtain hung neatly and was intact.

The bath mat was neatly folded over the side of the tub and it, too, was devoid of blood. He took off the stopper from the sink's drain and stuck a gloved finger down the pipe. There was some hair, but not very much. And the hair was loose bits—no roots. He peered underneath the sink. Eventually, he closed the cabinet door a disappointed man.

He moved on to the hallway linen closet. It had vented doors and six shelves. The linens were neatly stacked and organized: the bath towels with the bath towels, the hand towels with the hand towels, the washcloths with the washcloths. Some of the towels were mismatched in color and style and age, but everything was tidy. There were two extra pillows sitting next to a folded stack of pillowcases. There was also a pile of fitted sheets in beiges, yellows, ivories, and white—whatever worked, he supposed. Then his eye moved over to a pile of top sheets. The stack wasn't *as* precise and one of the sheets had actually fallen to the floor.

As if someone had quickly grabbed from the pile, causing the sheet directly underneath it to tumble to the ground. Snatching the linen in a panic because he needed to wrap up a body. It was far easier to drag a wrapped package than a loose corpse with floppy limbs.

Suppose . . . just suppose Katrina Belfort had been injured in an altercation with the killer? Maybe she was pushed and hurt her head, not enough to kill her but enough to knock her out. Then suppose the killer *thought* she was dead. He panicked, dragged her into the woods, and then he tried to obliterate the injury with a gunshot to throw detectives off track?

Okay, if that's the theory, Decker thought about how she could have hit the back of her head hard enough to knock her out. Maybe she was shoved into a wall or tripped and fell backward. Sometimes those injuries leave a lot of spatter, but sometimes they don't. Those types of injuries weren't usually lethal—not right away at least. Maybe it was even an accident. Maybe it wasn't. It really didn't matter. The outcome would have been the same. The killer thought she was dead and panicked. Rather than call the police, he chose to get rid of the body himself, figuring her absence would give him time to escape and create a story. So he wrapped her in a sheet, dragged her into the woods, and shot her in the location of where she hit her head. Then he walked back to the house, covering his tracks in the snow while he went along. Maybe he even called up a trusted friend for help . . . which would make Decker's life easier. The more people involved, the faster these things get solved.

Okay, so assuming that Katrina fell backward, she had to have hit her cranium on something hard like a floor or a wall, or a piece of furniture like a sharp edge from a table. The floors and tiles were devoid of any dents or dings, so he moved on to the walls: a banged head might have left a ding or a crater, but the plaster looked intact.

The last thing to do was scrutinize the corners and ledges of the furniture. Decker started with the granite kitchen countertops, moved on to the bookcase and the sofa table, then the end tables. It always paid to be patient. Sometimes it was the last item checked— in his case a square end table with a marble top inserted into a brass frame. With the naked eye, the corners looked clean, but luminol told a different story. The back left corner had been tucked under the sofa's upholstered arm. When he sprayed the table, it lit up like holiday Hanukkah lights.

Murder *Gadol Haya Sham.*

There was also a tiny amount of hair trapped between the brass frame and the marble inset. Decker took out a pair of tweezers and pulled it from the space. Some of the hair still had root and skin attached, which made it perfect for DNA testing. He placed it in an evidence bag.

He dropped to a squat and smelled the floor right in front of the end table.

Dishwashing liquid.

He sprayed the area.

It was speckled with blue—a leaking wound rather than arterial spray.

The house needed to be gone over by the pros millimeter by millimeter. In clean crime scenes—any crime scene, for that matter—there was no such thing as being too meticulous.

BACK AT THE station house, Decker regarded McAdams typing away on Katrina Belfort's computer. "How's it going?"

McAdams looked up. "I got into her research files but they're meaningless to me. I did print them out so we could take them up to Dr. Gold."

"What about her e-mail?"

"Not so lucky."

"We'll get a court order. I'm convinced she was murdered. Her death may have been accidental, but the shooting was not." Decker filled him in. "Someone not only cleaned the floor and an end table, he or she turned it around to hide the corner where Katrina most likely hit her head. Forensics is up there now doing their thing. I also had them dust Katrina's keyboard and mouse for prints."

"What'd they find?"

"Nothing. It was wiped clean. Now, Katrina was a neat freak, but it's still odd to write a suicide note and then wipe down the keyboard." Decker popped a piece of gum in his mouth. "Are you hungry?"

"Starving."

"Rina made dinner. Let's go home and we can talk about it there."

"What do I do with her computer?"

"We'll lock it up. Take her research with you. I'd sure like a better idea of what she was working on."

"You think it was academics that got her killed?"

"Can't say. But the more we know about her the better."

"What about her cadre of admirers? Specifically her young male admirers. One of them might have been hoping for more. You know how impulsive college kids can be."

"I spoke to her brother."

"So Ryan is the brother?"

"Yes. When Katrina lived in Maryland, her lover had been a married man."

"So she made poor choices before, maybe she made even worse choices this time. Who do we ask about that kind of thing? I mean it could be a fellow faculty member, but it also could be a student."

"Except students don't own cars. I keep thinking about that occasional late-night sedan parked in front of her house."

"Then let's eliminate the students and go on to the faculty."

Decker said, "Good idea. Let's start with Damodar Batra and Mallon Euler. They're rooming together. We'll tackle them after dinner. By the way, did you ever connect with Dean Zhou?"

"She's been out of town for the past two days."

"Where?"

"Her office wouldn't tell me."

"Find out where she was and verify it. If she was truly out of town, then she's out of the running as a suspect in Katrina's death."

"Why do you suspect her?"

"Just because she's in the department and seemed keen on looking at Eli's papers. What about Lennaeus Tolvard? Did you connect with him?"

"We keep missing each other. Want me to try again?"

"Yes, I do. He and Eli were doing something hush-hush. I want to know what it was." Decker checked his watch. It was almost seven. "Let's eat first."

"Fine." McAdams stood up and hoisted the computer to bring it to the evidence cage.

"We need to reinterview everyone. While we're concentrating on the college, I'll have Kevin and Karen talk to the neighbors again. Then you and I will go up to Boston and show Eli's papers to Dr. Gold. See what the fuck he has to say."

"You're swearing. You must be tired."

"I'm beat." Decker rubbed his eyes. "Let's go home and get some grub. Man does not detect on bread alone."

THE CONVERSATION, WHICH centered on Katrina's murder, continued all through dinner and lasted over tea and coffee. Dressed in sweats, Rina listened as the boys talked. It was toasty inside the house. So much so that she turned down the heat because the boys were complaining.

She waited until there was a lull in the discussion. Then she said, "If you're going to interview the college kids again, how about if I come with you?"

Decker regarded his wife over the rim of his coffee mug. "Why may I ask?"

"How many times have you talked to Mallon? If she's being manipulative—and I'm not saying she is—but if she is, she's got your number down by now. Another person in the room alters her script."

"It's not a bad idea," McAdams said.

"And you know that I was a math major in college . . . although I never made it past linear algebra." Rina looked at McAdams. "I quit college and moved to Israel when I was nineteen. It went over very big with my parents."

The kid grinned. "I knew there was a rebel somewhere."

"Obviously I liked the traditional life it led to because here I am."
She turned back to her husband. "How about it?"

"About what?"

"Let me come with you to talk to the students."

Decker put down his mug. "How well do you remember your
math, darlin'?"

"I haven't done a complex calculation in over three decades. But
I overheard you talking about Fourier transforms and eigenvectors
and eigenvalues and I looked up the concepts. The computer is a
wonderful thing sometimes. They have all these mini-lectures, and
after a fashion, you get a smattering of what's going on. You've just
got to familiarize yourself with the terminology."

"How big is a smattering?" McAdams asked.

"This is what I took away from listening to the lectures. Eigenvectors are represented by matrices and can be used as an alternative
coordinate system, and Fourier analysis is a way of breaking down
complex waves into simple trigonometric functions. Who is studying what?"

Decker was searching through his notes. "We had Eli studying
eigen*values* . . . what is the difference between an eigenvalue and an
eigenvector?"

"A value is a scalar—a number. A vector is a line moving in a
direction. An eigenvector is a specialized vector that is a multiple of
itself. The scalar or number that multiplies the eigenvector is called
an eigenvalue. Are you with me?"

"What do you mean an alternative coordinate system?" Tyler
asked.

"Usually when you represent a point in space, you think of it as
something on an x-, y-, or z-axis, right?"

"If you say so," Decker answered.

Rina continued on. "Eigenvectors are another way to locate
points. And from what I've been overhearing, Eli was studying eigenvectors and eigenvalues and Fourier analysis."

Decker said, "It might have been Fourier transforms."

"I'm betting all the Fourier thingies are related," McAdams said.

Rina said, "And I believe you said it was also Katrina Belfort's area of expertise: fast Fourier transforms. It was probably the reason why Eli had wanted to switch advisers from Rosser to Belfort."

"You were really listening to us," McAdams said.

"I have great powers of concentration when I want to. What is Rosser's area of expertise?"

"No idea, but it doesn't matter," McAdams said. "He'd want the brilliant student no matter what he was studying."

"Makes sense." Decker turned to Rina. "You're about to make a pronouncement."

"Why do you say that?"

"You have the look."

Rina said, "I'm trying to find an academic connection between the fields of study—eigenvectors and Fourier analysis and Dr. Tolvard and cosmology. One intersection might be charting complex waves in space."

McAdams crossed his arms and regarded Rina. "I like that."

"I'm a nerd. Only nerds rebel by becoming super religious."

"Well, you're the prettiest nerd on the planet," Decker said.

"Aw . . ." Rina leaned over and kissed his cheek. "You are the handsomest man on the planet."

"Well, that's not true."

"It is to me."

"Ahem . . ." McAdams interrupted. "What Rina said about the intersection of the two fields: it may be why Eli moved from math to physics."

Decker shrugged. "That may be. But Elijah Wolf has been ruled a suicide. Katrina is probably a homicide. I'm more interested in her right now."

"And you don't think the two cases are related?" McAdams said.

"Not a clue." Decker checked his watch. "We should go."

Rina said, "And me?"

"You should come," McAdams said.

"I believe that's my decision to make," Decker said. McAdams and Rina turned their eyes on his face. "You can come."

"Only if you say please."

"Don't push it."

"I'm not doing anything tomorrow, either. I could also come with you to visit Dr. Gold."

"Are you getting a little bored, darlin'?"

"Just a tad housebound. It's been snowing a lot and I need motivation to get out of my reading chair."

"I think it's a great idea," McAdams said. "Gold likes her better than either of us."

"Everyone likes her better than us." Decker shrugged. "Sure, come with us, Rina. I love your company and you always pack a great lunch."

"I'll listen in and tell you what I think," Rina said.

Decker said, "Yeah, I suppose we can always use a fly on the wall."

"I was thinking more along the lines of an irritating gnat that simply won't go away."

CHAPTER 20

THE QUICKEST WAY to get students in your corner was an offer of free food and drink. Once again, Mallon chose ·Rajah's, the Indian café with lots of vegan options. She was hiding behind a menu when Decker, McAdams, and Rina showed up. A brief nod from her and the trio sat down and were given menus. Damodar Batra came in a few minutes later, wearing a parka, jeans, and boots. He hung up his coat on a rack, took in a deep whiff, and let it out slowly.

"Feels like home." He pulled up a chair on the outside of a booth meant for four people.

"Where have you been?" Mallon's face was still obscured by endless lists of entrées. She sounded peeved.

"I had an interview with Newberg."

"Newberg?" Mallon set down the menu and gave him the death stare. "How'd you arrange that?"

"I begged. He gave me twenty minutes."

"Is he taking you on?"

"Probably not. What about you? Any luck?"

"No. I may have to look outside the department." She folded her hands. "Rosser's not helping me. He hates me."

"He hates everyone."

"Not Eli."

"No, Eli was about the only one he liked. Then Wolf had the nerve to rock the boat and all was not well." Batra shook his head and looked at Decker. "We're scrambling to find new advisers and it's hard because the department is so small. It's our senior year, for God's sake. I was just about done with my thesis. This has been a nightmare."

"I guess it would be a nightmare for Katrina Belfort except she's dead," McAdams said.

"Yeah, well . . ." Batra looked sheepish. "Thanks for dinner."

"Who is Newberg?" Decker asked.

"Faculty," Batra said. "Also new, but he's jammed up apparently. Asshole."

Decker said, "There are ladies present."

Batra bit his lip. "Sorry." He looked at Rina. "I don't think we've met."

Rina smiled. "Rina Decker. No blood relationship."

"That's a big coincid—oh . . ." He hit his forehead. "You're Detective Decker's wife?"

"I am. It's nice to meet you."

"Same."

"Can we order?" Mallon had gone beyond peeved to full-out grumpy. "I've got a shitload of work waiting for me."

Decker signaled the waiter. The two kids both ordered dinner specials. McAdams ordered a chai tea and two regular teas for Decker and Rina since all three had eaten.

Mallon kept folding and unfolding her hands. "Well, the feeling is mutual."

Decker said, "Pardon?"

"Rosser. I hate Rosser as much as he hates me. What a pompous little prig!"

Batra said, "More like a twit."

"How'd he get along with Dr. Belfort?" McAdams asked.

Mallon shrugged. "I never heard her go off on him, but she did think he was a misogynist. It's like kinda obvious."

Batra said, "Why are you asking about Rosser?"

"Katrina's dead. I'm talking to a lot of people."

"He's a jerk," Mallon said, "but I don't think it was his fault that she killed herself."

Decker said, "So you think Dr. Belfort committed suicide?"

"That's what everyone is saying." Batra paused. "Do you have other ideas?"

"Was she depressed?" Decker asked.

"I didn't think so, but I didn't know her well."

"You knew her well enough to call her by her first name."

"We all did," Mallon said. "She wasn't that much older than us and it was her idea."

"Yeah, exactly," Batra said. "Our relationship was strictly professional."

"Professional but you've been to her house."

Batra tensed. "So have Mallon and Ari and Eli and a bunch of other students. She had an open-door policy on weekends. She liked being available to her students. All you had to do was call before you came. What of it?"

"What of what?"

"Stop obfuscating. There was nothing going on between her and me or any of her students that didn't have to do with math. She wasn't like that."

"No need to get defensive, Batra," McAdams said. "We have to ask."

"And you got your answer. Anything else?"

"Stop being peeved," Decker said. "And for your information, we'll be asking a lot more questions. That's what you do in a murder investigation."

Mallon's eyes grew wide. "She was *murdered*?"

Decker sidestepped her question. "I've got a forensics team going through her place, bit by bit by bit. Plus I have her cell phone and computer. Most of her calls and texts were to students, colleagues, and her brother: times and dates of meetings and things like that. So when you tell me the relationship was professional, I have no reason to doubt you."

"Well, that's good to hear, thank you very much," Batra said.

"Keep up the snotty attitude and I'll really start coming down on you," Decker said. "Until I know better, you're all suspects. Got it?"

The kids said nothing. Batra finally said, "Are you arresting me or something?"

"If you're asking if you're free to go, the answer is yes. I wouldn't recommend it, though. Makes you look bad." When Batra didn't answer, Decker said, "You know, once we break into her e-mail, we'll probably find out a lot more about her life. So if either of you has something to share, now's a good time."

Mallon was fidgety. "I'm with Batra. I don't know much about Katrina's outside life. We almost always talked math."

"What kind of math?" Rina asked.

Mallon looked at her as if she just realized she was at the table. "Fourier analysis."

Rina said, "I'm no expert, but it seems like that is a wide-open field when it comes to practical applications."

"It has about a billion uses."

Decker said, "So maybe you can narrow it down a little for us? For instance, what was Dr. Belfort's doctorate thesis in?"

Batra lunged back into his chair and sighed. "The interplay between Fourier transforms and the stochastic oscillator." He glanced at Mallon. "No need for the death stare. They can find out about her dissertation in a heartbeat. And if they've confiscated her computer, they're eventually gonna find out what she was doing."

McAdams said, "And what exactly was she doing?"

"Nothing illegal, if that's what you're thinking," Mallon said. "It was just frowned upon by the department."

Silence. Decker said, "Okay, kids. Out with it. Let's hear the specifics."

Batra said, "Katrina took on a number of outside consultant jobs with major-league hedge funds. To do things like that—on such a large scale—she had to get permission from the department. They have to check for conflict of interest and that kind of thing. I, for one, think it's a stupid policy."

"Your opinion is duly noted," McAdams said. "You're saying her extracurricular activities could have gotten her fired."

"It would have gotten her in hot water with Rosser. Especially because she doesn't have tenure."

"Why'd she take such a risk?"

"Money, of course," Mallon said. "It paid like five times her salary."

"So why didn't she quit the college and become a personal consultant?" McAdams asked.

"She was waiting for tenure," Batra said. "That would have given her even more prestige. And the more prestige, the more money. Titles impress a lot of people."

Decker said, "And I take it you two were involved with her outside activities?" His question was met with silence. "It's all going to come out. Just start from the beginning."

"She asked us in," Mallon said. "It's not like we thought of it."

"I wish we did," Batra said. "She must have been making a boatload of bucks because she was paying each of us around fifteen hundred a month. And there were four of us . . . well, three now that Eli's gone. That's six grand a month out of her pocket."

"I don't think he needs specific amounts, Damodar," Mallon said.

"Why don't you let us decide what we need?" Decker now knew where Eli's pocket money was coming from. "So tell me what did you all do for her?"

Batra said, "She had a very practical dissertation, good theories that could be put to use by a lot of people. So she began to outsource her ideas to several hedge funds. She got a bite, then another, then another. It became too much for her. So she had us doing most of the calculations."

"And her dissertation was about Fourier transforms and stochastic oscillation?"

"Oscillator," Mallon said.

McAdams had taken out his iPad. "A stochastic oscillator is a market-momentum indicator. It tells the direction of movement of a stock not by price or volume but by momentum because momentum usually antecedes price."

"Exactly," Batra said.

"I have no idea what that means," Decker said.

Mallon said, "It's a percentage indicator that predicts whether or not a stock will go up or down by seeing how it moves in very small increments. If you get a positive momentum indicator—meaning momentum is up, you can buy in before the price actually moves. We're talking like in nanoseconds."

"It's a quant thing?" McAdams said.

"Yeah," Mallon said. "It's in and out trading."

Rina said, "I thought 'stochastic' in math means random."

"It does," Batra said. "But 'stochastic' in probability theory means a randomness through which order is found."

"It's like this," Mallon said. "You take a huge set of data . . . thousands of random facts. To make sense out of it, you begin to sort things together. Maybe eventually you see a pattern."

"Like flipping a coin," Batra said. "If you flip it at any given time, you have no way of predicting whether it will land on heads or tails. Even if you flip it a thousand times and get a thousand heads, the next flip will not guarantee a tails. But if you flip it zillions of times, you will eventually see that you have a fifty percent chance of the coin landing on heads and a fifty percent chance at it being tails."

"Making sense out of randomness," Mallon repeated.

"So where do Fourier transforms and analysis come in?" Rina asked. "She had you breaking down the stock movement into simpler waves to help her predict movement?"

Batra snapped his fingers and pointed to her. "You're good."

Mallon said, "Katrina had us analyzing the momentum of a zillion stocks on any given day to feed into her data bank so she could make recommendations to her companies."

"There must be an existing software program that can do this," McAdams said.

"I'm sure there are software programs for everything," Batra said. "Katrina was working on something much more sensitive and sophisticated. I think her end goal was to sell out to someone for big bucks. If you break down her hard drive, I'm sure it'll be filled with what we were doing."

Mallon looked down. "I'd appreciate it if you didn't bring us into the equation unless you absolutely have to do it. I mean technically I didn't do anything wrong . . . just working for a professor . . . but I'm sure it would give Rosser just another reason to hate me."

Batra said, "The guy has a stainless-steel stick up his butt."

McAdams said, "Why do you think Rosser hates his students?"

"He's just that kind of guy," Mallon said. "He takes on one pet student and hates the rest of us."

"And Elijah Wolf was the pet?" Decker said.

"He was until Eli went to the dark side, asking to switch advisers," Batra said.

"Since then, Rosser has been especially obnoxious to everyone,"

Mallon said. "He gets bad student ratings but he's head of the department, so I guess it doesn't matter."

Decker said, "I want to go over where you guys were last night—again."

The kids reiterated their stories. Mallon said, "As if I wasn't freaked out enough about last night, now you tell me Dr. Belfort was *murdered*. I don't know how much more stress I can handle. If I wasn't a senior, I'd take a leave of absence. Right now all I want to do is get the hell out of here."

Decker said, "Mallon, are you sure you don't have anything worth stealing in your room? Like possibly data from your venture with Dr. Belfort?"

"First of all, all that data is in my computer. Secondly, anything that we do by hand computation was left at Katrina's house. So no. Nothing in my room was worth stealing."

But Decker wasn't so sure. He felt that the break-in was part of the puzzle. But he had yet to form the grand picture, let alone how all the pieces fit together. "So neither of you has any papers from Dr. Belfort's extracurricular activities?"

"Nope," Batra said.

"Nothing," Mallon said.

More information to process. More things that could have gotten Katrina Belfort murdered. He was trying to narrow things down. Instead the gulf between unsolved and solved was widening. There was always that chasm to cross. It was always a challenge not to fall in.

WALKING HOME, MCADAMS turned to Rina. "You're awfully quiet."

"I was thinking. Over dinner, you mentioned the possibility of Katrina Belfort breaking into Mallon's dorm room because she was looking for something."

"And?"

"What if Katrina was hiding something in Mallon's room instead of looking for something? Wouldn't that make just as much sense?"

"I don't know, Rina. Maybe Katrina thought that Mallon had her data and was worried she was going to do something with it—either go to Rosser or use it for her own benefit."

"Mallon wouldn't go to Rosser because she was just as involved as Katrina was. And she probably didn't know all the intricacies of Katrina's program. But maybe Katrina thought that Rosser was closing in on her." Rina paused. "Just maybe Katrina took all of her papers and went to Mallon's room to hide them for safekeeping. Maybe that's what Eli's hidden papers are about."

"She had all the stuff on the computer, Rina," Decker said.

"But it's harder to break into a computer than to find hand computations. I'm sure at some point she became very protective of her work. And Rosser certainly disapproved of what she was doing. So perhaps she decided to stash them in a safe place."

"Okay," Decker said. "So she hid papers in Mallon's dorm room. Except we didn't find any papers."

"I know."

"And how did the hidden papers lead to her murder?"

"I don't know if they did."

McAdams said, "Maybe Rosser came to Belfort's house to confront her about her outside job. They argued and he accidentally killed her. But he still didn't find the papers linked to the hedge funds. So he goes to Mallon's room, hoping to find something incriminating there. When he comes away empty, he returns to Katrina's house to bury her up in the woods. Or more like leave her in the woods. There was no attempt to hide her. On the contrary, whoever brought her up there wanted to make it look like a suicide similar to Eli's death."

"That's a lot of hypotheses and a very short time frame to work with," Decker said.

"Why would Katrina go to Mallon's room?" McAdams said. "And why would she toss the room? What purpose would that have?"

"Misdirect?" Decker said.

"Personally, I don't see Katrina tossing Mallon's room to look for papers she already has. That's taking a big chance."

Rina said, "Then if it wasn't Katrina, who was it?"

"Maybe it was Mallon," Decker said. "Maybe she was doing it for attention."

McAdams said, "Just this morning you were saying she seemed genuinely shaken."

"Things change. Especially since Mallon and Batra were doing something iffy with Katrina."

"Why would Mallon sneak into her dorm room, toss it, go back to the library, and then call me in a panic?" McAdams said.

"If she was guilty of something, she wouldn't want to draw attention to herself," Rina said. "So if it isn't Mallon or Katrina who broke into the dorm room, our mysterious woman is still at large."

Decker said, "You're great at squashing ideas. Do you have anything positive to add?"

"Such as?"

"The identity of your mystery woman?"

"Nope."

Decker smiled. "Some help you are."

"When are you going to see Eli's parents?" Rina asked.

"I was going to go on Sunday. But now it looks like I'm going to Manhattan to visit Katrina's brother. I suppose I can do it tomorrow if the investigation doesn't take any sudden turns. I could stop by the farm, and then take him back to Cambridge."

"Uh, the him is right here. Since when am I leaving tomorrow?"

"You need to study."

"Oh joy."

"I'm still coming with you," Rina said. "I would like to see Ruth Anne again."

"Ah, let her come," McAdams said. "I like her company."

"Whose side are you on?"

"Don't go there, pard, unless you really want to hear my answer."

"Fine. Come with us. You're way better company than he is."

McAdams said, "I was about to say the same thing."

Rina laughed. "As long as you are going to the farm, you might want to ask Jacob if Eli sent him a package—his research or maybe copies of what he was doing with Katrina Belfort. A lot of times, sibs keep secrets from their parents."

Decker said, "Jacob said he wasn't particularly close to Eli."

"You only have Jacob's word for that."

"Why would he lie?"

"Misrepresent the relationship possibly. If you thought they weren't close, you stop asking questions."

"What are you getting at, Rina?"

"If Eli sent Jacob private stuff for safekeeping, he most likely told his brother to keep it under lock and key. Jacob's not going to volunteer information like that. Sometimes you need to ask the right questions to get the answers you want."

CHAPTER 21

RINA WAS IN the backseat, half listening to one of her audiobooks, half listening to the boys, who were up front, talking business. It was nine in the morning and they were a half hour away from the Wolf farmstead. It was a pleasant forty degrees outside with a blue sky and a shining sun. Peter was driving, while Tyler drummed the dashboard nervously with his left hand. Theoretically, he had packed up for Boston, but Rina wondered if that was going to happen. He seemed way more interested in Katrina Belfort's suspicious death than he was in passing his law finals.

"No one had the perfect alibi." McAdams sipped coffee.

"People rarely do at three in the morning," Decker answered.

"Ferraga and Rosser were at home, but either of them could have slipped out after the wife went to bed. Then there's Mallon, who was at the library, but even though people saw her, no one can account for every minute of her time." McAdams paused. "What about phone calls on her cell to verify where she was?"

"She showed me her phone," Decker said. "There's nothing from ten at night until she called you at three-ten in the morning. The calls could have been deleted from the phone's software. She'd be savvy enough to know how to do it. But any call she made would still be logged into the phone-company records. Right now we can't get a warrant to look through her log because we don't have probable cause."

"What about if we get her permission to look at her phone records?" McAdams asked.

"Sure, we can ask. How do you think she'll react to that?"

"No idea. But if she agrees, it'll help her case if she's innocent."

"It will definitely put her further down the suspect list. Give her a call and ask."

McAdams made the call. It went to voice mail. He asked her to call him back, not wanting to leave a request over the phone. "Further down the list? So she's still a main suspect?"

"Everyone who knew Katrina is a suspect because we don't know how it happened." Decker paused. "Katrina may have accidentally died. But she wasn't *accidentally* dragged into the woods."

Rina was having a hard time concentrating on the book's narration. She gave up and pulled the pods from her ears. She said, "Do you see Mallon as having the muscle power to drag a corpse into the forest?"

"Not on her own, no," Decker said. "She could have had help. Damodar Batra comes to mind. But like I said, no records of any phone calls from ten to three."

"Do you really like her as a suspect?"

"No. Well, when we talked to her, she was agitated."

"Have you given any thought to *my* theory?" Rina said.

"Sure, once you come up with a mystery woman."

Rina thought a moment. "I still think it's *possible* that Katrina was hiding her extracurricular activities in Mallon's room."

"We went over this before, Rina. Batra said that her activities would be on her computer. Why would she go about hiding papers?"

"Maybe it wasn't papers," McAdams said. "She could have hidden a memory stick and then erased her files so there wouldn't be any record of them in her computer. Memory sticks would be impossible to find."

"What's troubling you, Peter?" Rina asked.

"I'm just thinking. It takes me a while to integrate all of your suggestions." Then Decker said, "Everything that you two have been saying makes sense. But for some reason, I keep thinking about the 'so-called' suicide note."

McAdams said, "Written on a keyboard that had been wiped clean."

"It's still speaking to me."

"What's it saying to you?" Rina asked.

"If you're faking a suicide note, why make it sound so personal? From what we've discovered about Katrina, she doesn't seem to have much in the way of personal connections."

"That's why it was a very badly forged note," McAdams said.

"I have to agree with Tyler," Rina said. "It doesn't sound personal to me. It sounds like stock words for a faked suicide note."

McAdams said, "The murderer was attempting to make the death look similar to Eli's suicide. The whole thing was completely staged."

"I agree," Decker said. "Except Eli Wolf didn't leave a note. Why bother with it at all? And why bother saying the pain is too much? Katrina seemed to be pretty well put together."

"But she was doing something behind the college's back," McAdams said. "Maybe Rosser found out and was going to expose her."

Decker said, "Her murder would make more sense if she was threatening to expose Rosser or someone else."

No one spoke.

Decker said, "Katrina had to have had some kind of personal life."

"Some people live for work." Rina smiled. "Maybe her work was her life."

"I'm certain she was hiding more than her sideline with the hedge funds. Mike Radar has a tech guy coming in to the station house around noon. He's going to attempt to recover everything on her hard drive. I want to read her personal correspondence. Something . . . anything to tell me why someone would want to murder her."

McAdams made a face. "I'm still puzzled why you're so interested in an obviously fraudulent note. Why you think it's the key to her personal life? It seems almost like a throwaway."

"And maybe it is."

McAdams said, "Just remember what they say about hearing hoofbeats."

"You think I'm hearing zebras instead of horses."

"It's just something to keep in mind," McAdams said.

"What do you think, Rina?" Decker asked.

"Could be Tyler's right," Rina said. "Then again, perhaps you live on the savanna. In that case, hearing zebras would make total sense."

WHILE EZRA AND Jacob Wolf were outside repairing the lambing shed, Ruth Anne had set the table with a spread: fruit, nuts, cookies, and coffee. She couldn't quite decide what to do with her hands, so she elected to stick them in the pockets of the apron that covered her brown dress. Her blond hair was pulled back and her face wore an expression of resigned sorrow. "The coroner called us. You didn't have to come all this way. But it was gracious for you to do so."

Decker said, "I wanted to tell you how sorry I am, face-to-face."

"Thank you." She busied herself in pouring coffee. "I've been thinking a lot these past few days. I think . . ." She took a breath and let it out. "It's all because of the accident. It did funny things to his head."

Decker nodded.

Ruth Anne smiled. "Please sit."

"After you."

"Only for a moment." The woman sat down. "Ezra and Jacob should be in soon. I'll need to prepare their lunch."

"Need help with that?" Rina said.

"Sure." Another smile. "We can catch up." She poured herself a half cup of coffee and sipped. "Good." Then she picked up the fruit tray. "Please."

Rina picked a bunch of grapes and placed it on a china plate. "Thank you."

Tyler took a cookie. "I don't think we've met, Mrs. Wolf. I'm Detective McAdams. I also want to tell you how sorry I am for your loss."

"Thank you." She paused. "We live in a very tight-knit community. Everyone has been very kind and helpful. To my surprise, no one . . ." She wiped a tear from her eye. "Everyone's been remarkably nonjudgmental, especially because suicide is a sin."

"Eli's death is a loss for the whole community," Rina said. "I'm sure they care deeply about your family and about Elijah."

"I'd like to think so, yes."

"I'm not a religious guy," McAdams said. "I come from a privileged background. By all rights, people like me shouldn't have a care in the world. I don't know how many times I've seen the rich and powerful just hanging by a thread. We're all fragile creatures, Mrs. Wolf."

Ruth Anne nodded and wiped another tear away. "Kind of you to say."

At that moment, Ezra and Jacob Wolf showed up. The two men took off their boots, placed them on a mat, and hung up their heavy jackets. Ezra quickly disappeared into the house, so Jacob spoke for the both of them. "We need to wash up before we eat. Be back in a minute."

"I'd better get lunch started." Ruth Anne got up from the table.

"I'll come with you," Rina said.

Once both women were gone, Decker gave the kid a pat on the back.

"What was that for?"

"You've come a ways in the empathy department."

"This is just such a sad case." He paused. "Do you think there's a possibility that Katrina's murder is connected to Eli's suicide?"

"Until we get it solved, there's always a possibility," Decker said. "Katrina was doing a no-no as far as the department was concerned and Eli was helping her out. Maybe he felt guilty about it . . . coming from an environment where ethics are stressed. Maybe it pushed him over the line. Especially with his personality changes due to the accident. Who knows how his actions interacted with his injured mind."

Jacob reemerged wearing a long-sleeved black T-shirt and jeans, and clean socks. He said, "Thanks for coming all the way out. You know, the coroner called us already. You didn't have to bother."

"I wanted to express my sympathies in person."

The kid sighed. "Well, life goes on." He sat down. "Eli hasn't really been one of us for a long time."

He tried to sound matter-of-fact, but there was an overlay of harshness. Decker said, "This is Detective McAdams, by the way. He and I are currently working a case together."

Tyler stuck out his hand and Jacob shook it. McAdams said, "The case we're on . . . it involves one of Eli's math teachers."

Jacob picked his head up. "What kind of case?"

"A suspicious death."

Jacob opened and closed his mouth. "Suicide or a murder?"

"It looks like murder."

"Oh Lord." Jacob shook his head. "That's terrible. Is it a coincidence or . . ."

"I wish I could tell you." Decker paused. "Jacob, I know that Eli had been distant from the family. But brothers sometimes tell things to each other when the parents aren't around. I'm just wondering if maybe he said anything to you that sticks in your mind."

Jacob shrugged.

Decker said, "Or maybe he left something with you for safe-keeping."

The boy was quiet. Then he said, "Like what?"

Ezra came back, dressed in denim farmer's overalls. He had on a clean pair of work shoes. "I'm going to stop into Miller's and check the mail."

Jacob stood up. "I'll do it for you, Dad."

"Nah, you stay here and entertain our guests."

"I don't mind. Really."

Ezra put a hand on his son's shoulder and lowered him back into the chair. "The co-ops got a shipment of oranges in from Florida. Tell your mother I'll bring her home a case." He nodded to Decker. "I'll be back in ten minutes."

After he left, Decker said, "We're not here as guests and we certainly don't need entertaining. I hope your father doesn't feel put upon by us showing up here."

Jacob threw up his hands. "It's hard to tell what he's feeling. I could say it was because of Eli's death, but he's always been that way."

The table fell silent. Jacob took a cookie and chewed it slowly. "I reckon you want an answer to your question."

"I do."

"The last time I saw Eli, he did give me an envelope. He told me to keep it under my bed or something because he didn't want anyone at school to find it."

"Did you ask him what it was?" McAdams asked.

"Of course I did. He was vague. He said something about changing his thesis and he didn't want his teacher to know. Does this mean anything to you?"

"It's consistent with what we've heard," McAdams said. "Eli wasn't happy with his current adviser."

Jacob nodded. "Yeah. Okay. So he was telling the truth."

"Did you suspect he wasn't?"

"Eli's been known to tell a tall tale. And he changed after the accident. I had a hard time reading him. But I'll tell you one thing. He did seem upset . . . maybe 'upset' isn't the right word."

"What *is* the right word?"

"I don't know. After the accident, he spoke more or less in a drone. It took a while to get used to it. Last time we spoke, his voice seemed more . . . normal. Not totally normal, not by a long shot, but a little more fluctuation, maybe. I hadn't heard from him in a while. His voice took me by surprise."

Decker said, "Did he tell you anything else? Take your time, Jacob."

Jacob thought a moment and then shook his head. "Not that I recall. I suppose you'll want the envelope?"

"Yes, that would be helpful."

"I doubt it," Jacob said. "It's all math formulas. I looked at the papers after he died. I was thinking that maybe it could be a suicide note. Of course it wasn't. I don't think there were more than ten English words on any of the papers."

"Do you understand anything about the math?"

"Not really, no. He told me it was some kind of analysis."

"Fourier analysis?" When Jacob shrugged, McAdams said, "How about stochastic oscillator."

"No, that doesn't sound even a little familiar." Jacob paused for a few seconds. "You know, he did tell me that he was working outside the math department on an extra project."

"We have our suspicions about the extra project," McAdams said. "And Eli wasn't the only one working on it."

"So you know about this? What was it? That stochastic whatever you said?"

"Maybe that, maybe something else," Decker said. "Anything else that he confessed to you?"

"It wasn't a confession . . . exactly," Jacob said. "He told me that there was this girl and she brought him into something. But he didn't want anyone to know about it because it could mess up his scholarship and he didn't want to create problems. Whatever it was, he didn't want Mom and Dad to know about it. Especially the girl part."

"Why's that?"

"Once you mention a girl in this community, it creates all sorts of talk."

"Did he mention the girl's name?" McAdams said.

"No. I asked him but he wouldn't say. He said she wasn't important. Just that she spurred his interests in other directions and that's why he was unhappy with his teacher. But he couldn't say anything to his teacher because he might lose his scholarship. So he was working on his own."

"Did he ask you for advice?"

"No . . ." He shook his head. "I did tell him to follow his heart and his conscience and the rest would be okay. Obviously, it wasn't okay. He killed himself." A long pause. "He didn't know what he was doing when he did it. He wasn't in his right mind."

"I'm sure you're right."

"I knew he wasn't all there. I should have been more vigilant."

"These kinds of things are almost impossible to anticipate and even harder to stop."

The kid let out a sigh. "I suppose I should have told you about the papers the last time you were here, Detective. But then we didn't know if Eli was murdered or not. And there wasn't a good time to give them to you. And then I forgot about it." Jacob looked down. "Sorry."

"I'm sure you had many other things on your mind," Decker said.

"Maybe." He stood up. "I'll get them for you. But don't mention it to my parents. I don't want them to think that Eli and I had secrets from them even though we did."

Decker turned to Tyler. "Go with him. In case his mother comes out."

A minute later, the women returned to the dining room. Rina was holding a salad bowl. Ruth Anne held a plate of sizzling chicken breasts. She said, "Where did everyone go?"

"Your husband went down to pick up the mail and get a crate of oranges from Florida that just came into the co-op."

"Where's Jacob?"

"Washing up. He'll be back in a moment."

"Well, if Ezra wants to eat cold meat, that's his problem." She sat down and forked a chicken breast for herself. "I'm not going to wait."

Jacob and Tyler returned to the table. "Hi, Mom."

"It seems your father took off on one of his jaunts." She passed him the plate. "Help yourself."

"It's been hard for him," Jacob said.

"And it isn't hard for me?"

"Of course, Mom."

The table fell silent. Ruth Anne said, "I don't know why I'm being peckish with you."

"It's fine." He gave her the salad bowl.

Ruth Anne huffed to herself. Then she said, "Where are my manners? Can I get anyone a fresh pot of coffee?"

"We're all fine," Rina said. "Eat, Ruth Anne. It smells good."

"Next time you come, I'll get a separate pan and a kosher chicken. Then you can eat with us."

"I'll take you up on it."

"Like there'll be a next time." Ruth Anne shook her head. "This wasn't exactly a social call."

Rina leaned over and looked the faded woman in the eye. "My husband and I just moved into this part of the country a little over a year ago. I will take any friend who wants me as long as you reciprocate and come down to visit me."

"I don't think I've left this area in over a year."

"Well, maybe it's time for a road trip. You're an hour away from me."

"I just have so much to do." She looked at Rina. "Why don't you come up in the fall when it's jam time. Do you do jam?"

"I do jam."

Ruth Anne smiled. "We do get wonderful fruit from the orchard. And there's lots of fresh produce from the co-op. I could sign you up for the co-op. But you'll have to pay if you don't bring anything to barter with."

"I pay the supermarkets. I'd rather pay you. Thank you."

The door opened and closed. Ezra was carrying a crate of oranges. On top of the crate were two bouquets of flowers. "I'll put the crate in the kitchen. One of these is for you, Ruthie."

A genuine smile formed on her lips. "They're lovely. I'll put them in a vase." She looked at Jacob. "The other one must be for you."

Jacob glared at his father. "I'm capable of buying my own flowers, Dad."

"Thought I'd save you the trouble." Ezra's face was expressionless. "Go on. Put them in water or else they'll dry up."

Ruth Anne said, "I'll do it for him. You sit and eat your lunch. And don't blame me if it's cold."

"First I got to put the oranges in the kitchen," Ezra said.

"I'll take it."

"It's too heavy for you."

"Fine. Come in the kitchen and set it down. Do you have the mail?"

"Yeah, I have the mail. It's in my pocket."

The two of them disappeared into the kitchen. Jacob shook his head, then he laughed. "Now you see why Eli didn't want me mentioning a girl. Someone in the community and I have been going out for two months and they're already planning a wedding. Jeez!"

"It's a parent's prerogative to meddle." Decker smiled.

"They certainly think so." Jacob picked up a forkful of chicken and chewed it down. "Ah well. With this mess, there's certainly been enough rain in their lives. I suppose it won't hurt me to give them a drop of sunshine now and then."

CHAPTER 22

AS THE CAR edged into Cambridge—traffic was always heavy in Boston—Rina noticed a thinning of the conversation up front. Tyler had drawn inward, as if the mere presence of the university had sucked the life from him. It was all the more puzzling because Harvard was the only college that McAdams had ever known. Perhaps the institution was the embodiment of his father's authority—odd because Jack McAdams had gone to Duxbury, one of the five colleges of upstate. Apparently Peter noticed Tyler's silence as well.

"You look thrilled to be back," he said.

"Over the moon," McAdams said.

Rina said, "Harvard is one of the finest universities in the world. You should feel privileged to be a part of that."

"Everyone here feels privileged, and not in a good way," McAdams said. "Go to graduation, Rina. Hear the valedictories. 'Since we're so brilliant and privileged and special, it's now our responsibility to shoulder the burden of leadership and guide the planet to a better place.' They'd be appalled to realize that they're restating TR's White Man's Burden."

"Somebody's not happy about upcoming finals," Decker said.

"I'm right here, Old Man. No need to talk in third person. And I still have over a week to study, FYI."

Rina said, "I know the guys at the station house kid you, but they'd all trade places with you given a chance."

"Oh, come on, Rina," Decker said. "Seriously? Why on earth would any of us trade a life of paramilitary bureaucracy and endless paperwork for the rarefied gift of brilliance and opportunity?"

McAdams said, "Privilege is not what it's cracked up to be."

Decker said, "Neither is the noble workingman, Bruce Springsteen. Idealized things seldom are. There's no harm in getting a law degree, Tyler. You can even do some good with it. Even I learned a great deal by going to law school."

"You can stop right there, Old Man. You're sounding like my dad." McAdams paused. "Although if you were my dad, you'd be screaming instead of speaking. My life is fine. I'm just bitching right now because I'd rather be working on Katrina Belfort's case. I can study at your place. I don't see why I can't stick around to see it through."

"Because it could take a lot of time and you're distracted at our house."

"I'll be even more distracted wondering what's going on. I know you think it's debatable, but I am a grown man."

"Honestly, Tyler, I don't want this case screwing up your schooling."

No answer. The car turned quiet. Rina looked out the window. Near the university, Cambridge was a mixture of quaint clapboard bungalows, small, colorful Victorian houses, and soulless, cheap apartment buildings that housed students as well as local residents. The streets held the typical college stores and clothing outlets along with lots of fast food in lots of ethnic varieties. The co-op was the official Harvard bookstore that featured almost as many insignia items as it featured textbooks and school supplies. There were some good restaurants and a half-dozen places to stay for parents visiting overnight as well as guests of the university. The Inn at Harvard sat on the edge of campus, fashioned in brick with evenly spaced windows, a semicircular roofline, and a redbrick pathway that led up to the door: a modern take on a Federal style with a hint of Amsterdam thrown into the mix. The town was a mishmash, but it worked nicely.

The campus was also a combination of old and new architecture, the buildings interspersed among wide lawns currently covered in snowdrifts. Since it wasn't raining or snowing, students were everywhere, huddled in their parkas, trudging from place to place with heavy boots on their feet. Parking was always a problem, but Peter lucked out, snagging a space after a car pulled out.

McAdams said, "I'm leaving my stuff in the trunk of your car, Peter. I don't want to schlepp it with me."

"Where do you live? Are you on campus?"

"No, I'm in an apartment that reeks of eye-watering kimchi because my neighbors are Korean. Nice people, but you get tired of the smell. It wafts through the rather thin walls and settles into my clothing."

"At least you won't be attacked by a vampire."

"Nonsense." McAdams slammed the door shut. "This place is filled with bloodsuckers, and garlic hasn't stopped any of them."

It was a short walk to the math building. Professor Mordechai Gold had a spacious, wood-paneled corner office, the walls covered with degrees, awards, and certificates. The bookshelves were overflowing with reference material. The floors were covered with authentic Persian carpets. The place was big enough for a sofa and a few chairs as well as Dr. Gold's enormous desk. He had prepared for their arrival with coffee and cookies.

"They're kosher," he told Rina. "Sit, sit."

"How's the family?" Rina asked.

"Great. It's nice to see everyone again. Certainly the circumstances are better . . . well, maybe not for you. I heard about Professor Belfort's demise. That's just terrible. Can I ask what happened?"

"Single gunshot wound to the head."

"God, that's terrible. Was she depressed or . . . should I not be asking questions."

"It's fine." Decker sat down on one end of the sofa, McAdams sat on the other end, and Rina was in the middle. "We haven't received the coroner's report, but we're treating it as a suspicious death."

"Murder?"

"Yes, but that's not official."

"Oh my goodness. That makes it even worse." Gold turned to Rina. "At least you're doing okay, right?"

"No overt interference from our friends overseas, if that's what you're asking," Rina told him. "We do find a hidden electronic bug from time to time. I don't mind when they're in the kitchen or living room. It feels a little weird when we find one in the bedroom. How do they get in to place them with the alarm on?"

"The spooks have their ways," Gold told her. "Don't worry. Eventually they give up."

"They should," Rina said. "We're just not that interesting."

Gold smiled. "Coffee? Tea? Hot water? I'm taking some tea myself."

"What do you have?" Rina sorted through the tea bags and pulled out mint-flavored and gave it to him. "I can fix it."

"I'll do it. You're in my house. How are you, Tyler? How's law school. Isn't it finals time?"

"It is. I was studying at the Deckers' house. It's quieter and the food is better. But then someone decided to kick me out."

"He's getting overly involved in a police matter when he should be studying," Decker said.

"Not overly involved . . . just involved."

Gold poured Rina tea. "What can I pour for you two gentlemen?"

"I'm fine," Decker said. "Tyler?"

"I'm okay. I know you're a busy man, Professor." McAdams opened a briefcase. "This is regarding that case I shouldn't be involved with."

"Belfort?"

"Yes." McAdams took out a set of papers. "We downloaded these off her computer. If you wouldn't mind, could you take a look and tell us what you think?"

Gold took the pages and flipped through them. "What am I looking for?"

"We're just interested in what you have to tell us about them," Decker said.

"They're Fourier transforms. Without knowing the context, I can't tell you what she was analyzing. You know what Fourier transforms are?"

"Changing a function of time to a function of frequency," McAdams said. "Could she have been using the math to track the momentum of the stock market?"

"As a stochastic oscillator? Sure. It also could be a thousand other things." He continued to flip through the pages. "It's certainly nothing earth-shattering."

"No new ideas?"

"None at all. I mean she could have been using these particular formulas in a novel way, but the analysis is basic upper-division math."

"So it's nothing worth murdering over," Decker said.

"The math isn't, God no." Gold handed the papers back to McAdams. "Do you know if she was tracking the market?"

"According to her students, she was consulting to several high-worth money managers using a unique algorithm. So that would seem likely."

"So there you go," Gold said.

"But the math isn't a big deal?"

"Put it this way." Gold chuckled. "She isn't going to win the Fields Medal."

"Thanks," McAdams said. "These pages here were given to a math student's brother for safekeeping. Later, that student committed suicide."

Gold took the papers. "Yes, I heard something about that as well. What a terrible tragedy. What was his name?"

"Elijah Wolf."

"Oh dear." Gold shook his head. "I remember that name. He applied here and was accepted. We offered him a full scholarship, but he turned it down."

"His family wanted to keep him closer to home. He decided on Kneed Loft."

"It's certainly a fine college. He committed suicide? What happened, if I can ask?"

"We don't know, Mordy," Decker said. "By all accounts, he was a quiet, well-mannered kid who was obsessed with math. His friends didn't see any telltale signs. But I don't think most of them were close friends, nor were they clued in to his emotional ups and downs. No note was left. The tox screen was negative. Who knows what he was thinking?"

"And you're sure it's suicide?"

"That is the coroner's ruling. In light of Belfort's death, we might have another look at the case."

Gold flipped through Eli's pages. "This is Fourier analysis . . . that's a cousin to Fourier transforms, but the uses are different. These pages seem to be dealing with the analysis of complex waves and breaking them down into smaller simpler waves." A pause. "Could I see the first set of papers again?"

"Of course." McAdams handed him the pages.

"Okay . . ." Gold looked at the math side by side. "Two different things going on here. She's using transforms, and in light of what you told me, the calculations probably are related to the stock market. Eli's doing integration that involves eigenvectors . . . you know what an eigenvector is?"

Decker said, "Something where a part represents a whole?"

"No, that's more like fractals."

"You can start at the beginning," Decker said. "Math wasn't my strong suit."

"Math is one of those things that you either love or hate. No one feels neutral about it. Anyway, a vector is simply a line with direction. It's marked by a starting point on one end and an arrow on the end representing infinity. When you stretch a vector in space, it warps. Most vectors will change directions. An eigenvector is a specialized subset of vectors. When you stretch an eigenvector, the direction remains the same no matter how you stretch it. It's an important concept that is used in a variety of applied sciences. In engineering, for instance, if you apply an outside force onto a building, like a wind shear, you want to know how it will affect the stability of the components—the steel, the cement, the wood, the bolts and nuts. Eigenvectors will move in the same direction. The amount of stretch they move by is a multiple of a scalar, which is nothing more than a number. That number is called an eigenvalue. This is probably way more than you need to know."

McAdams said, "Actually your explanation is almost identical to what Rina had told us."

"You were a math major in college?" Gold asked her.

"I got as far as linear algebra," Rina said. "I had a baby at home and then another one on the way, so college was a lot for me to take on. Then we moved to Israel."

"You lived in Israel?" Gold asked Decker.

"This was with her first husband, Isaac."

"He passed when we were both very young." Rina's eyes watered. She hit Decker's shoulder. "Then this bum came around."

"Poor you." Decker smiled. "You know, Rina? Tyler's right. You're a very good teacher."

Gold said, "Maybe you should think about finishing your BA. We're open to applications."

"Now, there's a thought." She turned to Decker. "What do you think?"

"Go for it."

"Right."

"I'm serious. 'If not now, when?' to quote Hillel."

McAdams cleared his throat. "Uh, I do have a study group to catch, so can we get back to the case?" To Gold: "You were saying that Eli's papers are different from Belfort's papers?"

"Related, but not the same thing."

McAdams handed Gold a final set of papers. "These are also from Elijah Wolf. We found them hidden behind a drawer in his dorm room."

"Okay . . ." Gold gave them a once-through. "These equations seem to be more related to Dr. Belfort's papers. These are Fourier transforms. They are different calculations from the ones pulled from Belfort, but it's the same methodology."

"Okay," Decker said. "So the papers that Elijah asked his brother to hide are dealing with something different from the first and third set?"

"I can't tell you positively without knowing the context," Gold told him. "All I'm saying is that the calculations in the first and third set are dealing with Fourier transforms and the second set is Fourier analysis and eigenvectors. And I don't know what the math was being used for."

"Got it," Decker said. "There's nothing unusual about the math in the second set of papers that deal with eigenvectors?"

"Nope. Of course, Elijah could have been using the math to solve a revolutionary problem, but the math is simple."

"Thanks," Decker said. "That was helpful."

"Great." Gold looked at his watch. "That took all of twenty minutes. Lunch? I got some kosher sandwiches. If you don't have time, you can pack them up and take them with you."

Decker looked at Rina, who said, "I'm in no hurry."

Gold clapped his hands. "Great. I'll have my secretary bring them here. We can really catch up. I am curious about the Belfort case."

"You and me both," McAdams said. "Unfortunately, there's a study group due to convene in about a half hour."

"Good man," Decker said.

"Can I talk to you in private for a moment?"

Decker tried to read the kid's face. He was stoic. "Sure."

The two men got up and went outside into the hallway. McAdams said, "Can we strike a deal? If I spend the next couple of hours deep in my law books, can I please come back with you?"

"Tyler—"

"Don't make me beg, boss."

"And here I thought you pulled me aside to lay some insights on me after our meeting with Gold."

"I have a couple of those as well."

"I'm listening."

"How about we save them for the ride back." McAdams smiled. "Please let me sleep without the sounds of inebriated students banging into walls and/or throwing up? As I said, my walls are very thin. *Please*?"

Decker rolled his eyes. "You'd better fucking pass."

"I know what's at stake. I *promise* you I'll pass."

Decker shook his head and headed back into Gold's office.

McAdams grinned as he shouted, "I'll take that as a yes."

WITH HIS HEAD swimming in facts and case history, McAdams cornered the building and collided with Mallon Euler. She was wrapped in a knee-length wool coat, a scarf around her neck, a ski hat on her head, gloves on her hands, and combat boots on her feet. Her big blue eyes were cast downward.

"Mallon?" he said. "What are you *doing* here?"

"I heard you went to Boston. I was wondering if I could stay with you."

"I thought you were staying with Damodar."

"I was, but I don't fully trust him. I think he may be part of the problem. Can I?"

"Can you what?"

"Can I stay with you?"

"No, Mallon, you can't stay with me. First of all, I'm not staying here. I'm going back to Greenbury."

"Why?"

"Because I'm still working on the case with Detective Decker."

"Tyler, I'm scared to be alone and I'm scared to be with Damodar. I don't know who to trust except I trust you."

"Thank you for your confidence in me, but that doesn't mean we can be roomies."

"It's just temporary."

"No, you may not move in with me." McAdams shuffled his feet. "Look, I'm meeting up with the Deckers, and the three of us are going home together. How about if we talk when we're all back in Greenbury, okay?"

"If you're going back, can I hitch a ride back with you?"

"Oh God . . ."

"Please? Please, please, *please*?"

"Stop, stop." He exhaled. "I'll ask them. Come on."

He fast-walked ahead of her, but she caught up. "This is a very big campus."

"It's a university, not a college."

"All you geniuses walking around . . . you must feel very special."

"Don't you start on me! I get enough crap from Greenbury police."

"I'd feel special."

"Fine. You can take my special. It's never done me any good."

She suddenly brightened. "You know, I could sleep in Decker's car."

"Absolutely not. For one thing, you'll freeze to death."

"They don't garage it?"

"It's out of the question."

"How about the police station? I'll bring my own bedding."

"No."

"Could you slow down?"

McAdams complied. "Look, Mallon. I know you're freaked out. I understand completely. I was really antsy after I was shot. It's a real violation. But you have to make some workable arrangements for your living quarters. If you don't trust Damodar, find someone else."

"Fine, fine. I'll just stay with Damodar. I suppose it'll be okay since you'll be there . . . in town, I mean."

"I'll be there for about a week. Then I really have to come back here and take my finals. And you can't bunk down in my apartment. It's too small and it's totally unprofessional. No, no, no!"

"You don't have to be so rude about it."

McAdams stopped and held her bundled shoulders. "Look, Mallon. You're a very smart girl. And maybe once you graduate from Kneed Loft and the case is all done and resolved and it isn't ten below outside, we can go out for a nice dinner . . . at least, a dinner other than Indian buffet. But not now, okay? Now is not the right time for either of us. Got it?"

A big smile graced her lips. "You want to take me out for dinner?"

McAdams slapped his forehead. "Let's get going before Peter decides to leave without me."

"He wouldn't do that."

"Rina wouldn't, but Decker would with a cherry on top."

CHAPTER 23

MCADAMS DROVE, DECKER sat shotgun, while the women took up the backseat. The car was quiet for the first half hour since business wasn't discussed with Mallon in tow. Rina was drifting off. The silence gave Decker a chance to close his eyes and think. A few minutes later, Mallon spoke up.

"Thank you for taking me back."

"No problem." Rina opened her eyes and stretched. "Who wants coffee?"

"I'm off caffeine," Mallon told her.

"Then I guess you won't be drinking coffee."

"I'm gonna just put this out there," McAdams said. "You follow us up here and it's not just to feel safe. You've got to level with us. What are you after?"

Mallon crossed her arms in a huff. "I assume you're talking to me."

"Correct."

"Maybe this conversation is best held another time," Rina said.

"No, Tyler's right," Decker said. "What's going on, Mallon?"

"Nothing!" she insisted.

Silence.

Then more silence.

She sighed. "You had Eli's papers looked at?"

"Aha!" McAdams said. "Now we're getting to the root of all evil."

"Yes, we had the papers looked at," Decker said. "Eli wasn't working on any revolutionary math."

"How do you know that?" Mallon asked.

"*I* don't know," McAdams said. "But the guy at Harvard does. He told us the math was simple."

"Maybe he's lying."

Decker said, "Why would he do that?"

"Oh rubbish!" Mallon said. "I'm just going to put it all out there since you put it all out there, okay?"

"That would be refreshing," McAdams said.

"Ha, ha, ha." Mallon paused. "The papers that have to do with Dr. Belfort . . . I'm not interested, okay. I know all about them. And you know all about them. Or at least you know what she was doing because Damodar told you."

"Is he leveling with us?" Decker asked.

"Yeah, he is as far as I know."

"Could he have also been doing something else for her?"

"Sure. We're not close. He doesn't trust me and I don't trust him. At least we both know where we stand, and that's more than I can say for most of the people I know."

Decker said, "Mallon, if you're not interested in Belfort's shenanigans, what are you interested in?"

She exhaled. "Before Eli died, he told me that he was doing important research somewhere else. He didn't want anyone to find out about it because he could get into trouble and also get the professor in trouble."

"Which professor?"

"He didn't say."

"So he never mentioned Lennaeus Tolvard?" Decker asked.

"Oh . . . so you know."

"Apparently we do, and some faculty members know as well."

"Oh . . . okay. He swore me to secrecy."

"What was the research about?"

"I don't know—"

"Mal—"

"Honestly, I don't know. I'm sure it had to do with eigenvalues and eigenvectors and Fourier analysis, which is what he was studying. Anyway, he told me he wanted *me* to take over his research if something happened to him." Her eyes suddenly watered. "I asked him what could possibly happen to him . . . what he was worried about."

"And?"

"He told me everything was fine. But this was a just-in-case . . . because he trusted me with his stuff. I had no idea he was thinking about suicide. If I knew, I would have said something. He was never an emotional guy, but certainly he didn't seem upset or depressed. It was just an odd conversation. He brought it up once and he never mentioned it again."

"When was this?" McAdams asked.

"About three months ago."

Decker said, "And you never thought to tell us about this conversation?"

"He wanted to keep it private and I was trying to honor his request, especially since I wasn't sure how he died. Then this all happened with Professor Belfort. I thought everything might be related."

"Which is why you should have told us," McAdams replied.

"Mallon, do you think Eli's death and Katrina's murder are related?" Decker asked.

"How should I know? That's *your* job, right?"

"You're a smart lady. I'm just interested in your thoughts."

She was quiet. Then she said, "I dunno. Maybe the timing was a coincidence, but it's a weird one if it is, right?"

Decker nodded. "Right."

"All I'm saying is if you have Eli's personal research papers, he would have wanted me to have them. Do you have his papers?"

"I have some papers that he had stashed with his brother," Decker said. "And you can't tell the context of the research from the math."

"Are you going to ask Tolvard about it?"

"That was my next step."

"He won't admit working with Eli," Mallon said. "It's tantamount to admitting he stole Dr. Rosser's student. If you'd just let me take a look at the pages, there must be something I can figure out. And if he thought I could assume the mantle of his work, I would be happy to honor him. Why should his brilliance go to waste?"

"This is the deal, Mallon," Decker said. "Until we figure out what happened with Dr. Belfort and we're absolutely positive that Elijah's suicide isn't related to her death, we cannot show you anything. Maybe once the crimes are completely resolved, we can talk about giving you the papers."

"Fine!" Mallon crossed her arms again. "This is so frustrating."

"Well, as long as you're in here, in the backseat of my car, how about if you tell us everything you knew about Dr. Belfort's operation."

"I told you everything. She was using stochastic oscillator for market momentum. I have no idea what algorithms she was using. If you have her computer, you could probably find out. I'm sure everything's in there."

Decker thought about her words. If someone was after Belfort's algorithm, why not just steal the computer when she wasn't home? As he mulled that over, he thought maybe Belfort, like Mallon, always had her computer with her. In that case, if someone had wanted it, he or she would have to break into her house during the night when she was in bed sleeping, and swipe the computer without waking her up. Maybe she caught the thief in the act and there was a confrontation and he pushed her—

"Peter, Mallon is talking to you," Rina said.

"Sorry, what were you saying?"

"I'm just saying even if the algorithm is on her computer, you probably wouldn't have any idea how to differentiate it from all of her other math."

"No, probably not."

"I can help you, you know. I could be like an expert witness or whatever."

Decker smiled. "Thank you for your generous offer. And maybe we'll take you up on it. But not now."

She threw up her hands. "Just remember when this is all over, Eli's papers belong to me."

"Duly noted."

No one spoke.

The rest of the ride home was mercifully silent.

HOME SWEET HOME, except it was freezing. Rina took off her cashmere tam and laid it on the entry hall table, but kept her jacket on until it warmed up inside. "Did you turn down the heat?"

"Have you seen our oil bills?" When Rina didn't answer, Decker said, "Mea culpa. I apologize."

"Just for that, I'm not cooking," she announced.

"You don't need an excuse not to cook."

"I know that, but this is a convenient one. I'm too tired. So either we're going out to eat or we're getting takeout. And I don't want meat. I just had deli for lunch."

Decker said, "If you don't want meat, how about Falafel King?"

"That's meat."

"I'll get a shawarma, you can get a falafel."

"How about Vegan Paradise?"

"I'd rather go to Falafel King."

"I don't want a falafel."

"Okay, how about this?" Decker said. "I'll go to Simon's and get a brisket sandwich for myself and get you whatever you want at Vegan Paradise."

"Fine. I'll have a vegan taco plate and a minestrone soup." Rina was beginning to warm up. It put her in a better mood. "You don't mind making two stops?"

"Not a problem, my love. What about you, Tyler?"

"A brisket sandwich sounds good."

Rina said, "I'll thaw out, and open a good bottle of wine."

"Sounds like a plan." Decker slipped on gloves, a scarf, and a hat. "I've been in the car all day. I'm going to walk."

Forty minutes later, Decker rewarmed the food and within five minutes everyone was eating. Tyler had started a fire in the hearth, and with the heat turned up, the house had turned pleasant. A gentle snow was falling on the ground. It was the perfect time to stay indoors and read a book in a comfy chair while sipping an extra glass of wine.

Rina said, "Are you two done for the night?"

Decker checked his watch. It was seven. "Well, no one called with any news updates, so I guess the answer is yes."

"I got a bunch of syllabi today," McAdams said. "I'm going to read them over and see what I need to concentrate on. What's on the agenda tomorrow, Peter?"

"First, I want to see if the tech got anywhere with Dr. Belfort's computer. I'd also like to meet with Tolvard. Find out what Eli was doing."

"Do you think the research had anything to do with his suicide?"

"Beats me," Decker said. "But it certainly wouldn't hurt to flesh him out a little. Speaking of an enigma, if there's nothing new on Belfort, I want to go to Manhattan and visit Katrina's brother on Sunday."

"Did you say Manhattan?" Rina said.

"Yes, you can call the kids."

"Dinner?"

"Whatever you and the kids want."

"I'll have all Saturday to study," McAdams said. "I'll hitch a ride with you guys. While you're out to dinner with the family, I'll study at my stepgrandmother's house."

"You can come to dinner," Rina said.

"That's okay. Nina's not home and it'll be quiet."

"Where is she?"

"Staycationing in Rhodes at her villa."

"Lucky her," Decker said. "And you have the key to her Park Avenue apartment?"

"I have many keys, boss." He grinned. "And a few have even opened some doors."

CHAPTER 24

SLAPPING ON AFTERSHAVE, Decker realized that he hadn't changed his look for fifty years. But this year he had hit it right because mustaches, especially thick ones like his, had come back in style. Everything cycled. All you had to do was stick around long enough.

McAdams and Rina were already at the dining room table, drinking coffee and nibbling whole wheat toast. Rina was reading the paper while McAdams had his nose in a book. She looked up when Decker came in. "Good morning."

"Good morning." Decker went into the kitchen, poured himself a big mug of steaming coffee, and sat down at the table. He took a slice of toast. "How are you?"

"I'm great. We're having company for Shabbat tonight. Five students and you've met all of them. Tomorrow it'll just be us."

"Which students?"

"Hannah, Ben, Jennette, Mike, and Lenny."

"A congenial group. I look forward to it."

"Am I invited?" McAdams asked.

"You are if you behave yourself." Decker checked his phone messages. "Still nothing regarding Belfort's computer. You'd think they could have hacked into it by now."

"Maybe Belfort had everything encrypted and then encrypted again. She *is* a math professor." McAdams put down his book. "Lennaeus Tolvard said he can meet us today at eight at his office. I left him a message that we'll be there."

"Is that eight in the morning?"

"Hence I am up and ready."

Decker looked at his watch. The appointment was in forty minutes, enough time to finish a cup of coffee. He took the front section of the *Wall Street Journal*. As usual, the world was a mess. It was easier for him to deal with true criminals, although one might argue that politicians and felons were one and the same. At least with the bad guys, he knew exactly where they stood. He skimmed the paper until it was time to leave, and twenty minutes later, he and McAdams were out the door, trekking through drifts with snow crunching under their feet.

It was a frigid ten-minute walk to Kneed Loft and it took another five minutes to find Tolvard's office. His secretary was a student, probably on work-study and this was his assignment. He said, "Dr. Tolvard is expecting you, so you can go right in."

"Thank you," Decker said.

He and McAdams walked into the spacious office. Tolvard got up from his desk and extended his hand. "Lennaeus Tolvard. Sorry it took so long to connect."

"No problem." Decker shook his hand. The man was tall and thin with an aquiline nose, deep brown eyes, dark kinky hair, and mocha skin. Decker recognized the look instantly because he had seen it a thousand times on his son-in-law Koby as well as his twin grandsons, who resembled their father. The boys were lighter in skin tone and had looser curls, making them look more Israeli than Ethiopian. "Thank you for seeing us."

"Please have a seat." Tolvard sat back down and clasped his hands. "How can I help you? I assume it has something to do with this terrible business with Dr. Belfort."

"We are investigating her death, yes. What can you tell us about her?"

"Nothing really. We knew each other, of course. It's a small school, but I didn't have much to do with her socially or academically. Just the occasional hi in the hallways, in the libraries, and at the annual Christmas party."

"Okay." Decker took out his notebook. "So you wouldn't have had any occasion to call her up recently?"

"No. I don't think I've ever called her, period."

"So you were just colleagues and . . ."

"That's it. Just colleagues."

"What about her students? Are you involved academically with any of them?"

"You mean as an adviser?" Tolvard made a face. "No. I don't even know who her students are."

"Mallon Euler, Damodar Batra, and Ari Weissberg."

"I know the students. Mallon was in my class in electromagnetism and wave theory, Batra and Weissberg took that class and another one . . . particle physics, I want to say. But they were math majors. They have to take some physics classes to meet their requirements."

"What about Elijah Wolf," Decker said, "did he ever take any of your classes?"

"Okay, I know where this is going." Tolvard leaned forward. "If you want to talk about Elijah Wolf, we can talk about Elijah Wolf. His adviser was always Theo Rosser in the math department. And that's the truth despite what you may have heard."

"What we heard is that you were working with Eli without Dr. Rosser's consent."

"I did not steal Eli from Theo. I had no intention of stealing him from Theo. I know gossip said otherwise, but it wasn't true. I thought of actually talking to Theo directly about the rumors, but then the poor kid died and it just seemed so stupid and petty."

"So you weren't working with Eli on the sly," Decker said.

"It had to be on the sly because Theo wouldn't have tolerated it otherwise. So I was stuck between a rock and a hard place. I suppose I could have refused to deal with him." Tolvard rolled his eyes. "College is a place to inspire academic curiosity, not suppress it, for God's sake!"

"Why don't you just start at the beginning," Decker said. "It's easier that way."

Tolvard rolled his eyes. "He came to me about a year ago. He had some thoughts that coincided more with my research than with Theo's expertise. He wanted to change advisers. He thought Theo was stifling his creativity. But I told him that because he was an upper-division student, it was too late. It wouldn't do to take him on. Besides, I knew the flak that Theo gave Katrina when Eli first suggested a switch. I didn't want any drama."

A pause.

"But I didn't want to stifle him, either. He was a brilliant boy. I told him that if he had interests that he wanted to pursue outside his thesis and he thought I could help him, I'd be happy to share what I knew. But I did tell him it was probably better to keep it between us. Of course I knew it would come out eventually. But I thought if Theo knew that I wasn't interfering with Eli's thesis, he wouldn't care. Silly me."

"What happened?"

"Well, Eli died, for one thing. Right afterward . . . I mean the body wasn't even in the ground . . . Rosser started demanding that

I give him Eli's research. I pretended I didn't know what he was talking about just for spite. He doesn't believe me, of course."

"Does he own Eli's research or do you?" McAdams asked.

"That's a good question. I'm not in possession of most of his papers. But I do know what he was working on."

"Want to tell us about it?" Decker said.

"Not particularly."

McAdams said, "The course book has you teaching two classes this year: particle physics and electromagnetism and wave theory. And your field is cosmology, right?"

"I'm assuming you're wondering why Eli thought his interests might benefit from my expertise."

"Eli was studying Fourier analysis and eigenvectors," Decker said.

"Do you know what an eigenvector is?"

Decker paged through his notes. "It's a subset of vectors that doesn't change its direction when it's stretched."

"You've done your homework."

"It was explained to us several times, including yesterday by a Harvard math professor," Decker said. "Eli's research may be relevant to both investigations. I'm not Theo Rosser. I don't want drama, either. But we'll both get it unless you come forward. What was Eli interested in?"

"I suppose it's the right thing to do . . . to tell you." Tolvard sighed. "Eli was mapping space junk."

The room fell quiet. Then Decker said, "Okay, I'll bite. What is space junk?"

"Just what it says—junk floating around in space: old satellites, spent rocket stages, and a lot of fragments from collisions and disintegration in the cosmos. The official name is disambiguation. Most of the material is very small, but that doesn't mean it can't cause problems with current satellites and other operable space vehicles. Even paint dust and paint flakes are dangerous if they collide with something solid at the speeds that you deal with in space."

"How much space junk is there?" McAdams asked.

"A lot. For instance, just recently the Chinese government thought it would be fun to fire an antisatellite missile from earth at one of its old weather satellites, exploding thousands of shards in that already crowded lane, exposing the entire geostationary orbit region to Kessler syndrome. It really is a legitimate problem."

"And my next question is . . ." Decker said.

"What is Kessler syndrome? It's also called collisional cascading, which tells you what it is. Did you see the movie *Gravity*? It came out maybe four, five years ago."

"George Clooney and Sandra Bullock," McAdams said. "Aha! I get it. The space vehicle they were working on got whacked with some kind of floating shit . . . er, debris, and that caused all sorts of problems."

"Exactly," Tolvard said. "The theory is that a single collision could form debris which in turn could cause another collision which in turn causes more debris, etcetera, until low outer space is completely destroyed along with all operable satellites within it. That would completely destroy technology as we know it today, not to mention the possibility of debris colliding with earth and possibly throwing it off axis."

"A real gloom and doom scenario," Decker said.

"Yes, I know it makes good science fiction, but it really is a problem because lower outer space is only going to get busier and busier. The world needs more bandwidth, and huge tech companies like Google and Facebook want it before anyone else. Currently, Google is launching high-altitude balloons twelve miles up in the stratosphere to increase its bandwidth. But as you can imagine, balloons have their issues. For one thing, you'd need a lot of balloons to cover the earth properly. Plus balloons are less stable and more fragile than geostationary satellites.

"Satellites orbit much higher in space—twenty-two *thousand miles* from the surface of the earth. They are bigger, more powerful, and you'd only need about three or four of them to get all the coverage you'd want. But satellites cost exponentially more than balloons. If you're going to go about investing billions in a satellite, you might want to know what crap is floating around and where it is so your very expensive machinery doesn't get whacked to smithereens."

"Okay," Decker said. "So Eli was trying to map all this debris?"

"He was trying to create a prototype on how to map the orbits, yes. It's a nascent field, but the implications are tremendous."

McAdams said, "And potentially highly profitable."

"Potentially yes. I don't think Eli cared about that. He was just excited to be doing something original with eigenvectors, although they've been used for decades as coordinates in space."

"How do you map debris if it's changing locations all the time?"

"That's why I said 'map the orbit.'"

"How would you map the orbit of a paint flake?" McAdams asked.

"You bounce waves off of it. Your FM radio for instance. It gives off rogue waves that have the capacity to bounce off objects in space. If you have the capacity to pick up the waves with a specialized dish—for instance, let's say an FM dish—you can map the item by the defection."

"Even a paint flake."

"Even a paint flake weighs more than a radio wave, Detective. Eli had begun working on his own mapping system using Fourier analysis to break down the complex waves to see where they were coming from and using eigenvectors as his coordinates in space. He'd been working on it for over a year. Then . . ."

Tolvard threw up his hands.

"Just terrible. I still . . ."

"You'd been working with him for over a year?" Decker asked.

"On and off, yes."

"Did you notice any change in him these past months?"

The room went quiet. Tolvard said, "He wasn't depressed or anything like that. If anything, he seemed a little more engaged. I had assumed it was because he was so excited about what he was doing. But at times, he also seemed . . . distracted . . . like he couldn't quite concentrate. At one point, I thought he might be burning out. That's always a possibility. Students get this initial rush, but then get bogged down in the nitty-gritty of calculations. I asked him if maybe he wanted to take a break for a while to finish up his thesis with Rosser. But he said his thesis was done and he insisted he was fine. But obviously he wasn't fine."

The professor shook his head.

"In hindsight, I should have pressed him about it, but I didn't want to pry into his personal life. I should have. From my own anecdotal evidence, I've found that students have two peak periods for suicide. When they enter and right before they leave. Thesis panic, job panic, life panic."

Decker said, "From what I've learned, it didn't seem to me that Eli was panicky over anything."

"Something must have been bothering him. I feel terribly guilty. I should have been a little more directive."

Decker said, "You know that people who are determined to commit suicide will do it no matter what the obstacles are."

"Nice thing to say but . . . I just wish I knew what was distracting him."

McAdams said, "Did you know that he was also working with Katrina Belfort?"

"No." Tolvard looked genuinely perplexed. "No, I didn't. What was he doing with her?"

"She was doing some outside consulting with some financial companies," Decker said. "Eli was helping her out with some calculations."

"Really?" He shrugged. "I had no idea. No wonder Eli was distracted. His mind must have been pulled in many directions." He smiled. "My God, that must have ruffled Rosser's feathers. It was bad enough that Eli wanted to work with me. At least I'm not in the math department. Belfort was."

"It might have irked him if he knew about it."

"Ah yes, that makes sense." A pause. "Outside work is frowned upon in the math department."

McAdams said. "Not so in physics?"

"People can take outside work if the department head allows it. And he usually does. He understands about the paltry salaries of academics and economic necessities. I have several consulting jobs. Of course, it's easier with me because I have tenure." He paused. "Do you think that Belfort's death and Eli's death are related to the work he was doing with her?"

"We're working on all kinds of theories," Decker said.

Tolvard looked at the clock. "I do have a class to catch in twenty minutes."

"I understand." Decker stood up. "Thank you very much for taking the time to talk to us."

"I hope I've helped you. You can feel free to call me anytime if you think of something else."

"You have and I will," Decker said.

Tolvard smiled. "You know you're one of the few people I've met who hasn't asked me about my name. What they're obviously asking about is the disconnect between my name and my race."

"Scandinavian name and the Ethiopian face," Decker said. "My son-in-law is Ethiopian. They have distinct features."

"Yes, we do. So ask me the question."

"How'd you get a Scandinavian name?"

"My biological parents were farmers. They died during a famine along with a great deal of my biological relatives. My older brother and I were placed in an orphanage and adopted out to a wonderful

Swedish family who didn't have children of their own. Both my adopted parents were scientists. My brother is a chemical engineer. I'm a physicist. My biological parents were illiterate. So what does that say about nature/nurture and genetics?"

Decker said, "To me it says that if your biological parents had been raised in the same environment as your adopted parents, they might have been scientists, too."

"Of course, of course," Tolvard said. "I suppose I'm saying that I am who I am because of both sets of parents. A fluke of the right set of circumstances coming together at the right time. What does your son-in-law do?"

"He's a neonatal nurse who went back to medical school."

"We're bright people . . . Ethiopians. I still think of myself as Ethiopian. It smacks me in the face every time I look in the mirror. But I'm eternally grateful for my Swedish parents. For one thing, they gave me a real cool name."

CHAPTER 25

AFTER REINTERVIEWING BELFORT'S neighbors and coming up dry, Decker returned to the station house at one in the afternoon. McAdams was at his spot on the opposite side of their shared partners desk. He was reading intently and had his feet up on the desktop.

"What are you doing here?" Decker's voice was testy. "You should be studying."

"I *am* studying." He held up a law book. "Precisely what bee has entered your bonnet?"

"That idiom is very retro."

"Yeah, way classier than asking about the stick up your ass."

Decker sat down. "None of Belfort's neighbors remember seeing anything or hearing anything."

"What about the one next door?"

"Now she isn't even sure she saw anything. Maybe the shadow was a trick of the night. She certainly doesn't remember seeing a car or hearing a motor spring to life. How can you drag a body in an open backyard and up the mountain with no witnesses?"

"It's called three in the morning." McAdams put down his book. "I've been thinking. What about Tolvard?"

"What about him?"

"Do you like him as the bad guy? Maybe Belfort was trying to muscle in on Eli's research. Maybe Eli told Tolvard and the prof went to her house to confront her and things got out of hand."

Decker began going through his phone-call memos. "Don't see it."

"Why? Because he reminds you of your son-in-law?"

Decker looked up. "Where did that come from?"

"I'm just saying . . ."

"It's not because he reminds me of Koby. I don't see Tolvard as the bad guy because he talked freely. There were no phone calls or e-mails between them."

"What about using the college phones?"

"Of course. You can always find a way to communicate, but it just doesn't seem logical. Besides, Tolvard was just helping Eli along."

"So says Tolvard."

"Why don't you believe him?"

"I'm idling in neutral with Tolvard. But that doesn't stop my brain from thinking up possibilities. Like how about this? Maybe Tolvard was trying to muscle the project away from Eli. The project, if successful, could potentially be beaucoup lucrative to billion-dollar companies. Maybe Belfort was trying to defend Eli against Tolvard. She called him up to talk about things, he went over to her house, and then things got out of hand."

"Well, speculation could be cleared up if we had Belfort's phone records since he claimed he's never called her." Decker felt himself getting peeved. "How long does it take to get a phone record? You'd think I asked for a Gutenberg Bible."

"This isn't L.A., Old Man."

"It's 'Lieutenant' to you."

"I stand corrected, sir."

"By the way, I got Eli's phone records two days ago."

"You didn't tell me." McAdams made a sour face. "Typical. Why do I even try?"

"Sorry. You were studying and I didn't want to disturb you. Anyway, there was nothing illuminating in them. He rarely used his phone, and when he did, he texted instead of called. Since the phone record doesn't record the contents of the text, I don't know what they were about. On the day of his death, there were a couple of outgoing texts to Mallon. That corresponds to the texts she showed us when we first talked to her—that she had asked him to meet her at the college dining hall. Obviously the texts went unanswered. But I went through the days prior to his suicide. I didn't find any texts or calls from Rosser or Belfort or Tolvard. If any of them was the motivating factor behind his suicide, I haven't found any evidence to back that up."

"What about the actual contents from the server?"

"I'm still waiting. That takes even longer than getting a phone record. I could be wrong, but I don't expect anything revolutionary."

"I'm not saying his professors had anything to do with his suicide. What I'm saying is maybe Rosser or Tolvard had something to do with Katrina's death and Eli was the catalyst. Could be Rosser was angry at her for involving Eli in her outside activities. Or maybe Katrina was trying to steal Eli's research with Tolvard and Tolvard got mad."

"Anything's possible. It would help if we had the contents of her computer."

Mike Radar came into the detectives' room from his office. "Hello, gentlemen."

"Hi, Mike," Decker said. "Have you had any luck obtaining Katrina Belfort's phone records?"

"They haven't come through yet?"

"No, they have not, and I could really use them."

"We were approved from the judge."

"Can you call them and maybe ask for the company to e-mail them to me?"

"No, they send them in the mail. Sometimes it takes an extra day to get here. It's only been a couple of days."

Decker sighed. "I can't do anything without her phone records and without her e-mail. What about the warrant to get the contents from the server? I'll need her entire computer, of course, but the e-mail contents would be a great start."

"I haven't applied for it since we have the tech."

"He seems to be having a little trouble. I'm getting frustrated."

"Speaking of that . . ." Radar cleared his throat. "The tech called me about two hours ago. He came down with a fever last night. He tried popping Tylenols and working, but he couldn't concentrate and was afraid he'd do more harm than good. So he'll try again once he's feeling better."

"You are kidding me," Decker said. "Can't we get someone else?"

"Your L.A. is showing," McAdams said.

Radar smiled. "It's faster to wait for him to get better. If he can't do it, we'll petition for the files. She has quite a few servers, FYI. She has the school, but in addition she has Gmail, Hotmail, Yahoo, and there may be even more. That's why I'm loath to petition a judge because I need separate warrants. In the meantime, I've got a callout for you. It isn't murder, but it is in our job description. Lydia Tucker reported her car missing."

"I'm pleased it isn't murder. When did she call?"

"About a half hour ago." Radar handed Decker a slip. "Check it out."

"Do you know her?"

"Lydia? Sure. She's about ninety. I'm shocked that she was still driving."

"Maybe she just forgot where she parked it," McAdams said.

Radar turned to Decker. "Smug, isn't he." To McAdams, "Wait until you get there."

"I'm just saying . . ."

"Go to her house and take a report, Pete. Then go home. I know it's a short day for you, so there's no sense hanging around unless there's a reason for it. Remember this was to be your semiretirement job."

"Fine." Decker exhaled. "If anything should come in tonight, could you call me and leave a message. If we get hold of Belfort's communications, I'll come in to the station house on Saturday night."

"Decker, relax. It'll keep until Sunday. Just relax."

"Uh, yeah. I forgot to tell you. I'm going to Manhattan on Sunday."

"That's good. Go see the kids and have a wonderful time."

"I'm going mainly to speak to Ryan Belfort, Katrina's brother. I figured maybe he might be able to tell me more about her face-to-face than over the phone. And yes, I'll combine it with dinner with the kids."

"You're nothing if not efficient. How close was Ryan to his sister?"

"It was just the two of them. He knew her well enough to tell me that she had an affair while she was a graduate student in Maryland. I checked out the guy. He moved to California and was there when she died. He hasn't communicated with her in over two years."

Radar said, "Well, the affair's still interesting. Any affairs while she was here?"

"I haven't turned up anything, but affairs are usually kept quiet . . . until they're not. That's why I want her phone records, texts, and e-mail. They may point me somewhere."

Radar nodded. "Okay. See what the brother tells you. I'll put in an allowance for gas and meals for you." He turned to McAdams. "Are you going with him?"

"I am."

"Do you want a meal allowance?"

"I will pass on your generosity, Captain. Give my portion to charity."

"That would be the police department," Radar said.

Decker slapped the memo in the palm of his hand. "I'll see what I can do about Lydia Tucker's car." He looked at McAdams. "Call me if anything comes through . . . like a phone log. I'll see you later."

"Want me to come with you?"

"No need. Just keep studying. There's a lot that's riding on your passing the exams."

"I'm well aware of that, thank you very much."

"You don't appear nervous."

"That's because I'm *not* nervous. I will pass. I might not burn up the test but I'll do well enough, and that is good enough."

"I admire your confidence. Or are you just a good actor?"

"Look at this, Old Man." McAdams held out his hands in front of him. "Not a shake or a tremor. I'm as steady as she blows."

MAKING GOOD PROGRESS with his studies, McAdams decided to take a midmorning break while the Deckers were at synagogue for daytime services. He stood up and stretched and turned his phone back on. It immediately sprang to life with an incoming call. It was an out-of-town area code, and that made sense. Most of the people who called him didn't live in Greenbury.

"This is Tyler."

"Darling, you called your sister. I'm so proud."

"Who is this?" McAdams looked at his phone. "Iris?"

"You made her so happy."

"Really? The conversation lasted a total of two minutes."

"But it was a *meaningful* two minutes."

"I'm happy I made you proud. What's up?"

"Mallon Euler."

"Yes, right. Dr. Kent called me. She left early to apply to college."

"Ah, but there's more to it than that."

McAdams grabbed a pen. "I'm all ears, Iris."

"The impetus was a cheating scandal."

"Oh." A pause. "Mallon cheated?"

"Let me explain. At the end of her sophomore year, four girls turned in the exact same objective final for American history: Mallon, Mackenzie, and her friends Misha and Ellen. All of them had the same correct answers, and all of them had the same wrong answers."

"That's quite a feat."

"Something wasn't kosher. How all of them copied off one another . . . I'm not sure. Maybe hand signals. Kids are very resourceful these days. Anyway, the teacher, Dr. Kalish . . . do you remember Dr. Kalish?"

"Exoskeletal man with a Polish accent. What in the world was he doing teaching American history? He's a chemist."

"Mrs. Mallard was out having a baby. We were short-staffed and I believe he only taught the last six weeks. He's not a dumb man, our Dr. Kalish. As soon as he graded the tests, he knew that there had been cheating. But rather than confront the girls, he was clever. He had the girls come in, one by one, and told them that each one was between an A-minus and an A. So he was going to ask them a couple of questions to help put them over the hump."

"Ah. Who got the questions right?"

"Mallon, of course. She was the cheatee, not the cheater. So she got her A and everyone thought that was the end of it."

"What happened to Mackenzie, et al?"

"You know who their parents are, darling."

"Nothing happened."

"They swore up and down that they didn't cheat. Their answers were the same because they all studied together. And since no one could prove otherwise, it was business as usual. No harm done since Mallon got the benefit of their stupidity by upping her grade. So everyone walked away happy. Or so the administration thought. Somehow Mallon got wind of what the oral test really was about and she became very testy that Mackenzie, Ellen, and Misha remained unscathed. According to her adviser, she started asking a lot of questions. She was very persistent . . . read it as a pest."

"So what did they offer her in return for her cooperation?"

"Ah, darling, you always were a sharp one. They offered to graduate her early. Since she was having social issues and she was very smart, it was in her best interest."

"She graduated at fifteen?"

"Sixteen. She was way ahead in math and science and the school paid for a few home tutors to complete her humanities courses. From what was reported, Mallon was thrilled. The school gave her great recommendations and Kneed Loft offered her admission plus a free ride. She was all of seventeen years old."

"What did she do with herself between sixteen and seventeen?"

"The school hired her as an SAT tutor: a much better use of her brain. And it also showed there were no hard feelings. The school makes a point of supporting its own."

"Don't tell me she tutored Mackenzie, Misha, and Ellen?"

"From what I heard, the girls did very well."

"Lovely to know that nothing has changed since I left."

"Oh, Tyler, it's just the usual politics masking as academics. I'm sure you're faced with it all the time, working with the five colleges of upstate."

"I don't work for the colleges, Iris."

"But Greenbury is a college town and the administration has long tentacles. Don't be angry with your alma mater. It's a part of who you are. And by the way, have you thought about speaking to the student body about what you do? The police work, not the law student."

"I'm in the middle of finals."

"How about talking during spring break?"

"You don't have school during spring break."

"Oh. You're right. Then do it right after spring break. And need I remind you of the favor I just did."

"Okay. I will speak to the student body about police work. And I'll have street cred because I was actually shot."

A long pause. "I heard about that. If it's too hard to talk about it . . ."

"No, I'm fine, Iris, I shouldn't have even brought it up. I'm just acting petty."

"Did it hurt?"

McAdams laughed. "Of course it hurt! I will speak as a favor for you, Iris."

"You see how it works, Tyler. One hand scratches the other's back."

"I suppose that's okay just as long as no one gouges me."

CHAPTER 26

SUNDAY MORNING JUST before sunup, Rina had finished packing the car. She closed the trunk, turned around, and bumped into Mallon Euler. The girl was bundled head to toe, but she was still shivering.

Rina said, "Don't tell me you were just in the neighborhood."

"I was just walking to Bagelmania. It opens at six."

"It's in the opposite direction." When Mallon didn't answer, Rina said, "Come in and warm up. It must be ten degrees outside."

"Where are you going?"

Rina walked back to the house and opened the door. She let Mallon in first. "We're going to Manhattan to visit family."

"Can I come? Not to visit your family, of course. I just want to get away from Kneed Loft. I'm creeped out."

McAdams stopped in his tracks when he saw Mallon. "What are you *doing* here?"

The young woman's eyes watered. "I must seem stalkery, kinda."

"Uh, yes."

Tears were falling down her cheeks. "I'm sorry. I'm not myself."

Decker came into the room. "Hey, what's up, Mallon?"

"She wants to go to Manhattan with us," Rina said.

"The answer is still the same about Eli's papers," Decker said. "No, you can't have them."

"It's not that. I just want to get away from the college. Everyone's staring at me like I had something to do with Dr. Belfort's death."

"Did you?"

"*NO!*" She wiped the tears from her face with her coat sleeve. "No, I did not."

"Do you have somewhere to stay in Manhattan?" Decker asked.

"I can study at Columbia. They have a math library. And I think Butler is open all the time." Silence. "I just want to be in the company of someone I trust—for the most part."

"Not exactly a rousing endorsement . . . for the most part."

"Peter, could you help me in the kitchen, please?" Rina asked.

Decker regarded his wife, trying to figure out what was on her mind. "Sure."

After the door was closed, Rina said, "If she's truly frightened, I can understand her attachment to you and Tyler. And if she's faking it, it's probably better to keep her within reach."

"Do you think she's faking it?"

"I don't know. But what harm would it do to let her come with us?"

"For one thing she's still a suspect. For all I know, she's going to make a break for it."

"While riding in your car?"

McAdams walked in. "If it's a tie vote, I vote no."

"There you have it," Decker said. "You're outvoted."

"Didn't you just tell me that she was unjustly treated at your old school, Tyler?"

"They graduated her early, gave her glowing recommendations for college, and gave her a paying job."

"It sounds like she's had to work for everything she's gotten."

"Like most people," Decker said.

"Aw, c'mon, guys. Stop being so hard-hearted."

"It's not professional."

"This isn't L.A., Peter, no one's going to report you to IA."

"If she goes with us, I'm *not* sitting next to her," McAdams said.

"I'll sit with her in the backseat," Rina said. "Where does Dr. Belfort's brother live?"

"In Brooklyn. Columbia is way out of the way."

"So drop her off at NYU."

A long pause. Then Decker said, "She's *not* coming for dinner."

"I agree," Rina said. "But we can pick her up before we leave back for Greenbury."

Decker shook his head. "Why are you *always* taking in strays and oddballs?"

"I don't know," Rina said. "I guess I feel sorry for underdogs."

"Sometimes those dogs bite."

"You're right." She shrugged. "Up to you."

Decker sighed. "Is there any particular *reason* why we should take Mallon to New York?"

"She might be able to tell you the latest gossip . . . you know, glean information from her."

Decker looked at McAdams. "What do you think?"

"Ordinarily, I'd say no, but Rina's usually right about things."

"Fine. We'll take her." Decker threw up his hands. Then he turned to Tyler. "Tell her she can come but give her some ground rules."

"Like what?"

"Like no pumping for information. I will get very annoyed if she does that. If she doesn't like it, she can stay where she is."

"But say it nicely, Tyler," Rina said.

"That may be beyond my job description." McAdams left.

Decker turned to her. "Hopefully she isn't carrying any lethal weapons on her person."

"Tyler can pat her down before we leave," Rina said.

"Good idea. The way he complains about his love life, it'll probably be the most action he'll see in a while."

"What is *with* you?"

Decker exhaled. "Sorry."

"You don't have to apologize for being grumpy. It's early in the morning and you haven't had your second cup of coffee. But I'm also wondering if there's anything on your mind."

"No, I'm fine."

"No, you're not, but that's okay. You can't be fine all the time. Just try not to air your grievances in front of the kid, please."

"Yeah, that was not cool." He poured another cup of coffee for himself. "I'm slipping into old work habits." A pause. "I don't want you to think badly of me, like I'm incapable of relaxing."

"So what if you are?" Rina slipped her arms around his neck. "Ooh, you are tense." She gave him a quick massage.

"Feels good. Thank you."

"No prob." She patted his neck and dropped her hands. "Look, Peter. I won't get mad at you for being a workaholic if you don't get mad at me for picking up strays. We're who we are at this age and that's just that."

"Sure. Whatever. Invite anyone you want for Shabbos dinner."

"Including the homeless guy who stands in front of Frozenfest Yogurt."

"No, he may not come into my house. He smells."

"But I can buy him takeout?"

"Once in a while."

"Then we have a deal?"

"We have a deal."

ON THE RIDE to New York, Mallon said, "I heard you met with Lennaeus Tolvard." When no one spoke, she said, "I'm not asking questions, I'm making a statement."

Decker turned onto the highway. He and McAdams were in the front. "News travels fast."

"It's a small school."

"As everyone keeps reminding me. What else have you heard?"

"I thought there'd be no questions asked."

"No, you can't ask questions, but we can."

"That seems inequitable."

"No one said life was fair, kid."

"It doesn't matter," Mallon said. "I have nothing to ask. Thanks for taking me."

"You're very welcome. It was Rina's idea."

"I figured." Mallon smiled. "Did you guys hear about the big showdown last night?"

"What's that?" McAdams asked.

"Rosser versus Tolvard. They came to blows. Security had to break it up."

McAdams turned around. "Elaborate, please?"

"It was in the dining hall around eight. I texted you and then I tried calling you afterward, but it went straight to voice mail."

McAdams took out his cell and made a face. "I was studying. I forgot to turn it on."

"What happened, Mallon?" Decker asked.

"Apparently Rosser heard that you had visited Tolvard and asked about Eli and what he was studying. Anyway, when I met with him, he was furious."

"Who was? Rosser?"

"No, Tolvard was. Rosser had called him up and they got into a big fight. Did I tell you that Tolvard took me on as my adviser?"

"No." McAdams took out a paper pad and started writing down notes. "When did this happen?"

"Friday."

"And Rosser approved it?"

"This was part of the big fight. See, I was being shuffled around from professor to professor. Tolvard was willing to take me on, but Rosser wouldn't approve it since he wasn't a math professor. So Tolvard appealed to the dean because of the unusual circumstances and he totally got my thesis anyway. The dean approved."

"Which dean? Zhou?"

"No, she's the dean of residency and student life meaning housing, personal problems, illness, if you want to take a leave of absence, things like that. Tolvard went to Dean Crane—Malcolm Crane. He's the dean of student academics and he approved it. Rosser went apeshit. He stormed into the dining hall where Dr. Tolvard and I were having a thesis meeting and started *screaming* at him. It was wild!"

"What went down?" McAdams asked.

"Rosser was ballistic. He kept accusing Tolvard of stealing his students—first Eli, and then me. And that he was keeping Eli's research from him and that anything Eli did with Tolvard belonged to him. And then Tolvard started yelling back, screaming that Rosser wasn't fit to run a department and hadn't published anything meaningful since the Stone Age. And then they literally went nose to nose. That's when the pushing started. There was a lot of pushing and shoving and a chair and table got knocked down and food was all over the floor and each one said the other started it. Between you and me, Tolvard started the shoving, but I didn't tell security that. Rosser is an asshole." She turned to Rina. "Excuse my language."

"What happened after security broke up the fight?"

"Rosser stormed off. I heard they both met with Dean Crane. I don't know what was said, but Tolvard called me about two hours later and told me both he and Dean Crane thought it would be in my best interest to switch to the physics department, which means I would get a dual B.A. in physics and math, but it would also mean that I'd have to take four classes in summer school to meet the physics requirements for a B.A. But the good news is that the school would extend my scholarship. I'd also have to do a physics thesis and I'm totally not thrilled about that, either. I had no idea what to do, but then Tolvard said that I could carry on Eli's research once he's cleared it with the dean so that Rosser doesn't feel he owns it, which he doesn't. So I don't need Eli's papers from you because once Tolvard clears it with Dean Crane, he'll give me the papers that Eli was working on."

"Fantastic," Decker said.

"So I really did want to come just because I'm creeped out, especially after what happened last night. You want to know what I think?"

"Of course."

"I think Rosser is crazy enough to have killed Dr. Belfort. Before, I thought he was just a jerk. Now I'm not so sure. Certainly I wouldn't want to be alone with him even in his office. He's totally unhinged."

"What about Tolvard?" McAdams asked. "You said he did the first push."

"Tolvard was just reacting. When I spoke to him later, he was very calm. We're meeting on Monday at his office in the afternoon unless you suspect him of something, in which case I'll wait until he's been cleared in your mind because like I said to you, Detective Decker, I don't know who to trust at all in the school. All of us are walking around with this paranoia which I suppose isn't really paranoia because Dr. Belfort was murdered."

Mallon turned to Rina.

"Is there any coffee left?"

"Do you think you need caffeine?" McAdams said.

"Ha, ha. I'm wired because who wouldn't be wired after that. Besides, I hardly slept at all. I need something to keep me alert."

"Coffee's only going to make you shaky," Rina said. "Why don't you close your eyes and take a nap. We're going to be in the car for a while."

"I'm not tired."

"Give it a try."

"Sure, why not." She took her backpack from the floor and pulled out her phone. She stuck a headphone jack into it and popped in earbuds. Then she slumped back and closed her eyes. Within ten minutes, she was sleeping deeply.

McAdams said to Decker, "What do you think?"

"I think all academics are crazy."

"I could have told you that. What do you think of Rosser as . . ." He lowered his voice even further. "As our number one suspect?"

"He's a big guy." Decker was also whispering. "Big enough to drag a body up the hill by himself. They lifted lots of prints from the house. Mainly I'm interested in doorknobs that had been smeared but not wiped clean, which I found interesting. That someone would take the time to confound the prints without a clean swipe."

"Someone with intelligence."

"Very much so. This is the thing. They lifted a partial from the end table where I found the hair and blood. I've been trying to enhance it to make it more readable, but we might just have to go with it. Tomorrow, I'll start printing all the usual suspects—Rosser, Batra, Weissberg, Tolvard, Ferraga—"

"What does he have to do with anything?"

"I don't know that he does. But he was on Eli's committee."

"What about our little miss back there?"

"Absolutely," Decker said. "And what about Dean Zhou? Is she back from her conference yet?"

"Let me check my phone and see if she called or texted . . . oh, here we go. She texted me last night at nine in the evening, saying she's back in town but can't talk because she's going into an emergency meeting with Dean Crane and the administration."

"Get her alibi for where she was on the night Katrina died so we can rule her out."

"She was at a math conference. I think it was held in Atlanta."

"Then verify it. Get a statement from people who saw her."

"You think she had something to do with it?"

"Not necessarily. We're just hunting everyone down."

"I'll call her now." McAdams punched in the numbers. "Hello, Dean Zhou? This is Detective Tyler McAdams, I'm sorry to have to call you so early, but . . . yes, I heard about the incident . . . how unfortunate . . . okay . . . okay . . . okay, but I would still like to talk to you . . . no, I can't do it today, either. How about sometime tomorrow? . . . Twelve would be fine. In the meantime, I'd like to talk to some people who saw you at the conference, just to verify . . . no, it's strictly routine. Just to eliminate you . . . wait, hold on."

McAdams took out a sheet of paper.

"Could you spell that for me again? . . . Sure, you can text me, but in case I don't get reception, if you could just give the names to me now . . . James Wallach and Ralph Kidder . . . Alf Kidder. Do you have their phone num—. . . okay, text me the numbers, that's fine. Anyone else? . . . Mary Michelson. Thank you so much. By the way, about what happened last night. What's the upshot? . . . I mean who owns what research? . . . okay, I understand. No, I was just curious. It's just that we're working with a suicide and a possible murder . . . I don't know if their argument is relevant. I'm just collecting facts . . . thank you . . . and you'll text those num—"

McAdams looked at the phone.

"She hung up. She didn't like me poking around in what she called school affairs."

"All the more reason to get her alibi squared away," Decker said. "She was one of the first people who asked to see Eli's papers. Kinda pushy about it, too."

McAdams said, "Do you think she was part of Belfort's sideline?"

"Maybe she was. Or maybe she wasn't and wanted a piece of the action."

Rina leaned forward. "Or maybe *she* was the one who ransacked Mallon's room, looking for hidden papers."

Decker said, "Rina, she wasn't in town and she's Chinese."

"How do you know she wasn't in town, and haven't you ever heard of makeup and a wig?" When he didn't answer, Rina said, "Is she slender built?"

"She is," McAdams said.

"You asked me to name another mystery woman," Rina said. "Don't get peeved when I make a suggestion."

Decker sighed. "You're right. It's a good suggestion. Just not one I was expecting. I've got a lot of suspects and nothing concrete. I'm sure Ryan Belfort is going to be displeased by the progress of this investigation."

"It's only been a couple of days, Peter."

"No it's been four days. Seven days since Eli committed suicide. God created the world in seven days. You think I could solve something by then."

"You can't work miracles, Peter. You're not God."

"And don't I know it."

CHAPTER 27

ONCE IN NEW York City, Decker did a mental map because everyone was being dropped off at a different destination. Tyler was the first: the address, his stepgrandmother's posh Park Avenue apartment. The street was three lanes in each direction with a median divider filled with flowers in the appropriate seasons. Now it was flat and overlaid with snow, with the exception of a few melting ice sculptures. Traffic, as usual, was clogged with the ritual horn honking that served little purpose except to add to the urban symphony. Decker pulled over to the curb and the doorman rushed out to open the car door and greet McAdams as if he were coming back from military action. Immediately the uniformed man relieved him of his lightweight briefcase.

"Welcome back, Mr. McAdams."

"Thanks, Martin. How's it going?"

"You know . . . little of this, little of that."

"The usual."

"You got it, Mr. McAdams."

Tyler poked his head in the passenger window, talking to Decker. "You'll call me later?"

"I will," Decker said. "Get some studying done."

"Unfortunately, that'll happen because there's nothing to distract me." He tapped the car's hood as he walked away, personified wealth in a cashmere coat with a fur collar.

Decker pulled the car out into thick traffic, going south.

Mallon rolled her eyes. "Figures" was all she said.

"There's no shame in being rich," Rina said.

"Did you see how the doorman rushed over like, God forbid, Tyler should carry his own briefcase?"

"It's the doorman's job and it's honest wages."

"Being professional ass-kissers."

"Now there's where you're wrong. They and the super are the fabric of these fancy buildings. Without them, the residents are helpless. I guarantee you it's not an easy job."

Mallon didn't answer.

"I may be biased," Rina said. "I do like the uniform. I've seen pictures of Detective Decker in the early days, dressed in his uniform. Very handsome."

"You're making me blush."

"You were a doorman?" Mallon asked.

Rina laughed. "No, I meant as a police officer."

"Oh." Mallon sounded less than enthusiastic. "Right. When was that? Like the sixties?"

Decker said, "Early seventies. I'm not that old. But the country was still in turmoil."

"The Vietnam War?"

"Yes."

"Did you beat up the protesters?"

"You have a way with words, Mallon."

"I just meant there were a lot of protests and people got beat up."

"A few got hurt. Most of them were simply arrested and let go a few hours later."

"So what was the point of arresting them?"

"Not a good idea to sanction chaos in the streets, Mallon, no matter how futile the effort. Then people really do get hurt." Decker turned onto Fifth, headed downtown. "I feel sorry for you kids nowadays. You're always groping around to get the sixties going again and it never quite happens. And in answer to your question, I never beat up anyone."

"But you arrested people."

"Some idiots . . . including my ex-wife."

"His ex-wife is a very nice woman," Rina said. "That came out wrong."

"If you say so," Decker said.

From the back, Rina gave him a gentle slug.

"Did you always want to be a cop?" Mallon asked.

"Not a lifelong dream, but it was a natural coming out of the military."

"You were in the army?"

"I was."

"Did you like it?"

"*Like* it? No, I didn't *like* it. I hated every moment of it. It was a nonstop brutal and bloody nightmare. I was drafted. Where I lived, if you were drafted, you served."

"Sorry to bring it up."

She sounded chastened. Decker said, "No problem. It's part of my history. Even with the war going on, you could tell that the Vietnamese people were a nice lot when they weren't sniping at you. Rina and I went back on a tour last year. I hardly recognized the country. We had a fantastic time. I kept trying to use my Vietnamese and I made everyone laugh. I served my country. I'm very proud of my country. I'm American through and through. But revisiting the country, I just kept wondering what the hell were we doing there? The passage of time . . . you see things differently."

"What about you, Mrs. Decker?"

"What about me?"

"What's your background?"

"Why don't you go first, Mallon."

"Nothing to tell, really. My parents divorced when I was seven. My father left to teach math in Leipzig and my mother is depressed all the time. I have a little sister who's two years younger and way smarter than I am. She's almost autistic. She's at Berkeley and I don't think she'll ever return to the East Coast. They totally loved her. She not only found herself, she found others like her."

"Do you keep in touch?"

"E-mail."

"That's good. Family is important."

"So they tell me," Mallon answered. "Now you, Mrs. Decker."

"California born and bred. I grew up in Beverly Hills, which sounds a lot ritzier than it was. We had a duplex. Our family was on the top and my uncle and aunt and my two cousins lived on the bottom. My dad came from a family of eight and he and his uncle were the only ones who survived the Holocaust."

Mallon bit her bottom lip. "Wow. Uh, I mean sorry. Did I just stick my foot in my mouth?"

"Not at all. I had a nice childhood. Our duplex was Spanish style with red roof tiles and big picture windows with lots of stained glass inserts called accidentals. It had beautiful old wood floors and original built-ins but no air-conditioning. In the summer, we sweltered, especially since we were on the top floor and heat rises. Eventually my uncle died and the place was sold, and by that time my father was doing well and we moved into a beautiful house in the swanky area of Beverly Hills when I was in my senior year of high school. By that time, I had turned so religious that I eschewed anything material, dumb cluck that I was. Most kids have pictures of rock stars on their walls. I had rabbis. It drove my parents nuts, which I suppose was the point."

"What did your father do?" Mallon asked.

"He owned a glass installation company. He was one of the first dealers in L.A. to move to all-glass shower enclosures. My poor papa. He worked incredibly long hours. I rarely saw him except on Saturday morning when we went to synagogue. He looked so handsome, all dressed up." Her eyes started watering.

"Has he passed?" Mallon paused. "Too personal?"

"No, he's still alive but not in the best of health. But he is ninety-six. My mother, who is ninety-four, is still as lucid as they come, much to Detective Decker's dismay."

"What are you talking about? It's wonderful that she's so with it."

"She's still telling him how to run his life."

Decker laughed. "That's true."

"Do you see them often?"

"Well, we moved to the East Coast and they moved to Florida, so we actually see them and the detective's mother a lot more now that we're all in the same time zone."

"Nice." Mallon turned quiet.

Decker had finally wended his way into the East Village. He stopped in front of one of NYU's scattered buildings, a purple flag waving in the winter breeze. Even on a Sunday with chilly temperatures, students took up Washington Square Park and its environs. Manhattan was a city in perpetual motion.

"I don't know where the library is, Mallon," Decker told her, "but if you ask, I'm sure someone will help you out."

"This is fine." Her voice had turned very quiet. "Thanks." She got out and closed the door.

"Wanna sit up front?" Decker asked his wife.

"Absolutely." Rina got out of the car and sat in the passenger's seat.

"I miss having you up here. I miss the conversations that we have when we take these long drives."

"Thank you. I do, too."

Decker scooted the car back into traffic and headed to Brooklyn. "What do you make of her?"

"Mallon? Another wounded animal. You want to hear a pronouncement?"

"Lay it on me."

"I think that she'd be perfect for Tyler provided that she isn't a suspect in anything."

Decker laughed. "That's still not a closed book."

"Yes, I know. Do you really suspect her or are you just saying that to cover your bases?"

"I don't know, Rina. Until we get into Belfort's computer, I have to be psychologically prepared for anything. If the tech doesn't crack it by this weekend, I'm just going to get the warrants to get the e-mail information from the server . . . servers. She used a lot of them."

"A different server for a different purpose?"

"My thoughts, too. She was wearing a lot of hats and probably one of them got her killed. Anyway, enough about my ignorance. What do you and Rachel and Lily have planned?"

"Actually, it worked out perfectly. Rachel has to go to work at the hospital until five, and I'm going to babysit."

"Meaning you're going to be exhausted."

"Lily is in pre-preschool. I'm going to pick her up in an hour. Rachel has left me a list of suggestions for both food and activities. I know how to get to the park. I know how to get to the JCC children's center, plus Lily still naps at around two. So I'm covered."

"I don't think this interview will take all that long. I could meet you at their apartment at around two."

"Great but call first. Never wake a sleeping toddler."

"I thought it was a sleeping lion."

"One and the same."

RYAN BELFORT HAD made his home near the waterfront in a posh condo that sat above a Starbucks, a tea shop and an organic vegan restaurant that boasted a raw-food health bar, which Decker interpreted as uncooked vegetables. The area was lively, the streets were packed, and parking was more of a concept than a reality. The closest spot was five blocks away, but the sun had managed to peek through the clouds and there was at least promise of a better day ahead.

The building was six stories with Belfort's unit on floor three. The man who answered the door was indeed the same guy in the pictures at Katrina's house: good-looking and in his thirties, tall with broad shoulders, blue eyes, and tawny colored hair. He was dressed in sweats and socks, and while he didn't exactly welcome Decker with open arms, Ryan allowed him past the threshold, which was enough in Decker's book. The living room was tidy and spare. Apparently neatness ran in the family. Ryan plopped onto a celadon-green couch and slapped his hands over his face in a dry wash. Then he looked up.

"Any news?"

"Not yet. I'm having her computer looked into. That should tell us something, maybe lead us in the right direction."

"Okay." Belfort pointed to a chair and Decker sat down. "So why the visit if nothing's new?"

"I wanted to offer my condolences in person. And I'm also wondering if there's *anything* you might be able to remember about Katrina that might help me. Sometimes the smallest thing turns out to be big."

"Nothing more than I told you over the phone."

"Tell me about your sister," Decker said. "What was she like? What would you want her legacy to be?"

"Interesting question." He sighed. "She was always in my corner. We got along great."

"Protective?"

"In a way that made you stick up for yourself. She . . . enabled others. That's what she was . . . an enabler but in a good way."

"Positive outlook?"

"Yes."

"How'd she get along with others growing up?"

"She had friends if that's what you mean."

"Life of the party?"

"I wouldn't say that. But I never remember her complaining about her social life."

"Boyfriends?"

"Nothing serious that I remember. She was always pretty, so she could be choosy." A long pause. "She was good with guys . . . with my friends, for sure. They'd talk about sports and cars and she'd join in like she was one of them. She was easy to talk to—the kind of girl you can take out for a beer. She could converse on almost any subject."

"Any specific topics that *she* liked to talk about?"

Belfort gave the question some thought. "You know, because she was such a math person, she rarely talked about what *she* was doing. Mostly it centered around what you were doing. Even in adulthood, when we got together, if we weren't gossiping about old friends, we talked about my work, not hers."

"But she felt close enough to you to confide that she was having an affair with a married man. She felt close enough to tell you his name."

Belfort winced. "Not her finest moment, but it wasn't serious. I only found out about it because I came down to visit her on her birthday and there was this big bouquet of expensive flowers that just overwhelmed her apartment. She told me it was from a friend, and when I started to tease her, she told me it wasn't at all serious. He was just someone that was convenient. And besides, he was married—which she said worked out well for both of them."

"Big bouquet of flowers. Maybe he was more serious than she was."

He shook his head and furrowed his brow. "Surely you don't think he hurt her. It ended over two years ago."

"You told us the name, so we checked him out. Jason Logan moved to California a year ago and is an associate professor at Pepperdine in Malibu. He lives a block from the beach and he claims he hasn't left the West Coast in over three months. His last trip was to Hawaii with the family in November. I have no reason to doubt him."

"Well, like I said, she never mentioned having problems with him."

"Unfortunately, she must have been having problems with someone."

"You don't think it was an accident? Her death? You never told me the specifics."

"Her death wasn't accidental. That's a definite. Suicide? Perhaps. More likely someone was trying to make it look like a suicide."

"How? A fake note? Pills by her side? A gun in her hand?"

"A and C. It was a slapped-together job, Mr. Belfort. Something that wasn't well thought out."

"Oh dear God!" He shook his head. "Well, she never said anything to me about problems with anyone. So whoever it was, she might not have perceived that person as a serious threat."

"I agree with you there."

Belfort blew out air. "The whole thing is so unreal. I just can't believe she's gone. One minute she's in my life, and then poof. She had years in front of her, things to accomplish." His eyes watered. "It isn't fair. You must see that all the time. How unfair life is."

"I do," Decker said. "And it's frustrating."

"How often do you solve these things to your satisfaction?"

"Good question," Decker said. "I'm still at it. So I guess I get enough to keep me going."

"Do you think you'll find my sister's killer?"

"It wasn't a random murder. It just may take time to button everything down, but I'll get an arrest. I'm confident of it. Greenbury is a small town. There are only so many places where people can hide."

"So you're pretty sure it was someone she knew."

"I'm pretty certain, yes."

"I can't picture her making anyone that mad. It's so unfair."

"Yes, it is. And I'm sorry about that. I can't do anything about the unfairness, Mr. Belfort. Hopefully, I can do something about the justice."

CHAPTER 28

THERE WERE THIRTEEN for dinner including the grandchildren: Cindy, Koby, and the twins, Rachel, Sammy, and Lily plus the couples—Jacob and Ilana, Hannah and Rafy, and Gabe and Yasmine. The majority of the conversation happened between the kids, while Rina and Decker entertained the grandchildren. The twins, Akiva and Aaron, were now six and the size of ten-year-olds. The boys could read a little: mostly statistics from basketball cards.

"I see you're training them early," Decker said.

Koby said, "They're on a team with eight-year-olds."

Rina furrowed her brow. "It's not too much for them?"

"They're the tallest on the team and the fastest runners."

"They seem to enjoy it," Cindy said.

The pride was evident. Decker had the height but never the speed. Football had been his thing.

Hannah said, "If you have the talent, you should start early. Look at Gabe. How old were you when you first started playing?"

"Two, but I lost my childhood." Gabe thought a moment. "Actually, that wasn't because of the piano. My parents are two of the most childish people on the face of the earth. Someone had to be the adult. I'll tell you this much. Good scholarship potential for them—smart, athletic—"

"And they're black," Koby said. When everyone stared at him, he shrugged. "True is true."

"It's a little early to start planning their lives." Rina was holding Lily on her lap, feeding her chicken soup.

"We already made out a list of colleges," Koby said. "Penn has a very good team for an Ivy school."

"He's just kidding," Cindy said.

"No, I'm not," Koby said.

"No, he's not kidding," Cindy admitted.

"Well, Lily's going to have to make it on her brains," Sammy said. "She's the shortest kid in pre-preschool."

"She's two." Jacob lectured his brother. "A lot can change."

"You guys are rushing everything," Decker said. "Take your time. Enjoy them while they're still manageable."

"Yeah, yeah," Sammy said. "Is that how you felt when we were all young?"

"Probably not."

And so the conversation went, ebbing and flowing with a lot of laughter in between. The meal lasted over two hours, and would have probably gone on longer but Decker glanced at his watch and asked for the check. When it came, he reached for it, but Jacob got to it first.

"It's on us."

"We're taking you out," Hannah said.

"Are you sure?" Decker said.

"Decided before we all sat down," Koby told him.

"It's our treat," Sammy said.

"No need for that." But Decker had already put away his wallet.

"Thank you. The treat was unexpected and unnecessary, but very nice," Rina said.

"The way we figure," Jacob said, "is that you've taken care of us for all this time. Now it's time for you to take care of you."

"I take care of me?" Decker was confused. "Does that mean I pay for my own dinner?"

"No, of course we'll pay," Sammy said.

"You can pay tip if you want," Jacob said.

"I knew there was a catch."

Gabe laughed. "He's kidding."

"No, he's not," Ilana said.

"I'll pay tip," Gabe said. "I just got a paycheck from my agent."

"Large?" Jacob asked.

"Substantive."

"You pay tip."

"Nonsense, we're all going to split the tip," Sammy said. "This is a joint venture."

Jacob said, "How much do you want to leave for tip?"

At that point, Decker stood up. "I hate to eat and run, guys, but we've got a long ride back."

"Yeah, sure," Sammy said.

Yasmine said, "We should leave twenty percent."

Rina handed Lily back to Rachel. "At least twenty percent. There were a lot of us."

There were kisses and the good-byes, and the kids were still figuring out each one's share as Decker and Rina walked out the door.

She said, "That was nice."

"It was." Decker paused. "It's good to have a little fresh air. It was pretty stuffy inside."

"You have a headache? It was also a little noisy inside."

"A *little* noisy?"

"You want an Advil?"

"Two, please. I thought your hearing goes as you age."

"Not fast enough apparently." Rina laughed. "My head is ringing."

"The boys are adorable but they talk over each other, and as they do, their voices get louder and louder."

"That's good. Then their teammates will be able to hear them across the court."

"Yeah, what was that all about, making lists of colleges?"

"Koby's just fantasizing. It's easier to do that than realize how vulnerable the little ones are and how helpless you are as a parent."

"Yeah, you're right. You usually are."

"Thank you." She leaned over and kissed his chilled cheek. Decker took her gloved hand in his own mitten. As they walked back to the car, no romantic words were needed. Being together was enough.

RINA DROVE AS Decker checked his phone messages. "Finally!"

"Good news?"

"Yes." He stowed his phone in his jacket pocket. "The tech got into the computer and pulled transcripts from two of Belfort's e-mail accounts. I was all set to get a warrant for the servers, but this saves me time, aggravation, and best of all, it may actually help break the case."

Decker checked his watch. It was almost eight. They wouldn't get back into Greenbury until eleven. But this couldn't afford to wait.

"I'm going to have to work late. I could bring the transcripts home, but honestly it's easier for cross-referencing to work at my desk."

"It's fine, Peter. Do what you need to do."

"Promise me you won't wait up. I might pull an all-nighter."

"Not a problem, although I'll miss you."

"You'll be sleeping."

"I can feel when you're there and when you're not. Your aura is all around."

"More like my weight when I move around. Are you okay with driving home?"

"Fine."

"Are you sure?"

"Yes, I'm positive. Take a nap, Peter. Rest your brain until it's needed." Rina slowed the car and squinted out the window. "I think that's her." She pulled in front of a purple-flagged NYU building and a swaddled Mallon hopped in the backseat.

"Where's Tyler?" she asked while rubbing her shoulders.

Rina said, "We're getting him now. Do you want me to turn up the heat?"

"Yeah. I'm freezing. It's freezing outside."

"How long were you waiting?"

"Five minutes. You're driving, Rina?"

"I am."

"If you need a replacement, I do have my license."

"I'm fine, but I'll keep it in mind."

Fifteen minutes later, Tyler came out and opened the front passenger door. When he saw Decker in his seat, he got in the back next to Mallon. "You're driving, Rina?"

"Yes, I am. It seems to be a rather big deal. I'm from L.A. We drive a lot there."

"I'm just used to him driving. No offense meant."

"I want to take a nap," Decker said. "I have some work to do tonight."

"What kind of work?" McAdams asked.

"I'll tell you about it later."

"I'll plug my ears if you want," Mallon said.

Decker ignored her. "You and Rina go back to the house. You need your rest."

"If you work, I'll work. I can also nap while Rina drives."

"Everyone can nap," Rina said. "I'm wide-awake after three cups of coffee."

"Well, I'm not tired," Mallon answered.

"Then you're lucky that napping is not a requirement for passage home," Rina said.

Decker stifled a laugh, leaned back, and threw his scarf over his eyes. Within twenty minutes, all three of them were out. Rina didn't mind. She found the silence was a welcome friend.

THE PILE ON his desk was thick with paper and topped with a note. *More to come.*

Decker leafed through the pages. He glanced at McAdams, who was sitting at his desk and literally twiddling his thumbs. It was almost eleven-thirty. "I'm really fine doing this by myself."

McAdams said, "I'm *wait . . . ing.*"

Decker gave up being Mr. Nice Guy. He could use the help. "I'll take her Gmail account as well as her kneedloft.edu messages and you go through her Hotmail. I think there are IMs as well as e-mails."

He plopped a stack of papers onto McAdams's desk. It didn't take too long. Ten minutes later, McAdams said, "Whoa! Inappropriate."

Decker looked up. "What?"

"Hold on, hold on." McAdams read for another thirty seconds in silence. "And getting more inappropriate by the moment. These are IMs from Belfort to Aldo Ferraga."

"*Ferraga?*"

"Yeah, Ferraga. I wonder how he hacked into her IMs. I didn't know you could do that. I thought they weren't retrievable."

"The wonders of modern technology. What does it *say,* McAdams?"

"Oh . . . sorry. It starts out with flirtation but evolves into something pretty darn steamy. See for yourself." He handed Decker around ten pages of transcription.

Ferraga: *Great lunch . . . great conversation. Let's do it again sometime.*
Belfort: *Let's.*

Next day.
Ferraga: *Free for lunch?*
Belfort: *Coffee at 3? My office?*
Ferraga: *See you then.*

Next day.
Ferraga: *Can't stop thinking about you.*
Belfort: *Hmm . . . sounds intriguing.*
Ferraga: *When can I see you?*
Belfort: *Not today.*
Ferraga: *When?*
Belfort: *I'll get back to you.*

Next day.
Ferraga: *????*
Belfort: *Not today. Rosser's on my back.*
Ferraga: *I hope that isn't literal.*
Belfort: ☺
Ferraga: *When?*
Belfort: *I'm pretty tied up.*
Ferraga: *I hope that is literal.*
Belfort: *lol. If you're desperate, you can drop by my house tomorrow. It'll have to be late.*
Ferraga: *How late?*
Belfort: *Around 11.*

Ferraga: *I'll be there.*
Belfort: *ttyl.*

Apparently it was more than just talk.

Ferraga: *I need to see you again.*
Belfort: *You mean you need to fuck me again.*
Ferraga: *Why are you Americans so unromantic?*
Belfort: *Are you complaining?*
Ferraga: *No, of course not. But I'd like to think of it as more than just a fuck. But if it was just a fuck to you, I will accept that.*
Belfort: *Of course, it was just a fuck. You're married. But it was a very good fuck.*
Ferraga: *It was sublime.*
Belfort: ☺
Ferraga: *When can I see you again?*

And so on and so forth. It was the same thing for several more pages with increasingly raunchier language and graphic descriptions of body parts.

McAdams said, "Anything on your end?"

"I've been reading her Kneed Loft correspondence, which mostly consists of indecipherable math and a lot of meetings. Rosser and Belfort find it hard to be civil even in school-related e-mails. Most of the time, it has this underpinning of hostility."

"Like what?"

"Give me a minute. Okay, it's like this note here. They're talking about a faculty meeting. Rosser ends it by saying 'this time please be punctual' followed by three boldface exclamation points."

"Did she respond?"

"She wrote: 'I'm always punctual if given the *correct* information.' At one point, she was probably reprimanded for being late. The hostility between them is in sync with what we've been told. Your exchanges are definitely the more interesting."

Decker got up and stood behind McAdams, reading over his shoulder. The kid looked up. "Excuse me?"

"I hope you don't mind."

"And if I did?"

"I'd just take the pages from you. This way we can read it together and save some time."

McAdams pulled up a chair. "Sit down. I'll put the stuff in the middle."

The two of them read in silence for a few minutes. McAdams read faster and kept passing the pages to Decker, who had pulled out his pad and started taking notes. Then McAdams said, "Look at this."

"What? Where?"

"Here. It's a variation on the same theme except she's starting to lose interest . . . at least that's how I see it." He handed Decker the pages.

Ferraga: *Same time?*
Belfort: *Not tonight.*
Ferraga: *Why?*
Belfort: *I can't.*
Ferraga: *Why. I miss you. I want you.*
Belfort: *Not going to work tonight. I think Rosser's onto us.*
Did you say anything?
Ferraga: *Of course not!*
Belfort: *Maybe your wife?*
Ferraga: *She doesn't know a thing. Why do you think either*
one is onto us?
Belfort: *I don't know about your wife. Rosser's been a real*
shit this past week. He's totally fucking me over because

Eli has the nerve to want to change advisers. If you want to get me in the sack, get Rosser off my back. Tell him it wasn't my idea for Eli to request the change. I've told him about a billion times, but he doesn't believe me.

Ferraga: *It would look suspicious if I suddenly started defending you on something trivial.*

She didn't react defensively. Instead, she was eminently practical.

Belfort: *You're right. Tell him Eli also asked you to be his adviser and you also turned him down. Tell him that and maybe it'll dawn on him that I'm not trying to steal his students even if that's what the student wants.*

Ferraga: *But it's not true. Eli never approached me.*

Belfort: *So fucking lie. You must be good at that by now.*

Ferraga: *You're getting emotional about this. Just calm down. Let's talk and we'll figure out the best strategy.*

Belfort: *I've already figured out a good strategy. You just have to have the balls to pull it off!*

Ferraga: *Let me come over tonight and we'll think of something.*

Belfort: *Aldo, you don't seem to understand. I'm stressed out about this. He's threatening to **report** me for something I didn't do. I keep telling him that but he doesn't believe me.*

Ferraga: *Rosser can be a jackass.*

Belfort: *So if you know that, tell him that Eli asked you to be his adviser or, at the very least, tell him you heard that Eli was talking to other professors . . . not just me. We both know that's true. He's been talking to Tolvard in physics.*

Ferraga: *What about?*

Belfort: *Who cares? Don't get distracted. All I'm saying is if Rosser knows there's another full tenured professor in my court, he'll probably back down . . . Please?*

Ferraga: *Katy, you can be quite emotional. But I do care about you, so I'll see what I can do.*

Belfort: *Can you do it today? I know you're meeting with him at four.*

Ferraga: *How do you know that?*

Belfort: *I have my ears to the wall all the time. That's what happens when the chairman of the department hates your guts. Are you going to help me or not?*

Ferraga: *Are you going to fuck me or not?*

Belfort: *You come through, and then I'll come through.*

Ferraga: *You're a whore.*

Belfort: *No, I'm not a whore. I just don't have tenure yet.*

Ferraga: *I meant it as a compliment.*

Belfort: *No you didn't, but I took it as a compliment. Call me whatever you like: bitch, cunt, whore, slut . . . just come the fuck through for me. See you tonight at eleven.*

McAdams blew out air. "She certainly wasn't sensitive when it came to pejoratives."

"Words weren't the problem," Decker said. "It was sticks and stones that got her in the end."

CHAPTER 29

GOING THROUGH STACKS of Belfort's e-mails, Decker paused as his eyes landed on a specific text. He said, "Harvard, listen to this." He read out loud.

It's been an incredibly high-pressured day as all of them have been for the last couple of weeks. You have no idea of the stress that I've been going through because no matter what is said about you, you have the shield of tenure to bounce off the slings and arrows. And after the Christmas party, it was patently obvious that all is not cozy for you as well.

Neither one of us wanted it to come to this, but the situation is untenable. I cannot look in your wife's eyes and pretend. ***I can't go on. The pain is too much.*** *It is with great reluctance when I say to you that things must end now. It's inevitable anyway because the chances of my staying here are very low. Tenure—although well deserved by what I've accomplished—will be impossible with Rosser at the helm.*

I always have and will always think fondly of you. You're a great man and a great mind. I cherish our time together, but we must be practical—a hallmark of our species. Think of me with fondness and perhaps a little love.

"Ferraga lifted the phrase for the fake suicide note from her breakup e-mail," McAdams said. "That's pretty simplistic for a guy of his intelligence."

"Maybe it was the first thing he could think of for a faked suicide note."

"Maybe, but it's still pretty dumb."

"Yes, it is," Decker said. "It points the finger at him."

"Or maybe someone else wanted that finger pointed at him." McAdams leaned back and stretched. He looked at the clock. "Jesus, it's quarter past two."

"I don't have that much more from this pile. I want to finish up."

"How long do you think it'll take?"

"I take notes while I read. I'd say another half hour or so. You can take the car and go home. I can walk."

"I'll wait. I have to file all this stuff anyway." McAdams began to put the correspondence that he had gone over into dated folders. "So Belfort broke it off with Ferraga."

Decker was reading and didn't answer. The room was still for ten minutes, no sounds except for the hum of the heater, the ticking of the clock, and human breathing. Then Decker said, "Okay, listen to this. It was written a week before she died. It's her response to an e-mail he must have written to her . . . which isn't here. This is odd. How did it get deleted from the computer's hard drive?"

"Check further down in her e-mail. Sometimes the previous correspondence is there."

"No, it is *not* there. I checked."

"Jeez, don't bite my head off," McAdams said.

"It's late, I'm snappy, I make no apologies. Just listen." Decker read the text.

> When I mean I can't go on, I mean I can't go on, Aldo. I just don't have that kind of energy inside. We had a good run, but it is really and truly over. Within a few months, I'll probably be leaving, so let's just get a jump-start on our lives, accept the inevitable, and move on.

McAdams said, "Ferraga wasn't ready to let go."

"Yeah, he was still carrying the torch even though it was daylight." Decker kept reading, and then shuffled through the pages for a few minutes. "Nothing from her to him after that. Could be they communicated in some other way."

"Phone or text."

"The phone records should be in tomorrow." Decker lifted his arms way above his head. "They should add to what we already have."

"But we're both thinking how it would play out," McAdams told him. "Ferraga goes over to her house to beg her for a last fling. She refuses. He insists. Things get crazy. She pushes, he pushes, she pushes, and then he pushes again but this time a little too hard. She hits her head on the side table."

"Sure."

"Ferraga panics. He doesn't know what to do. But he realizes he has to do something. He remembers Eli's suicide just days ago and decides to link the two: that makes sense to him because Eli was working for Belfort. He even suggested that there was a strong bond between the two of them when we talked to him. So Ferraga lugs her up the mountain and invents this mythical suicide using the same phrase she used to dump him: 'I can't go on. The pain is too much' or whatever. Poetic justice and all that."

"Sure."

"Why are you being so noncommittal?"

"I am seeing the same scenario you are, Tyler. Ferraga is way up on our list of suspects, but let's not get tunnel vision. We now have a spurned wife to consider. From what Belfort wrote, she might have known what was going on. Maybe she went to Belfort's house and confronted her."

"At one in the morning?"

"She went earlier and Belfort wasn't home."

"So where was Belfort?"

"Trashing Mallon Euler's room? Hiding papers in Mallon's room? Out taking a walk? Who knows? Maybe Ferraga's wife waited outside until Belfort came home and had it out with her."

"Do you see a woman lugging a body up a mountain?"

"That's a good point. It could be that after she killed Belfort, she realized she was in deep trouble and enlisted her husband's help in lugging the body up the mountain. Out of guilt, Ferraga felt obliged to help his wife out."

"Could be."

"While I'm surmising, let's consider Theo Rosser. He and Belfort hated each other. Their e-mail exchanges were always hostile, and from what we've heard, he was trying to get her kicked out of the department. And then there was Belfort's little sideline with the hedge funds. Maybe her extracurricular activities got her into hot water. Maybe she lost someone a lot of money."

McAdams paused. "If it was Belfort's stochastic oscillator that got her into trouble, it could explain why someone other than Belfort broke into Mallon Euler's dorm room."

"Looking for evidence of Belfort's system in Mallon's room."

"So the room trashing could be connected to Belfort's murder." His eyes widened. "Maybe Mallon really is in trouble. Is she safe staying with Damodar Batra?"

"I wouldn't know for sure." Decker smiled. "You're worried?"

"I wouldn't want to see her whacked if that's what you're asking."

"*Whacked?*"

"C'mon. Yes or no? Do you think she's safe?"

"Call her, McAdams. She's probably still up. She's a night owl and she had a nap in the car."

"I'll text her."

"You young 'uns with your fancy phone machines."

McAdams rolled his eyes and texted Mallon. When he was done, he said, "Are you going to pick Ferraga up?"

"Of course I am. I'd like to see if the phone records on Belfort's cell came in. If I see a large amount of traffic between them the night she died, then I'll have even more ammunition when I question him."

"You're not concerned about him running?"

"He hasn't run yet, but he has to know that the affair is going to come out and it'll look bad for him." Decker started neatening the piles of e-mails. "Someone probably should be on watch at his house."

McAdams's phone beeped. He looked down. His fingers flew over the phone window.

"What did she text to you?"

"That she was fine. But I want to make sure it was from her and not Damodar."

"So what did you text back?"

"I asked her where she was today and where she went." His phone beeped. "Okay, she gave me the right answer. I know it's her." Again his fingers tapped the phone screen and then he stowed his cell. "I told her that I'll keep my phone on so she can call me if she needs to. I know I'm encouraging her, but it's that or feeling guilty if something bad happens to her. For some odd reason, she brings out some kind of primal protectiveness."

"Admit it. She's wormed her nerdy way into your heart."

"It's more like I can be around her without getting irritated. You said someone should be watching Ferraga's house. By someone, do you mean us?"

"For me, the night is shot anyway. My mind is reeling, I've had three cups of caffeinated coffee since I got here, and I'm not at all tired. You however might be able to salvage a couple hours of sleep. I can watch Ferraga's house by my lonesome."

"No, no, no," McAdams said. "The Three Musketeers and all that jazz."

"There're only two of us."

"Well, I'm not about to crap out now," McAdams said. "It's a matter of pride."

"I won't argue," Decker said. "And for the record, this is the one time you can be as annoying as you'd like. You can even completely piss me off."

"Anger keeps you awake, right."

"Anger and anxiety," Decker said.

"Same here."

"You've had a lot of sleepless nights, Tyler?"

"More than I care to remember."

AT SIX IN the morning, Decker called in a relief man and went to sleep for four hours, dead to the world. When he woke up at ten, he wiped the cobwebs from his brain with a hot shower, a good breakfast, and the ever-present caffeine fix. He wore a shirt and tie under a black V-neck sweater, a black blazer, and gray wool pants. To Rina, he said, "Kid still sleeping?"

"Yes." She was dressed. Decker hadn't even heard her wake up.

"Don't wake him."

"What's your schedule for today?"

"I have a couple of interviews to do. Anyone call?"

"Ben Roiters said that Ferraga left the house at eight and drove to Kneed Loft. He assigned someone young from the department—had him dress like a student. He's hanging around the hallways, keeping an eye on Ferraga."

"Okay. Good."

"Toni also called. Belfort's last month's phone records are in."

"Then I have work to do." Decker took a final sip of coffee. "What are your plans?"

Rina held up a finger. "One more thing. Tyler said it's important."

"Oh. What?"

"He forgot to tell you last night. He apologizes. He made calls to Professor Zhou's math conference. After talking to a lot of people, he thinks that Professor Zhou actually left the conference early enough to put her back in Greenbury on the night that Belfort died. Tyler has no idea of her whereabouts, but he'll follow it this morning and get a timeline for her movements."

"Huh." Decker stood up. "Well, that changes things."

"What does?" McAdams came shuffling into the kitchen in his pajamas and robe. His hair was a mess and his eyes were red.

"Your revelation about Professor Zhou," Decker said.

"Right. I'm following it up this morning. Give me a minute to shower and change."

"You should eat something," Rina said.

"I'll grab a bagel." He shuffled out of the kitchen and Rina and Decker heard the door close.

"I'm really worried he's not going to do well on his exams," Decker said.

"So solve the case so he can go back to school."

"Sure. Why didn't I think of that?"

Rina laughed, stood on tiptoes, and kissed his cheek. "He's a big boy. He can take care of himself."

"You're right." Decker took out his phone. "Let me just make a quick call."

"Take your time. I'm going to Hillel and meet with the student board. They're planning an on-campus Shabbat Challah Day this Friday . . . get it? Challah Day as holi-day?"

Decker rolled his eyes. "What exactly is Challah Day?"

"We're baking a zillion challahs and distributing them around the campuses. What a hoot."

"You don't have to do it."

"It's fine. I like the kids. I can hear about their problems, be really sympathetic, and not be concerned because I'm not their mothers." Decker didn't answer. Rina said, "You haven't heard a word I said. What's going on?"

"Sorry. I'm just wondering if Belfort and Zhou were on the outs."

McAdams came back in. He was dressed in a suit, but his hair was still wet. "I have no idea. But since she was back in town the night Belfort was murdered, we have to consider Rina's idea. That maybe she trashed Mallon's room. She was pretty darn anxious to get hold of Eli's papers. Maybe she thought that Mallon had them."

"Like I said, makeup and a wig can do wonders," Rina answered.

Decker was still thinking. "I seem to recall e-mails between them—Zhou and Belfort—but it was centered on a thesis committee where I think Zhou was the adviser." He paused. "It was in Belfort's kneedloft.edu account."

"Who was the student?"

"It wasn't Elijah Wolf or Damodar Batra, that much I remember. But the name was familiar. I think I need to start a flowchart."

Rina gave McAdams a paper bag. "Bagel and cream cheese with an apple and an orange. You can get coffee at the station house, although the coffee is terrible. And you should dry your hair before it freezes." She picked up a window scraper. "I'll see you both later."

Decker took it from her. "I'll do that."

"The car has been warming up for fifteen minutes."

"So it shouldn't take me long." He left the warmth of the kitchen without a jacket.

She turned to McAdams. "It makes him feel good."

"He adores you."

"And why not?" McAdams laughed, and Rina said, "How's the studying coming?"

"Fine."

"He's worried about you. I keep telling him you can handle it. And I think you can. But I'm also a little concerned."

McAdams fidgeted. "No need."

"Tyler, crime won't go away after you graduate law school."

"I know. I'm fine, Rina."

Decker came back. "All done." He kissed his wife. "Have a fun time baking."

"At least it will be warm," Rina said.

After she left, McAdams turned to Decker. "Peter, I know you're concerned about my studies. I want you to know that I had a really good day yesterday. I'll come in to the station house for a couple of hours: maybe do the flowchart and pick up the loose ends. I'll be back here in the afternoon to study. So don't worry and we'll both be okay."

Decker blew out air. "What happens if you don't pass?"

"I think I'm put on probation, but I'm not sure. Don't worry. It's not going to happen. I may not ace the exam, but I'll pass."

Decker smoothed his mustache. "All right. Let's get going."

"When are you bringing in Ferraga?"

"As soon as I'm done checking Belfort's phone records. It probably won't be until late afternoon. You'll be studying."

"Maybe." When Decker gave him the stink eye, McAdams said, "Joke. Get it? Joke."

"I'd get it if it was funny. Passing exams isn't a joke."

"You know what? You nag me way more than my parents ever did."

"Too bad about that, Harvard," Decker said. "It's the price you pay for a photo on the piano."

CHAPTER 30

"YOU HAD TO know it would come out."

"Yes, I knew." Under his breath, Ferraga whispered something unintelligible.

"Excuse me?" Decker said. "I didn't catch that."

"I said I'm not an idiot."

"No one thinks you're an idiot. I'm just wondering why you didn't tell me when we first spoke."

"It is an error of omission. I haven't lied about anything."

"That remains an open question," Decker said.

Ferraga's lips pursed, marring his good looks. He had a good head of curly hair and regular features with eyes that were constantly in motion—scanning the small interview room, up at the ceiling then down at the table. He sneaked a quick glance at Decker, and then another at the tape recorder, until his eyes rested on his clasped hands. He wore a white shirt, a brown corduroy jacket with patch pockets, and dark brown pants: very professorial, even down to the sneakers on his feet. He said, "I knew you'd think the worst. I needed time to reflect before I said anything."

"You've been reflecting for five days." Decker leaned over the table. They were sitting in one of the two interview rooms at the station house. "What have you come up with?"

His eyes met Decker's. "If you want to nose into my affairs, I will answer your questions."

"That's good because I'm going to ask you questions. I'm investigating a murder. So why don't you stop stalling and start at the beginning."

"The beginning of the affair?"

"Yes. How did it start?"

A deep sigh. "It was the biggest mistake of my life."

Ferraga's e-mails to Belfort sounded anything but regretful. In fact, they suggested that he wanted more, and more often. He was slow to get the initial words out, but once he started talking, he laid out their relationship with a bantam cock's strut, adding more detail than was necessary. Decker already knew the dates and times from Belfort's communications, but he wanted to hear Ferraga's story to see if his times and dates roughly matched. According to him, their final breakup date was a week before Belfort's death.

"You didn't see her after that?"

"Of course I saw her. She worked down the hall from me. But our communication after that was strictly professional."

Decker said, "We have phone calls between the two of you the afternoon before she died."

"If you say so."

"It's not what I say, it's what her phone records say."

Ferraga suddenly looked defeated. "I did not *kill* her."

"We're not talking about that right now, Aldo." Decker leaned forward. "You called her the afternoon before she died. Three times. What did you two talk about?"

"Nothing important."

"Let me be the judge of that. Do you want to tell me now or do you need another five days to *think* about it?"

"It wasn't personal. It was professional. She had been complaining to me about Theo Rosser, as usual. If you read her e-mails, you must know how she feels about him."

"So you called her up to hear her complain?"

"No, no, no. We were talking in her office. And it was the day *before* she died. Check with her secretary if you don't believe me."

"I will. But we're not talking about that right now. We're talking about phone calls on the *day* she died. Why did *you* call *her* up?"

"Okay." He took a deep breath and let it out slowly. "I'll explain. We're on quite a lot of thesis committees together. Our faculty is small and our students rotate the same ten professors." A pause. "I had some questions about the logic in one of her student's paper."

"Which student?"

"Mallon Euler. Naturally, she launched into a diatribe about Rosser, claiming that Mallon was having a very hard time with him because he's a misogynist—which has some truth to it. But I just kept my mouth shut and let her talk."

"You called her three times."

"Okay, okay." Ferraga picked up a glass of water and drank half of it. "After she had done some initial ranting about Rosser, I mentioned a problem with Mallon's line of thought that should be addressed, something that *potentially* Rosser could take issue with when Mallon defended. Katrina appreciated my heads-up. Normally, it isn't correct protocol to warn a student ahead of time, but I thought that Mallon deserved a little help. Rosser is hard on her."

"That explains one phone call. Two more to go, Aldo."

"Right. About a minute or two later, I called her back. I asked her if she'd like to meet with me so we could talk about Mallon's issue in person. She said no. She understood my concerns. She thanked me and we hung up."

"That brings it up to two calls."

"The third call was a mistake. I missed a call at my desk and thought it might be her. That she had changed her mind about talking in person. But she claimed it wasn't she who had called me. That call lasted fifteen seconds. And, by your own admission, there were no calls beyond that afternoon."

"It doesn't mean you didn't go over there."

"I didn't *kill* her."

"We're still not up to that part yet."

"Why on earth would I kill her?"

"Do you want me to answer that?"

"My wife already knew."

That might have been the truth. Katrina had intimated in her e-mails that the wife did know. Decker said, "How did she take it?"

"Olivia is a mature woman. We Europeans have a different concept of affairs."

"If Olivia had such a mature attitude, why try to hide it in the first place. And I read the e-mails, Aldo. You two were sneaking around her all the time."

"There's no need to throw things in her face." He looked down. "Olivia and I have both . . . experimented from time to time."

The professor wouldn't make eye contact. Decker knew he was telling half-truths. "This wasn't just an experiment, Aldo. By the depths of your letters, it was clear you were obsessed with Katrina Belfort."

"The sex was good, I will admit. But there are always others."

"This brings us back to my first question. Why didn't you tell me about the affair the first time I spoke to you, if you have such a casual attitude toward trysts?"

"I wasn't worried about Olivia, I was worried what you would think. And by these questions, I see that my fears have been borne out. It's a small town with a small-town police department. People jump to conclusions."

"It's not jumping to conclusions, it's reality. You and Katrina were having sex."

No response.

Decker kept his face flat. "Let's go over the three phone calls again."

"That's not necessary. Either arrest me or let me go."

"I thought you were going to answer all my questions?"

"Arrest me or let me go."

There was only one person in the room who dictated the terms of an interview. "Fine." Decker stood up and took out a set of hand-cuffs. "Stand up, please. Aldo Ferraga, you are under arrest for the murder—"

"Wait, wait, wait." His face had gone pale. "You can't be serious."

"You gave me the ultimatum. I have no trouble arresting you."

"On what basis?"

"You don't really want me to answer that."

"What do you *want* from me?"

Decker pointed to the chair and they both sat down. He said, "Aldo, you could have e-mailed Katrina any questions you had about Mallon, but you chose to call her."

"No I couldn't e-mail Katrina. I was already compromised by telling her my concerns. I didn't dare put it in writing. It's not the usual protocol to give feedback before a student defends unless it's *your* student. And Mallon wasn't my student."

Decker looked up from his notepad. "Or perhaps you were hoping to curry favor with Katrina by helping Mallon."

"I was doing something nice for Katrina and for Mallon. I didn't expect anything back. And it was the reason why I suggested that Katrina and I meet in person. I didn't want to discuss this at length over the phone. I don't believe that anyone was listening in, but I thought it was more prudent to talk face-to-face."

"I can believe your first phone call. I can even believe the second one. I'm having a hard time with the third. That you just thought you had a missed call from her."

Ferraga fidgeted and looked down.

"Aldo, this is a murder investigation. I'm sensing that you don't believe the gravity of the situation. Just tell the truth."

"I called her to ask her to reconsider meeting in person. I told her to bring Mallon if she thought my intentions were less than honorable."

"Okay." Decker smiled. "That makes more sense. See how easy that was?"

Ferraga was silent.

Decker said, "Katrina still refused?"

"Yes. I didn't call her after that and I certainly didn't meet with her. It was my last interaction with her." He whispered, "I'm glad I was nice."

Decker regarded the man, played the conversation in his head. He was inclined to believe him—so far. "Tell me about the night she died. Where you were and what you were doing."

"I told you, I was home the entire time. My wife can vouch for that."

"She vouches for you, you vouch for her. I have no way of knowing if either one of you is telling the truth. For all I know, Olivia could have gone over there and had it out with Katrina Belfort."

"That is completely ridiculous!"

"Not from where I'm sitting. I can see her having a heated conversation with your ex-lover and things escalating to the point of disaster. She murders her and then calls you up asking for help to cart her up the mountain." Decker again leaned over the table. "There might just be a late-night phone call from your wife on the night that Katrina died. Do you mind if I check your cell phone?"

Ferraga blanched. "You haven't invaded my privacy enough?"

"Do you want to clear yourself or not?"

Ferraga looked at the ceiling. "Shit!"

Decker leaned back and paused. Then he spoke gently. "What's wrong, Aldo? Tell me. Get it off your chest. You'll feel lighter."

"I did not *kill* her!"

"And your wife?"

"No, of course not!"

"And yet you do not want me to see your phone calls?"

Ferraga took out his phone and gave it to him.

After scrolling through to find the date, Decker stopped when he reached a number. "You called your house at eleven-fifteen the night Katrina died. What was that about?"

"I told Olivia I was working late."

"You talked for twenty minutes. Telling your spouse you're working late is a two-minute call."

Silence. Decker waited him out.

Ferraga said, "We had words."

"About?"

"She thought I was with Katrina."

"And?"

"I wasn't. I was in my office working." When Decker didn't respond, Ferraga said, "I do work."

"I don't suppose that there's anyone out there who saw you in your office?"

"What do you think?"

"So now Olivia can't alibi you even though she did. You both lied. This is a problem."

"I loved Katrina!"

"I don't doubt that, Aldo. But lots of women are murdered by people who love them."

"I didn't . . ." He slapped his forehead and then he talked with animation. "Dr. Zhou. She has the office right next to mine. She was in her office that night. It must have been close to one."

"She saw you at one in the morning in your office?"

"No, she didn't see me, but I could certainly hear her. It was her voice. I remember being surprised because I thought she was still away at the Preston conference. She was having words with a man and it got loud. I was concerned. I knocked on her door—which was locked—and asked if everything was okay."

"And?"

"She said she was fine. She apologized for the disturbance. After that, I went back to my work and came home around two-thirty. When I got into bed, Olivia stirred and glanced at the clock. She will tell you that." When Decker didn't answer, Ferraga said, "I swear that is the truth."

"Are you willing to swear on a polygraph?"

Ferraga made a face. "Is that really necessary? It isn't admissible in court, but I suppose you know that."

"It helps us rule out people sometimes. And if you're telling the truth, you shouldn't have any objections."

"I don't have any objections." He paused. "I'd like this to be done as discreetly as possible."

"I'll be discreet as long as you show up. So it's a go?"

"Yes . . ." Ferraga was resigned. "When would this be?"

"The polygraph? I could probably set something up tomorrow."

"That soon?"

"Why? Do you need to reflect again?"

Ferraga's face held a pained expression. "What time?"

"Let me call up the examiner and I'll let you know."

"May I leave now?"

Decker didn't answer. Instead he said, "So she never opened the door . . . Dr. Zhou."

"No. Under the circumstances, I wish she would have. Just ask her."

"You said she was arguing with a man."

"Yes."

"Did you hear any of the contents of the argument?"

"No. I wasn't eavesdropping. But when it got very loud, I became concerned."

"No words at all?"

"Let me think . . ." He sighed. "Something about a thesis, I believe. Maybe Katrina's name came up."

"Are you saying that for my benefit? To deflect suspicion onto someone else?"

"You *asked* me."

"Yes, I did. So you heard Dr. Zhou arguing with a man."

"Yes."

"Any idea who the man was?"

"No."

"But you're sure you heard Dr. Zhou's voice."

"She answered me when I asked if everything was okay. I assumed it was her. Who else would be in her office?"

"Did she often have arguments?"

"Not often."

"Occasionally?"

"I've heard her voice get loud now and then. I'm sure I get loud now and then."

"Any idea who she has argued with in the past?"

Ferraga shrugged. "If I knew, I don't remember now."

Decker said, "How did she get along with Rosser?"

"Why don't you ask her that question?"

"I will, but right now I'm asking you. You said that Rosser was a misogynist, so I was wondering about his relationship with Dr. Zhou."

"Katrina said Rosser was a misogynist. I did not."

"But you said there was some truth in it."

Ferraga was getting exasperated. "So far as I knew, Zhou and Rosser got along fine. Their duties were quite different. There wasn't much . . ." He winced. "Academic competition."

"What are Zhou's duties?"

"She's the dean of residency and student life at Kneed Loft."

"Does she have tenure?"

"Of course."

"I know she's in the math department. Does she still teach or publish?"

"I think her publishing days are behind her."

"She still goes to conferences."

"She likes to keep current. But she doesn't care about publishing. She's a full professor. She's been with the school longer than Rosser."

Decker said, "And you have no idea who she might have been arguing with?"

"No."

"And you're sure she wasn't arguing with Rosser?"

"I'm not positive, but it didn't sound like his voice."

"Did the voice sound familiar?"

Ferraga gave the question some thought. "If I had to guess—and it is a guess—I'd say she was arguing with a student."

"A student?"

"There was that mention of a thesis. And it didn't sound like she was talking to a faculty member. She was really dressing him down. Only a student would take that without storming out."

"Which students would she be talking to?"

"It could have been anyone in the college. More likely it was probably one of her RAs who messed up."

"You think it was an RA."

"I don't know for certain, but probably."

"How many male RAs does she supervise?"

"I don't know offhand. Maybe ten."

"Was she particularly close to any of them?"

"I don't know. Why would I know?"

"Well, you know more than I do," Decker said. "Take a guess."

Ferraga said, "Lin has a couple of graduate students who also work as RAs—Scott Sumpter and Alistair Dixon."

Decker perked up at Dixon's name. He was the graduate student who had first recognized Eli from the postmortem photo. He was anxious to help when Decker and McAdams first started investigating Eli's death. "And you didn't recognize the voice as belonging to either of them?"

"Maybe Alistair, although I'm not sure. Both of them are bright boys but no geniuses. Otherwise why would they be here for graduate school instead of Princeton or Berkeley?"

"Elijah Wolf was here."

"That's because his parents refused to let him go anywhere else."

Probably the first true statement that had come out of Ferraga's mouth. Decker handed him back his phone and said, "I'll set up the polygraph. You're free to go, but stick close to Greenbury."

After Ferraga left, Decker took out his cell and called McAdams. He took out his cell and called McAdams. "How's the studying coming?"

"Do you need me? I'm dying to take a break. It's been three straight hours."

"Tell me again why Professor Zhou returned early to Greenbury?"

"Migraine. That part seems to be true. I talked to several people at the conference who said that Zhou had been complaining of awful headaches the entire time."

"What time did she arrive in Greenbury?"

"Around nine in the evening."

"What did she do when she got in?"

"She said she went home and straight to bed."

"Really." Decker recapped his conversation with Ferraga.

"So she was lying."

"Or Ferraga is lying. We already know he lies. I'm withholding judgment on Zhou until proven guilty."

"You're going to talk to her, right?"

"Yes, I am. Do you want to come?"

"I thought you'd never ask."

CHAPTER 31

PACING IN HER meticulously appointed office, Dr. Zhou stomped back and forth in black pumps, her heels clomping on the wooden floor. Her hand was touching her forehead.

"Yes, I left because of a migraine. I get migraines all the time. *This* place gives me migraines." She wore a red knit dress. There was a black blazer hanging on the back of her desk chair. "And yes, Dr. Ferraga did knock on my door at around one in the morning that night . . . what was it, Wednesday? It was the night poor Katrina . . . anyway, he knocked, asking if I was okay. I wasn't okay, but it was none of his business. By the time I left my office, it was close to daylight. I had a pile of work to catch up on, and since I couldn't sleep, I thought I might as well clear my desk."

Decker nodded. "You left your office around . . . what? Five? Six?"

"It was almost six. I stopped by Bagelmania and picked up breakfast. Then I went home and attempted a nap, but my head was pounding and I was sick to my stomach. Finally, the medicine kicked in and I came back to my office to finish up my work. After that, I nursed myself at home for two days because I wasn't supposed to be in town anyway. I turned off the lights, turned off the phone, took a sedative, and slept for two days straight. I didn't even hear about poor Katrina until the following Saturday when I returned to my office. Then that nonsense with Theo and Lennaeus happened, drawing me out of my cocoon. God, they are morons!"

"What time did you return to your office on Saturday, Dean Zhou?"

"Around eleven in the morning." She sat in her desk chair and opened the drawer. She popped another pill in her mouth. "All this has been terrible for my health. Poor Katrina. I suppose I'm still in shock."

"What do you know about it?"

"The affair or her demise? I don't know anything about her death."

"But you knew about the affair?"

"Everyone knew about the affair. No one cared except maybe Aldo's wife."

"What about Theo Rosser?"

"Yes, he'd care if he knew."

"So not everyone knew."

"Theo isn't perceptive when it comes to his faculty and students. I'm left to pick up the pieces. By the way, did you ever find out what was in Elijah Wolf's math papers?"

"We did."

"Anything significant?"

"No."

She was waiting for more information. Decker changed the subject. "Who were you arguing with the night Katrina died?"

"Pardon?"

"When Ferraga knocked on your door and asked if you were all right. Who were you arguing with?"

"What I was shouting about has nothing to do with poor Katrina. But I'll answer you anyway. I was arguing with Alistair Dixon. He's one of my grad students."

McAdams glanced at Decker. He said, "We met Alistair when we met you: the night we were asking questions about Elijah's death."

"Yes. Right, of course. I remember now."

"What were you two arguing about?"

"His sloppy work." She shook her head then regretted the movement. "For God's sake, this isn't Princeton. It's not *that* hard to get an M.A. We're not asking for a proof of Fermat's Theorem, we're asking for a simple mathematical idea that might be expanded upon in the future."

"I thought someone proved Fermat's Last Theorem," McAdams said.

"Andrew Wiles. What does that have to do with anything?"

"Nothing," Decker said. "What is Alistair Dixon working on?"

"I can't tell you that. That would violate his privacy. But you can ask Alistair if you're so *curious*." She realized her tone was sarcastic. "I'm not feeling well. You'll have to give me a pass if I seem snide."

"We're aware of that," Decker said. "Thank you for talking to us."

Her answer was a dismissive wave.

"If I name a few possible math topics, could you give me a yes or no?"

"No, I will not give you a yes or no. But feel free to ask."

Something was brewing in Decker's head. He couldn't quite place it yet, but the idea would blossom eventually. He said, "Does it have to do with Fourier analysis? It seems to be a very popular subject around here."

She appeared surprised. "It is not and was never *my* field of interest."

"But it was Katrina Belfort's field of interest."

"Alistair was working with me, not Katrina."

"Does it have to do with Fourier analysis?" Decker repeated. "A simple yes or no."

When she didn't answer, McAdams leaned over to Decker and showed him his notepad. Decker said, "Go ahead and ask her."

McAdams said, "Does it have to do with stochastic oscillator momentum and stock theory?"

She flushed with anger. "So if you already talked to Alistair, why are you bothering me?"

"We haven't talked to Alistair," Decker said.

"Yet," McAdams added.

Zhou opened and closed her mouth. "Don't tell me it was a lucky guess." She stood up, winced, and then sat back down. "What's going on?"

Decker said, "Did you know that Dr. Belfort had been employed by hedge funds? She was using her own variation of the stochastic oscillator index to predict daily market movement."

The woman ran her tongue in her mouth several times. "How did you find this out?"

"Never mind about my sources, what do you know about Belfort's moonlighting?"

"This is the first I've heard about it."

"You wouldn't be lying to me, right?"

"Why would I lie to you?"

"Because employment outside of the department is usually frowned upon. If you knew about it, it could reflect poorly on you."

"I'm not lying. I didn't know about it. And I'm *positive* that Theo doesn't know about it. He would *not* approve."

"How did Alistair Dixon decide upon his topic?"

"He started out on something different and switched to Fourier and stochastic oscillator theory about a year ago."

"And you approved the change of topic?"

"I did, but with reservations. It's only a two-year program. That's not a lot of time to develop a thesis. He had a lot of catch-up to do, but he assured me it wasn't a problem. Then when I read a draft of his thesis coming home on the train from the conference, I was utterly shocked by how many holes he had in his logic. It wasn't as if he had to prove something ingenious, but there had to be some mathematical basis for what he was suggesting."

"What was Dixon's relationship to Dr. Belfort?"

"So far as I knew, there was no relationship. This is very bizarre. Who told you that Katrina was moonlighting?"

Decker sidestepped the question. "If Theo Rosser found out about her extra job, how do you think he'd handle it?"

"What do you mean?"

"We're working on the assumption that Dr. Belfort was murdered."

A pause. Then Zhou said, "Oh please! Theo didn't murder Katrina because she moonlighted. Had he found out, he'd use it to fire her and ruin her chances of getting another job. He detested her."

"So we've heard," McAdams said. "Any idea why he hated her other than misogyny?"

"Theo has no love for women, but if you flatter him the right way, he's a pussycat. She could have had him eat—" She didn't finish. "Never mind."

Decker smiled. "Eating out of the palm of her hand?"

The dean was quiet. McAdams thought a moment. "Okay. I get it. He had a thing for her and it wasn't reciprocated."

"No, you're wrong," Zhou insisted. "He hated her."

"Fine line between love and hate and all that jazz."

Zhou didn't argue. "I don't know. Could be. He started off very enthused about her, but it quickly changed. Katrina could be a charmer, but she also was ambitious. Maybe Theo just didn't like the combination."

"How do you think he would have reacted if he'd known about the affair? Do you think Theo would have actually fired her?"

"It's very difficult to fire a person for moral turpitude once there is tenure."

"She didn't have tenure."

"But Aldo did. He would have had to go as well or else we risk opening ourselves up to sexual discrimination."

"Let's get back to where you were the night of Katrina's death," Decker said. "You say that Ferraga knocked on your door at about one in the morning?"

"Yes."

"Okay. When did Dixon come to your office?"

"It must have been a half hour before."

"Around twelve-thirty?" Decker made a face. "A little late for an academic meeting."

"When I got home, I e-mailed him my concerns. He asked if we might meet as soon as possible. Since I couldn't sleep and I was in my office anyway, I told him if he wanted to drop by, I'd talk to him. Students are up late. So yes, he came in around twelve-thirty."

"How did he respond when you told him your concerns about the paper?"

"He wasn't happy, of course. He said it was a work in progress." She paused. "He got upset. I really reamed him out. I could have handled it better."

"When did he leave your office?"

"I didn't look at the clock. I think we talked for around forty-five minutes, so he probably left around fifteen after one."

"Do you know where he went after that?"

"No idea. I would think he'd gone back to his dorm or the library."

"But you don't know."

"No, I do not know."

"Did you talk to him the following morning?"

"I talked to him the following day. It was in the afternoon, I believe. He was still very upset. I would have thought he'd be over it by now."

Maybe he was upset for other reasons. Decker folded his notebook and handed her his card. "If you should think of anything else, give me a call."

"I have a question," McAdams said. "Did Rosser ever appear jealous of Ferraga?"

"Nothing naked, but Theo is, by nature, a jealous man."

"How is his jealousy manifested?"

"I might have spoken out of turn. It's just my opinion."

"Please," Decker said. "Tell us what you think."

"Theo isn't a team player. He isn't wild about the successes of his faculty, even though they reflect well on him as head of the department. He especially doesn't like ambitious women. Katrina wasn't the first woman with whom he has had conflict."

"You mean Mallon Euler?" McAdams asked.

"No, I was referring to another female faculty member, who left four years ago. But yes, I do believe he is a little rough on Mallon."

"Have you ever talked to him about it?" Decker asked.

"I've made some small talk about it. He just denies the problem. That's Theo's style."

"Being pigheaded?" Decker asked.

"That's a bit harsh."

"How would you put it?"

"Theo is a remarkable man. He should have been full-time faculty at Harvard or Princeton or Berkeley. But he gets fixated on a person or an idea and he won't let go. Persistence is helpful in math *if* you're on the right track. But sometimes you've got to stop working an idea to death no matter how brilliant you think it is. Sometimes you've got to learn to switch gears."

AFTER THEY LEFT the building, McAdams said, "When you think of venal professions, mathematics doesn't jump right out at you. But I guess the pettiness of academia cuts across the board."

"People are people."

"Profound."

"You don't have to be profound to be right."

McAdams chuckled, pulled up the collar on his navy cashmere coat, and tightened his scarf. "Want me to call Alistair Dixon?"

"Yes. Let's set something up in an hour if you can. I'm going to Bagelmania to try to confirm Lin's alibi the morning after the murder. Want me to grab you anything?"

"No, I'm fine right now." McAdams took out his phone to look up Alistair Dixon's cell number. "She still could have done it, you know. There was plenty of time between two and six to get in an argument with someone and push Katrina into a table."

"Of course."

"But you don't suspect her." McAdams punched in the numbers. "I can tell that by now—who you think is innocent and who you think has something to hide."

"She sounded truthful. She said she was in Bagelmania at six in the morning. If she was lying about that, then I'll change my mind."

"Voice mail, hold on."

"Give him my number as a callback."

"Don't trust me?"

"I want to talk to him."

"Whatever."

Decker paused until McAdams stowed his phone into his pocket. Then he said, "Dean Zhou was right about switching gears. We're working on the assumption that Theo Rosser hates Katrina, and then you mention that he had a thing for her . . . it potentially changes the entire complexion of the case. Good for you, Harvard."

"Thanks." He thought a moment. "So, you suspect Rosser?"

"If he felt that Katrina had spurned him, who knows what was boiling up inside him. Then we also have Dixon, who was doing his master's thesis on the stochastic oscillator indicator, switching to the topic a year into the program. Where did that come from?"

"Maybe he was also working for Katrina."

"Mallon and Damodar never mentioned Dixon on the team, but maybe Katrina had several teams helping her out."

"Want me to call up Mallon and ask her about it?"

"Not yet." Decker paused. "Something hit me when I was talking to Zhou. It just came to me. She mentioned that Dixon's paper was sloppy. Maybe he needed better data. How do you like the idea that he broke into Mallon's room trying to find *her* data?"

"Uh, I don't think you can turn Dixon into Mallon no matter how professional the wig or the makeup job. He's a beefy guy."

"So he hired someone to break in."

McAdams shrugged. "And when he couldn't find what he needed in Mallon's room, he went to Belfort's house. They argued and he pushed her."

"Or he broke into Belfort's house hoping to find her data. Maybe she heard him, woke up, and that's when he pushed her."

Decker's phone rang: it was Dixon. After introductions, Decker said, "I am trying to establish where people were on the night of Katrina Belfort's death. Dr. Ferraga said he knocked on Dr. Zhou's door at about one in the morning and you were there . . . yes, Dr. Zhou told me . . . yes, I know that you didn't see him. But I need a statement. Could you come in to the station house . . . no, not over the phone. I'll need a signature. It will only take a few minutes . . ." Decker looked at his watch. "Around four? Okay, I'll see you then. Thank you . . ." He hung up.

"How'd he sound?" McAdams asked.

"Nervous, but all people sound nervous when dealing with the police."

McAdams checked his watch. "That's two hours from now."

"The boy can add."

"See what four years of college can do."

Decker smiled. "I can follow up on Dean Zhou's alibi by myself. Go home and study."

"Okay."

Decker held his chest. "Uh, what did you say? Did you actually agree with me?"

"Very funny."

"I should video rare moments like this. It's *almost* as rare as one of my kids agreeing with me."

"Don't play that benighted detective crap on me, Decker. You don't brook shit from no one. Which technically means you brook shit from everyone. Anyway, you get the gist of what I'm saying. You're as shrewd as they come. You just mask it better than someone like my dad."

"Anyone could mask it better than your dad."

"Now, that is true. I still want to be there when you interview Dixon. He's my age. I think I'd be an asset."

"Definitely."

Tyler smiled. "Why, thank you, boss."

"You're welcome." Decker threw his arm around the kid. "We make a good team, Harvard. You give me youth and I give you gravitas."

CHAPTER 32

DIXON WAS ESCORTED into one of the two interview rooms at the station house. The area was small, accommodating a table where Decker sat with a pad of paper and three chairs. McAdams was setting up a video recorder that had been mounted on the wall. Decker looked up, saw Dixon, and poured three glasses of water. "Have a seat."

"Uh, I thought I was here to sign a statement." The young man's eyes traveled between the tape recorder and the lone empty chair. A bead of sweat traveled down his forehead.

"Yes, that's right," Decker said. "You can take your jacket off. No sense becoming overheated."

"How long is this going to take?"

"Not too long," Decker said.

"Can you give me an approximation?"

"Have a seat, Alistair. The quicker we do this, the quicker you're out of here."

Dixon took off his parka, his hat and gloves, and his scarf. He laid them on the back of the chair and sat down. The kid was solidly built, but his stature was on the shorter side. He had brown curly hair, light brown eyes. His cheeks were probably red from the cold. Decker slid a blank pad of paper over to him.

"Write down what time you went to see Dr. Zhou, what time Dr. Ferraga knocked on the door, and what time you left Dr. Zhou's office. Also, write down where you went when you left Dr. Zhou's office and what time you arrived there."

"Why? I thought all you wanted me to do is write an official statement."

"That's what I'm asking you to do. Write an official statement."

"I thought this was about Dr. Ferraga."

"It is about him."

"So why do you need to know where I went?"

Decker said to McAdams, "Is the video on?"

"It is." McAdams stepped down from the stepladder. "At least, that's what the indicator light says."

"Good enough." Decker spoke into a table mic. "This is Detective Peter Decker and I'm talking to Alistair Dixon." He looked at his watch and gave the date and the time.

Dixon's eyes darted from man to man. "Why are you recording me?"

"Do you have a problem with it?"

"Uh, yeah."

"Why's that?"

"It just makes me look . . ." Dixon's voice trailed off. Decker waited him out. "I'm just uncomfortable being recorded."

"It's the way it's done officially."

"Yeah, if you're a suspect in something."

Decker smiled. "You watch too many cop shows. We record everything. It's routine. Are you finished writing your statement?"

"I haven't even started." Dixon sighed. "What do you want? Like just the times?"

"The times and what you were doing."

"Right." It took Alistair about ten minutes. Afterward, he said, "Can I go now?"

"I want to go over the statement with you. It shouldn't take long."

An exaggerated and exasperated sigh. "Why?"

"So I don't make mistakes." Decker read the statement to himself and then gave it to McAdams to scan. "You went to Dr. Zhou's office at around twelve-thirty at night."

"Yes."

"A little late to be working," Decker said.

"What is this?" His expression was angry. "Are you going to question me?"

"Do you have any objection to my asking you a few questions?"

"I do if they're pointed questions."

"Just questions of clarification."

"When you say it's a little late to be working, it sounds like I did something wrong."

"No, no, no. I'm just wondering if you normally meet with Dr. Zhou in the late hours of the night. Maybe it's the only time she can see you."

Dixon sat back in his seat. "Okay. So I know you talked to Zhou. What did she tell you?"

"This is what I do know. I know you were having a heated argument with her and it was loud enough for Dr. Ferraga to knock on the door and ask if everything was all right."

"We were having a healthy academic debate. That's all."

"Free speech is still part of America," McAdams said. "What was the debate over?"

"You wouldn't understand."

"Why's that?"

"The math is complicated."

"So you were arguing over esoterica in your math thesis?"

"How do you know it was about my math thesis? Did she tell you that?"

Decker said, "From what Dr. Ferraga told us, it sounded like Dr. Zhou was doing most of the arguing. What was she so angry about?"

"This is beginning to sound like more than a few questions."

"Alistair . . ." Decker leaned over. "Dr. Zhou told us some things. Dr. Ferraga told us some things. The department is small and Katrina Belfort is dead. We're just trying to verify where everyone was on that night and what they were doing."

"So this is about Katrina Belfort."

"Of course. What did you think it was about?"

Dixon didn't answer. Then he said, "I was with Lin from roughly twelve-thirty to around one-thirty. Can I go now?"

"Where did you go after you left Dr. Zhou's office?"

"I went back to the dorm and went to bed."

"About what time was that?"

"I walked home." He averted his glance. "It was around two in the morning."

Decker scribbled on his notepad. "Is there anyone who saw you at your dorm around that time?"

"No." He was offended. "Everyone was sleeping."

McAdams said, "Everyone was sleeping in a college dorm at two in the morning? Man, things have changed in three years."

Decker said, "Alistair, we both know it's impossible to get privacy in a dorm. There are always some night owls lurking around the common room fridge, looking for munchies."

"I didn't see anyone. Look, I answered your questions. I'm going to go now."

Decker said, "So if we checked the electronic swipes hooked up to the entrance to your dormitory, we'd find that you clocked into the building sometime between one-thirty and two?"

Dixon's face went pale. "Uh, someone opened the door for me."

"So someone saw you enter your dorm," Decker said. "Even better. I need the name."

Dixon exhaled. "I don't know who it was."

"Wasn't it you who told me that Kneed Loft was a very small school?"

"I don't know everyone in the school and I don't know everyone in the consortium."

"But you should know everyone in your dorm since you're the RA," McAdams said. "And you should know if a stranger is entering your dorm at two in the morning."

Decker said, "Obviously you didn't go home. Where'd you go?"

Dixon answered with feigned anger. "Do I need a lawyer?"

"You tell me."

"Unless you have a legal reason to detain me, I'm done here."

"This is the deal, Alistair," Decker said. "You can go. But we're working on a murder investigation. We're also trying to figure out who broke into Mallon Euler's dorm room because the two events may be tied together. What do you know about that?"

"Nothing! How could I? I was with Dr. Zhou when it happened."

"Okay, let's break down that sentence, Alistair," Decker said. "Yes, you were with Dr. Zhou. That means you couldn't have ransacked her room. But that does not mean that you didn't have something to do with the break-in."

"Why would I break into Mallon's room?" More emphatic. "*Why?*"

McAdams said, "Maybe you were looking for data on stochastic oscillator indicators. We both know that Mallon was doing analysis in the field."

Dixon opened and closed his mouth. He couldn't seem to get the words out.

He stood up, pitched forward, and used his chair to regain his balance. "I'm going now."

"That's fine," Decker said. "But let me leave you with this thought. If you did have something to do with Mallon's break-in and you did ask someone to help you find her data for your 'work-in-progress' thesis, we're going to find out about your involvement.

And in a school this small, it won't take long. And if you leave without telling us what you know about it, it will look very, very bad for you. And because we're investigating Katrina Belfort's death, your name is going to go to the top of the list. Because that's what happens when you lie to the police."

Dixon's brow got moist and his hands started shaking. "I had nothing to do with Katrina's death! *Nothing!*"

"Just like you had nothing to do with Mallon's break-in?"

"Shit!" The kid sat back down and covered his face with his hands. He then looked at Decker. "I did not *kill* Katrina Belfort. I barely had anything to do with her when she was alive. *Why* would I kill her?"

"We're not up to that part yet, Alistair." Decker paused. "We're not even up to Mallon Euler's break-in. Talk to me about the stochastic oscillator indicator. How did you become interested in exploring it for your thesis?"

"It was something I was always interested in."

"That's not true, Alistair. Dr. Zhou told us you switched topics after a year."

Dixon looked at the tabletop. He was silent.

McAdams said, "Alistair, I did a senior thesis at Harvard. It's hard to find something new. It is a pure pain in the butt. And it's not unusual to switch topics."

"So I switched topics. So what?"

Decker said, "So how'd you decide upon doing the mathematics of the stochastic oscillator indicator for your master's thesis?"

"My first topic wasn't going in the direction I wanted. I was fooling around with applications of Fourier analysis and waves and I hit on the stochastic oscillator indicator. It was something of practical use that interested me."

"The indicator has been around for ages. You obviously were looking at it from a new perspective."

"Right. Exactly."

"Tell us about it."

"It's very mathematical."

"Oh for Christ's sake!" McAdams blurted out. "Stop hiding behind numbers. We know that there was a group looking at the indicator with fresh sets of eyes. We know that Mallon Euler was in that group. So just tell the goddamn truth so we don't have to constantly repeat ourselves."

Decker was surprised by the outburst, but it seemed to wake Dixon up. He said, "Let's try it from the beginning—again. Who told you about the stochastic oscillator index, Alistair?"

"It's a well-known mathematical indicator."

"Answer the question, Dixon," McAdams said. "Who told you about it?"

A resigned exhale. "Damodar Batra. We just got to talking one day and he mentioned he was doing some innovative work on the stochastic oscillator indicator. It sounded . . . promising." He looked down, then back up. "Like I said, I was struggling with my first topic. It just . . . and Lin can be . . . whatever. What Damodar was doing sounded interesting and not too difficult. So I asked Lin if I could switch topics, and after some convincing, she said okay."

"And it went okay for a while, but then you got stuck," McAdams said. "So you went back to Damodar to ask some questions and he had reservations about helping you."

"Have you talked to Damodar already?" Dixon asked.

"Not yet," McAdams said. "But we will. We'll need confirmation. So just get it all out there. Like Detective Decker said, it looks bad to hold back."

Dixon shook his head. "Batra got super pissed when he found out that I had changed my thesis topic. He said the information that he had given me wasn't for public consumption, and if anyone found out, he'd be in deep shit. I told him that the stochastic oscillator indicator had been around for a long time. That all I was doing was a practical application of Fourier analysis with my own spin."

Decker said, "What was your own spin?"

"I don't want to sound like a snob, but it really involves a lot of math."

"Let me guess. You were using Dr. Belfort's algorithm. Except that piece of intellectual property didn't belong to you. It didn't even belong to Damodar."

Dixon blew out air. His eyes got wet.

McAdams said, "Batra threatened to report you."

"He did." Dixon looked down. "But then I threatened to report him. Because what Dr. Belfort was doing wasn't sanctioned by the department. It could have screwed both of them. In the end, neither of us reported anything and we stopped speaking to each other. If anyone had a grudge against Belfort, it would be Batra, not me."

"Why would Damodar have a grudge against Belfort?" McAdams asked.

"He felt she wasn't paying him nearly enough to do the grunt work."

"But you're the one co-opting Belfort's work as your own," Decker said. "Maybe she found out about it. Maybe she was going to expose you."

"She couldn't expose me without exposing herself," Dixon said.

"So you had spoken to Dr. Belfort on the topic."

"No!" Dixon was adamant. "I don't think she even knew about my thesis. She wasn't on my committee, so there wouldn't be any reason that she'd know about it."

"Maybe she found out," Decker said. "Maybe Batra told her."

"That would put him in the weeds. I guarantee you that he never told her." Dixon dry-washed his face. "Look. I did . . . borrow the topic. But honestly, I was trying to put my own spin on it."

"But your own spin wasn't working too well," Decker said. "We know that Dr. Zhou read your paper and had problems with it. She called you when she came back from her conference and expressed her concerns."

"She told us your paper was a mess," McAdams said.

"It wasn't a mess!" Dixon lowered his voice. "Of course, it needed some adjustments, but it wasn't a mess."

"But you needed help," Decker said. "You needed data. You couldn't break into Batra's room because he'd immediately suspect you. Eli was dead and his room cleaned out, so there was no luck with him. That left Ari and Mallon. You had no idea where Ari was, so you couldn't take the chance of breaking into his room. He could walk in at any moment. But you knew Mallon went to the library that night. So it had to be Mallon by default."

The room fell silent.

"Okay . . ." Dixon whispered. He put his hands together as if in prayer and touched the fingertips to his lips. Then he said, "I admit that I asked a friend to go to Mallon's room and see if she had any papers that might help me."

"How would your friend know what to look for?" McAdams asked.

"She's a math major."

"And she agreed?"

"She was a friend." He paused. "She has a thing for me."

"Did she find anything?"

"Unfortunately no. Dr. Belfort must have kept all the paperwork at her house."

"So you left Dr. Zhou's office and then you met up with your accomplice," Decker said.

"She wasn't an accomplice. She was just doing me a favor."

"She broke into Mallon's dorm room and ransacked it trying to steal data for you. That would qualify in my dictionary as an accomplice. I'll need a name."

"*Please* keep her out of it."

"I have to talk to her. What's her name?"

"God, I've made a mess of things."

"Name, Alistair."

"Lucinda Rinaldi." He spelled it for Decker. "I'll take the blame. Please just *try* to leave her out of it."

"I can't promise you anything, but if you tell me the truth, it'll make it easier on everyone. After Lucinda told you that she couldn't find any data, what did you do?"

Dixon turned white. "I didn't do anything."

"Let me rephrase the question," Decker said. "Where did you go after your meeting with Dr. Zhou? And don't tell me you went back to your dorm room. We know you didn't." When Dixon was silent, Decker said. "Okay. Don't answer the question. We know where you went. You went to break into Dr. Belfort's house to find the data yourself."

"I think I should get a—"

"What happened?" Decker interrupted. "Did you wake her up? Did you catch her by surprise?"

"No!"

"Did things get out of hand? Was there a struggle?"

"No, I swear! No, no, no!"

"Look, Alistair, I know it was an accident. You didn't mean to kill her."

"I didn't kill her!" Fat tears were running down his cheeks. "I didn't kill her because she was already *dead* when I got there!"

CHAPTER 33

WHEN DIXON REALIZED what he'd blurted out, he covered his face with his hands. "I am so screwed!"

Decker spoke soothingly. "We'll get through this together."

"What do you want?" Dixon dropped his hands to the tabletop and looked up with wet eyes that beseeched. "Just tell me what you *want*!"

"Are you hungry, Alistair?"

"God no. I'm nauseated."

"Thirsty? Maybe you'd like a soda to calm your stomach, or something hot like herbal tea? You may be here for a while."

He shook his head.

McAdams said, "I'll get us all some coffee."

After he left, Dixon said, "I didn't *kill* her. I was horrified when . . ." Again he covered his face as if that would blot out the memory. "I didn't kill her."

"I believe you."

He took in a deep breath and slowly let it out. "So what do you want?"

Decker paused. "Let's go back a little bit. What time did you leave Dr. Zhou's office?"

"Around one-thirty in the morning."

"And where did you go after that?"

"I walked back to my dorm room."

"But you didn't *go* to your dorm room."

"No."

"Why not?"

"I texted Lucinda."

"The girl who was doing you a favor."

"Yeah, please keep her out of it."

"I'll do what I can. Can I see the text?"

"Deleted. It's gone."

"I'll still need your phone. You know that texts are often retrievable." Dixon was quiet. Decker said, "Go on. What did you text Lucinda?"

"I asked if she had any luck. So she texted me back saying that she didn't find any papers in Mallon's room at all, let alone anything that related to the stochastic oscillator algorithm. Mallon must keep her work with her."

"What time did Lucinda text you?"

"I might have deleted her text as well." He pulled out his phone and scrolled through his texts. "No, I didn't. One thirty-six." He showed the phone to Decker, who wrote the time down on his pad.

"Good. You're doing great. Then what happened?"

"I probably made the worst decision of my life."

McAdams came back into the room with a tray. He set the coffee, paper cups, and powdered creamer and sugar on the table. He handed Decker a cup and said, "What was the worst decision of your life?"

"I was almost at my dorm. It was late, I was tired, and I guess I was in panic mode. My thesis was at a standstill, Damodar was pissed at me, you wouldn't let me look at Eli's papers, and I had hit a total roadblock. So instead of going back home, I turned around and walked over to Dr. Belfort's house."

Decker said, "How long did it take you to walk there?"

"About twenty minutes."

"So you arrived at her house around two in the morning."

"About."

"What happened once you got there?"

"I just wanted to talk to her. Maybe she would be willing to help me out in exchange for me helping her out."

"How would you help her out?"

"I was going to offer to help her like Damodar and Mallon. I was going to offer my services."

"If she agreed to help you with your thesis."

"Yes. And I didn't break into her house. I want to make that clear."

"Okay," Decker said. "So what did you do once you arrived at her house?"

"A light was on in her living room. Several lights were on, actually. I knocked at the door. I figured she was working late."

"All right. You knocked on the door. Go on."

"Obviously no one answered. So I went around to the back, figuring that maybe she didn't hear me or she was working at the back part of the house." Dixon licked his lips. "When I knocked on her back door, it opened up."

"The back door was unlocked?"

"Not just unlocked. It was unlatched. When I touched it, the door opened."

"So what did you do?"

"I made another bad decision." His voice was filled with self-loathing. "I went in and called out. 'Hello, anyone home?' That kind of thing. I walked into her living room and saw her lying there." His voice dropped to a hush. "It was awful. I've never seen a dead body before."

"And you're sure she was dead."

"Yeah."

"What position was she in?"

He closed his eyes trying to remember something that was impossible for him to forget. "She was on the floor, her upper body leaning against the couch. Her head was canted to the side, her chin was resting against her chest . . . her mouth was slack, her eyes were closed. I tried to wake her up. I shook her arm . . . gently at first, then harder. She didn't respond. She . . . fell over to the side."

"Which side?"

"The left, I think. That's when I freaked. I just got the hell out of there."

"And you didn't at any time call the police or an ambulance?"

"No." A pause. "That looks bad, right?" When Decker didn't answer, Dixon said, "It wouldn't have mattered. She was dead."

"Where exactly was she in relation to the couch: right side, left side, or in the middle?"

"On the left side, I want to say." Again his eyes closed. "An end table was knocked down. There was a pool of blood on the floor. Blood was also running down her shirt." He paused. "There were also two coffee cups on the sofa table—like hand-made ceramic mugs with three-dimensional faces on them. I guess you saw that when you searched the house."

"You know that we didn't find Dr. Belfort in her house, Alistair."

"Right. She was in the woods."

"And that meant someone dragged her into the woods."

"I didn't do it. I got out of there and went straight back to the dorm."

"What time was this?"

"Around two forty-five. You can check with the electronic swipe on my dorm door because I had to swipe in." Silence. "I swear she was already dead."

"You took her pulse? You checked her breathing?" When Dixon didn't answer, Decker said, "If you had called us right away, even anonymously, we would have come down right away. We could have checked her pulse. We could have checked her breathing. She could have still been alive."

"If you would have seen her, you would know she was dead."

"And you're an expert? Someone who has never seen a dead body?"

Dixon's eyes moistened. He whispered, "I'm sorry."

"Even if she had been dead, if you had called us, the integrity of the crime scene would have remained intact. She wouldn't have been dragged into the woods. Her back skull would have been whole instead of being obliterated by a gunshot wound in a weak attempt to make it look like a suicide. And even more important, we might have been able to nab whoever shot her because that person was probably in the house when you went inside."

The room went silent.

"This is the point where everything gets sticky, Alistair," Decker said. "Do I arrest you for murder or do I arrest you for unlawful entry and tampering with a crime scene?"

"I told you that the door was unlocked."

"You can't go into a house just because the back door happens to be open. That isn't an invitation to come on in!"

Dixon looked down. "I didn't kill her."

"Okay, suppose that I believe you. I want to know what exactly you did once you were inside."

"I told you, I shook her. She didn't respond."

"Afterward. For instance, did you look around the room for her math papers?"

"I saw her and freaked out."

"You didn't answer the question, Alistair. Once you were inside her house, did you look around the room to try to find her math papers?"

Tears spilled out of his eyes. He nodded yes.

"Did you look at her computer?" The kid didn't answer. "We've recovered the hard drive. Even if you erased your search, we'll find evidence. Not to mention fingerprints." When Dixon remained quiet, Decker said, "Unless you wiped the keyboard down. The question is, did you wipe it down perfectly?"

He was met with silence.

"Did you look at her computer? Yes or no?"

"Yes."

"And?"

"I just glanced because I heard noises."

"What kind of noises?"

"Like shuffling."

"Shuffling?"

"Shoes or slippers on a floor. Muffled. Sounded like it was coming from another room. That's when I really got scared. I swear to God, that's when I left."

"What else did you hear?"

"Just that. I got the hell out." He looked down.

"Did you see anyone?"

"No, I didn't see anyone. I ran out and ran home."

Decker sat back in his chair and thought a moment. "Alistair, when you got to Belfort's house, did you see or hear anything unusual before you knocked?"

"No. Just the light on in her house, which I thought was a little unusual given the hour."

"Did you hear anything unusual?"

"No."

"Were there any cars parked in front of the house?"

He thought for a moment. "Not right in front of the house. I remember thinking how empty the street was."

"So there were no cars parked on her street?"

"I don't remember."

"So think about it for a moment. It was under a week ago. Do you remember any cars parked on Belfort's street?"

"Well . . ." Dixon cleared his throat. "I remember passing parked cars on the way to her house."

"That's a good start. Now think back to her street. Were there any parked cars on her street?"

Dixon closed his eyes. "I'm not sure if this is a false memory or . . . I believe . . . there was a car in front of her neighbor's house . . . or maybe it was two doors down . . . on the right side."

"Good. Do you remember anything about it?"

"No model or license plate, if that's what you're asking."

"Nothing caught your attention?"

"No."

"What kind of car? Van? SUV? Sedan? Truck?"

"Minivan."

"A minivan?" Decker was hoping for the mysterious late-night sedan.

"Yeah, a minivan." Dixon opened his eyes. "Yeah, I remember now. It was in front of the neighbors. I remember thinking that the car was clean for being parked outside. You know what snow and grime do to cars in the winter. It wrecks them. The car had obviously been garaged."

"That's very good, Alistair. Really good. Do you remember anything about the minivan other than how clean it was?"

"Not really."

"Was it a light or dark color?"

"Everything looked dark because it was nighttime." He paused. "It wasn't white. Maybe black or dark blue. I wouldn't swear to it."

"But you saw a minivan parked near Belfort's house?"

"I *think* so."

Decker said, "Let's go back to the crime scene."

"Do we have to?" When Decker didn't answer, he said, "What do you want to know?"

"How long were you on Dr. Belfort's computer before you heard the noise?"

"About five minutes."

"Did you find the data for Dr. Belfort's stochastic oscillator indicator on her computer?" McAdams asked.

"Everything was encrypted."

"How did you pull up her files?"

"They were already on the screen. She must have been working on them when, you know, it happened."

"We have her computer," Decker said. "We can verify whatever you are telling us."

"So verify it. I'm telling the truth."

"Maybe you are this time, but you've been lying to us from the get-go," McAdams said. "Why should we believe you now?"

"I swear I'm telling the truth now."

"So prove it," Decker said. "Take a polygraph. While it won't eliminate you as a suspect, it'll go a long way in helping us decide whether you're being truthful or not."

"I am being truthful. I admitted being there. But I didn't kill her."

"I already have a few people who are willing to take—"

"Who?"

"Can't tell you that. What I want to know is can I count *you* in?"

A deep breath in and out. "Sure. I'll take a polygraph. I didn't kill her. Can I go now?"

"Not quite. I'm still in a quandary—do I charge and hold you for a day courtesy of the great state of New York? Or . . . do I let you go."

"I didn't *kill* her."

"You could be a flight risk. You're single with no ties to the community. Plus, I can actually put you at the crime scene by your own admission."

"I . . . did . . . not . . . kill her."

"I believe you. But I'm still going to charge you for obstruction of justice, illegal entry, and tampering with a crime scene. I have to put you through the legal process. It would be negligent if I didn't."

Dixon withered. "Please don't do this to me." Silence. "Please, Detective. I've cooperated with you."

"And that's precisely why I'm not going to charge you with murder."

"You've got to be kidding!"

"Do I look like I'm kidding?"

"Why are you doing this to me? Please!"

"You know, I'm going to cut you a break right now. I'll let you call your lawyer on your cell phone so you can get started on getting out of here."

"I don't have a lawyer. Do I look like I can afford a private lawyer?"

"Then the state of New York will get one for you. I tell you that when I Mirandize you."

"I didn't murder anyone. You've got to believe me."

"I do believe you, Alistair, but I'm still going to hold you for a while. Stand up." The young man broke into tears when Decker started reading him his rights. "Try not to take it too hard or too personally. If you're innocent, one day this'll be a great story to tell your children."

"I'm gay."

"First of all, being gay doesn't preclude having children. Second of all, a night in prison will give you street cred, Dixon. People are going to start asking you lots of questions. It's not going to be a pleasant time for you, son. You need to toughen up a bit. A night in the cage will go a long way toward achieving that goal."

CHAPTER 34

I T TOOK LESS than three hours for Alistair Dixon to be released on his own recognizance. By that time, it was almost nine in the evening and Decker still had to finish paperwork. When he came home, he was famished and worn out. He glanced at McAdams, who had left the station house before the official booking, two hours earlier. The lad was sitting at the dining table, open books in front of him.

"Rina said she'd be back at ten." Tyler checked his watch. "Which was five minutes ago. How did the booking go?"

"He's already out. Any idea where my wife went?"

"She didn't say. Just that we should wait for her to come home for dinner. I hope it's soon. I'm starving."

"If she waited for me, I'll certainly wait for her." He pulled out his phone in the kitchen and made a quick call to Kevin Nickweed. Then he returned to the dining room. "I'll just take a quick shower. Be back in a few."

"What's with the secretive phone call?" McAdams said.

"No secret at all. Just didn't want to disturb you. I called Kevin about the CCTV tapes on the night of the murder. There are no security cameras on Belfort's block, either on the street or on the houses. That's to be expected. Most people here don't even have alarms. The closest camera is at the intersection of Forest and Main, which is three blocks away. But it's a big intersection."

"You're hoping to find the minivan."

"I'm sure I'll find *a* minivan. I'm hoping it'll be an *important* minivan. I told Kevin to pull the tape. See if we have any luck."

"Good idea."

"I shouldn't be long. Just want to get clean."

"Yeah. Take your time, boss. A hot shower is very therapeutic."

When Decker came back into the dining room, Rina had returned and the table had been cleared and set. She came out of the kitchen with a smile and kissed his cheek. "I heard you arrested someone for the professor's murder."

"We arrested someone but not for the murder, unfortunately." Decker had dressed in sweats. "But he was at the scene and in the house illegally. Plus he never called the cops. Where were you, by the way?"

"I teach an evening class two times a week."

"Of course." He smiled. "Need help in the kitchen?"

"Sure. There's a platter of salmon over buckwheat. Salad's in the fridge."

"I'll get it," McAdams said.

"Thanks." Rina regarded her weary husband. "I'm glad you're making progress."

"Two steps forward and one step back."

"Better than the other way around."

"I don't think it's him by the way," Decker said. "The guy we arrested. Alistair Dixon."

"The RA?"

"What a memory."

"Why don't you think it's him?"

"He's sneaky and a weasel, but he doesn't seem like the kind of guy who would drag a body up a hill, shoot the woman in the head, and be cool enough to go on with his life. Plus, he agreed to take a polygraph."

"I agree with you, for what it's worth." McAdams put down the tray and the bowl of salad. "He's a terrible liar. When he finally started talking, he talked details."

Decker dumped salad on his plate then topped it with two fillets and a spoonful of buckwheat. "After his meeting with Dr. Zhou, he said he walked over to Belfort's house. He remembers seeing a minivan parked on the street. He also remembers that the van was clean, meaning it had recently been washed and garaged." He turned to McAdams. "It might not be significant, but let's see if the neighbor owns a minivan. If he or she doesn't, let's check out Ferraga or Rosser and find out what cars they drive."

"Right," McAdams said. "What about Zhou?"

"She was at Bagelmania at around six in the morning. And as of right now, I don't have a clear motive for her killing Belfort."

"So she's out of the running?" McAdams said.

"No, but she's not at the top of the list. But as long as you have DMV on the phone, check her vehicles as well."

"Who is on the top of your list?" Rina asked.

"It changes. Right now I'm really interested in Dixon, but I'm also really interested in Ferraga and Rosser. Both have motivation. Ferraga loved her too much: Rosser hated her too much. Anyway, call up DMV, Tyler. Find out their vehicles."

Rina said, "Can you let the boy eat first?"

"No."

McAdams said, "He just wants to steal my salmon. He's ravenous."

"I'll guard it for you, Tyler."

"Thank you, Rina, someone cares." He got up from the table and went inside the kitchen to use the house phone.

To Decker, she said, "Don't you dare put your fork anywhere near Tyler's plate."

"Who? Me?"

"I bet you were the type of kid who ate the fudge ribbon out of the chocolate ripple ice cream."

"And I bet you were the type of kid who lectured my type of kid on the meaning of fairness."

"Yes, I was a goody-goody." She paused. "I really don't miss that aspect of my personality and I have you to thank for it."

"Why's that?"

"You have a bit of psycho and liar in you. Not enough to be callous and amoral, but enough to get your job done."

"As I recall, you were always a pretty good liar."

"Just for *shalom bayit*."

"So now you're just justifying your bad behavior. I just may have to steal his fish."

"You will not."

"How did your class go?"

"Big turnout tonight."

"What was the topic?"

"The Purim story. I think they thought I was serving free booze."

McAdams came back. "Zhou drives a Toyota. Rosser drives a Lexus, Ferraga drives a black Beemer. But Rosser's wife, Shannon, has a dark blue Sierra minivan, and Ferraga's wife, Olivia, has a Sienna minivan in black."

"That is interesting. What about the neighbor?"

"Michael and Kristen Canterbury. Neither owns a minivan. But that's only one person on the block."

Decker pondered over a forkful of fish. "Maybe we can get Alistair Dixon to remember a few more details about the minivan."

"Maybe." McAdams sat down and speared a piece of fish. "This is good."

"Thanks." Rina thought a moment. "Which one had the older-model minivan?"

McAdams checked his notes. "Rosser's is five years old, Ferraga's is two years old."

"Okay. And if the minivan was garaged, someone was taking good care of it. Who has the younger children?"

"Right." Decker waved a fork in her direction. "Good."

McAdams got up and came back with his pad. He began his search. "Rosser is fifty-seven years old and Ferraga is forty-two. Both have children, according to their bios."

"How old are the kids?" Rina asked.

"Doesn't say," McAdams answered. "Let me just . . . hold on . . . nope, that's not going to work." A minute passed. "Okay, here we go. There's an Alexis Rosser who got into Harvard a year ago."

"How'd you find that out?" Decker said.

"I am connected with the university directory. So she's probably around nineteen. Hold on . . ." His hands flew over the keyboard. "There is a boy named Steven Rosser who graduated last year. So if they are Rosser's kids, they're older. And even if they aren't his progeny, he may have others at home who are younger."

"What about Ferraga?" Decker asked.

"Nothing in the Harvard directory under that name. But that doesn't mean anything, as you well know. I'm just figuring that a guy like Rosser would want his kids in Harvard."

"Who doesn't?"

"Anyway, Ferraga is forty-two. The kids could be college-aged."

Decker said, "It would mean he had a kid in his early twenties. It's possible."

"But all things considered, he's more likely to have younger kids than Rosser," Rina concluded. "A lot of the houses here have one-car garages. After dinner, why don't you drive by both houses and see which if any of them has a minivan parked outside the house."

"Good idea," Decker said. "Let me change out of sweats."

"First finish your dinner," Rina said.

"I'd like to get going. It might be a long night."

"That's why you need to finish your dinner. You can't work on empty. And don't wolf the food down. You'll get indigestion."

"Rina, I may be getting on in years but I know how to eat, okay."

"Okay, darling." She raised her eyebrows.

The rest of the meal was silent. Finally, Decker stood up. "May I be excused?"

"Stop it." After he stomped out of the room, Rina said, "He does get indigestion. Just trying to save him a night of misery."

Tyler said, "His age is a touchy subject."

"I know." She stood up and began to clear the dishes. "I shouldn't have said anything, especially in front of you. Oh well. Like bad gas, it'll eventually pass."

McAdams laughed and helped her clear.

A minute later, Decker was dressed and walked into the kitchen, where Rina was rinsing dishes. "Leave them in the sink. I'll do them when I get home."

"Don't bother. I'm going to throw them into the dishwasher." She turned around, straightened his tie, and grinned. "You look dapper."

"I've worn this suit a million times."

"You still look dapper." She kissed his cheek. "Can I pack you something?"

"Don't bother. Indigestion and all."

"Oh, stop." She hit his shoulder.

McAdams said, "I'll wait for you outside."

Rina turned to her husband. "I'm sorry."

"Ah, it's not you. I'm just tired. I was looking forward to some R and R until someone mentioned a drive-by."

"Oops."

"It's a good idea, damn it. Maybe you should quit your day job and work for Greenbury PD. Then again, it's hard enough living with me. Working for me would be impossible."

"You're not hard to live with . . . mostly."

"Thanks a lot."

"Go." She stood on her tiptoes and kissed his lips.

He kissed her back. "I'm off. The night isn't getting any younger and neither am I."

"Peter, stop it."

"Rina, complaining at my age is like Social Security and Medicare. It's an entitlement. To take that right away from me is just plain un-American."

ROSSER LIVED IN a modest brick-and-wood-sided bungalow. And typical for the area, it had a one-car garage. The minivan, registered in his wife's name, was parked on the street and caked with several layers of dirt and salt. The windshield was covered with a thin layer of grime. It was in the high teens outside, but with the wind chill, it felt like it was blowing zero.

"Cars can get very dirty, very fast," Decker said. "But this one doesn't look like it's been washed in a long time."

McAdams was shivering. "Where's the Lexus?"

"Either he's out or it's in the garage."

"He uses the garage and keeps his wife's car on the street," McAdams said. "That sounds like Rosser."

Decker rocked on his toes. "It's ten-thirty at night and Rosser's not going anywhere. We can deal with him tomorrow. Let's go check out Ferraga. As a suspect, he's still right there at the top."

The address put them in front of another brick bungalow. This one had a two-car garage. No minivans were parked on the street.

Decker pulled up in front of the house, but didn't get out. He said, "Looks like both cars are garaged."

"Meaning between the two of them, it's more likely to be Ferraga's minivan than Rosser's. But since there are gazillions of minivans, we can't say for sure whose car it was."

"Except that it didn't belong to her neighbor on the right." Decker cranked up the heat and said, "I was thinking . . ."

"That's always dangerous."

"Listen to me. Dixon told us there were two coffee cups on the living room table."

"Yeah, the ceramic mugs with the faces. Which we did not see when we were in her house."

"Someone cleaned up. That's a given. But if Dixon is to be believed, she was drinking coffee with someone before she was murdered. So what does that sound like to you, McAdams?"

"She was friendly to whoever showed up."

"Friendly . . . cordial . . . civil. If Ferraga would have showed up at past one in the morning—because we know where he was until one in the morning—do you think she would have bothered serving him coffee? Do you think she would have even opened the door?"

"Yeah, she was pretty fed up with the relationship."

"What about Rosser?"

"Katrina hated him, but he was head of the department. No way she'd have slammed a door in his face."

"I agree. She would have invited him in. Do you think she'd have made him coffee?"

"Like I said, he was the head of the department."

"Maybe she would have made him coffee. But do you think she would have served him coffee in cute little ceramic mugs with faces?"

"Yeah, that sounds a little girlie." McAdams paused, then said, "Ferraga's wife, Olivia."

"Bingo," Decker said. "Ferraga admitted having words with his wife around eleven-fifteen in the evening. He swore to her that the affair was over and he really was working late at his office. But it didn't sound like she believed him."

"She goes over to the house to check up on him."

"She knocks on the door and Belfort invites her in."

"Why would she do that?" McAdams said.

"I don't know that she did. But knowing the kind of woman Belfort was, I would think she would have been polite. Maybe Katrina invited Olivia inside because she wanted to apologize. Maybe Olivia asked to look around to make sure her husband wasn't hiding and Belfort agreed. And they got into an argument and Olivia pushed her."

"Would you really sit down and have coffee with your husband's mistress?"

"Like Aldo Ferraga said: Olivia Ferraga is from Europe. Civilized women put up with their men's sexual vagaries."

"I suppose, but only up to a point, don't you think?"

"Yes, I do think. And for Olivia Ferraga, perhaps that point had finally been reached."

CHAPTER 35

FERRAGA ANSWERED THE door, his dark eyes fluttering when he saw who it was. He was dressed in sweats and a cardigan with slippers on his feet. He gave a quick shudder, reacting to the cold air. "Give me a minute." He closed the door and came back wearing a parka and a scarf. He stepped outside and regarded his watch. "Can't whatever it is wait until the morning?"

Decker said, "Actually we came here to talk to your wife."

"Olivia?"

"Yes, Olivia."

"Why?"

"Can we come in? It's cold." Decker rubbed his arms to prove the point.

"I don't want you upsetting Olivia."

"But you must know why we're here." Silence. "We have a witness, Aldo. Someone who can put Olivia at Katrina's house on the night she was murdered."

"But that's impossi—" Ferraga stopped talking.

"Impossible?" Decker finished the word. "Why would that be impossible?"

"I will be happy to answer any questions. I will even come to the station house. But please. Do not drag my wife into this."

"Unfortunately, she dragged herself."

"Do you have an arrest warrant?"

"No."

"Then please leave—"

The front door opened.

Olivia was a wraith of a woman with long wavy blond hair, blue eyes, and sunken cheeks. A cable-knit sweater hung on her body; her legs were housed in baggy jeans. She appeared as if she hadn't eaten in decades. "Please come in."

"Olivia—"

"It's all right, Aldo. I've had enough." She turned to Decker and McAdams. "Please come in."

It was warm inside—stifling after standing in the cold for five minutes. The living room was immaculate and a fire was going in the hearth. Decker said, "Thank you for your cooperation, Mrs. Ferraga. Actually, we'd like to talk to you at the station house. We'd like to talk to both of you there."

"I can come down," Olivia told them. "But my children are asleep. Aldo must stay."

"I'll call someone to watch them for you."

"No." Olivia shook her head and the mass of tresses that came along with it. "The kids need at least one parent to guide them through life. Aldo will stay until I get back. Just let me get my coat."

She turned and walked away. Ferraga said, "This is outrageous!" His cheeks were red. "I'm calling my lawyer right now!"

Decker heard his rant, but didn't answer. Olivia's odd words were picking his brain.

The kids need at least one parent to guide them through life.

"Shit!" Decker slapped his face. "Do you own guns, Ferraga?"

"Oh God!" Ferraga ran to the bedroom and jiggled the locked knob. He pounded on the door and shouted, "Olivia, open up!" A pause and more banging. *"Open up!"*

"Move aside." Decker rammed his shoulder into the door. With McAdams's help, they splintered the wood. The hole was just big enough for Decker's hand to slip through. He unlocked the door and swung it open.

She stood there with a gun pointed at her temple.

"Olivia, drop the gun." Decker took a half step backward so as not to crowd her space. "Please don't hurt yourself. You have children. They need a mother. They need you. Drop the gun."

"I'm useless to them now."

"Don't say that. Don't ever say that. Children can't live without their mother. You know that. We both know who the real parent is. Put the gun down. We all know it was an accident. There is a better solution."

The barrel was still touching her temple. Abruptly, she shifted positions, her arm coming forward, aiming the barrel of the gun toward Ferraga's chest. In an instant, Decker jumped on top of Ferraga, bringing him down to the floor just as the gun exploded. A bullet sang through the air, going over their heads. At the same instant, McAdams charged Olivia's legs, knocking her over with the gun going off a second time before it finally skittered to the floor. Decker lunged toward the gun and grabbed the grip. Still on the floor, he opened the chamber and pulled out the bullets. He stood up and, with shaking hands, pocketed the bullets. Tyler was still wrestling with Olivia. His expensive cashmere coat had been ripped at the right shoulder, with the tear oozing blood. Decker got the woman facedown on the floor with her hand behind her back. "I'll need a belt."

McAdams complied and ripped it off his pants. He handed it to Decker. Suddenly his shoulder felt like it was on fire. He touched it and regarded his fingertips. "Fuck." He winced. "Lightning really does strike twice."

Decker shouted as he secured her wrists. "Ferraga, call an ambulance."

A teenage boy came into the room, dazed and scared. "What's going on?"

Ferraga said, "Go back to sleep, Tommaso."

"What'd you do to her this time?" the boy screamed.

"Go back to bed!" Ferraga screamed.

"You tried to kill her, you bastard!"

Decker said, "Will someone call an ambulance now!"

"Tommaso, go back to bed or I'll—"

"You'll what?"

Decker stood and brought Olivia to her feet. "Son, go back to your room now! We need to sort this out and you're getting in the way."

Olivia smiled angelically at her son. "I'm fine, Tommaso. Please do as the policeman says."

Reluctantly, the furious boy went back to his room and slammed the door. To Ferraga, Decker yelled, "Did you call an ambulance?"

"Don't bother." McAdams rotated his shoulder. "It's just a graze. I mean it hurts, but I'll be fine. The bullet must be somewhere in the room. I'll get Forensics on it."

"You need an ambulance, Tyler," Decker said.

"I'm fine. We need a team down here. They're going to ask questions since a firearm was discharged. I'll take care of it, Decker." McAdams picked up his cell and went into the corner to talk. Then he hung up. "They'll be down ASAP. You can take her down to the station house—"

Ferraga blurted out, "I'm coming with her. I'm bringing a lawyer." To Olivia, he said, "Don't admit anything until you've talked to him."

Olivia sneered at her husband. "You're in no position to tell me what or what not to do."

"I'll handle Forensics," McAdams said. "With a shooting, Radar will probably come down."

"You need to get that looked at, Tyler."

"After we've got this sorted out," McAdams said. "I'm okay. Actually, I'm real pissed. She ruined my coat."

What McAdams had said made perfect sense. The kid was remarkably sanguine. The captain would come down and he would certainly be able to direct everything. Decker's heartbeat still had yet to come down. Adrenaline was pounding through his veins, making him jittery. He was definitely too old for this. "You need to have a doctor check you out."

"It's just a little blood—"

"Tyler—"

"I'll get it taken care of, but it's not serious. If I can say that without fainting, you know I'm telling the truth." Someone was thumping at the door. "It's our backup. I'll get it."

With Olivia's arms behind her back, Decker led her to the front door with Ferraga in tow.

"Don't say anything, Olivia." When she didn't answer, Ferraga implored, "Please, don't say anything."

Her reaction was to turn her face away.

Decker briefed the two uniformed officers. Afterward, he blew out air and looked at Tyler. "So you'll take it from here until Radar comes down?"

"I said I would." He winced.

"You're in pain."

"I was shot, so yes I'm in pain. But I'm okay. I swear. Go."

Decker regarded the kid's eyes. He felt his voice choke up. "Risky move there, Harvard, taking her down with a gun in her hand. But knowing where she was pointing, I sincerely thank you for it." A pause. "Thank you, thank you, and thank you."

"All in a day's work." He winced again. "Just don't pat me on the shoulder for a while."

FACE-TO-FACE IN THE interview room, Olivia rubbed her wrists and said, "Thank you for taking off the belt."

Decker said, "Do you want some water?"

"No, thank you."

"Anything to eat?"

"Nothing."

Given her physical appearance, food was probably not a top priority. Decker turned on the tape machine and tested it. When he saw that it was working, he identified himself and Olivia Ferraga, and gave the time, date, and the location. He turned his attention to her.

"Would you like to start from the beginning?"

"Aldo said I should ask for a lawyer, but first I want to hear what you have to say."

"We have CCTV cameras," Decker lied. "We know it's your van parked outside Dr. Belfort's house. We know where Aldo was at that hour. So we know it was you who drove over there. And we have a witness."

Olivia looked down. "I don't know what to do. Should I ask for a lawyer?"

She had an ever-so-slight Italian accent. Decker said, "We know it was an accident, Olivia. There are mitigating circumstances. You're a good woman and a great mother."

"How do you know that?"

"Because I know who's been running the household while Aldo runs around. It's obvious." She was quiet. Decker leaned forward and dropped his voice. "Good people can have accidents—terrible accidents. Just tell me what happened."

She sighed. "Things happen."

"Yes, they do."

"I did not mean to hurt your partner, for instance."

"I know."

"He came at me. It was an accident."

"I realize that."

"Are you going to charge me?"

"I'd like to talk about Katrina Belfort first."

She hesitated. "What's to talk about?"

"Why did you go there in the first place?"

"To see if Aldo was telling me the truth. To see for myself if he was there."

"Around what time was that?"

She looked down. "I'm a terrible mother."

"How can you say that? Your son obviously adores you."

"I left them alone."

"When you went to Katrina's house, you mean?"

"Yes." She looked at him, tears in her eyes. "I left them *alone*!"

"How old's your son?"

"Fourteen."

"He's old enough to babysit. You wouldn't be charged for any-thing."

"Maybe not legally. Morally I was negligent."

"Olivia, what time did you go to Katrina Belfort's house?"

"You have CCTV cameras. You should know."

"I do know. I want to hear it from you."

She was quiet. Decker waited her out.

"Around eleven-thirty," she said.

Finally. Now that she had put herself at the scene, Decker knew the rest would eventually follow. "Go on. What happened next?"

"I didn't see Aldo's car. But that means nothing. Sometimes he walks from his office to her house. I know because I've followed him. He is so dense, he never even noticed. Or maybe he did and just didn't care."

"I understand. So you showed up at Katrina Belfort's house at eleven-thirty in the evening. What happened next?"

"I knock on her door."

Her face grew flat, devoid of emotion. She seemed to be replaying the events in her head.

"She opens the door. I ask her if Aldo is there and she says no. I ask her if I can look around and she says yes and she invites me in."

Recited in present tense. "Good," Decker said. "You go into the house. And then?"

"I look around. Aldo is not there. I'm going to leave, but she asks me if I want coffee. Like we're friends having social time together. So casual. At that moment, I hated her even more, which was silly. If it wasn't her, it would be someone else. Stupid man."

"But you sat down with her anyway."

"Yes. It was a mistake." She rubbed her wrists again. "A big mistake. I should have left. But curiosity got the better of me. Who is this woman and why is she dating a married man? Is she sorry? Does she feel shame? I wanted to know."

The room was quiet.

"We talked. She was quite charming. I might have liked her in a different situation, but her affable nature made it worse."

"How did the conversation begin?"

"A little of this and a little of that. Then she looks me in the eye. She apologizes for her bad behavior. There is no sincerity in it."

"Okay."

"She tells me it's over and that it won't happen ever again. But I don't believe her. Why should I believe her? I tell her that. I say, 'Why should I believe you?' "

"I understand."

"She keeps at it—repeating herself—it's over, it's over. Then she says . . ." Her face grew hard. "Then she says to me that she's no longer *interested* in Aldo. That he means *nothing* to her. Anything that she has ever felt for him has vanished. Discarding Aldo like he is spoiled milk!"

"That made you mad."

"Furious! I know she is lying. That she really does love him. Like I love him. So I tell her that. That she is lying. That it is Aldo who doesn't want her. That she can't have him." Tears fell down her cheeks. "She kept saying she doesn't want him. *She* didn't want him! I remain faithful to him for eighteen years, loving him all that time, and that whore doesn't *want* him. I tell her I don't believe her. Then do you know what happened?"

"Tell me."

"She got up and said, 'You can believe whatever you want. Just make sure your goddamn husband stays away from me. Otherwise I'll take out a restraining order.' That whore seduces him away from his wife and then has the nerve to threaten him with a *restraining* order?"

"Outrageous."

"It was mean-spirited and unforgivable. I push her. I said, 'You wouldn't dare.' She pushes me back and says that she would. So I push her again." She stopped talking.

"Go on, Olivia. I want to hear it all. Tell me exactly what happened."

"It was an accident."

"I know it was. But you need to tell me how it occurred."

Olivia shrugged. "She fell backward. She . . . hit her head on something, then fell to the floor and hit her head again. I heard her skull crack. I saw the blood pour from her head. I didn't mean to hurt her. It . . . it just happened."

"I believe you. So what did you do after she fell?"

"I was in shock."

"I'm sure you were. Did you try to help her?"

"No."

"Did you call 911?"

"No."

"Did you call anyone?"

"Not right away, no."

"So think back, Olivia. What did you do immediately after Katrina Belfort hit her head?"

Olivia's dry eyes focused on Decker's face. She shrugged again. "I watched her die."

CHAPTER 36

SHE CALLED ME on my office phone," Ferraga told Decker. He was with a lawyer named John Granger—white-haired man in his early seventies. Greenbury was filled with semiretirees in a variety of professions.

"When was this?" Decker asked.

"It was after I had knocked on Dr. Zhou's door. So it must have been around one-fifteen or maybe one-thirty."

"Olivia called you at around one-thirty?"

"Around that time, yes."

Silence.

"What did she say?"

"She was distraught. She told me that something terrible had happened. I thought it was one of the children. Then she said she was at Katrina Belfort's house. My heart sank."

"What did you do?"

"I grabbed my keys and sprinted over to her house. I didn't have my car." He shook his head, his eyes far away. "She's on medication, you know."

"Who is?"

"Olivia."

"What kind of medication?"

"Antipsychotics. She doesn't always take it. She doesn't like how it makes her feel. She forgets, but sometimes I know it's deliberate. Her mother was like that. She ended up in a mental institution. I didn't want to subject Olivia . . . I tried to look after her. We have a person come in for a couple of hours each day to look in on her. I wish I could afford someone full-time, but I just don't have the money."

"What happened when you arrived at Katrina's house?"

"The door was unlocked. I walked in and saw what had happened." He looked at his lawyer, who gave him a nod. "Katrina was dead. She appeared as if she had been lying there dead for some time."

"Why do you say that?"

"Her complexion was gray. There was a pool of blood on the floor. The blood did not appear fresh."

"Where was Olivia?"

"Sitting on a chair . . . mute, paralyzed, terror-stricken, blood on her clothes. I . . ." He took in a deep breath and let it out. "I was about to call the police from Katrina's home phone. Leave an anonymous message until I could think clearly. But I heard knocking on her front door: someone calling out her name."

"So what did you do?"

"I panicked. I grabbed Olivia's arm and we hid in her bedroom. I had locked the door behind us. That's why I know it was impossible that a witness saw us."

"Nothing is ever impossible, Dr. Ferraga. Did you know who it was at the time?"

"Not at that time, no. But once I found out you arrested Alistair Dixon, I recognized the voice . . . in my head." He pointed to his temple. "But when we were hiding, I was in an altered state. All of my senses had shut down."

Ferraga closed his eyes and opened them. "It was horrible being in her bedroom. It was doing awful things to Olivia's mind. She kept looking at the bed. No matter how many times I told her to be still, she kept pacing back and forth."

The shuffling that Dixon heard. Decker said, "About how long were you in the bedroom?"

"The alarm clock on her nightstand read one fifty-six when we went inside the bedroom. Around fifteen minutes later, it became quiet. We left the bedroom around two-thirty. Alistair was gone."

"Then what did you do?"

"I drove Olivia home, gave her a sedative, and put her to sleep."

"And then what?"

Again Ferraga looked at his attorney. Granger whispered in his ear. "I went back to Katrina's house. It was almost three."

"Why didn't you call the police then?"

"I was not thinking clearly. I had no conception of time or even where I was or what I was doing. I was very confused."

So that's going to be his defense—diminished capacity because he was in an altered state of mind. Decker said, "So, for whatever reason, you didn't call the police."

Again, the lawyer whispered in Ferraga's ear. "I was not thinking clearly."

"Okay. You weren't thinking clearly. Do you remember what you did when you went back to Katrina Belfort's house?"

"Not exactly."

Inside, Decker was growing impatient. He had to use another approach. "The more you forget about what happened, the more it seems like you're protecting yourself—or even Olivia. I mean how do I know you took her home, gave her a sedative, and put her to sleep? Maybe she was the one who cleaned up the crime scene."

"No," Ferraga said. When Granger tried to talk to him, he shook his head. "No, it was me. But I wasn't thinking clearly. I wasn't in my right mind."

"I believe you. Just tell me what you were thinking even if it was crazy," Decker said. "I have to know what happened; otherwise it all falls on Olivia."

Granger said, "You don't have to tell him any more."

Ferraga ignored him. "For some reason, I kept on thinking about Elijah Wolf's suicide. No one knew why he did it. In my scrambled thoughts, I supposed that if I could imply that their deaths were a pact between them—a love affair gone wrong—I could convince everyone that she killed herself like Elijah. As I said, I was confused and deranged."

"So you decided to shoot her and make it look like suicide."

Granger said, "He already admitted to accessory after the fact."

"I need to hear what he has to say, Counselor." Decker turned to Ferraga. "Where'd you get the gun?"

"It was Katrina's."

"Okay. So you decided to make it look like suicide. Why drag her into the mountains?"

"To make it look similar to Elijah Wolf's suicide, of course."

"Any other reason?" Decker said. "For instance, you knew that firing a gun in her house would make too much noise? That it might arouse the neighbors?"

"I was only thinking that Elijah had killed himself in the woods. So I figured, she had to kill herself in the woods. How many times do I have to tell you that I wasn't in my right mind?"

"But you were aware enough to make it look like Elijah Wolf's suicide."

"Yes. It was an obsessive thought that was running through my mind."

"Okay. So when you came back, what exactly did you do? Think about it, Aldo. I want a step-by-step."

"First, I removed her bloody clothing and placed that in a bag. Then I washed her off with a towel and placed the towel in the same bag as her clothing. Then I grabbed some clean folded clothing from her drawers . . . to make it look like Elijah Wolf's suicide. Then I wrapped her body in a sheet and dragged her up the hillside.

"I dragged her up until my arms were breaking off and I could go no farther. I took her out of the sheet and . . . I took the folded clothes and placed them by her body . . . just like Elijah."

Silence.

"And then what did you do?" Decker asked.

"I came back to the house."

"You left out a few things."

"Yes, I tried to obliterate my footsteps and the drag marks. I admit that."

"And I suppose you weren't thinking clearly when you shot her in the back of her head?"

Ferraga said nothing.

"Why don't you tell me in your own words how you shot her?"

"What's to tell?" Granger told him. "She was already dead."

"So if she was already dead, why not just leave her in the woods? Why *shoot* her in the back of her head?"

Ferraga said, "I told you I was trying to make it look like suicide . . . to tie it to Elijah Wolf's suicide. So she had to shoot herself."

Decker said, "Obviously she couldn't shoot herself."

"Obviously," Ferraga admitted. "I put the gun in her hand and pulled the trigger with her finger."

"Aldo, you didn't shoot her in the temple. That's the obvious place to do it. That's where Elijah shot himself. You, on the other hand, shot her in the *back* of her head. You shot her in a way to obliterate the injury she sustained when she fell on the corner of the end table."

Ferraga looked down. "I wasn't thinking clearly."

"On the contrary, I'd say that you were thinking very clearly."

"My client has already given you an answer," Granger said. "Please move on."

Decker said, "When did you type her suicide note?"

"After I . . . when I came back to her house."

"You used the very words she used when she wanted to end your love affair."

"I used them because it sounded like Katrina. I wanted it to be as authentic as possible."

"Her suicide."

"Yes." Ferraga shook his head. "It was insane what I did. I was insane! I was . . . crazy. I will admit my part in this charade. But I didn't kill her. You must believe me."

Decker's face remained flat. "What did you do after you left her body in the woods?"

"I went back to Katrina's house and mopped up the mess with paper towels and threw them in with the bloody clothing. I washed the floor with dishwashing liquid." He wiped his wet eyes.

Granger said, "In his confused mind, Ferraga felt like he was helping Olivia. Certainly he wasn't helping himself by doing that."

"Or just maybe he thought he could get away with something."

"I don't know what I was thinking," Ferraga said. "I don't remember."

"What time did you leave Katrina's house? Do you remember that?"

"I suppose it was around five."

"And you went straight home after that?"

"Yes." His eyes watered. "She was already dead. You have to believe me. If she was even the least bit alive, I would have called the ambulance. I loved her. I wasn't ready to end our relationship. I kept telling her I would never leave Olivia, that she didn't have to worry about the affair being too serious." He swallowed hard. "She must have tired of me."

Decker said, "You got to your house around what time again?"

"Maybe five-thirty."

"You walked home or drove home?"

"I had Olivia's car."

"Okay. You drove home and it was around five-thirty."

"Maybe a little later. It was still dark."

"What did you do with the clothes you were wearing? I assumed you changed your clothes."

"I did change my clothes."

"So what did you do with your bloody clothing?"

"I must have put them in the same bag with all the other blood-stained clothes."

"Where is the bag?"

"I threw it away."

"Where?"

"I don't remember." When Ferraga's comment was met with silence, he said, "I swear I don't remember. I was completely insane by that time."

"Aldo, our techs found remnants of cloth in your fireplace." That part was true. Probably not enough to use for forensics, but there were definitely bits of cloth that survived even after Ferraga cleaned up.

Granger said, "That means nothing."

"He burned his clothes in the fireplace," Decker said. "That shows intent!"

"If I burned them, I don't remember," Ferraga said. "All I remember is showering a very long time. Then I shaved and went to work around seven. When I heard the news, I was truly horrified. It was as if I heard about it for the first time. It was as if someone else had to have done it." He put his hands over his mouth and shook his head. "I was in a dissociative state."

"Did you learn that word from your lawyer?"

Granger said, "We're cooperating with you. No need to get snide."

"Sometimes you just do things," Ferraga said. "You know you're not thinking optimally. You know you're really not thinking clearly at all. But you've come this far and you see no other way out. You just go to the bitter end and hope for the best." He looked up at Decker. "I'm not a criminal. I'm not a psychopath. I'm just a man who was trying to do the best I could."

"You were having an affair."

"Olivia and I have not been intimate for a very long time. It's part of her medication. You lose the drive."

"Did she know about the affair?"

"She found out about three months ago."

"Was she surprised by it?"

"Excuse me?"

"Katrina couldn't have been the first."

Ferraga looked down. "She told me to end it and I told her I would."

"You would what?"

"I told her I would end the affair."

"But you didn't."

"I knew Katrina was tiring of me. It really was over by the time this tragedy happened." Again he caught Decker's eye. "What will happen to my children?"

"Do you have relatives who'd be willing to take them?"

"My brother, perhaps. He's divorced. He doesn't see his own kids very often." His eyes leaked tears. "What charges do I face?"

"Tampering with evidence, defacing a body, obstruction of justice, aiding and abetting."

"I will face prison time."

Granger said, "Not necessarily."

Decker said, "Diminished capacity. I get it. You know, Aldo, if you had called up right away—even anonymously—you wouldn't have faced jail time. Yes, you were trying to shield your wife, to spare her for the ordeal, but judges understand mitigating circumstances."

"I told you I wasn't in my right mind. But whatever I did, I did it to protect my wife. She can't go to prison. She isn't stable."

Decker said, "Aldo, if she isn't stable, why in the world do you have a gun in the house?"

There was a long pause. Granger said, "You don't have to answer that."

"I will answer that because the answer is innocent," Ferraga said. "Frequently, I am gone at night. And please do not snicker. It was not just the affair. I actually work in my office at night. I find the peace and quiet conducive to getting things done. Olivia told me when the hour gets late and I'm not home, she feels vulnerable and scared."

A pause.

"She asked me to buy her a gun because she couldn't buy one— her mental state is on record. So I bought it for her. I felt . . . I owed it to her."

"You owed it to her?" Decker was floored. "You knew she was unstable. She could have killed one of your children."

"She would never do that."

"She could have killed you. She could have killed herself. She almost did kill herself." Decker paused. "Or maybe that was the ulterior motive."

"That's a horrible, untrue, vicious thing to say. I have given my life to that woman."

Decker said, "I apologize if my comment seemed rude."

"It was . . ." Ferraga didn't finish his sentence.

That was okay.

They both knew the truth when they heard it.

MCADAMS CLOSED HIS duffel. His shoulder was still sore, but since it could have been a lot worse, he refused to complain. He hoisted up the bag with his good arm and walked into the hallway, where Decker immediately relieved him of it.

"I can do it, Old Man."

"I know, but why should you?" Decker smiled. "You're used to people doing your bidding anyway. I'm just one of many."

"That's true. Do I tip you?"

"Don't bother. You've already done your good deed for the month."

"Her gun wasn't anywhere near you," McAdams said.

"It was pointed right at me . . . or at Ferraga. It was pointed at both of us. Whether or not she would have hit him or me is another question. I'm glad you acted before we both found out."

"I wasn't thinking," McAdams said.

"Not consciously, no. But your subconscious was thinking very well. You were there when it mattered. I'm proud of you, kiddo. You are the consummate professional."

McAdams smiled broadly. "Thank you, Old Man. How about we do Kevlar next time?"

"How about if there is no next time?"

"Even better."

Rina came in. "Here's your lunch." She handed Decker a paper bag. She turned to Tyler. "And here's lunch and dinner for you."

McAdams took the proffered bag. "Thanks, although I probably won't eat too much. Not good to study on a full stomach. It shunts the blood to the gut instead of the brain and I'll need every bit of brainpower I have."

"You'll do fine."

"Yeah, I'm really not worried."

Decker said, "When do you find out the results?"

"At the end of the next week. I still have the weekend to prepare. I'll be fine. You know the administration told me that if I need more time to recuperate, I can take the exams a week later."

"And?"

"I told them it was only a graze, that I'd be fine. Besides, you don't know how venal people can be. For all I know, some of my classmates will think I shot myself to get more study time. I wouldn't be surprised if a few of them attempted a copycat."

Rina laughed. She kissed his cheek. "Good luck."

"Thank you." He turned to Decker. "You know I really can hire a car."

"I'm playing chauffeur for the day. Just don't ask me to wear a uniform. I have a little business to do on the way back, so it's no problem."

"Okay. Let's rock-and-roll."

They stepped outside and Decker popped the trunk. After placing McAdams's duffel inside, he slammed the trunk and turned around. From the corner of his eye, he saw Mallon Euler obscured by a bush. Gently, he nudged McAdams's good arm. "I'll wait inside."

"What? Wait a sec."

But Decker was already gone. McAdams made a face. "You can come out of hiding, Mallon." She stepped out of the blind swaddled in a white parka, white pants, and white boots. She looked like a snowman. "How long have you been waiting there?"

"About a half hour."

"You're allowed to ring the doorbell."

"I was gonna do it, but then you came out." A pause. "I heard." Her lower lip quivered. "Are you okay?"

"I'm fine, but thanks for asking." Tears streamed down her cheek. "Really I'm fine. Stop." His insistence turned the waterworks on full blast. He said, "Oh Christ. C'mere."

She walked toward him and he embraced her in a big hug. "I'm *fine*."

"I just . . . care."

"Thank you. I'm glad you care."

She pulled away. "You're going back to Harvard?"

"Yes. I'm still officially enrolled."

Her eyes looked at her boots. "Okay. So I'll see you maybe . . ."

"I'm sure I'll see you again before you graduate." But she made no attempt to excuse herself. "Something on your mind?"

"I had a long talk with Dr. Tolvard. I'm taking over Eli's work for my thesis. Tolvard said I could have it. He even said he'd work with me."

"Eli's research on space junk?"

She nodded but still couldn't look him in the eye. "Yeah, I have to go to summer school anyway, now that I'm getting two degrees. Actually, Rosser, by being a butthead, did me a favor. I get to honor Eli by continuing his work."

"That's lovely, Mallon. I'm sure he would have wanted it that way."

"Maybe." She shrugged. "Besides, his ideas were way better than mine. It'll make a much better thesis in both departments."

McAdams laughed. "No sin in being practical." He gave her a brief smile that she didn't see because she was still looking down. "Any plans after summer school and graduation?"

"Actually yes." She cleared her throat. "Eli must have written to Google at one point, telling someone what he was doing. He must have listed Dr. Tolvard as a reference. Dr. Tolvard got a call and referred them to me."

She stopped talking. McAdams could see where this was going. "You've landed an internship at Google?"

"Actually, a job . . . in the fall."

"Plotting space junk?"

"Yes. Satellites are expensive. No sense launching something if it's going to collide with crap. Obviously, it's what Eli would have wanted to do. Why let all his hard work go to waste?"

"Why indeed." He placed a hand on her shoulder and she looked up. "Any organization that has you on board is very lucky. Congratulations."

Again her eyes teared up. "I can finally visit my sister." A pause. "I've never been to the West Coast."

"The bay area is beautiful. The weather is lovely and it's truly scenic country. All you have to remember is that the ocean is to the west instead of the east."

There was an awkward pause. She said, "Can I e-mail you?"

"Anytime."

"Can I text you?"

"Yeah, you can even call me."

"I like texting better."

McAdams laughed. "Whatever, Mallon. I would like it if we keep in touch."

"You would?"

"Yes."

"You're not just saying that?"

"No. Let's keep in touch."

Another awkward moment. She kissed his lips gently. "Thank you for taking me seriously."

"And thank you for having faith in my ability as a cop." This time he kissed her gently. "I need to go now, I'll miss my bus."

"I thought Decker was taking you up."

"Yeah, that's right. He is. But I still need to go."

"Trying to get rid of me."

McAdams ignored her comment. "I'll talk to you soon. I mean I'll text you soon."

"What*ever*!" She walked away, then she turned to him and smiled. It was a radiant grin.

CHAPTER 37

THE DAY WAS crystal: deep blue skies, cotton-ball clouds, and a bright full sun. Decker pulled down the car's visor to deflect the glare from the acres of snow-covered ground. The afternoon heat of forty-two degrees had melted some of the drifts and that made driving on the rutted road a challenge as the tires ground and stalled in mud and slush. He arrived at the farm just as the sun was sinking against a flat, white horizon.

Ruth Anne opened the door, in her eyes a mixture of surprise and alarm. "Detective Decker." A pause. "How nice of you to visit."

"I was in the area, so I decided to pop in. I hope that's okay."

"Of course." She hesitated, but then she caught herself. "I'm so sorry. Where are my manners? Do come in."

"Thank you." He wiped his feet on the mat. "Am I interrupting anything important?"

"No, not at all." She stepped aside and wiped her hands on an apron. "Is Mrs. Decker with you?"

"Unfortunately, no."

"Please sit down. How about some coffee?"

"I'd love a cup of coffee."

"Ezra's gone to market. He won't be back for a while. Do you need to talk to him?"

"Actually, I'd love to speak to Jacob if he's available."

Ruth Anne hesitated. "I think he's in the barn." She was fidgety. She probably wasn't used to being alone with a nonrelative man in the house. "How about if I put on a pot of coffee and then get Jacob for you?"

"Don't bother. Just point me in the right direction."

"Well, all right." She licked her lips. "Anything new?"

"Concerning Elijah? Nothing, I'm afraid."

"How about the death of that teacher?"

"We have someone in custody."

"I see." She continued to fidget and didn't ask for details.

Knowing her faith, Decker said, "This won't be a death-penalty case, Ruth Anne. It was just one of those unfortunate things that shouldn't have happened."

"I'm glad no one is seeking revenge. Decisions like that are best left up to God." A pause. "Well, then." She led him to the back door. "You can see the barn from here . . . that little peak of red."

"Yep."

"It's about a five-minute walk. But be careful. It's muddy and some ice is still on the ground."

"Yeah, my car tires have been taking a beating. It was a beautiful day, though."

"It is nice to see the sun. Even though we're not even in February, it feels like spring's around the corner."

She seemed to be speaking metaphorically, as if she deigned to hope that one day her dark winter might lift. The loss of a child was forever sadness. No joy could ever be felt without an "if only." But Ruth Anne was making a valiant effort to keep up her dignity as well as her privacy. She had her family, she had her community, and she had her faith in God. Decker smiled. "It's never too early for spring."

"And bring Jacob back with you. He's been out there for a while. He can use a little thawing out."

"I'll do that." Slowly, Decker worked his way through the icy trail. The dusk was incredibly quiet, the loudest sound being his breathing. He felt warm air from his lungs on his cold nose, which was probably rosy by now. Stepping carefully, he followed melted footprints that had already paved the pathway. As he approached the structure, he could hear the bleating of the sheep. When he opened the door, he found that the inside of the barn was almost as cold as the outside. It reeked of wet hay and sheep dung. Jacob was tending to a lambkin, feeding it from a bottle. He looked up, but then he went back to his business.

"Where's the ewe?" Decker asked.

"She's in the isolation crib—infection." He stood up and wiped his gloved hands on his overalls. His face was wet with perspiration and his hair was wet from water dripping through the rafters. "She's getting better, but she's on antibiotics, which isn't too good for the baby. I've gone about milking her by hand to keep her ducts open. Hopefully the lamb will be able to nurse from his mom in a couple of days."

He held up the bottle.

"He has an appetite. That's a good thing."

"Sign of health," Decker said.

"Yes, it is," Jacob said.

"How's your appetite, Jacob?"

"I'm fine." He wiped his face with a handkerchief. Under his breath, he said, "Just peachy."

Decker said, "The shock has worn off and now you're pissed at him." When Jacob didn't answer, he said, "I'd be pissed if I were you."

"Why should I be pissed at Eli? You are talking about Eli, right?"

"Of course." Decker took in a deep breath and let it out. "You know, Jacob, I talked to a lot of people about Eli's frame of mind before it happened. No one told me that Eli had seemed depressed. As a matter of fact, people said that he had been more social and more outgoing than anyone had remembered. That kept sticking in my craw. Why would he end it if he wasn't depressed?"

"You tell me." Jacob hesitated. "Did you find a note or something?"

"No, we didn't find a note. Did he send you a note?"

"Why would he do that? You think I'd hide it from you?"

"You might want to protect your parents." When Jacob didn't answer, Decker said, "I know he talked to you. You two were close."

"Yeah, right."

Bitterness had crept into the young man's voice. Decker said, "The thing is, Jacob, before I could start thinking about why Eli did it, I had to make sure that his death wasn't connected to Katrina Belfort's murder."

"Was it?"

"No. And once I realized the incidents were completely unrelated, I couldn't stop thinking about your brother."

"Well, good luck with that."

Decker kept his voice soft. "Eli had told you what was happening to him, didn't he."

"I don't know what you mean."

"What I mean is that his brain was starting to heal from the accident, that he was finally starting to feel and act like his old self again."

Jacob wiped his nose with his glove. "His old goofy self was how he put it." Anger welled up in his eyes. "He always was a stupid idiot."

"And as he healed—as your brother started returning to his

former life—his prodigious mind was crashing. His mathematical talents that once came so easy to him were slipping away."

The barn fell quiet except for the bleating of the sheep.

"He was stuck in this no-man's-land," Decker said. "Not himself entirely, but no longer the math whiz kid. It was tearing him apart."

"We weren't good enough for him anymore." Jacob was whispering.

"You know that wasn't it."

"Then give me another reason." Jacob's nostrils flared with fury. "His family who loved him for whatever he was, for whatever he would be in the future, we just weren't good enough."

Tears fell from his eyes.

"He swore he wouldn't do it. Even so I made him swear on the Bible that he wouldn't do it." He looked at Decker. "He looked me square in the eye and *lied* to me. Now I'm carrying this horrible . . . it's on my shoulders. I'll never forgive him for that. Never!"

His lip trembled.

"I failed my parents. I failed myself. Mostly I failed him."

"You didn't *fail*, Jacob." The young man looked up. "There was *nothing* you could do to prevent it. If someone is determined to kill himself, it's going to happen. All we can do is try to understand. It must have been torture for him to see his brilliant mind collapsing as his brain healed. Maybe he figured if he couldn't live as a genius, then at least he'd die as one."

"And so he did, stupid ass."

"I'm sure your religion teaches you compassion."

"I'm way beyond that. All I think about is what a jackass he was. It's bad enough he lied to me. But he lied on the Bible. And to do this to my parents. They don't deserve this shit. How could he do that to them?"

"Suicide is a selfish act. But it's also an act of desperation. He couldn't see any way out. He must have felt very lonely."

"How the hell does he come off feeling *lonely*! He was the one who ditched his family." Jacob spat at the ground. "He swore me to silence. Well, he can break his word, but I won't. And now I'm stuck with this horrible burden. I can't tell my parents. It would hurt them beyond anything." He looked at Decker with red eyes. "If he wouldn't have sworn on a Bible, I would have said something. He knew what swearing on a Bible meant and he did it anyway. And now I'm responsible. I am so damn *pissed* at him."

"Eli put you in an untenable spot. There was no way you could win."

"I hate him for doing what he did to me. I also hate him because our love and faith couldn't compete with his desire for immortality or whatever."

"It wasn't that, Jacob."

"I beg to differ. That's exactly what it was."

Decker didn't argue. The kid was entitled to his feelings and there was probably some truth to what he felt. "This burden you carry, Jacob. It's a lot for you to hold inside. I can understand why you wouldn't upset your parents. But if you ever want to talk about it, I'm a phone call away. And if you want to talk more about it, I can get you someone more useful than me."

"Like a shrink? You think I'm weak?"

"Not at all. To take on this burden in silence shows a towering strength of character. I'm anything but weak, Jacob. I've sought out help from time to time. But it's up to you."

"Why would I want to talk about it to you or anyone, for that matter?" he snapped. "I wish I could forget I ever talked to that idiot!" Jacob bit his lip. "I know you mean well, Detective. But I'm not the talking kind."

"I respect that, but the offer is always open," Decker said. "Your mother made a pot of coffee. She told me to tell you to come inside and thaw out."

"You go. I'll be there in around ten minutes."

"I think your mom's a little edgy about being alone with me."

"Oh . . . right. That's a religious thing. I've still got work to do. I've got to feed a few more cossets and then I've got to clean out some pens."

"I can help you out with that. My uncle had a farm in Florida. I used to spend my summers with him. It was mostly orange groves, but he did own some livestock. I mucked the horses' stalls, baled hay, and fed a lot of piglets. I also put up fences so the gators couldn't come in and snatch the babies."

Jacob laughed but there was no joy in it. "I think you're putting me on."

"Jacob, it is not something that I would make up to impress you."

"Okay, then. You asked for it." He handed Decker a bottle. "You can feed the one in the corner if you can wrassle him down. He's feisty."

"Not a problem."

Actually, it was a problem. The baby not only ruined his shirt and pants with his muddy hooves, his resistance caused Decker to break into a sweat. At least he was providing amusement for the kid, who smiled at Decker's grief. Finally, he managed to hold the lamb steady and pop the bottle into its mouth. Once the baby realized that there was a pot of gold at the end of the rainbow, he drained his dinner in roughly five minutes. Decker and Jacob worked in silence until the chores were done.

Afterward, as they were walking back to the house, Jacob said, "Thanks."

"For what?"

"I don't know exactly. Not judging me, I guess."

"Oh hell no." He put his arm around the kid's shoulder. To his surprise, the kid didn't resist. "Your parents lean on you a lot. It's natural. You're the oldest and you've been tagged the responsible one. But a little fun goes a long way. It's good for the soul."

Jacob didn't answer. Then he said, "I got engaged yesterday."

"Congratulations."

"Quick, huh? Like two and a half months."

"You know when it's right." Decker paused. "Are you happy about it?"

"Yeah." He scratched his chin. "Yeah, I really am happy about it. We're good together."

"I'm happy for you."

"Weddings are community affairs. You can come if you want. You can also bring your wife."

"That's good because we usually do go together." The kid smiled. "I'm sure she'd love to come. She likes ethnic things, being ethnic herself."

"Yeah, all ethnic mothers are pretty much the same." Jacob went quiet. "I really don't hate Eli."

"I know that."

"We were close growing up. We had our assigned roles—I was the responsible one, he was the goof. I just . . . I don't know. It must have been hard for him to see it all going south. He just didn't want to stick around for the crash. He was never too good at picking up the pieces. He always left that to me."

"You carried him as well as anyone."

"I suppose. Still, I wish I could do something for him beyond visiting the cemetery."

"You know a friend of his from college is taking over his research in his honor. In his short years as a math prodigy, he did a lot of good things. Maybe his impact will be felt beyond the grave."

"I hope so." He shook his head. "Although I still think he was a selfish jerk." Tears followed. "There's always one in every family."

Decker didn't answer. His mind said, *Amen to that, brother.*

WHEN RINA ANSWERED the phone, McAdams didn't bother with the pleasantries. Instead, he said, "I didn't want to bother the old man at work. But I thought I'd let you know that I passed."

"Congratulations. I had no doubts."

"I did. I got very lucky."

"I'm sure that's not true."

"It is very true. There were tons of things the tests could have featured that I knew nothing about. But someone upstairs took pity on me."

"I've never known you as a religious man."

"In trenches and in finals," McAdams told her. "I passed with honors if you must know."

"I must know."

"I suddenly have people clamoring for me for a summer internship. I've got my pick of some really good jobs."

"That's great!"

"Shame I'm already booked for the summer."

"Nonsense, Tyler, take advantage of the opportunities. Greenbury PD will survive without you."

"Woman, you cut me to the quick."

"You know what I mean."

"I do know. And I'm happy to be a hot property. Unfortunately, we all know that I'm not a team player. And I really don't like bosses giving me dog assignments and telling me what to do. I'm horrible at corporate structure."

"I heard these top firms buy you expensive dinners and take you yachting on weekends."

"After working you to death."

"At three grand a week. Tyler, at least give it a try."

"It takes a lot more than a sail to Nantucket to buy me off. My mind is already made up so why argue. In the meantime, I'm off on vacation."

"Where to?"

"I'm going to work on my tan. My stepgrandmother has a villa in Rhodes, bought with my grandfather's money, of course. But since Nina is so lovely, I can't begrudge her anything. She says hello, by the way. I'm sure she'd extend the invitation to you and the old man."

"That's so nice, but we've made some arrangements next week to visit the children."

"Next time."

"Next time it is." Rina hesitated. "Tyler, you really should consider one of those prestigious internships. You may even find it interesting."

"I doubt it." A pause. "Rina, I'm independently wealthy, which means I don't ever have to work, let alone work under a boss. But like any rule, there's always an exception. So tell Mr. Exception that I'll see him in the summer."

"We'll see you then."

"Bye." McAdams cut the line, but didn't pocket his phone. Instead, he thought a moment. Then his fingers flew across the pop-up keyboard on his iPhone.

Hey.

A moment later, he heard the beep. He read the text.

Hey.

How's it going?

Good. Eli was really onto something. I miss him in my own nerdy way. Have you heard about your exams?

I passed.

Congrats.

Thanks.

We have break next week. Maybe I can come up to Harvard? See what it's like?

I won't be around. I'm taking some time off.

Okay. Maybe next time.

McAdams smiled. He texted: *This may seem a little odd, but I'm gonna just throw it out there because I'm just that kind of guy.*

What?

Have you ever been to Greece?

No. I've never been outside the country. Lack of funds. Why?

Would it interest you to go?

Of course it would interest me. Like big-time.

McAdams smiled broadly. He texted: *Well then, sister, today's your lucky day.*

ABOUT THE AUTHOR

FAYE KELLERMAN lives with her husband, *New York Times* bestselling author Jonathan Kellerman, in Los Angeles, California, and Santa Fe, New Mexico.

35674055863493

Chase Branch Library
17731 W. Seven Mile Rd.
Detroit, MI 48235